Is It Today?

Fantasies

It's Crying Gas, Girl!
H J Furl

Is It Today?

Fantasies

HJ Furl

For my true friends

CONTENTS

The sublime and the ridiculous are often so nearly related that it is difficult to class them separately. One step above the sublime makes the ridiculous…
…and one step above the ridiculous makes the sublime.

Thomas Paine, Age of Reason, II, ad finem

Come into the garden, Maud,
For the black bat, night, has flown,
Come into the garden, Maud,
I am here at the gate alone.

TENNYSON, Maud, xxii, St. I

The Arrival

IT WAS UNUSUAL FOR IZZY to find a midult lying by the hewn oak logs in the clearing at twilight. There were rabbits scarpering into the bushes. Foxes returning from raiding hens' eggs on the allotments. Deer foraging. Izzy even spotted a badger once, squashed across the forest road. It was unheard of for her to find a midult though, in the forest, the vast triangular swathe of silver birch, ancient beech, and oak that teemed with wildlife.

There were new-borns, seen but not heard, sickly-sweet dummies stuck into their bleating mouths. Izzy had found one, screaming, abandoned by his mother in the peat bog. She'd left him there in case his parent returned.

Then there were toddlers, babies who could walk unaided but spent their time being walked around the west loop in buggies until they fell asleep. Izzy would sit on a tree stump and watch them perambulating, some of them as old as seven. She never saw a child at play in the forest.

After dark, Izzy invariably stumbled across drunken adolescents petting on the stubbled heath, coupling in lengths of grassy meadow, inside a sleepy hollow, kissing behind a lightning-dead tree. Her attempts to communicate with them invariably impeded by headsets. In broad daylight, adolescents were seen in their natural habitat, the high street, terrorizing old-aged shoppers with shiny new garden implements bought at the town's hardware shop, or ripping wing mirrors off of parked 4x4's.

The commonest forms of wildlife found in the forest were the youths, midults and senults, which co-existed in classes: working, new money and middle class. These sub-classes or phyla, frequented the woodland at differing times of the day depending on the clemency of the weather, their mood and motivation. Izzy made a point of hiding in the blackberry bushes to study their distinctive rituals.

First to rise, at civil twilight, were male runners, identified by their pouting bare chest and determined expression. Izzy noticed that the female joggers, dressed in plastic ear plugs and lycra leotards, always looked the other way when the lusty males cried their mating calls.

Cyclists and mountain-bikers presented a dangerous occupational hazard to Izzy. There had been numerous occasions when a cruising hybrid, sporting a broken bell or failed front brake, narrowly missed careering into her and hurling her callously to the ground. Izzy wondered if she would hurt when he did. Wondered if he would stop and tend her wounds. Or would he shoot off mercilessly down the gravelled hill towards Marten. Leaving her, just another push-bike injury statistic strewn across the wayside, black tyre burns etched into her slender thighs like grotesque rubberized railway tracks.

The die-hard ramblers and experienced walkers gathered in the carpark for the 10:30 send-off. Mainly retired or redundant midults and active senults keen to find companions to alleviate the boredom of their cosseted, house-bound lives. Cheery, chatty, souls who waved at Izzy as she perched on a convenient oak branch, happily tanning her arms and legs under the warm sunshine.

Sometimes, she watched them change out of their hiking boots, gossiping about charity coffee mornings, or coach trips to heritage railway lines. Or just helping each other come to terms with Death and Bereavement, two unpleasant issues Izzy would never have to face. Afterwards, they slowly filed out of the pot-holed carpark, leaving by the wrong exit, fearful of shredding their tyres on the scary yellowed crocodile teeth.

Senults only entered the forest in organised groups, living in a society where human life feared growing old. Violence against the elderly had soared to new highs. Increasingly, senults were abused by those they should be able to trust. Neglected in care homes. Treated as easy financial targets. Assaulted by thugs who knew they'd get away with a legal slap on the wrist. Petrified of leaving their own home, senults represented an obstacle to THE ARRIVAL that would have to be overcome utilizing the radical solution.

Other, more unsavoury characters could be found in the shadier recesses. Izzy knew where. Drug dealers. Criminals. Weirdos daubed in body paint, squatting peacefully as they pipe-smoked dirty weed under the shelter of makeshift tepees. All of them lurking, skulking about. In the forest. On one occasion, ramblers were stunned to see a coachload of colourful strangers hastily disembark in the carpark, run off up the hill path, and disperse among the dingy copses.

And then there was Izzy. An extraordinary young adult by any standard. Izzy the enigma. She stood over the midult.

'Are you alright?' she said.

Izzy was always asking questions. On this occasion, a particularly stupid one. It was clear from her traumatized demeanour, that this midult was not alright. She was distressed. There were brambles tangled in her honey blonde hair. Her cheesecloth dress flapped open in the cool breeze. Her stockings were bunched round her ankles. She crouched by the pink shale track, mewling quietly. So quietly that Izzy couldn't understand a word.

'Sorry, you'll have to speak up, I can't hear you,' she said.

The midult gabbled something about love-in-the-mist.

'Love? Mist?'

The midult stared blankly at Izzy.

'Where? Here, in the forest?'

'In the forest?' Izzy repeated impatiently.

The midult remained silent.

'Try, won't you?'

She was beyond help. In any case, Izzy couldn't help her, not even if she wanted to. Being familiar with the midult's mate: a tall, slim, male midult with a cock's crest quiff, she reasoned that her predicament was the result of coital concerns such as:

Where's my lacy underwear?

Did I just fake it for him?

The earth was supposed to move for me, right?

Did I feel okay?

Did I just dislocate my leg for him?'

And: Surely, he doesn't want sex with me again tonight, does he?

Izzy strongly suspected his request for repeated sex had caused an altercation which spilt out of their luxury apartment, onto the village green, into the churchyard, through the meadows, and into the forest. In other words, they had a tiff, went to the woods, made it up, and had sex. In the mist. That kind of made sense. She glimpsed at the female whimpering at her feet. So, what happened to you afterwards, eh?

Not that the midult's plight was her concern. Her mating partner had made it abundantly clear to Izzy that she was not to get emotionally involved with female midults under any circumstances. Female midults were obstacles to THE ARRIVAL. Izzy muttered her a heartfelt apology, skipped over her feet, and walked away.

Iain waited until Izzy had gone, rode up to the midult on his metallic grey hybrid mountain bicycle and rang its prawn pink RING ME ANY TIME bell. Irin's initial reaction was one of shock. She ceased mewling as an appalling notion shattered her addled mind: the cyclist might be an alien.

It was tough for Irin to tell what the bloody thing was from its bizarre apparel. An enclosed blue cycling helmet, fitted with a customized amber visor, concealed its face. A thermonuclear protective vest and red-lined road bib, with an integrated rubber jock strap, hid its body. The cyclist sported trendy coyote light assault boots, built-in shock absorbers, studded cycle gloves, and it spoke.

'It's only me!'

She panicked and crawled off on all fours. He dismounted, shouldered off his rucksack, and grounded her. She bleated like a little lamb. Ignoring her gibberish, he reached inside his sack, extracted a misshapen object, and untied its brown wrapping paper. Her spirits sank when he rolled her onto her back. Her scared eyes haunted him. She pleaded for her life. He felt for her.

She kneed him in the groin. He winced. She wriggled free of him, snaking across the dirt. He exhaled. She made it as far as the undergrowth. Abruptly, he took the jagged garden rock and clumped her round the head. She dropped, her arms splaying as if trying to break her final fall. Removing his gloves, he knelt next to her, pushed back her bloodied hair, and felt her neck.

She was dead.

He looked around.

They were alone in the moonlight.

'Can't let them see you like this, Irin.'

Iain rolled Irin onto her back and dressed her, rolling her stockings up her taut calves, over her knees, and up her thighs, carefully re-attaching them to her ruby and black suspender belt.

Irin watched Iain with her dead eyes as he smoothed the scarlet-tinged curls from her face. He lifted her cold hands. Her poppy red fingernails were soiled with dirt. He picked them clean. He sucked them. Her face was dirty. He cleansed her. Iain took a deep breath, pausing over Irin's precious mound, broke down, and cried. His tears subsided.

He recovered quickly, his nimble fingers moving deftly, sealing her corpse inside her dress. Her membrane had adhered to one side of her mouth as she bit her lip, baring her sparkly white teeth. He took her head in his hands and kissed her cyan lips. A single teardrop rolled down her cheek. Irin had been loyal, loving, and faithful to him. Iain would always love her. He had to leave her. To care for Izzy.

Wearily, he lifted Irin in his arms and carried her far into the woods where he laid her to rest in a dry ditch covering her with soil and broken twigs to keep her warm. Then he mounted his bicycle and ascended the winding hill.

Izzy tied her teak hair back in a crude knot and ran. Iain watched as she danced up the hill in her grey sports bra and red fitness pants: young, free. He wanted her. His heart fluttered as she vanished in the gloom, his bright elusive butterfly of love. She had the face of an angel: teardrop eyes, her spoilt lips divinely pursed, rather droopy at the corners, the faintest brown moustache.

Iain closed his eyes and imagined her naked. The light faded. He tightened the stiff strap on his helmet and pedalled to where the path forked. He would ride the west loop, past dewpond, bog, marsh, climb the steepest inclines, descend the deepest troughs, until he found her in the mist.

The sun set in the velvet sky presaging rain at dawn, freshening the stale air. Izzy shivered as the fresh breeze cooled her midriff. Goose-bumps bristled on her tummy, caressed her waist, massaged her back.

A swarm of marauding mosquitoes descended on her, a kamikaze death squadron. Flapping her arms, slapping her neck, Izzy fought to stave off their impending feast. The females adored her, settling in her scalp, nestling in her folds, pricking her skin, injecting their saliva, sucking her blood. She fell to earth cowering until the pests had had their fill of her, itching, scratching, rows of puce bumps erupting in blunt infant volcanoes along her jawline, her armpits, her soft creases.

Apart from the plagues of mosquitoes, Izzy loved summer evenings, her favourite time of day, the only time she felt at one with nature. She checked her illuminated wristband. They would all be fast asleep now, the midults, snug in their luxurious cots. Whereas she was made to sleep on a bunk inside a box.

Relishing the soft earth under her bare feet, the tightness pulling at her hot calves, she slid down a shallow slope into a dry hollow, crushing twigs and early-fallen acorns, squashing beechnuts. Izzy picked up the pace, feeling the burn, stretching her supple limbs to the limit, grinding her way uphill past clusters of felled silver birch until the track levelled out.

The going was good to firm made treacherous by sprawls of tangled beech roots. She cherished the peace of night, the reassuring natural noises, nocturnal animals: fallow deer, rabbits, foxes, badgers, all strays scampering in the thicket. That is what she was: a stray, who came out to play at twilight, a nocturnal animal released from captivity to run wild, run free, in search of her dream.

The sky faded to black. She entered the wood's heart, where peat bogs fermented, and let her imagination run wild. Were there fire-flies? Will o' the wisps? Faeries? Witches? Magic?

What… the fuck… was that?

The mist descended out of nowhere, immersing, absorbing her. Izzy breathed its acrid vapour, inhaling the damp, dewy musk. The temperature plummeted. The chill shot icy shards into her body.

She froze, then twitched, jerked and jumped like a shattered porcelain marionette thrown in the air by a demented puppeteer. They passed through her, knife-like, unknown entities, etching their sordid intimate imprints on her soul. Her mind grappled with the absurdity of intruders permeating her numbed brain, writhing inside her vital organs.

What are you? Leave me alone! Get out of me, won't you?

The intrusion ceased as suddenly as it began. Izzy collapsed, exhausted, in an untidy heap.

Why do I feel so tired? What's happening to me?

The mist lifted. The sky cleared. She stared at the heavens, the blue void filling with crescent moons, glitterball stars, gasping, awed by what came next…

'Can't take much more of this!' she protested.

Her walnut eyeballs rolled, revealing their whites. Her heavy lids sagged, drooped and shut. Izzy surrendered to her deathly fatigue. Rolling onto one side, curling up in the foetal position, she fell asleep and dreamed the strangest dreams.

When she woke up, Izzy was lying flat on her back, emotionally drained, staring at the starlit sky. In time, she regained her strength, clambering to her feet unsteadily, as if she were a young doe rising out of her bracken bed. Her head span. She staggered up the steep slope, stumbled, fell into his arms, and passed out.

He had a body to die for: race-fit, solid muscle, tuned for speed, ready for the heart-pounding sprint. He was one-of-a-kind: his open-edged brows maximized his field of vision. His neon red night eyes enabled him to see more. His advanced snub nose bridge opened out his airflow, combating fogging, preventing his internal body from overheating. He suffered from alien drug rash, hooded brows, teal eyes, chiselled jaw, sticky-out ears, bum fluff, hooked nose, dry lips, pipe neck.

He appraised Izzy's sleeping face. She looked beautiful.

He threw her over his shoulder, took his bicycle in one hand and tore round the east loop, down the winding hill, through the meadow to the main road. His resilient fit moved with Izzy instead of against her, built for longer ride comfort. He had hidden reflectivity in his backside. His legs wore smooth edgings with rubbery grips to help him to stay in place.

From the road it was a short jog: past the church, right at the crossroads, over the cricket pitch, to an overgrown path skirting the allotments, to the grey clay lane that led to the remarkable little box he gave her to live in.

Iain threw the door open, stomped into the box, and dumped Izzy's inert form on her bed.

He'd fashioned the box for her with his bare hands, erecting a central plasterboard partition to create two cubes. The solid oak door, with its deceptively ornate devil knocker and doorbell, led the occupant off the tarmac lane onto bare wooden floorboards. The living cube, Iain had determined, was primarily suited to nocturnal activities: sleep and sex. With such functions in mind, he had installed blinds over the front and back windows. He drew them down and locked the door.

A sawn-out bolthole in the partition led to the sanitary cube, a cork-tiled conurbation of ceramic splendour in angelica, a beautiful toilet and wash hand basin suite that added elegance to any converted garage. There was a curved shower unit in the corner, a blacked-out oval glass portal, and an integrated fan unit. Cooking facilities, food storage and waste disposal units were unnecessary. Izzy fed carnivorously, metabolizing her own waste, methane, and by-products.

Iain regarded her inert body, sprawled haphazardly on the bed. She'd be out cold for half an hour. He lifted his burly right arm, followed by a well-muscled right leg, and sniffed himself like an animal, baulking at the stink of stale sweat, sediment and soil deposition. Microclimatic conditions for THE

ARRIVAL depended on body purity, fertility, and compliance with hygiene, health & safety due diligence in the profligate progenitor. Prior to procreation with a suitable progenitive who could produce progesterone in preparation for her progeny.

As he discarded his foetid, outer layers, he prognosticated. Izzy was producing oxytocin and seemed pretty relaxed, if not proactive about pregnancy. Her high prolactin level would enable healthy nutrition for her progeny, pending THE ARRIVAL. Iain stood in the shower, scrubbing his tainted torso clean, and tried to prioritize process.

Izzy would reproduce with him tonight. His dead mate, Irin, would be interred and moved to a deeper grave in the churchyard. Her burial would require assistance from Irma, the local gravedigger, who was open to bribes. He made a mental note to contact her in the morning. Irun, manager of the charitable recycling facility, would arrange for the collection of Irin's clothing and incinerate her underwear, stockings, perfume, cosmetics and toiletries on the local allotment bonfire. Izzy would then move out of the box and bring up her progeny in the spare room of his apartment overlooking a village green famous for its Donkey Derby and Firework Display. He would meet Ilene at The Gate tomorrow night for drinks, and float the idea of her relocating into Izzy's box, in return for a leading role in Senult Control.

Iain had been left with no choice but to kill Irin: she was an obstacle, like all female midults. She *had* to die. Just as all male midults *had* to be assimilated. Just as Ilene *had* to coordinate the cottage industry of processing all senults, transgressing them through the village halls. Iain bore ultimate executive responsibility for enaction of all operational aspects of THE ARRIVAL.

Satisfied that he had made detailed plans for THE ARRIVAL, he stepped out of the shower, towelled himself dry, sprayed his body with musk, switched off the fan-light, and made his way silently into the living cube.

His angel was lying on the bed waiting for him to inseminate her with his alien spermatozoa. He went and knelt beside the bed so that he could examine her. Izzy was still unconscious. She was perspiring lightly; the tips of her teak hair were dark and wet; her brow was covered with tiny beads of perspiration. He brushed a stray strand out of her mouth, rubbing her lips gently with his thumb, so that her face grinned at him. Her eyelids were closed. Iain flicked one open to reveal the walnut iris. The eyeball was lustrous, clear of the tell-tale threads which would manifest her whites once full parasitic infection had set in.

He ran the edge of his hand down her neck and appraised Izzy's body. Her jawline, shoulders, armpits, midriff, the creases and folds in her limbs, were spattered with bright red hives. Iain reached for his rucksack, took out the tube of antihistamine balm he kept for insect bites, squeezed a little onto his fingertips, then lightly massaged the soothing lotion into Izzy's inflamed skin. Izzy smiled to herself, enjoying the sensation of her body being explored by his tender touch. She felt the lump swell between her breasts, like a large raised hiatus hernia. He rubbed the cream into her legs, screwed the cap back onto the tube, dropped it on the floor and took out the sachet of weed, hiding it under the bed. He looked up. Izzy was awake. She feigned surprise when he brushed her cheek with his hand. The lump grew in her chest.

'Where am I?' she said.

Iain sat her up in bed, took her in his arms and embraced her, patting her back as if he were winding a baby. She smelled his musk and smiled. He was clean for once; he must have washed. She felt the spur rise up her oesophagus, felt uncertain.

'You're safe in the box, Izzy,' he told her, reassuringly.

She let Iain pull her grey sports bra off over her head. 'Safe?'

He held her tight, loving the thrill of her naked breasts pressed against his manly alien chest.

'I found you asleep in the forest,' he said.

Izzy looked puzzled. 'Asleep? Why would I want to sleep in the forest?'

He ran his fingers through her damp hair. She was beautiful. Had the face of an angel. He wanted her so badly. He slid his hands down her slender back and tucked his fingers inside her fitness pants. Izzy smiled as her lump grew. The spur extended as far her throat. She was ready.

'I have no idea, but you're safe with me now, that's all that matters,' he said.

She let him pull off her fitness pants. Izzy was wearing a pale grey thong. A frisson passed thru them. Izzy took the weed and put it in her mouth like a naughty child. It was dark brown and tasted bitter like dust and bark that had been ground to a must by a sorcerer's pestle. She masticated, grinding her teeth, kneading the ayahuasca with her tongue, crushing the greens and stems into a pulpy spinach mulch. Izzy suspected the ayahuasca was dirty, full of toxic impurities, like her mating partner. Rumours abounded that dirty weed masquerading as ayahuasca liquid, mulched vine of the dead or synthetic DMT had led to the deaths of countless teenagers at wild parties and rock festivals. Izzy needed it to sleep. Chewing the psychedelic cud was Iain's idea.

'Take the weed to relieve the tedium, Izzy,' he said. 'Open your mind.'

Her oval face drew with doubt at first. Still, she supposed, if the natives enjoyed this shit in the jungle, why couldn't she get off on it in bed? She duly took the weed, took off her thong, opened her mind, opened her legs to him, and enjoyed their best sex since her arrival. Once he had finished, Izzy lay on top of him, playing with his wet hair, rubbing his lips with her thumb.

'Do you love me, Iain?' she asked.

He saw Irin lying in her shallow grave. 'I love you more than life itself, Izzy,' he replied.

'Then let me kiss you.'

He opened his mouth to her tongue. Too late, he felt her spur slide down his throat, extend as far as his oesophagus, and suffocate him. Izzy relaxed as the tubular organ drew neurotoxin, pumping poison out of the swelling in her chest. Her secreted toxin entered Iain's bloodstream, stunning him. Izzy felt her lump contract as she squirted her volatile secondary fluid into Iain's digestive tract. His dying body twitched involuntarily as the molecular acid dissolved his flesh, his muscle, tissues, his organs, his bone, turning his torso into a skin-encapsulated sac of mulch.

She fed on him for five hours…

As a result of one night's gay abandon, Izzy was lip-hooked, tongue-set, utterly dependent on her dead boyfriend. In time, her stomach extracted the liquid entheogenic from her digested prey, vomiting it into the glass bowl she kept by her bed. She was drenched in a brilliant white light. Purged out, Izzy felt herself leave her body and travel the void, transiting into a fluffy world. Effortlessly rebirthed, she popped out, releasing all her negative energy, her bad emotions. Izzy descended into a realm of inner peace. Her mind and body united by subliminal blood rushes, congealed alien flesh, liquified organs and body fluids; she regurgitated Iain, spat him out in pellets. Then she slipped on her pyjamas, climbed between the sheets, and fell asleep.

Slowly swinging her slender legs off the bunk, Izzy fumbled with the camelia satin waist band around her midriff, divesting herself of her wondrous, velvet-piped jim jams and playful toys and dolls. She tried to stand. She was groggy, permeated by weed and alien residue. Her addled brain swelled like sodden sponge. Her heavy head whirled. She slumped onto the bed.

Izzy clenched the edge of the bunk tightly. Her throbbing head hung below her knees, the lemon extensions attached to her burnt sienna hair drizzling down her calves, kissing her feet. She instructed herself not to overextend her abs for fear of an unsightly acid reflux. Pretty soon, her retching abated. Fisting her slim arms deep into the duvet, Izzy pushed herself up onto the balls of her feet.

Beside the bed lay a modacrylic sheepskin rug which, judging by its squashed, sorry look, had never been shampooed. This rug was where Izzy performed her post-digestive stretches. Other than the built-in bunk and radiator, the black hole's only other feature was the full-length gilt-edged mirror, a car boot sale bargain that hung despondently off the crumbling plaster wall, facing her quilted cot.

Izzy appraised herself in the mirror. She had a pallid complexion, anaemic milky white skin.

Her body started to bloat…

*****

They spread quickly through the mist and infected her. They thrived in her maternal body. Izzy really mattered now! She carried them inside her cells. They mutated with her ova. Izzy had a body to die for. They lived inside that body as parasites. She carried within her the hopes and aspirations of future generations. Izzy was selected for her stamina, resilience and endurance. Her absorption rate for male midults and reproduction capacity were phenomenal. She bred…

THE ARRIVAL

The fog emanated from a dewpond in the forest, an unfurling blanket of phosphorescent blue. A minuscule hole appeared at the epicentre, spreading rapidly like spilt ink, rippling in a pool of indigo. The pool burst into a swirling kaleidoscope: a distant galaxy, the faint glimmer of a dying star, a solitary sea-green planet.

They ARRIVED, shrouded in mystery, freed from all physical constraints, finding sanctuary.

They found a host in Izzy, then another, Morgan, then Ilene…

Soon, there would be millions of them:

ARRIVING

Apocalypse

'YOU'RE CHEATING! COVER YOUR EYES! Count to 10!' the boy laughed.

The girl covered her eyes and turned to face the steamy kitchen window. It was lunchtime. Her mother smiled benignly at her through the mist as she drained off the boiled potatoes. A delicious smell of freshly baked gingerbread men teased her nostrils.

She started to count. '1, 2, 3, 4, 7, 10.'

'I heard that, cheat. Start again!'

She counted again, properly this time, '1, 2, 3, 4, 5, 6, 7, 8, 9, 10.'

Now, where are you hiding? The garage? The outhouse? The potting shed?

She shook her head. *He must be in the woods.* As she entered the forest, she stung her arm on a nettle. Her frock caught on a bramble thorn. It was dark in the woods. She was scared. She wanted to go home. She was about to give up when a thick shaft of sunlight burst through the trees. There was a clearing ahead. Freshly hewn pine logs, scattered in the bracken. He was sitting on a tree stump, head in his hands, frothing spit at the mouth, twitching. Having a fit. Seeing his little sister watching him, he begged her not to tell. But she ran home as fast as she could and told her mother. Father was out, doing the weekly chopping.

Next day, the men in white coats came to the house to take the boy to the asylum, trussed in a straitjacket. That night his grey smoke poured out of the tall chimney at the hospital crematorium.

'Martin's sudden death remains a mystery to us,' his mother said over supper.

Maria told tell-tales at a very young age.

Maria told tales. The paid-up Purist Party member informed the local militia where to find undesirables within the community, indifferent to their dreadful fate. When her valiant man, Stephen, died fighting the indestructible enemy, she moved out of their house in the historic city centre to a discreet abode in the suburbs, fearful of recriminations for her extreme views. After inheriting his self-drive car business, she became a wealthy woman who could afford the best for her children: a Purist kindergarten for Keira, an elite sporting academy for Kiran. But all the money in the world couldn't put Maria's warped mind back together again.

She read her daughter the fairy tale in which the princess consents to a prince kissing her awake in a far-off fantasy world where good always triumphs over evil. The ruby crystal wall softened, artificial dusk turned to twilight, and the girl closed her eyes. Her mother kissed her goodnight, then she searched under the bed until she found her battered rag doll, a doll which reminded her of her childhood when she played hide and seek in the forest near her parents' old summer house. She tucked the doll up in bed and prayed for her daughter's purity. Keira was her war baby; she had never known peace. Maria crept out of the room, leaving the door open, a lamp alight. Her little girl was scared of the dark.

She crossed the landing to the sapphire room. Kiran was fast asleep - cradling his ginger teddy bear. Her knight was difficult to control at the best of times, without Stephen to exert much-needed discipline. Calm one minute, temperamental and disobedient the next. Kiran frequently threw tantrums for no apparent reason, the disturbingly dark trait that ran in their family. She ruffled his silky blond hair. Her son looked just like his father. He would be so proud. Every night she prayed that her knight would grow up healthy and strong, without the affliction.

Keira and Kiran were perfect, unblemished children, role models for future generations of the super-race, the ultimate human dream. Maria endorsed and participated in the separation of undesirables, the cruel apartheid that had divided the city since the insurrection, when the once-unthinkable purges of the weak and diseased returned to haunt the nation. Although the war was far from over according to the deluge of state propaganda, it alarmed Maria to hear of a decisive enemy advance up to the city border. More than 60,000 refugees now lived in the city, fugitives from the brutal killing machines that annihilated humans with impunity. She was under no illusion; the Robots would kill her first. Then they would kill her children. Maria was steeling herself in preparation for her family's death.

She went to her bedroom and admired herself in front of the vanity mirror suspended on the amethyst wall.

'Mirror, mirror on the wall, who's the fairest of them all?'

The mirror was voice-activated. The wall turned red. Maria had been a widow three years. Still only thirty, she was an attractive woman who could afford to pluck young gigolos fresh from the academy. But she could never love another, not after Stephen. Excited by her image, she undressed and washed herself, splashed a dab of scent behind each ear, slipped on her red satin gown and climbed on the quilted bed. Hugging herself to stay warm. She hated the long, lonely nights with no-one to caress her, and lived in fear of the inevitable invasion.

A young man's face appeared in the mirror. Maria felt like a child waiting for Santa Claus to climb down her chimney. Except that she couldn't wait. She closed her eyes and the neon walls softened. A virtual princess in red satin lay sleeping on a velvet bed with her handsome prince. Maria entered virtual reality, her private la-la land. She saw her dead man's bronzed face, his rugged muscular physique. Thrilled when Stephen communicated with her.

'May I have your consent to kiss you, Maria?' he said.

He was playing with her! She stroked his neatly trimmed blond beard, ran her hands over the twin cusps of solid barrelled chest, finding his downturned nipples. And gave them a tweak.

'I might let you! If you're nice to me!' she giggled, hopefully, as she missed him so much.

Haunting him with her hazel dew eyes, she drew him close. He thirsted for her. His parched dry mouth drank in her moist pink lips. She opened her mouth relishing his smoky breath. He savoured her sweet saliva as her tongue flickered playfully against his soft palate, then paused.

'Nice to you?' he frowned. 'I love you! It's been so long since I died. Have you missed me?'

'Missed you? Hardly a day goes by when I don't think of you. You're still with me, here.'

She pressed her fingers to her bared chest and crossed her heart. He was overwhelmed by her love, his heartstrings were torn to shreds of undying love for her, bursting out of his soul.

'How lovely of you, Maria. How very lovely.'

He asked after the children. She told him the children were well. Kiran was seven now, he missed his dad. He was lonely without his friends since the authority closed the academy. He rarely left the house, preferring to spend his time in virtual reality with Keira. They were best friends. Maria wished Stephen could meet them. But he couldn't, not in his virtual state. She told him Keira would start kindergarten when the horrid war ended. If it ended.

'They say the Robots have reached the city wall,' she said, 'I'm frightened of what they will do to us when they find us, I'm scared. Hold me, Stephen.'

The prince looked into the gathering gloom as death's dark clouds loomed on the horizon.

'I must go now. I'll always love you, Maria. I'll never forget you.'

'No! You can't leave me! Hold me, darling, one last time! My dream hasn't ended yet!'

'I can't, I'm not real! I only exist in your imagination!'

'You must! I'll never see you again! You must!'

His face was indistinct. She felt him ruffle her hair, licked her lips at the divine sensation, buried her head in the pillows. Her red satin rolled off her shoulders like crimson quicksilver. He parted her lush chocolate-cherry hair, revealing her gilded neck, the tell-tale curls of teak. She bristled at the touch of his lips. He nuzzled her. He kissed her there. She loved it when he kissed her there. Her virtual-beast, her lion-man.

Maria woke up to find him gone. She cried herself to sleep.

Nathan was an undesirable, an unemployed chef, a survivor of the cruel purge. A man who stayed alive through his wits, stealth and concealment, never staying in the same safe house more than one night. Even if that meant sleeping rough on the streets. Tonight, home was a mattress in a derelict warehouse beside an old railway marshalling yard. Nathan slept fully-dressed, in a black boiler suit with an infamous bright orange U patch, the distinctive brand label of the undesirable, stitched onto the chest. He slept soundly in his sleeping bag. He didn't hear them arrive.

They shed their cloaks of invisibility at twilight to reveal their beautiful charcoal-grey battle dress: a pointed nosecone, slash-back wings, an empty black cockpit, a stubby fuselage, and tall angular tail fins. The sting was in their tails. Before the attack began, each drone shed an electron bomb. The bombs' sensors hacked into the city's IT systems: networks, stand-alone and mobile devices. Severing all electronic communications and command and control units within six miles of the city centre. Creating widespread pandemonium among the inhabitants. The e-bombs drifted lazily to the ground attached to gaudy tangerine parachutes.

Maria was woken by the wail of air raid sirens, an unfamiliar loudspeaker blaring outside in the street.

'Warning! Warning! The enemy have appeared over the city centre!'

'Please, God, save us.' She prayed for their lives. Her face blanched with worry.

The petrified children ran into the room and leapt into her arms. She held them tight. They were all she had left. Keira touched her mother's tense face, felt her worn out laughter lines.

'Are we going to die, Mummy?' she asked.

Maria stroked her daughter's curly blonde hair. She felt so soft, young, vulnerable. The tears came fast, choking her up as she tried to speak.

'Of course not, darling, but I think we should get dressed in our warmest clothes and go to the cellar where it's safe, don't you?'

Kiran cried out in protest, 'No, not the cellar!' He clenched his hands into tight little fists, pummelling his mother's breasts. 'It's cold and dark! I hate it in there!'

Maria hugged him to calm him down. Scolding him wouldn't improve their chances of survival. The children didn't start this bloody war. She hoped they might live long enough to see a brave new world. A world at peace, without brutality, torture, killing and destruction. Oblivious to her tell-tales which resulted in 196 undesirables being sent to certain death in the asylums that flourished, like toadstools in the depths of the pine forests. Kiran had a hysterical fit, frothing at the mouth, twitching. Reminiscent of Martin.

He screamed, 'I'm not going! I hate it! Keira hates it! She's scared of the dark!'

Maria lost her tenuous self-control and rebuked him, 'Do as you're told! Bad boy!'

She slapped her challenging son hard, nine, ten times, stunning him, making his face sting.

Keira clawed at her arm and yelled, 'Stop it, Mummy! Stop it! You're hurting him!'

Humiliated more than hurt, Kiran ran from the room.

Immediately regretting what she had done, Maria called after him, 'Forgive me, Kiran!'

While Keira gripped her mother's hand and waggled the stupid doll. 'Can I take Gertie?'

'Of course, you can,' her mother retorted in a voice laced with sarcasm. 'We wouldn't want *her* to be lonely now, would we? Now, run along and get dressed.'

'Yes, Mummy,' nodded Keira, ever-obedient.

She ran upstairs to the brother she idolized. He was flying around on his interactive Action Man bed playing virtually real war games: East plays West, East takes West, West concedes.

'Are you hurt, Kiran?' she asked. 'Please say you'll be alright.'

'I'll have a bruise in the morning but I'll be okay. Thank you, Keira.'

'Kiran?'

'Yes?'

'If anything happens to Mummy, promise you'll look after me.'

'I promise. Cross my heart and hope to die.'

Nathan woke to the sound of a distant air raid siren. It was freezing in the granary. The floor was covered with fine, floury, dust. His face, hands and feet were blue, numb with cold. He was ravenously hungry. Stank to high heaven. It had been weeks since he enjoyed a hot bath. He envied the wealthy elite luxuriating, warm as waffles, in their glass houses. How many fat cats would survive the onslaught he wondered?

He puffed a frosty halo, enduring yet another coughing and sneezing fit, took the crumpled photo out of his breast pocket and stared fondly at Renate's chocolate face, her shiny ebony eyes, the flat nose, and toothy smile. Her hair was puffed up, like jet-black candyfloss tied in a pale blue vellum bow. She looked sensational. He tucked her away safely inside his boiler suit.

I hope she's okay, he thought. *I miss her like crazy. I hope I make it back to my sweet lady.*

After praying for her, Nathan wriggled out of his sleeping bag, grabbed his rucksack, and hurtled down the stone steps. Before he ventured into the street, he tore off the incriminating patch. Then he ran for his life, towards the river. Nathan had to reach the river if he was to have any chance of finding his woman alive.

Kiran stood in the doorway, hands-on-hips, looking very grown up in his bright blue puffer jacket, brown needlecords and trainers. His cheeks were streaked with dry tears from blubbing.

'Come on, Keira. Get dressed,' he said, sounding unusually quiet.

She told him she couldn't get her sock on. Keira's socks were the ultimate cotton nightmare: bunched around her heels and inside out.

Kiran looked up at the heavens, and sighed, 'Here, let me help,' knelt and pulled off her sock, turning it right-side-in, yanking it up over her foot.

In her satin bomber jacket, "Kids Will Change the World!" sweatshirt and skinny-fit, pink twill jeans, his sister looked as if she was going to a kid's birthday bash, rather than a night in the cellar.

'Thank you,' she said. Keira was ever so polite.

Kiran waited until she had pulled on her blue suede hi-tops. Took her hand and led her across the landing. Past their mother's bedroom. She was too preoccupied to notice them. They were about to descend the balustraded staircase when Keira stopped. Kiran toppled over her.

He shielded his mouth and hissed, 'What is it now?'

'I forgot Gertie. I'm sorry.'

Kiran looked her up and down as if she were crazy. 'Keira! Wait in the kitchen! I'll get her.'

'Thank you,' she mumbled, staring at her feet, shame-faced for all the trouble she caused. She looked pretty glum, as if she were about to burst into tears.

Kiran suddenly felt very old, positively ancient. 'It's alright, don't cry. I'll look after you.'

Keira cupped her hand to his ear and told him what she wanted to do. He smiled back at her, a naughty smile, went to her bedroom, turfed the candy pink bed inside out and found the doll.

Maria climbed out of bed, showered, shaved, brushed her hair, teeth, and dressed up in her most expensive clothes. If she was going to die tonight, she decided, she'd go out in style. She strolled out onto the landing like a fashion model strutting the catwalk, attired in grey turtleneck sweater, silk scarf, crinkled ankle-length jeans and a mock suede and fur coat with an integral fur-lined hood. In a furious bate. Her son hid from her in the closet while she shouted at them.

'Kiran? Keira? Are you ready yet?'

'Yes, Mummy!' Keira called, faking enthusiasm. 'I am waiting for you in the kitchen.'

Maria breathed a sigh of relief; the cellar door was in the kitchen. She went downstairs. Kiran left the closet and crept down the crimson staircase as far as the reception room. He paused to admire her two digitally-reproduced works of art: Water Lilies, The Annunciation. His father's antique walnut writing desk. The crystal chandelier that hung from the baroque ceiling.

Would they survive the blast?

Kiran walked into the dining room, past a shiny mahogany table, ten dusty balloon-back chairs, a chiffonier full of china, and an inlaid music cabinet bedecked with crystal glasses. He hid behind the door to the kitchen. Keira was standing like a sentry in front of the open cellar door. She wasn't holding Mummy's hand. They were turned away from him, staring at the dark cellar. The light bulb had gone out. The megamarket was closed. Forever.

Kiran entered the kitchen.

'Please don't make me go down there,' Keira was saying, 'There's a rat on the step, look!'

Maria raised an eyebrow. Perish the thought. 'A rat! Where?'

She craned her neck, leaned forward to get a better view. There was no rat, only cobwebs.

Kiran took a step forward.

'Where, darling?' her mother asked, impatiently. 'I can't see a rat.'

'There!'

They pushed her in the small of her back with all their strength. Down the stairs she fell! They slammed the door shut. Kiran locked the door, removed the key, stuffed it in his jacket pocket. Maria bumped her elegant backside on every single step until she reached the bottom. Where she promptly banged her head on the concrete floor and passed out.

Her cherished children punched their fists in triumph, 'Come on, let's go!'

Kiran passed Keira her doll and strode purposefully into the larder. Once inside the sacred vault, he prepared a late-night snack of chocolate, crisps, chicken and Coke and threw it all in a carrier bag. Then he dragged his bewildered sister outside into the garden.

'Quick!' he said. 'Follow me!'

'So where *are* we going?' Keira asked, ever so matter-of-factly.

They reached the garden gate.

'We're going on an adventure!'

Maria never let her children play outside and forbad them from leaving home after dark. They froze in the moonlight as an animal rustled the dead leaves under the hedge. A bird with a broken wing? A real rat? Kiran and Keira walked through the creaky gate, relieved to hear the crunch of gravel under their feet, and entered open space. They passed an old bandstand, where a young Stephen once sang patriotic songs, then walked down a broad tree-lined avenue into the gloom. The sweet chestnut trees cast strange shadows as they swayed fitfully in the chilly breeze. A pipistrelle fluttered by them, scuffing Keira's hair. Scared witless, she tugged at her brother's sleeve.

'I don't like it,' she said, shaking, 'I want to go home.'

Tiny stars pricked at the boy's eyes. His head spun. He felt sick. He had a migraine. Too much chocolate? Or too much responsibility? At too young an age? Kiran didn't have the heart to tell his sister, they couldn't go home. Mother would never forgive them for what they had done. He dreaded to think what cruel punishment she might inflict on them if they went back.

On the other hand, if they rescued her, released her from her cell, nursed her wounds and made her better, they would be her heroes. They could even pretend her fall was an accident. The children loved her really, with all their hearts. And she adored them. Perhaps she would forgive them and they would all live happily ever after. Like they did in fairy tales. Perhaps.

Until the bombs fell. And the Robots came.

He slumped in a heap on the damp grass, his head between his knees, and wondered what to do. Without a friend in the world to ask. Except for Keira. She was his friend. His shoulders heaved and he wept tears of frustration. Keira tried to wrap her short arms around him, only to find they didn't reach.

She cocked her head to one side. 'Why are you crying?'

'I don't feel well.' He did look pretty sick.

'Don't worry, I'll look after you,' his only-just-turned-four sister said.

He felt a little better. 'Oh, Keira,' he sniffed, 'what would I do without you?'

'Let's go home now, Kiran,' she pleaded.

They'd taught their mother a damn good lesson on the perils of being cruel to children. A lesson that she wouldn't forget in a hurry. Now they were missing her like mad. Keira's lower lip curled up and quivered. Soon they were both crying. But Kiran looked the more miserable.

'We can't go home,' he explained, 'Mother will kill us after what we did to her.'

They were interrupted by a shrill whining noise which grew louder until it deafened them. They rolled on the ground with their hands over their ears.

'What is it?' Keira shouted.

'I don't know!'

The noise stopped. A silver ball with a fluorescent green aurora lay by them, flattening the unmown grass. Kiran sprang up and examined the bizarre phenomenon. He ran his hand over the ball's smooth surface. The object was perfectly spherical, solid, heavy, warm to the touch. Fascinating. The eerie glow came from the instrumentation panels inserted into metallic green caps at either end. Caps that reminded Kiran of the Poles. He rolled the ball. Keira held back, wary, edgy, watching the back of his bobbing head.

'Look!' he said.

They inspected the illuminated panel, captivated by its magic. Hundreds of lemony yellow numerals, letters and symbols changed constantly on the flickering screen.

'Isn't it pretty?' Keira remarked, gripping her brother's hand. 'What do you think it is?'

Kiran scratched his head, 'Dunno! Could be a weather satellite, I suppose.'

The numerals reminded him of the codes on his virtual console, a kind of data stream.

'You don't suppose,' he started to say.

She interrupted him, holding up a tangerine bundle, a mess of linen and tangled string.

'I found this!' she announced, excitedly. 'By the bandstand!'

At first, he thought it was a damaged kite. Then he realised what it was. He jumped to his feet. Jerked her arm. Pulled her clear of the ball. Keira dropped the parachute, annoyed at his reaction.

'Keira, get back! It's a bomb!'

She wasn't listening…

'Keira?'

She was too busy watching the hundreds of grey moonlight shadows form in the night sky.

'What are those funny arrows?' she asked, pointing at the gathering drones.

The aerial raid on the city was a treble strike. The first wave of drones vaporized all of the military installations, militia headquarters and air defences. The second assault targeted the mediaeval Old Town with its congested and highly combustible buildings and exclusive Glass House area.

Each drone dropped a single high explosive bomb weighing seven thousand pounds. The affectionately-named Fast Roast Meat Cookers destroyed streets in seconds, rupturing water mains, blowing off roofs, doors and windows. They also created the rapid air flow needed to feed the wildfires caused by the drones' secondary payload: the deadly cluster incendiaries. The first bombs were released at 21:34, the last incendiaries fell at 21:54.

There were no rescue teams left alive to fight the fires. Hundreds of fires from the burning city could be seen sixty miles away on the ground and five hundred miles up in the air. Thick black smoke rose as high as 15,000 feet.

The Enemy Intelligence System rapidly decoded data transmitted to the central command unit by the drones. Then EIS autonomously elected to expand the target zone, far beyond the perimeter of the firestorm to include all airports, hospitals, ambulance stations, train, subway and bus stations. And any exit routes that escaped damage.

The third wave appeared at 22:14. An explicit executive order was issued to all drones not to strafe civilians. The sirens sounded but, since there was now no electricity, they were small hand-held sirens that could only be heard within a block. The city was defenceless.

Bombing recommenced at 22:24, aimed at a wide dispersal zone radiating outwards from the city centre. The last cluster fire bombs fell at 22:34. At least no civilians were strafed! All drones returned safely to their secret airbase.

Maria lay huddled on the damp cellar floor clutching her badly gashed head. *I'll have a nasty bump and bruise in the morning*, she thought, daftly. That was the least of her problems. She had no feeling in her legs. Couldn't move them. But she felt the explosions, their aftershocks, run up and down her spine, as the bombs rained down and the floor shook. She heard a man's scream in the distance. Another bomb fell. This time the whole building shook. Chunks of masonry fell from the ceiling. Maria was showered with bits of concrete and plaster, coated in fine white dust like a ball of dough being floured, ready to be aerially oven-baked. *It had to happen*, she rationalised sensibly. *My luck had to run out.*

The air was scented with the noxious by-product of an arson attack deliberately inflicted on defenceless humans by insensitive drones. The house trembled as yet another bomb exploded nearby. Maria had to leave before it was too late. She thought of the air raid shelter on the far side of the city filled to the brim with refugees. Maria wasn't aware of any other shelters. She'd have to take her chances. But first, she must find her children. They'd be terrified.

The incessant shelling would drive them mad. Most of all, she dreaded them dying. Life without Keira and Kiran would be unbearable. If they were killed in this war, she would kill herself. She shook the absurd notion out of her mind and rolled onto her bloodied front. Then Maria hauled herself up the cold stone staircase, her dead legs weighing her down like sacks of potatoes.

The shameful scenes at the riverside would haunt Matthew, an unemployed engineer, for the rest of his life. Hundreds of survivors had lined the quayside: a sea of terrified faces, roasted radiation red by the raging inferno. Any sense of order, dignity or respect was lost in the rush to escape. Grown men and women, clad in pyjamas or underwear, shoved mothers with young children and old folk out of the way then plunged head first into the ice-cold water. Matt and Renate watched from the safety of their stolen launch by the far bank as all but the strongest swimmers got swept away by the tidal current. Their eyes were elsewhere, constantly searching the screaming faces of survivors who poured out of the inferno in droves, into the death trap.

There was an explosion. The firestorm attacked those condemned, killing indiscriminately, carbon-dating their lives in seconds. Chaos ensued as the panicked crowd surged forward. Unlucky procrastinators on the front line were pushed over the edge. The river became a seething mass of vanquished souls, clawing each other, fighting to stay afloat. After a while, they relaxed, conceding defeat. The dead drifted off downstream in orderly fashion, bodies bobbing along like plastic ducks in their last race. Until they reached the weir.

Nathan raced down the narrow streets of the mediaeval town into the firestorm. He watched with horror as his best friend ran towards him through the flames. The man tripped and fell. For a moment, he screamed, gesticulating wildly with his hands. He dropped to the ground, starved of oxygen. Nathan covered his eyes, ears and nose while Luke was consumed by fire. An insane fear gripped him. But he willed himself on: *I won't burn to death. Don't let me burn.* He forgot how many bodies he tripped over as he ran. He only knew that he must not burn.

Maria stared up at the clouded night sky through the gaping hole in the roof. A blooming pall of black smoke blotted out the stars. The force of the explosions had blown the cellar door off. This revelation gave her renewed hope. She snaked up the slippery stairs, out of the cellar, rolled on her back and gulped in the fresh air, covered from head to foot in blood and soot. The house was a smouldering ruin. She looked around her wrecked home, tried to contain herself, but the tears streaked down her black face in soured cream-white runs.

Someone gripped her hand. Maria stared at her children's ghostly faces in the dark, their dust-blanched hair. They lay with her in the broken glass and rubble, guilt etched indelibly into their pained expressions. Keira immediately accused Kiran of wrongdoing.

'What have you done to Mummy?' she screamed. 'What have you done?'

He was appalled. His sister already knew how to blame someone else. Who taught her that?

'What do you mean?' he snapped. 'It was your idea.'

The children stopped bickering and embraced their mother.

'Please don't cry,' they told her, 'we'll look after you.'

Maria hugged them, held them tight.

'My darlings!' she said. 'You came back to save me. What would I do without you?'

Matt removed his broken glasses, rubbed his weary eyes, and drew a hand through his bristly beard. He had given up all hope of ever seeing Rachel alive again. He sat at the boat's helm, thinking of her. The cheeky smile on her soft strawberry lips. The cherry-rimmed spectacles perched on her beaky nose. Her tidy bob of copper hair. He remembered the red roses, their romantic candlelit dinners, moonlit strolls hand-in-hand by the river. How the simple things had meant so much to her: his handwritten love letters, breakfast in bed, having a cuddle.

He recalled his proudest moment when he held their new-born son Jacob in his arms while Rachel slept after giving birth. Then the militia had burst into the hospital bedroom and made them wear black boiler suits with U patches to show the watching world they were undesirables.

Understanding his pain, Renate wrapped her arm round his shoulder. She wondered if her man survived the holocaust. A deathly hush fell. The river lapped gently against the hull of the boat. Only a handful of swimmers had reached safety. It was a time for mourning, grieving, for grim reflection. She held Matt in a silent embrace: her frizzy hair slick with perspiration in the intense heat, her face lined with the strain of not knowing.

Matt steered the launch upstream away from the carnage. They crossed the river and moored at a wooden landing stage on the banks of the city's central park.

Nathan found the safe house with a cellar, a sanctuary full of screams for the injured and dying: men, women and children. The aftermath of the bombardment was far worse than his darkest nightmares. So many victims. So horribly burnt. It was hard to breathe. A grey-haired lady in curlers and a nightie, an angel of mercy, soaked tea towels in a sink of cold water and passed them round. Nathan thanked her, wrapping a wet cloth around his face to soothe his fire-burn. The safe house took a hit. The room went dark, pitch-black. Utter panic set in. He tried to escape. To his shame, he trampled on dying people to get out, forcibly shunted upstairs by the other survivors, desperately trying to escape behind him.

The scene outside was unimaginable. Entire streets were in flames. Hot ash rained down on his head. But most terrible of all was the firestorm. He covered his eyes when he saw the horrid, inhuman things. Whole families running around in flames. Burnt-out shells of trams, taxis, coaches crammed with cremated civilians, refugees, rescuers and soldiers. Lost babies. Lost children. Lost souls. The fire was everywhere. The hottest wind in recorded history, the evil firestorm, threw the fleeing survivors into the burning ruins, the same shelter of death they had just escaped from.

Nathan's heart sank. He had been running around in circles. The safe house had evaporated, consumed by the inferno. He wondered if anyone else managed to escape. Pictured the angel of mercy up there in heaven handing out wet tea towels, saving the dead and dying. Bless her.

Maria fingered the deep gash in her head. At least the blood had dried. She fell asleep in the arms of her beloved children. When she woke, the paralysis had spread. Numb below the waist, she lay still and told her son that she couldn't move her legs. Painfully slowly, he dragged his mother out of the ruin, through the shards of broken crystal, past piles of charred matchwood, shredded clothing, flaming artwork, fractured dolls, a blown-out teddy bear. He stumbled and fell, but got to his feet and continued to haul her dead weight until they reached the shattered kitchen door. Keira watched him as he heaved her outside. They lay on the garden lawn under the moonlight with nothing left but memories, a stupid rag doll, and a carrier bag. Kiran passed round the chocolates, crisps and chicken, and helped his mother sip Coke from the bottle. She burst into tears and kissed him on both cheeks. Maria was battered and bruised but she had never felt love like her son's love. The memory of her dear boy, so young, tender and caring, would stay with her forever.

The synchronised bombing of the city was over. The battle for survival was about to begin. Maria was under no illusion. The Robots would kill her children. She had steeled herself ready for their death. She ruffled her son's hair. He looked so like his father. Her treasured knight would grow up to be a strong young man. She kissed her daughter on both cheeks. One day she would be a beautiful woman. Maria struggled to find the words to express how dearly she loved them both.

'Now, children,' she said, 'you must leave me here and find help. Go through the park, past the bandstand and take the avenue with the sweet chestnut trees. Don't stop until you reach the river. You'll be safe there. I love you, Kiran. I love you, Keira. Now be good children and go.'

The children shook their heads and disagreed. 'No, Mother, we're not leaving you!'

'You must! Your lives are in terrible danger if you stay here with me.'

Kiran pictured the Robots exterminating everyone who survived the aerial bombardment.

'We won't go! We won't go!' he protested.

But even as he spoke, he knew that he must.

'Hold me, my darlings,' Maria cried, reaching for them.

They held their mother for the last time. They kissed their Queen. And said goodbye.

Renate, an unemployed megamarket cashier, stared at Matt tearing his grey hair out with worry. Fretting over Rachel and Jacob. Those beauties aren't coming back, she knew it, she felt their loss deep inside her heart. She really ought to tell the poor man. But she couldn't bring herself to tell him. Instead, they discussed the tide. Soon it would recede, revealing the thick grey slimy mud which full-grown men sank into, disappearing without a trace. If they missed the tide they went nowhere, just sat around, waiting for the Robots to arrive and electro-fry them. Matt stroked his cheek, deep in thought. It was Renate who broke the silence.

'We must leave, Matt,' she said.

Reluctantly, he agreed. Renate untied her sweaty blue hairband and smoothed back her sopping wet hair. Wishing she had brought a change of boiler suit. She sighed. Matt was a good man, kind and loving. He deserved better than this hell. She felt for him, hoped he found inner peace one day. They stood silently on the landing stage, wringing their hands, preparing to say farewell.

Nathan's clothes were saturated with sweat. His legs ached from running. His lungs were seared from the heat. He looked at the dense fog of black cloaking the narrow street, the blazing fires all around him, and flopped to the ground, trapped. Horizontal flumes of blue flame cork-screwed behind the gaping windows. There were piles of crisp ash everywhere. It occurred to him that he hadn't seen a living soul since he left the safe house. How many souls had perished, this night in the apocalypse? Hundreds? Thousands? Tens of thousands? He must stay alive. Must find a way out, for Luke, for Renate.

Rachel walked out of the smoke towards him in her soiled boiler suit, the golden-skinned unemployed teacher, carrying her tiny bundle, her baby, and gave him a weary smile. She had flare-burnt strawberry lips, shattered cherry-rimmed specs, a sunburnt nose, an untidy bob of filthy dirty, carbonized copper hair. Nathan couldn't believe his eyes. She was incredible, a mother in a million. He opened his arms wide.

'Rach? Is that really you?' he cried.

He embraced her and Jacob. If only they could reach Matt and Renate.

'Fancy meeting you here, Nat,' she jested. 'Now, let's leave, shall we? If we go left here, this lane will lead us past the old church and the mosque to the park. Cover your face and take a deep breath. Are you ready for this, Nathan?'

'Are you for real, Rach? Yeah, I'm ready! Let's do it!'

Rachel hugged her baby to her chest and took Nathan's hand. Together they walked into the smoke, past the old church and the mosque, which would never burn, until they reached the open space. Safe, at last, from the firestorm. From there it was a short walk through the park, round the bandstand, along the avenue lined with sweet chestnut trees. To the river.

Matt saw her first, walking unsteadily towards him, beaming, their baby son cradled in her arms. He ran the last steps, rushing to embrace them. Nothing could still his euphoria, the sheer joy uplifting his soul. His heart pounded with anticipation. He held their miracle child, hugged and kissed Rachel. She felt so fresh, so alive in his arms. And she reeked of coal. They were reunited, speechless, happy beyond their wildest dreams. They boarded the launch with their child, starry-eyed, so in love, and sat waiting for the new dawn to break on the distant horizon.

Renate tried to control herself, failed admirably, ran up and threw her arms around Nathan who thought he was dreaming, thrilled senseless to be back in her loving arms again.

She was crying. 'Want to love you till the day I die, Nat!'

He cried too. Tears of joy. He held her tight, popped the question, there and then, 'Say you'll marry me, Renate.'

'I'll think about it,' she answered, slyly.

The love of his life smothered him in kisses. He swore that he would never leave her side again. After the celebrations they would say a prayer for Luke who died in the name of freedom. They walked arm-in-arm to the landing stage and climbed into the launch. Matt took the helm. And they cast off.

'Wait!' Rachel cried. 'Look!'

The children stared in fear and awe of the blazing inferno surrounding them on three sides.

Maria opened the heart-shaped pendant on her necklace where she kept him, a cameo portrait of her valiant knight, resting against her heart. She prised out the bitter pill. Release would take seconds. She put the cyanide in her mouth and felt its dryness on her tongue. Someone gripped her hand. The pill fell out of her mouth. Onto the paved garden path.

'Please, don't!' Renate shouted.

Maria felt humbled. 'How can I ever thank you? You don't know what this means to me, to be saved.'

Matt and Nathan lifted her onto a makeshift stretcher. As a second woman spoke: radiant, proud, holding her baby aloft. Maria looked guiltily at the undesirables. How could she have been so cruel to these lovely people? Perhaps there *was* hope for a brighter future, a brave new world, after all? She vowed to atone, to repent for her sins. If she survived, she would devote her life to building a new city, a true community founded on love, hope and equality. Meanwhile, her eyes searched for her son and daughter.

'Don't worry, your children are here,' Rachel assured her. 'We nearly left you behind. If it hadn't been for Kiran and Keira leading us to you, we would have.'

Maria stared at Rachel's kind face as the first light of dawn brightened the horizon. She hoped that her baby lived long enough to see one world, the entire human race, living in peace.

'We *said* we would never leave you, Mummy,' Keira said, ever so matter-of-factly.

Kiran gave his sister a loving hug. They all cheered as she showed off her grubby sweatshirt:

Kids Will Change the World!

In 2017, one hundred and sixteen founders of robotics and AI companies signed a petition calling for an outright ban on killer robots and lethal autonomous weapons, claiming the use of such weapons crossed a moral red line.

Act of Kindness

THE GIRL APPEARS AT DUSK on platform one, slumped on a black bench. It is bitterly cold in early March. She is wearing a short, shiny leather zip-up jacket over a clingy cream dress. Covered in grime. Shivering with cold. The teenager wrings her hands and tries to stay warm. A blast of icy air chills your face. You smell a sweet aroma, pear drops. You don't understand. Until she waves a cannister of hairspray, sprays it in her face and inhales it. There is little that you can do to help her. Her eyes are glazed. She acts disorientated. High. But, deep in your heart, you know you must.

The station is deserted. The home signal changes to green. You perch on the edge of the wet seat in your warm winter coat and search the curve of the line for the train. An empty cup sits on the bench between you. She can't bring herself to say the words. How must she look? A dirty urchin in a clean, modern world. How can she stare you in the face and beg of you?

There is an announcement. You sigh with relief as the train appears like a phantom out of the freezing fog. You think of your husband waiting for you in the West End. Your romantic candlelit theatre supper in Covent Garden followed by the hit show. Your 46th birthday treat.

Feeling sorry for her, you plunge a hand in your bucket bag and draw out your purse. Only to find you have no loose change. In a moment of madness, you extract a crisp twenty-pound note, fold it in four, and drop it in the girl's cup. You shake your head. It breaks your heart to see her like this. So sad, cold and lonely. Out on the streets. Out of luck. Out of love.

She stares at you in disbelief, her voice nigh inaudible. 'Thank you, you're very kind.'

'Don't mention it, take care of yourself,' you mumble, feeling awkward.

The train glides to a halt. You walk as far as the yellow safety line. A freight train rumbles past on the opposite platform. You watch her slip the note inside her pocket. Your eyes meet. She yearns for you. Love in the mist. The girl clutches her chest then slides down the smooth bench, breathing in short sharp breaths. She is clearly in pain. You stare at her, frightened for her, filled with dread. Your heart is in your mouth. You avert your eyes. The train doors slide open. A blast of warmth hits your face.

She is desperate. She calls after you. 'Wait!'

You bite your lip. Watch her face strain.

She tries to shape words in her clumsy mouth. 'Excuse me! Sorry!' Her speech is slurred. 'Don't I know you?'

You tell her she's mistaken. Tell her you've never seen her before in your life. Her teak pupils dilate, occupying the whites of her eyes.

Her voice floats and flits, word to word, 'I have this feeling about you. Haven't we met?'

What can you do? Your toes go numb in your smart sling-back shoes. You stamp your feet. Board the train, muttering a heartfelt apology. Her pain grips your heart like a vice.

She hollers at you. 'We were in love?'

You stop dead in your tracks. She tumbles off the bench. The doors close. You didn't help her because you were not prepared to miss this train. You enter coach Q, for Quiet Zone. The train is held at a red signal. Straining in your reserved seat, you scan the platform. Search for her. Overwhelmed with guilt. Ashamed of yourself.

You travel on the sleek, new, green bullet train, slouched in the forward-facing seat, half-asleep. You can't stop thinking about the girl. What on earth possessed you to leave her like that? What if she was seriously ill? What if she died? What if someone saw you? The guard, the driver, a railwayman, the Police? You wonder what to do. What can you do? You decide not to tell a living soul what just happened. Not even your husband. No, definitely not him!

You dream you feel her holding your hand, even smell her chemical breath in your nostrils. The train skips some points. You wake up with a jolt, stare down the aisle. Your heart skips a beat as the girl staggers towards you.

The train pulls past a station and gathers speed. She topples into the seat opposite you. The girl is an emaciated, malnourished waif who deliberately inhales solvents to get high. She has these mood swings. Her nose is running.

So, she licks her upper lip with the tip of her tongue and swallows the snot. The girl changes personality. Lifting her aching head out of her hands, she eyes you. Your heart sinks when you see the sore scarlet rash bloom around her nose and mouth, her bloodshot eyes, her tangled knots of dirty hair. She'll kill herself if she carries on huffing like this. You know she will. She needs your compassion. Not your rejection.

She needs you. One act of kindness. That's all it takes. To show how much you love her.

You sit there dressed to kill in the chic navy blazer, satin blouse and pencil skirt you wore for today's board meeting. Wondering what to do. As she unzips her pockets. As she empties the contents on the table in front of you: the blue cannister of hairspray, a butane lighter fuel refill, an open bottle of nail varnish remover. That aroma of pear drops. Her lips quiver. Her eyes mist over and she bursts into tears.

'Please help me, Mum,' she says, 'I'm sorry. I love you.'

*****

Alison admires herself in the bedroom mirror. How lovely she looks in her wedding dress. A healthy glow lights up her tanned skin. She feels rejuvenated: a confident young woman who battled her solvent addiction and won. She smiles wistfully. You stand behind her and lift her veil. Her eyes are sparkling with happiness.

She whispers to herself, nigh inaudible, 'Excuse me! Don't I know you?'

You are so proud of her. She makes you go all teary.

You are about to lose the girl you found at dusk on platform one.

Thanks to the editor of Scribble where an earlier version of this story first appeared in December 2018.

Blue Infinity, Red Heart

WE MET BY CHANCE AFTER midnight on the last train home. I'd spent the evening dancing in the aisles to my favourite band at their sell-out concert at the London Arena. Worn their hallmark navy tee-shirt over my faded denims and scuffed plimsolls. Avidly read their unique message to me, their wonderful fan, in the glossy programme. By the time I changed trains at Stratford I was ready for my bed.

I stood in front of the yellow line and scanned the train indicator for signs of life. The eastbound platform was crowded: late-night revellers, drunken party-goers, baying football supporters in red-and-white scarves. A few residual fans. And a handful of shattered City slickers. All trying to stay cool in the stultifying, sudorific heatwave. The opposite platform was deserted, save for a young couple engaging in mock fisticuffs. I watched with alarm as the teenage girl ran off to the exit leaving the boy doubled up in pain beside the platform edge. Then my train arrived, erasing the scene from view, prompting unanswered questions.

A brace of exhausted passengers shoved their way off the train. I was swept aboard by the jostling throng. There was an end seat free. Instinctively, I glanced up. Seeing there wasn't a blue sign insisting that I vacate my seat for the disabled, pregnant or those less able to stand, I sat down. The unusual young woman sitting opposite me disappeared behind an incoming wave of wet tee-shirts, damp vests, and dry, short-sleeved summer shirts.

No sooner had the train entered the tunnel than it lurched to a halt. The driver told us not to lean on the doors. Nobody listened. The train edged forward with a jolt. An unpleasant yob swung onto me reeking of whisky, her affinity for me marred by her blue language. I cringed, breathing her stale, acrid sweat. I'm claustrophobic. The sweltering, airless, carriage was my cell. The driver announced we weren't going anywhere until passengers stopped leaning on the doors.

I reddened. The programme felt clammy in my hand. My mouth was saltpan-dry. Why did I throw away my half-drunken, strawberry-scented water? I pictured its plastic, dissipating on some far-off exotic beach, asphyxiating a sea turtle or baby dolphin. Returning to my body as particulates. Penetrating my stomach wall. Worming its way into my unsuspecting viscera. After that, I must have either fallen asleep or passed out.

I felt a zephyr on my face as the doors slid open. A female voice announced Woodford. My coach emptied. Our doors closed. Feeling refreshed, I scanned the carriage. It was empty, almost. I tried not to stare at the unusual young woman. Instead, I studied the advertisements.

The holiday scene featured a deliriously happy young couple cavorting on a sunny beach. The man was wearing a sky-blue tee-shirt, stone-beige summer shorts. The woman, a mustard swimsuit. She was piggy-backed onto him, twiddling her sandy toes, fascinated by the sky's blue affinity with the flat, foamy, azure sea. The header read:

Blue Infinity: The Holiday of a Lifetime!

My heart sank. I felt lonely. I couldn't help myself. My eyes fell on her. She was red-faced, full of blush, red-haired. Her deep, golden-red locks tumbled like a lion's mane over her bare shoulders. The strangest-looking, most beautiful woman I'd ever seen.

She wore a shiny red leather miniskirt, a lightweight geranium vest, pineapple leather-luxe trainers. Thick, ginger tufts of hair sprouted from her armpits. Her face was plastered with freckles. Unsightly tan blemishes dwelt in her scalp, clearly visible under her thin ginger hair. Congealed blotches of brown massed on her chest, into the crease of her breasts. Invasive speckling tanned her bare arms and legs.

I was intrigued by her bovine face, her cherry lips, her utterly wasted body. Every inch of her sun-bit, dappled, mottled, skin. She stared nervously at her hands as if she found the sheer intensity of her freckling embarrassing. I wondered if she only ventured out after dark to spare her blushes. Her little hands rested firmly in her lap. In those hands she clutched her package, about the size of my clenched fist. A parcel, that was clearly labelled:

Fragile! Handle with Care!

There was handwritten scrawl spread like italic graffiti on the waxed wrapping paper. Her message? What those symbols meant I couldn't imagine. She raised her eyes and scanned me.

'I noticed you watching me.'

I felt my cheeks turn puce, my mouth stumble on my lips. 'I'm sorry, I was only…'

'You were staring at my freckles, weren't you? Like other men do. Beautiful, aren't they?'

Her freckles intoxicated, wearied me. I rubbed my eyes, my bearded face. 'Yes, but I…'

'In case you were wondering, they go on forever,' she sighed. 'Like me.'

I shook my head. Had a long day, dreamy, wanted my bed. 'Sorry, what did you just say?'

'I go on forever,' she said, with a hint of pride. 'Would you like to live forever with me?'

I hesitated at first, admiring the smiling, bearded young man in the advert as he cavorted on the beach. The laughing, freckled redhead, piggy-backed to him, twiddling her sandy toes. Their love! The sky! It's blue infinity! And I asked myself: *What on Earth have I got to lose?*

'Yes, I would,' I declared.

As we approached murky Buckhurst Hill, she leaned forward and passed me her package. Inscribed beneath the label were the words:

Sacred! Blue Infinity!

If I'm absolutely honest, I was nervous. I had my doubts.

'Go on then!' she dared me. 'Open it!'

I tore open the sky-blue wrapper, unfolded the soft velvet pouch, pulled out the polythene bag, and dropped it on the floor. Splat! The bag split on impact, its contents spilling out in an untidy, sloppy, pool. Lying, beating rhythmically, in all the scarlet blood, her ruptured sac. Her red, bleeding, heart…

She leaned forward, careful to avoid all her slop spreading over the dirty floor, and seized my shaking hand. I felt her lift me up, taking me up to a higher place. We ascended, hand-in-hand. There was a wrench, a deafening cracking, splitting sound as the roof of the train was torn open and peeled off like the lid on a can of mackerel. The roof peeled off! Revealing a starry night sky, a crescent moon, shooting stars. I rose, in awe of her universe, her strange, compulsive, universe.

'Oh, my God!'

She spun above me like a freckled top whirling madly in outer space.

'My name's Blush,' she blew, free, alive, glowing with ruddy health, 'I live in sacred blue infinity. Like me to take you there?'

'Yes! Yes! I would!' I begged, forgetting to mention that I was Marc from Buckhurst Hill.

I stared down at the tube train: its severed roof, the crowd gathered on the platform star-gazing, cheering us on, thrilling for us, as we mounted her star and hurtled into space. Planet Earth. Its global warming. Its plastic-infused wildlife. Its PC insanity. All of it! Disappearing from view. Along with Buckhurst Hill Station...

I found myself on a sunny beach.

'Put me down! Put me down!' Blush shrieked.

She was so deliriously happy! I let her slide off my back onto the beach. She twiddled her wet, sandy toes, then dashed into the frothing surf.

'Come on in!' she shouted. 'The water's lovely and warm! Enjoy the moment!'

My spirits soared. I waded out to join: my love! Our love! Her sky!

Her sacred, blue infinity!

My red, bleeding heart...

B u g s

THE NIGHT SKY IS STARRY, the cabin is dark. Passengers sleep in masques and blankets. Or squint at late-night movies. Eyes glued to movie screens. Ears connected by flexi-tubes to plugs. After a stale pizza meal, Laura and Honey Spark cuddle up as best they can in the cramped economy seats to sleep on flight DO564 from Miami to Heathrow.

'Are we there yet, Mom?' the girl asks.

'We'll be there in the morning, Honey.'

Hints of pride swell Laura's throat, proud of her baby after all she went through at nursery school.

'What is it like in London?'

'Well, there's a queen who lives in a palace guarded by toytown soldiers and...'

Honey's face lights up. 'A real queen in a real palace?'

'Yes! And red buses, and another palace with a tall clock called Big Ben, and a riverboat, and a castle, and a big, big wheel. And lots for us to see and do and eat...'

'I wish Daddy was here.' Honey seems unusually glum.

Laura rubs her gold eternity band. 'I wish he was here, too. He's with the angels, poppet.'

Honey is too young to fully come to terms with what happened on that terrible day...

Avery Spark was a good man, a loyal and loving man. A devoted father who gave his life for children. An outstanding example to others, etched for all time in the conscience of the local community. Since the drug-crazed, deranged youth burst into his classroom, smiled his wicked smile and callously opened fire with a heavy, semi-automatic machine gun. Spraying the sweet, innocent children with bullets. Until they flopped at their desks. Soaked the floor in blood. Screamed with pain. Their pink mouths frothed. Their red eyes filled with terror.

Honey played dead, lay prone beneath her dead friends. He tried to kill her. The teacher bravely leapt in the way. Turned himself into a human shield. Separated the cold-hearted killer from Honey. Protected his cherished child as she held her frozen breath. Avery took ten bullets in the gut for her. Died instantly. Saved her life.

Then the maniac stalked about, cruelly popping his bullets into defenceless children, even as they lay dying, just to make sure they were all dead. Honey quaked with fear. Thankfully, he moved on to the next classroom, turned the gun on himself, and blew his brains out.

Twenty-eight infants and 3 teachers were slaughtered that dreadful day. How can that happen? Twenty-eight kids?

Laura struggles to keep her emotions in check, 'Think it's sleepy time, sweetheart, don't you?' then tucks in her pride and joy, snug-as-a-bug-in-a-rug.

Honey yawns, stretches her slender arms, all dreamy. 'Mm! Night, night, Mom. Love you.'

'Love you too.' Laura fondly kisses her girl's soft round cheeks. 'You sleep tight.'

She notices a bug, climbing the seat in front. Dark-brown, shiny, size of her ring fingernail. Sees an even bigger bug, crawl out from behind the TV monitor which is still showing "It's A Bug's Life!" Tries to grab it! Stub it out! It's too quick! It's gone! Irritated, itching, she reaches up, presses the illuminated service button, alerts the red-headed, red-faced, Irish-bred flight attendant. Coleen asks if she would mind keeping her voice down, so as not to disturb the other passengers. Tells Laura this flight's full. Explains there are no other seats available. Mumbles a huff goodnight and walks away. The plane isn't due to land for nine hours. Laura thinks she'll get bitten. She tries to relax. After a restless hour or so, she falls asleep and dreams.

She wakes just as the AE-380 airbus begins its descent to Heathrow, horrified to discover Honey is covered in bites. As they exit the plane, Jaxon, a flight attendant with oil-slick hair and a goatee, apologizes without prejudice and offers to upgrade their flight home to business class. Laura declines.

Honey's very quiet?

Worried, Laura drags her down the eternal queue at Passport Control. Freaks out waiting for their baggage. Tears through "Nothing to Declare" into "Arrivals".

Honey is slumped all over the trolley.

Laura leaves Terminal 5. Pushes her way to the front of a taxi queue. Offloads her sick daughter onto the back seat of a black cab. Asks the cabbie to take them to the Terminal Hotel. Cyril, who has driven cabs long enough to know a sick little girl when he sees one, slams his foot on the accelerator. They shoot off down the arterial road in a cloud of black diesel-fuelled particles polluting every lung in sight.

Honey trembles as the taxi screams into the hotel's forecourt. Her mother folds her palm over her forehead which is bubbling with tiny droplets of perspiration. Her girl is running a high fever.

Distraught, Laura checks in and begs for help. Celeste, a kind-hearted receptionist with black hair and skin, phones for an ambulance, tannoys medical assistance, ushers them to a first aid room, orders complimentary ice-cold drinks. *Poor woman looks as if she needs all the help she can get*, she thinks. After all, Celeste *is* one of life's vanishing breed of caring souls.

Honey rasps.

Hell-bent on justice, Laura lies her baby face down upon the bed, bares her sore calves, and snaps them on her phone. Lying amongst the fine white hairs are raised sores, twenty on her left leg, eleven on her right, all of them erupting lesions of golden pus, like dermal volcanoes.

'My poor kid must've scratched her bites all night long when she was asleep,' Laura reflects bitterly. Incandescent with rage, she shares the horrific shots with the watching world, adding this biting caption:
Each bug bit Honey then went into hiding. These images show my daughter's calves, but her arms are blooming bright red sores. That's more than just a few bloody bugs! Dream On tried to bribe me with an upgrade on the flight home. I told the nice young man; I didn't want an upgrade or refund. All I want is a flight home on a different plane, and to make sure the plane infested with bugs is taken care of. Must sign off now. The ambulance is here. Laura Spark xx

Within an hour the images go viral. She receives nine comments: two messages of support and, incredibly, seven disturbing likes saying how much they enjoyed the photos.

Dream On Airlines are forced to issue the following statement:
We have been in touch with our Customer to apologize and investigate the incident. Dream On operate over 110,000 flights every year and reports of bugs on board are extremely rare. Nevertheless, we remain vigilant and continue to monitor our aircraft...

The official inquiry into the Infestation of Flight DO564 from Miami heard Honey's legs ulcerated within hours of her arrival in the UK. She was admitted to intensive care in a state of shock. Happily, her legs responded favourably to treatment and she made a complete recovery.

The night sky is starry. The cabin is dark. Passengers sleep under masques, blankets. Laura and Honey cuddle up to sleep, to dream, on flight DO565 from Heathrow to Miami.

'Are we nearly home yet, Mom?'

'We'll be there in the morning. Think it's sleepy time, don't you?' Laura's voice is a loving hush.

Honey yawns and stretches her twizzle arms. 'Mm! Night, night, Mom. Love you.'

'Love you too, with all my heart. Night, night.' Laura proudly strokes her baby's gold hair, kisses her goodnight. Noticing she didn't finish her delicious mozzarella olive and pepperoni pizza! *One more slice won't do me harm*, she thinks, sinking her teeth into a gooey mouthful.

She opens her leather bucket bag to discover the bugs have hatched in its silk lining, bred, swollen in size to thumbnail, and multiplied. They swarm over her blanket. Disgusted, Laura pushes them away tipping contents of her handbag: tweezers, comb, lipsticks, mirror, tampons, passports, purse, hair brushes, tissues. Littering the dirty floor under her seat, scattering bugs everywhere.

She stands up, stamps her feet, tries to shake them off, but the super-resilient, shock-resistant strain survives, crawling up her bandy-thin legs, under her hand-woven linen embroidered dress, in search of her warmest breeding places. Desperately, she slaps, hits, squashes, pinches them in a bid to kill the devils.

Laura freezes stiff as several bugs crawl inside her comfortable waist-high briefs and nestle in her hairy crotch. Still more bugs scamper over her belly, traversing her shallow navel, and burrow under her taupe double-fashioned bra where they nip at the soft undersides of her breasts. They swarm over her body, reaching her chest, armpits, neck, face. Infesting her hair follicles. Penetrating her roots. Bristling with bugs, she staggers, sways and falls into the aisle, her arms held aloft in the shape of the cross, collapsing in a seething, dripping, running, living, black-treacle mess on the royal blue carpet.

The young man in an aqua blue, pink-striped shirt, ocean best shorts and a fat, copper-tinted quiff, stirs in the window seat, complaining as bugs stream up his legs and rapidly fill his boxer shorts. They file up the sweaty recesses around his scrotal sac, excoriating his flaking groin, scuttling like crabs up the anal crevice between his fleshy buttocks. He shrieks like a baby as they penetrate his fragile defences. Whelps of alarm emanate from other passengers, distressed sheep, all bleating for assistance from the beleaguered cabin crew.

Laura, who is frantically tearing off her clothing in a vain bid to shake out the infernal bugs, hears her daughter emit a blood-curdling scream. She rubs the bugs out of her eyes and looks over her shoulder. Honey's legs are pole-straight. Her arms hang limply by her sides. Her eyeballs bulge. Her lank hair is riddled with bugs. The jaw flaps open to show off her pearly white teeth. A fat bug rests on her petrified upper lip, then disappears inside her petrified mouth.

Meanwhile, in the opposite row, tourists scream in Japanese, plaster-boarded with bugs. A hysterical young mother brushes the greedy insects off of her baby. An elderly couple next row forward hug each other's infested torsos for dear life, unified in a congealed mass of shiny dun.

Hordes of bugs scurry up the aisle like bestial newlyweds, overwhelming the wretched cabin crew. Every passenger itches, whines, and scratches. The bugs feast on their bodies, infest the food galley, the zero-gravity toilets, a baby changer, even the linings of the luxury cots in First. Occupying every single crack, crevice, orifice, hole, nook and cranny.

After a minor delay, caused by an inconveniently narrow gap beneath the steel-reinforced door, the insectivorous terrorists make their way into the flight deck, assume control of the pilot, the co-pilot, and generally disrupt the whole aircraft.

The crippled aircraft makes a swift descent, nosediving. Its engines scream. Its cabin decompresses and the air rushes out. Twelve passengers get sucked outside, scudding off to their deaths across the grey dawn sky like human clay pigeons soaring into a shotgun oblivion. Oxygen masks flutter down, rubber butterflies, swinging in a flushing wind.

Time runs out for flight DO565.

Laura lies sprawled on the floor. Honey's dead. The passengers and crew are all dead. All except for the host and her ghastly bugs. They are alive and thriving.

Entomologists are concerned that insects will be forced to find new habitats as humans destroy the environment. They are increasingly alarmed that insects will be forced to live in us.

Laura gabbles insanely: 'Mind the bugs don't bite, Honey! Mind the bugs don't bite!'

Coming Out of the Rub

I HAD THE BATHROOM RE-CARPETED last week to hide the stains. The estate agents, Bunty Fleiss, assured me the house was fully refurbished, that every last stain was removed. But they are still there. The stains belong to Marcus Firman, a cardiovascular surgeon, and his jaunty wife Annette, the special needs teacher at our local primary school.

I climb out of the lukewarm shower, stand on the rug and towel my torso dry. She ambles up to me in her smart black shirt and trousers, I let the wet, turquoise towel slip. We embrace. She clings to me like a semi-permeable membrane in the humid heat.

'Made you wet,' I say to her, un-sticking her from me.

She presses her palms into the small of my back, 'Doesn't matter! Feels nice!'

Inhaling deeply, I savour the fragrance on her neck. 'You smell delicious. What is it?'

Her body tenses. 'Don't remember, do you? You bought it for me, duty-free?'

'Duty-free?'

'The flight to Crete?' She despairs of me, pinches my arm, vents her frustration. 'Try, won't you?'

'You lost me I'm afraid.'

She brushes my nipples with her soft lips and murmurs into my chest, 'Dirty Velvet.'

'I forgot.'

She wilts. I feel her body sag into mine. 'It doesn't matter.'

She glances at the glitzy watch I gave her for our fifth anniversary.

'It's nearly six. Have to go. See you!'

I let her go. 'Yeah, see you.'

'Darling?' she says, tucking her shirt into her waist as she reaches the door.

I look up from drying my veined feet, 'Yup?'

'You'd never hide anything from me, would you?'

I clutch the towel protectively to my chest. 'What an odd question, of course I wouldn't.'

'Just checking.'

I tell her I'll be in bed when she gets back. I always rest after lunch.

'Might just join you!' she chirps.

That pleases me. I want her to be happy every single day of her life. She leaves. I hear a door slam, and miss her already. Lonely, I wipe the steamed-up mirror clean with toilet tissue and study the spidery stress lines etched into my face, permanent dark rings around my eyes. My heart aches for her when we're apart. Silently, I pray I die first.

Most men spray their body head to foot after a shower. I prefer to beautify myself feet-up and leave my head till last. Stretching my muscled legs, propping them high, on the avocado toilet cistern, I spray my feet with refreshing mint, witch hazel and cypress. Skin allergies are the bane of my life. When I was at high school, I developed an allergy to copper sulphate and blue-vein cheese. Copper makes my lids swell. I love Stilton, Cambozola. But they bring me out in an embarrassing red rash, oral herpes. I flush the same way under my armpits when I use bad deodorant. Just to be sure, I use 48-hour, motion-sure sensitive roll-on. It contains aluminium chloralhydrate. Doesn't aluminium cause dementia? I honestly can't remember.

The brutal murder of Marcus and Annette Firman made the national headlines. The couple were slayed by a crazed maniac who stabbed them to death as they slept in separate beds. It marked them with three signs on their backs: a diamond, heart and club. Police are treating the killings as the work of a bizarre cult. Whatever culled them, and cut them up, is still at large.

I'm not frightened of dying, just petrified of getting old. Most men are, but are too scared to admit it. I wish I was female. At least they have a longer lifespan. Anyways, I'm not sure what it means to be male nowadays. I struggle to understand modern relationships. Are they based on love, sex, trust, consensus, equality, necessity? What are they based on? Are the flowers of romance dead and buried?

I keep a range of anti-aging solutions on the top shelf. Apart from the niggly osteoarthritis in my neck and back, my body is in good shape. Every day I perform stretches. Four times a week I work out at the gym. And I visit my sports physio for a punishing deep tissue massage once a month. It wouldn't be an understatement to say that Jason changed my life. I wrote him a personal testimonial:

I would like to record my appreciation for the excellent sports remedial therapy services provided by Jason Ashleigh. When we first met, I suffered from excruciating neck and back pain due to osteoarthritis and took ten painkillers a day. With Jason's caring support, his personal motivation and encouragement, I achieved recovery in under four months. I have improved my mobility, core strength and fitness to the extent that I returned to regular weight training and no longer require painkillers. This therapy was a positive life-changing experience for me. I really can't praise Jason enough for the undeniable improvement in wellbeing, health and fitness he brought into my life.

The challenge with staying young is in my head. The vitreous jelly behind my right eye shrunk last week. Now I see a thin line at the extremity of my vision, not a floater, a line that turns yellow at night. I had a bad fright that morning. Saw a shadow person. I try to control the devil with different glasses. Sutra, my exotic optician, tells me I should stay focused. Now, I wear multi-focal distance glasses for shaving, the same specs I wear when driving, and computer glasses to write a story. Today, I'll need sunglasses as she has planned on me going out in the glary sun to the market to buy fruit.

Jason was great, twenty years my junior. We argued about age, sex, men, sex, women, health, robots, age. I told him stories as he gouged the scar tissue out of my lumbar region. He made me tingle all over. He pulled the waistband down on my tracksuit bottoms and massaged my buttocks, then made me roll over, so that he could fondle my penis and testes. We grew close, kind of fond of each other?

I can't stop thinking about the knife. I shave carefully, gliding the blade round my cheeks, chin, neck, over, under, my lips without cutting myself. I rinse my face with aftershave from a blue energizer I bought from The Salon. Luba, my stupid Czech bald beauty therapist, told me it's the only male smell in a range dominated by female smells. That explains why it's so expensive, does it?

Still, the astringent is my only treat now that I can't afford to see Jason. Friday was my last appointment.

I clean my teeth with a dirt-cheap cavity protection caries paste, followed by a gargle of unbranded minty mouthwash that costs less than a bar of milk chocolate. Ross, my bronzed hygienist, doesn't want to see me for a year. I wonder what I'll look like when my teeth fall out. Perish the thought!

I miss Jason. He was my confidante, my closest friend, my lover. I worry about him; hope he doesn't do anything stupid. I wouldn't want him to come to any harm. We all have secrets.

My secret is my hair. At least, I *tell* everyone that it's my hair. It is really regrown head fluff stimulated by a prescription-only scalp solution and sky-blue finasteride. The tablets are meant to be cut in four. I cut them in half. Despite the warning on the label, I haven't experienced any side effects. I always make a point of wiping the knife on the dishcloth after cutting the tablets. Apparently, they can cause excessive body hair growth, hot flushes and nausea in women, and genetic defects in babies. A strip went missing last week. I think she took them! She doesn't appear to have suffered any tell-tale skin reactions. I still stashed them out of sight in my sock drawer - along with my Men's Health magazines.

I apply the rapid regrowth lotion to my scalp, combing the cloudy solution into my thin grey hair. Before I leave the room, I check the list pinned onto the back of the door, to ensure I haven't forgotten anything:

Darling, here's your bathroom list:

Left you a fresh towel to dry yourself with, babe.

Spray your feet, make them smell nice for me.

Use lots of deodorant for me, won't you?

Take care when you shave. Hate it when you cut yourself.

Don't forget your blue after-shave, my favourite.

Don't forget your hair tablet!

Love you,

xxx

I pad across the landing to her bedroom, proud to call myself her house husband. That doesn't mean I keep the place clean. The net curtains are filthy, so the neighbours can't see in. I throw the towel on the carpet, and perform stretches in front of the mirror. Jason taught me to contort my body into spectacular positions: the cat, doggie-style, the cobra. His pelvic thrust. When I feel especially brave, I perform them in front of the young on the mats in the gym's Core Strength Zone. Dawn, the shifty receptionist, tells me Jason hasn't been in since Friday.

My second list is lying on the bed. Ever since my amnesia started, she writes me a daily to-do list. My head is full of stories. But I can't write them until I complete the list. I flop on the bed in a bedraggled heap and read:

Darling, here's today's to-do-list:

Water garden. Don't forget my hanging baskets!

Spray my courgette plants with slug spray.

Empty the washing machine. Wait a minute before you open the door. Hang out our laundry.

Left you out a tin of Mackerel in Teriyaki Sauce. Make yourself a salad.

Take my party frock to the dry cleaners.

Buy me toothpaste and mouthwash. Can you buy milk and a paper, too?

Check our e-mails. Check WhatsApps from Li and Lou.

Water the allotment. See if the beans are ready to pick.

Go to the market, buy me clementine.

Good job! Very good job! Ha! Ha! Now you have a lovely day. Don't overdo it.

I love you,

xxx

I feel overwhelmed. Now, where to start? How to start? Go back to bed? No! Start getting dressed, something bright. It's a blistering hot day, a vest and shorts day. To my amazement, my silk-embossed tee-shirt from our Vietnam trip four years ago still fits. Think young, man! I unwrap my skimpy black shorts. Act your age? What the hell!

I pull out the sock drawer and they are still there: the azure and crimson ankle socks by Pepe I bought in Crete. I walked five kilometres in the blazing heat to find a shop that sold socks - as she lay in the health spa thrilling to a full body massage by Andreas. I quickly lace up my smelly trainers, and skip downstairs.

I found the dagger in its sheath soon after we moved in, strapped beneath a rafter in the garage. I climbed my spattered decorating ladder to examine it. The scabbard was made of black leather, stitched down each side, fastened with metal studs. Its back was badly frayed, stained with dry blood. The haft of the knife was stamped with symbols: a diamond, heart and club.

I drew the knife from its sheath. Its bevelled blade glinted in the early evening sun. I ran my thumb down one edge. It was razor sharp. The knife tip was bent as if it had been rammed against concrete, or a bone. I turned the weapon over in my hands. The obverse was speckled with dry blood. Hearing her calling me for supper, I replaced the knife in its sheath and hid it in my galvanised metal tool box.

I haven't told her about the dagger or the stains soaked into our bathroom floorboards. She'd only worry. Instead, I decided to inform the Police when they hold their next knife amnesty.

I stand in the hall, staring into the street, in disbelief. My personal organiser left the front door open. Fearing for my safety, I wedge it open with the doormat, step outside. We live in a three-bed, semi-detached in a quiet cul-de-sac surrounded by neighbours who mind their own business. The road is empty. Angry, I stomp inside and slam the door. Glossy pamphlets litter the castellated rug: another new pizza takeaway outlet, a special offer on double-glazing, the latest tree surgeon. I scoop them up and walk into the kitchen.

She's laid our fake pine table for my breakfast: pink grapefruit, honey granola, stoned prunes, seeded granary toast, stem ginger marmalade. Bless her! I'm just about to switch on our precision-pour kettle and make a coffee when I notice the back door isn't closed. I curse her, swearing at her like a fishwife in a rant.

I told him we were finished. He couldn't accept that. He held me tightly in his strong arms and tried to fuck me. I was stunned, I had never been fucked by a man before. I pulled myself off of him and got dressed. He started crying, saying he couldn't live without me. I left him heartbroken in the day nursery which doubled as my treatment room, with no-one to console him. I walked out of his life forever.

I step into the garden and take in the carnage before me. Our new lawn is dead, blanched to straw by the devastating heat. The dwarf apple tree will bear no fruit. All the tomato plants have wilted. I must save the leeks, water the leeks. The watering can is inside the garage. The door is shut. I swing it open. I step inside.

He is waiting for me in the shadows. He swaggers up to me, unshaven, and unwashed. His breath smells stale, as if he's been out drinking all night. He rolls up the sleeve of his navy sweatshirt and reveals three tattoos on his shaven wrist: a diamond, heart and club, then says:

'My, you're a handful today, aren't you, man?'

I won't keep still. I flail my arms, bite, tear, scratch and gouge. Anything to stay alive. But the murderous grip around my throat only tightens, constricting my strangulated windpipe, weakening any residual resolve, stifling my futile resistance. I am petrified! I fight back the asphyxiating nausea.

'Relax your neck.'

I give up all hope of survival, unable to fight back, to free myself from the relentless chiropractic grasp. One of his strong hands masks my mouth, its steely digits pinching shut my nostrils. The other is firmly clamped under my chin. The two hands entwine and I find myself being hauled up, barely able to stand tiptoed. A human flag hoisted by the scruff of my neck.

My flimsy body dangles like a wriggling caterpillar about to pupate. My heavy legs swing freely, like dead turkey legs, limp, numb, blued, dead. I swallow hard as a putrid lump swells in my throat. A sour-tasting sore-bud that blooms into a violet flower of bruises.

'That's better, boy!'

I burst into tears. My puffy cheeks stream sadly-salted tracks of abject despondency. Jason shows me no mercy, taking my prone head in both hands, double-twisting and bending my neck until the bones crack, sending intense waves of pain undulating down my spine.

Seemingly intent on tearing my head off, he rips open my lower jaw, stretching my mouth until it gapes. Forcibly pushing and pulling my throbbing bonce in-and-out, in-and-out, of my make-believe tortoise shell.

I hear her call me from inside the house. 'Hiya! It's only me! Forgot my glasses.'

I manage a howl, a pathetic, hoarse, strangled, whelp. One final strong-armed wrench and my neck snaps. My spinal life-cord severs. My thoracic vertebrae break, fracturing into bony fragments.

I exhale her name in my last breath: 'Cherith!'

My insignificant world fades to unwelcome release as her cheerful voice trails off into the distance.

'Honestly! Forget my head if it wasn't screwed on. See you!'

Dancers, Why?

SARAH WANDERED THROUGH THE FREEZING night, down the empty streets.
She was nervous, she bit her lip, smudging her teeth with poppy red lipstick.
She took a deep breath, composed herself, and entered the village hall. The
place throbbed with music, the sound of swing. Numb with cold, she removed
her woolly beret, knitted gloves and winter coat, and dashed to the powder
room. Fortunately for her there was an empty cubicle. Sarah lifted up her
lime-green polka-dot dress and rubbed the circulation back into her legs.
Luxuriating on the warm wooden seat, she felt her charm, and breathed a long
sigh of relief.

She walked out into the bright lights. Thirty-four and fading fast. Would
love pass her by? He watched her from the edge of the dancefloor. She looked
sad, lonely, different from all the other girls. He strolled up to her and said hi.
Her heart butterflied. She went all pins and needles.

'Come on, babe. How about you and me stepping out, huh? Gee, you're
cute, no kidding.'

This man could shoot a line. Sarah admired his rugged looks, the clean cut
of his uniform.

'Thank you, I'd love to,' she said.

He smoothed on. 'Can you dance jitterbug, babe?'

'Might be able to, if you show me,' she teased.

Sarah was playing stupid. She *knew* how to jitterbug, she'd practiced the
moves all day long. Pulse-step, step-drop, one-two, rock-step, up-down, lifting
her knees. She couldn't help herself! Hopelessly in love for the very first time.
She felt dizzy, light-headed. Her heart thumped like a toy drum. Her mouth was

moist and ready for his kiss. She swiped on more rouge. He could smudge it off her if he liked! Sarah had fallen head-over-heels in love with the most wonderful man in the world.

He took her by both hands. Pulled her sharply to her feet. She let herself fall into his muscly arms. Savoured the clean scent of his skin. His smoky breath. Her soft hands pressed against his chest, rubbing the shiny breast buttons on his airman's jacket.

'Come on then!' he barked. He was firm with her. She liked that: the manly, protective type. 'Let's hit the floor. What's your name?'

She struggled to make herself heard over all the noise. 'Sarah! Yours?'

'John!'

Her face glowed. He was her wildest dream come true: tall, dark, handsome, strong. They joined the swirl of the dancefloor. John was a masterful jitterbugger. Sarah took to the dance like a bee to nectar. She held his hand. Her arm went limp. He was gentle with her. Didn't pull her arm off. No more quick-quick-slow! She felt so alive!

The dancefloor heaved with servicemen and women swinging to the big band beat. This could be their last night. Tomorrow they might go missing, believed killed in action. As if sensing their fear, the band stepped up the tempo. Music filled the air: blaring trumpets, raucous trombones, a sexy sax, thrumming bass, beating drums. So loud, that the dancers could hardly hear themselves shout.

Sarah closed in on her man, wrapping her slender arm around his broad shoulder. John put his arm round her waist. Step-pulse, turn-out-a-little, face each other, step-pulse, rock-step, step-pulse. The dance finished. They panted like two lions after a heavy lunch. Hearts full of love. Lungs full of smoke.

'Can I get you a drink,' he asked, adding, 'there's Coca Cola or Coca Cola?'

'I'd love one,' she said, gasping.

Soft drinks flowed like champagne that night. There was plenty to eat. Sarah felt as if she'd discovered an oasis after a long trek through the desert. The lights went down and the band played a slow romantic number. She was in the mood for love. Her house-mate flashed her a nervy smile as she left the hall on the arm of a young GI. Daisy wouldn't be home until morning! Sarah winked at her and they burst out laughing. The dancers smooched. She slid her hand down his back to encourage him a little. Felt his arm tighten round her waist. Felt him draw her close. Felt wonderful!

'I'd like to go home now,' she said suddenly. 'Would you walk me home, please?'

'Course I will.' He could barely conceal his surprise. 'Take my arm, won't you?'

They stepped out into the starry night, the frost's chill on their faces, gazing at the full moon as they walked, arm-in-arm, down the deserted street. Lights shone out of every window. The endless nights of curfew, constant blackouts, wailing sirens, screams of the injured and dying, would soon be over. Soon there would be celebrations, street parties, congas. Huge crowds, waving Union Jacks in the Mall. The band would strike up Moonlight Serenade for the young airmen and their forces sweethearts.

They stopped and basked under the lamplight on a street corner.

John produced a packet of Camels. 'Cigarette?'

'Yes, please.'

Sarah slipped his fag between her lips, cupping her hands round his to keep him warm. Their red embers glowed. They blew halos in each other's faces. John reached inside his greatcoat, pulled out some crinkly packets, and stuffed them in her coat pocket. Sarah was delighted. She always wore anklet socks. There hadn't been nylons in the shops since war broke out.

'Happy Valentine's Day,' he said, sounding choked.

She was puzzled; Valentine's wasn't until next month.

He looked down at his feet. 'Think of me, won't you, while I'm away?'

Sarah realised. He was flying bombing raids over enemy territory. She threw her arm round his neck and kissed him. To her surprise, he pushed her away.

'I'm sorry I led you on. I should go. Be seeing you.'

She called after him as he crossed the street. 'Please, don't go. I love you.'

Sarah stood alone, staring at the clear night sky, and wished upon a star: come back safely to me, darling, you're all I have left in the world. Her lip quivered, her nose ran, and she started to cry. Crying never failed to break a man's heart.

He appeared at her side. 'Hey, don't cry...'

She told him it was the war. She said the war had been hard for her. This war was so hard.

He brushed the tears from her cheeks with the back of his hand, 'Come on, let's get you home. How far is home?'

'I share a house with two other girls,' she sniffed, 'I have my own room. It's a short walk from here.'

They arrived at the bleak, terraced house. The windows were blacked out. Daisy and Vera were smooching the night away with their GI dates. They wouldn't be disturbed tonight. Sarah turned the key in the lock and turned to face John.

'Would you like to stay the night?' she asked.

John saw her shadow in the gloom of the porch. Sarah had changed. She seemed distant. He was scared, but compelled by a stronger force. He desired her, he found her irresistible. She let him inside, shutting out the starry night. It was cold in the hallway: dank, musty smells. Sarah switched off the light, took his hand in hers, and led him up the dingy staircase. A cobweb brushed his cheek. *What kinda place is this?* he wondered.

'You live in this dump?'

'What choice do I have?' she replied, solemnly. 'What choice do any of us have in this war? I manage, I get by. I have my little room, a roof over my head, enough to eat. Which is more than many have after the bombing. Some of my closest friends have lost everything: family, home, possessions…'

'I'll take you away from all this, I'll take you home, I promise. When this crazy war ends.'

That's what all the airmen said. She looked him straight in the face. 'Will you, John, really?'

He looked away from her, remembering Oklahoma, golden fields swaying in the summer breeze. Josie's soft, round, brown face crying him goodbye behind the kitchen window. Sarah squeezed his hand as they reached the landing, and switched on the light. The modern house had three bedrooms, a bathroom, and a separate toilet. The door facing them was Sarah's room.

He felt awkward about Josie. 'I'm sorry, I think I should go.'

She gripped his wrist, holding him like a naughty schoolboy refusing to go to school. 'Please don't go.' She started to cry again. 'I want you to stay. I'm lonely. Stay with me.'

He brushed the tear-damp hair off her face. 'Okay, don't cry! I'll stay.'

Sarah let him inside, locked the door, and switched on the light. They slipped off their winter coats and shoes. She removed her mauve beret and shook out her wavy blonde hair. He gawped at her bare legs, the flimsy dress, her radiant face.

To his surprise, her little room was cosy and warm. A coal fire smouldered in the open fireplace. The heavy curtains added to the snug feel of the place, her warm welcome. He felt himself relax. The room was sparsely, if adequately, furnished with a single bed, tallboy, mirrored dressing table and chair. He noticed some faded brown photographs on the mantelpiece over the fireplace: a young mother holding her baby, a blond athletic youth, a pair of identical twins in a cot, a couple holding hands. He studied the last photograph closely. The faces were indistinct.

Sarah distracted him. 'I have a surprise for you.'

He felt energised by her, but remained suspicious. 'What kinda surprise...?'

'Stand still and I'll show you.'

He smiled contentedly as she undressed him, removing the airman's jacket, hanging it over the back of the chair. She unknotted his tie, unbuttoned his shirt, easing it over his shoulders, exposing his solid, hairy, well-muscled chest and flat stomach. Carefully, she folded his clothes, placing them in a neatly-folded pile. He reached for her, wanted to hold her tight. She resisted him, stayed his advances.

'Not yet!' She ran her finger down his chest, counting his ribs. 'Valentine's Day isn't until next month, is it?'

He explained. 'I wanted you to remember me while I was away.'

Sarah felt the surprise bloom inside her like a white rabbit inside a magician's hat.

'How could I forget *you*, darling?' she grinned.

Seeing the passion, burning in her sapphire eyes, John fell back onto the soft bed, forcing himself up onto his elbows. She leaned forward. Kissed him. Tasted his smoke with the tip of her tongue. Felt his hand wander up the soft inside of her thigh.

'Stop it, John!' she cried.

For a moment, Sarah stood perfectly still at the foot of the bed. Then, she reached behind her back, unzipped, and took off her dress. He stared up at her in disbelief. Other than her bullet bra and red anklet socks, Sarah was naked. Her stomach was daubed with a living painting, a shimmering, undulating tattoo, a magnificent scarlet rose in full bloom, its petals dripping dew.

At the rose's heart lay the solid diamond charm, sparkling with violet, indigo, amber, emerald, shards of light. Her beautiful phenomenon took his breath away. He sank deep into the bed, transfixed, dumb. Slowly, her petals unfurled. Her intimate charm protruded. She extracted her surprise from her navel and lay her iridescent gem in the palm of her hand.

He clearly saw his fate at that moment, he saw his fate shaped, entirely within her charm…

Valentine's Day, 1945:

Sarah wandered through the teeming rain, down the empty streets. She bit her lip, smudging her teeth with rouge, took a deep breath, and entered the village hall.

There were dancers.

Dancers, everywhere.

Dancers, why?

The Dare

HE KEPT ONE AS A trophy: white, hard and dimpled.

They were naughty boys with grubby shirts, shorts, wrinkled socks and scuffed shoes.

Jack was the bully. His coarse brothers: Don, Jude and Robin, picked on him because he was so small. He learnt to defend himself with his fists. Jack was in the lowest stream at school, intensely jealous of Bruce, the A stream know-all. He exerted an unpleasant influence over the younger boy, an untiring persecution which amounted to first-degree bullying.

Bruce was the patsy: tall, gangly and refined with a distinctive auburn coif. Jack taunted him, jeering: 'Ginger Nut!' but he still insisted that he was auburn.

Least of all was Danny, a short, shy, introverted child who owned one shirt which he wore to school as well as play. He was a mummy's boy. Dan put up with the bully for an easy life but Bruce was his real friend. He loved animals, and kept a guinea pig in a makeshift cage in the back garden. Even built it a six-foot run out of timber and wire mesh. So that it could earn its hay mowing the back lawn. The pathetic creature had a lump on its stomach the size of a snooker ball. Mummy couldn't afford to take it to the vets to have it put down. Whereas Dan didn't have the heart to wring its neck and kill the blighter with his bare hands.

The unlikely trio prattled on as they crossed the field of gold. Presently, Jack stooped and picked a fistful of straw. The younger boys obliged him, shutting their eyes, and craning their necks, as he pushed the stalks between their lips. Mindful of the dare, they sucked on in silence until they reached the thicket.

Danny peeped through his fingers at Bruce's face as he marbled with fright.

Jack's eyes issued him a stern warning. He shook his head despondently. Then they drew their first straw.

Inevitably, Jack drew the shortest, boasting triumphantly, 'Yay, I win! I go first!'

Avoiding the thicket, they strode onto the 18th green and stood with their skinny arms welded behind their backs, staring into the cloudless sky, like night-seers searching for shooting stars. Pretty soon, a male voice boomed 'four' in the distance. Before they could duck, a round white blur hurtled towards them, bounced upon a grassy hillock, passed a sand bunker, flew across a ditch, and rolled onto the green.

Danny watched, transfixed, as the ball slowly trundled to a halt at his feet. Jack pounced, and stuffed it in his pocket. They kicked divots and waited. In time, a thickset bald man with an indigo visor silhouetted the horizon. The man waddled, club in hand, down the fairway to the green and asked the boys if they had seen his ball.

Jack brushed his ziti face on his shoulder. 'Flew in the hedge. Want me to find it for you?'

'Would you, son?' the red-faced golfer puffed. 'That would be kind.'

'Course,' fawned Jack from underneath the prickled hedge, 'give me a minute.'

Minutes later, he emerged, covered in dry dirt, badly scratched, and empty-handed.

'Sorry!'

'No problem,' the golfer huffed and departed for the 19th hole.

Slyly, Jack retrieved the ball: a Bridgestone B330S, a bombers ball, a long ball with a soft, gradational core. Not the best, but his latest acquisition still left him with a decent feel, a sort of gastric fulfilment. He showed off his prize, smarming smugly at Bruce.

'Beat that, Ginger!' he dared.

Aghast, the tall boy flushed. 'Stop being so horrid. I am *not* a ginger. My hair's auburn.'

Sick to the molars of the bully, Danny mustered up all his courage and squared up to Jack.

'Leave him alone. He ain't done you no harm,' he blurted.

'Oh, I see,' smarted Jack, 'Danny the Superhero, come to save his puny little mate. Is this a challenge? Looking for a fight, are we?'

Confidently, he raised his clenched fists to his chest.

'No, I don't want a fight, thanks,' Dan mumbled.

'Well then,' said Jack, 'I won. Let's see who gets the dare next.'

Danny felt for Bruce as he drew the final straw from his mouth, his body trembling as if his fate was foreordained. Then he drew *his* straw, whooped and punched his fists in the air.

'I win! I go next!'

Feeling awfully guilty, he consoled his friend, comforting him, fondly stroking his ginger- auburn hair as he wept into his shoulder. Bruce's hot tears soaked his faded collar.

'You'll be fine,' he soothed, unconvinced. 'Would you like to go in first?'

Bruce sniffed. 'What an oafish thing to say, durr-brain. What difference will that make?'

He was right, of course. Bruce going in first made no difference. You see, Dan had the dare. It was his for the taking and he intended to use it wisely. He stared at the smug, melodramatic prig leering at him. They knew it would now fall upon Bruce to retrieve the trophy ball, with all the risks the final dare entailed.

'Time to go-o!' sang Jack, clearly enjoying Bruce's suffering.

Disgusted, Dan dragged his friend off the 18th green. They arrived at the thicket and stood staring into the gloomy black hole. There were no stars in there, just dark. Bruce pleaded for him not to go in but Jack, half-crazed with excitement, roared, 'Dare! Dare!' Danny hugged Bruce, v-signed Jack, sank down on all fours, and crawled inside.

Inside, the thicket was dark but not so dark that he couldn't make out the slowly recoiling shapes. Danny flared his nose at a dead bird, curling his fingers into the soft dry soil, stuffing his nails with dirt. In a while, after cracking several petrified twigs, snapping a rotten branch and flattening every bracken frond in sight, he saw the balls, scattered around a tree stump.

Was it him or was it getting hot in there? The dense canopy of brambles above Dan's head narrowed to a tunnel, catching in his curly hair. To reach the balls he had to wriggle on his belly, chin to dirt. There were ten golf balls in all: nine nestled in the soil, the tenth perched precariously in the branch of a bush. Danny shuffled into the sweltering den, earth tainting his taste buds, sweat dripping off the tip of his nose. He reached the nine. Careful not to disturb them, he plucked them one at a time, dusted them off on his tee-shirt and crammed the whole lot into his khaki shorts. Dan edged forward until he reached the fork. He thought of Bruce, gushing with fear, wetting himself, at the mercy of a vile bully who had predetermined his grisly fate.

Painstakingly, the boy reached up for the jewel in the crown, the holy grail, lying in its cradle and extracted it. To a poor boy like Dan this ball, the custom Titleist ProV1x tournament ball, was priceless. The ProV1x, one of the longest balls in golf, had a great feel and softness for a distance ball, pure off the putter, with a great roll. An expensive ball for a recreational golfer to lose at the local club. Proudly, Dan wiped the trophy ball clean and popped it in his mouth, to keep it safe. He unfolded the cradle of blue vellum. The fine, navy italic writing had faded with age and was barely discernible. Danny leaned on one elbow, held the letter to a ray of light, and read:

Dear Linda,

I lay awake thinking of you last night, the wind whistling in the eaves, the rain spattering on my window pane. I wondered about our love. What if we had never found our secret place?

I love you,

Daniel xx

What the words meant he couldn't begin to tell. Daniel? He felt cold and alone. He wanted to be with Bruce and Jack in the warm sunshine, as far away as possible from this foreboding place. Who was Linda? More to the point, who was Daniel? What happened to them? He was convinced that something terrible had happened. Badly frightened, he began to wriggle backwards out of the gloomy hole.

It watched him, waiting till he couldn't scream, unfurling from the fork, side-winding over the dirt. The adder lunged, sinking its bent fangs into the exposed flesh beneath his chin. Reflexively, he yipped and gulped, choking on the ball. His pain swelled in severity from searing hot to poker-hot. His scarlet neck bulged, infested with itching hives. The swelling spread up his neck. He was scared stiff, so scared that he couldn't cry. He lay in the thicket, paralysed, not daring to breathe. Felt the reptile's tourniquet tighten around his throat. Felt sick. Felt his tongue, gums and lips swell and numb up - like they do at the dentist's. He buried his head in his hands and wished the snake would leave him alone.

Danny cried out for his mum.

He kept one as a trophy: white, hard and dimpled. The rest of the balls were sold.

Dying Wish

JESS TOOK DOWN THE CARD from Charlie saving the blob of blue-tack, stuck on the back, for next year. If there was a next year. She placed it face-down on the oak side table and gazed out of the window wringing her hands. The morning light matched her mood: dull and dreary. Save for the first tentative shoots of spring, and autumn's clinging sulphur leaves, the front garden looked drab and featureless. Washed out, like her, on the twelfth day of Christmas. Christmas had held such promise...

Charlie escorted her down the high street in his green wellies and waxed jacket on the mildest of Christmas Eves to sing carols on the village green. They shared a plastic cup of hot mulled wine and a warm mince pie. An older man, wearing a bright yellow hazard vest, came around with a song sheet, shaking a bucket. Charlie put in a 20p piece as Jess sang Rudolph the Red-Nosed Reindeer.

Jess rose early the next morning to fetch some seasoned logs from the potting shed for the aga, stuff the turkey, and load the bird into the oven. Before she went back to bed, she hid seven sixpences in the pudding, then drenched it in brandy. The doorbell chimed Christmas Bells at noon. Charlie stood by the compactum, primed to disrobe guests and hang up coats while she embraced her family in the hall: Mum & Dad, Suzie & Mickey and Beattie & Debi with their screaming kids Charles II, Harry and Meghan. After pre-lunch drinks in the reception room, Jess ushered the guests into the dining room. They sat at the extended oak table and gawped at the elaborate candelabra, silver cutlery, crystal-cut glasses, and fine bone china. Jess had even bought stupid reindeer napkins from M&S for the occasion. They all bowed their heads as she said grace. All that is, except for Beattie, Debi and the children, who were devout atheists. Jess lit three red candles, opening the window in case they fell asleep, drowsy with carbon dioxide. Then everyone pulled a cracker, put on silly hats, and read silly jokes. Meghan found this year's good luck charm: a green plastic dragon.

Jess stuffed them like geese being fattened for pate foie de grâs. After they had watched the young King speak in the play room, it was time to open presents around the tree. Jess was given candy-striped pop socks by Mum, a tight-fitting purple sweater by Dad, and an e-book: Is It Today? by Suzie. As Beattie and Debi didn't believe in bearing gifts, Jess excluded their family from the proceedings. There were gasps all round as Charlie bent down on one knee, took out a sparkly diamond ring, and asked if Jess would marry him. Thrilled to bits, she burst into tears and told him she would. The family celebrated with a slice of rich iced fruit cake and glass of Prosecco. All too soon it was time for fond farewells, hugs and kisses, fleeting waves from a car rear window…

Charlie washed-up, dried, and put away the greasy leftovers for rechauffé while Jess went to bed for a well-earned rest. As she lay asleep in the dark, she felt her nose being tickled: her fiancé whispering sweet nothings in her ear.

'I love you, Jess.'

'Love you too, Charlie,' she replied, 'with all my heart.'

They kissed under a sprig of mistletoe. Jess giggled as she slipped off her satin pyjamas. He removed his naughty Italian kitchen apron and climbed into bed with her. She glowed with rude health next day. Suzie and Helen, passing acquaintances on the Boxing Day walk, admired the ring and told her how well she looked.

Life was wonderful.

She picked up the card: Happy Christmas to the One I Love, and read the message inside:

To Dearest Jess,

Have a wonderful Christmas.

With my fondest love, now and always,

Charlie xxx

Jess felt her mobile vibrate in the back pocket of her needlecords. Who could that be? She pulled it out and stared at an international number flashing on the screen. Just a nuisance call. Some turd pretending to be her internet service provider. She felt her chest tighten. What if it wasn't? She swiped the green button.

'Hello? Who is it?'

She didn't recognise the woman's voice: refined, genteel, public school, 'Is that Jess?'

Something about the taut articulation made her hackles rise. 'What do you want?'

'Hello, Jess. That is Jess, isn't it?'

She panicked. 'Who are you? Why are you calling me?'

'Charlie's alive.'

Jess froze, went to cut the call, paused, angry, intrigued. 'Is this some kind of sick joke?'

'Charlie's alive,' the woman repeated. 'Would you like to see him?'

Her lip trembled, she sniffed back tears, went to switch off the phone, couldn't, inhaled deeply, had trouble speaking. When she answered, she squeaked,

'He's dead! Charlie died in a head-on car crash driving home on Boxing Day.'

'He's here, with us. He wants to see you again. Wants to feel you touch him. Would you like to touch him, too?'

'You're sick! Leave me alone, won't you!'

'You haven't forgotten his dying wish, have you, Jess?'

Shaking, she swiped the red button, leaning against the table to steady herself. How could the bitch be so cruel? He was dead. God, how she loved him. He *was* dead... wasn't he? The call lasted less than a minute. She searched contacts, selected the number, swiped a green blur, dialled...

The Institute, a towering prism of olive-tinted glass, dwarfed the other buildings in the City. The pyramid's base occupied quarter of a square mile of wasteland overlooking the Thames. UV's Clinic took up eleven storeys below its zenith, and reception was on the 74th floor. Jess stepped out of the hi-velocity glass lift and made a beeline for the ladies' toilet. She stood in front of the full-length mirror and appraised herself. Charlie would have been so proud of her.

Jess was dressed to kill in a beige, wrap over mac with a broad white sash. Not ideal for a cold, drab January morning, but the colours flattered her appearance and she wanted to look her best for him. She inspected her hands: no rings, no nail varnish, plain as the day they met. Her wavy, brunette hair was cut short in a smart bob. *Suits you*, she thought. Jess didn't try to disguise the smears of tiredness under her sapphire eyes. She couldn't. She didn't wear make-up, other than the stunning ruby red rouge that she wore to complement her beige complexion. Satisfied, she had lost none of her natural beauty mourning, she tucked her pink tote bag under her arm and strode out to the spacious reception lounge.

The attractive couple were standing by the vast expanse of triangular glass panes, staring at a vista which stretched as far as Canary Wharf in the east to the misty downs in the south. Both of them were impeccably groomed. The woman wore a stunning, sleeveless, white dress with black trim worn above the knee, straight-seamed stockings, and black stilettoes. Her auburn hair was piled in a dome on top of her head. She looked positively statuesque compared to the little man standing next to her.

From where she stood Jess couldn't see his face, only the blow-waved, oak brown hair and well-cut charcoal grey suit. The man swung a soft black bag against his knee. He reminded Jess of the doctor who called round to see her when she was a child suffering with chickenpox. They were deep in conversation, didn't appear to notice her.

Jess sauntered up to the reception desk. The glass-topped block was surmounted with two huge ceramic bowls of pink orchids. As she approached, the receptionists stood in unison and left their service station to greet her. She had never seen anyone so strange, or beautiful, in her life. They were identical: tall and elegant with flat chests, tiny waists, angular arms and long spindly legs. The clones reminded her of giraffes, moving with the grace of gazelles, flexing their hips as they moved, as if disjointed. They had immaculate shoulder-length brunette hair - faintly-parted to the right - wild, starry eyes, and miniscule snub noses. Jess appreciated their Italian ¾ sleeve navy, square-neck tops, two-way stretch classic trousers in sand, and creamy stilettoes. UV clearly believed in their staff projecting an image as polished as the fabulous glass prism itself, no expense spared. There was something different about them, something indefinably pure. She admired their perfectly round pudenda, the missing tell-tale bulges, and moulded clefts. Jess was positive that they had no genitals.

'Welcome to Uncanny Valley,' they chanted, in sibilant voices, 'how may we help you?'

'I'm here to meet Amanda Irvine,' Jess smiled.

The clones had a relaxing effect, touching her with their presence.

'Thank you. May we ask who's speaking?'

'Jessica Belcher.'

'Thank you. May we take your coat?'

'I'll keep it on if you don't mind?'

'Thank you. May we offer you fine tea made from our freshly-cut leaves?'

'Tea would be lovely, thank you.'

Jess found herself mimicking the clones, bewitched by their charming grace and manners.

'Thank you. Would you prefer Earl Grey, Green, Assam, Strawberry, Peppermint, Lemon or Breakfast?'

'Green… please.'

'Thank you. Please take a seat by the window and complete this medical questionnaire…'

The clones were interrupted by the woman.

'Thank you, Lucy, Lucian, that will be all.'

Lucy? Lucian? Jess went to speak. The woman with the auburn hair spoke first.

'Hello, Jess. It is Jess, isn't it?'

She extended her perfectly-manicured hand. Her incredibly long, thin fingers reminded Jess of vulture talons, cat claws.

'Amanda Irvine.'

Jess couldn't take her eyes off of the clones.

'Beautiful, aren't they?' Irvine gushed. 'They're gender neutral. We create them here, you know, the perfect synergy between human and artificial life.'

Jess was shocked. 'You create them?'

'Yes, out of human embryos.'

'Are they, are they human?'

'Half human, half machine. Lucy and Lucian are artificials.'

Jess felt her jaw unhinge at the joint. 'Artificials?'

At that moment, Lucy and Lucian strutted up bearing trays: teas in silver pots, milks in decorous jugs, sugar in oriental bowls, and cylindrical drums: one turquoise, one lemon, which, she presumed, contained biscuits.

'Ah, here's tea!' Irvine announced with a flourish. 'Sit down and I'll explain what we did to Charlie.'

They sank into the black leather sofas. The woman crossed her long legs and looked away. *What you did to him?* Jess mused, taking an instant dislike to Irvine. *Not: How we saved Charlie's life?*

Lucian interrupted her, bending at the hip to pour tea: green for Jess, grey for Irvine. Lucy offered her milk and sugar.

She waved her hand, 'Thanks, but I prefer it neat.'

Jess took a sip and grimaced: the lukewarm tea tasted insipid. Lucy unscrewed the lemon drum and offered her a biscuit.

'Our zesty twist on the classic teatime biscuit,' it intoned, 'made with real lemon curd by our in-house chef for a delicious sweet-sharp taste. Would you like one?'

Jess keened, 'I'd love one.'

'Thank you. Can you stop at one? Why not take two, three, or four?'

She helped herself to three biscuits, nibbling around the edges. They were delicious, sickly, but delicious. She quite forgot where she was for a moment. The tea tray was set for three. A cup for the man who stared out of the vast window? The artificials turned away and pranced off to reception as Irvine reminded her of the reason for the meeting.

'I'm sorry for the dramatic phone call.'

The impassive grin on Irvine's face told Jess that she wasn't sorry at all.

'I had to be sure you came here quickly.' She regarded Jess pensively. 'We are under considerable pressure to release a statement, together with an image of your husband to the media.'

'Charlie wasn't my husband,' Jess corrected her, setting down her cup, 'he was my fiancé.'

Irvine seemed genuinely taken aback. 'You're not his next of kin then?'

'He proposed to me on Christmas Day.'

If Jessica Belcher expected an outpouring of emotion from Irvine, she was disappointed. She bit into her third biscuit.

'To release a statement and image of your fiancé to the media,' she reiterated, 'following his ground-breaking operation.'

Jess was confused. 'I can't keep up with you. What ground-breaking operation?'

Irvine licked her fat slug pink lips and set her teacup down on the saucer, with its handle set at exactly 90 degrees.

'Jess,' she said, lecturing her like a child, 'Charlie is the world's first…'

Jess gagged and retched, 'Sorry, I think I'm going to be sick.'

'You do look rather pasty…'

Jessica pushed out the glass-topped coffee table, slewing tea over it, ran to the toilet, threw a cubicle door open, hiked off her coat, knelt before the clean white ceramic bowl, and flipped open the lid. Shivery, she gripped the cold porcelain rim with both hands, bent at the waist, and sloughed out the contents of her stomach.

When she returned to her seat, she saw that Irvine had been joined by the man, attended by their ever-present sidekicks. Lucy unscrewed the turquoise drum and offered Jess a different biscuit.

'Crunchy, buttery biscuits made with chewy, ginger pieces!' it chanted. 'Just the thing to get you hot under the collar at teatime. They also settle upset stomachs. Would you like one?'

Jess found herself unable to resist, and took four. Irvine arched her brows, cringing with embarrassment, then glanced at the man, anxious to move on.

'How are you feeling, Jess, better?' she said. 'I guess that must have come as quite a shock.'

'I'll live.'

'In that case, shall we continue?' Jess nodded. 'Allow me to introduce Janus Ventil, the bio surgeon who led the team that gave Charlie his life back. Janus?'

Ventil extended his hairy hand at her like a puppy trained to put out its paw. Jess noticed the Rolex, hanging loosely off his limp wrist. *So, this is the house that Jack built*, she mused.

'Mrs Belcher,' he fawned, 'how lovely to meet you. Amanda's told me all about you.'

Has she now? Irvine was smirking to herself, the childish snob: *Belcher?*

'Please, call me Jess, and it's Miss not Mrs. Charles proposed to me on Christmas Day.'

'Really? How wonderfully romantic!' carped Ventil coldly. 'I am sorry for your loss.'

The ginger biscuit soured in Jess's mouth, a rough titbit stuck in her throat, she struggled to swallow, gagged it down in one, managed to speak. 'I don't understand.' She glared at Irvine. '*She* told me Charlie was alive.'

'Charlie is alive,' the bio surgeon stressed, 'but not in the conventional sense. I think it's only fair to tell you that your fiancé's life is being artificially sustained by UV. It belongs to us now, for us to experiment with as we see fit.'

'It! How can you say that?' screamed Jess. 'Charlie's a man, not an animal. You don't own him! I'm taking him home!'

'I'm afraid that won't be possible,' Irvine asserted.

'Why not? Charlie's mine! You have no right to hold him here against my will! I demand...'

Ventil cut in, 'I'm afraid we have every right. As you know, Charlie signed a dying wish, authorising us to use his head and body for medical research in the event of his death.'

Jess threw her arms about in frustration. 'But he isn't dead? He's alive... I want to see him!'

'Part of him is alive,' cautioned Ventil. 'He was delivered to UV clinically dead. His body was dead. But our scanners detected the faintest signs of brain activity.' He paused for effect. 'In the absence of next of kin, and you are not registered as his next of kin, Jessica, UV took the unilateral decision to proceed with the transplant. Your fiancé has made a remarkable recovery. He is now conscious, admittedly very weak and heavily sedated but stable, and able to speak when he is awake. You should be thrilled, Jess. Without our dramatic intervention his brain would have died within the hour. I must say you don't seem too pleased about it?'

'Of course, I'm pleased. I'm just concerned at how Charlie feels about the change, is all. How *does* he feel about... the change?'

'Jessica,' Irvine soothed, reaching across the table and gripping her hand, 'Charlie is grateful to us for just being alive. He wants to see you again. Wants to feel you touch him. Would you like to see him? I think she's ready for him now, don't you, Janus?' she whispered as an aside.

'I think so,' he muttered. 'It's recovering in our specialist ICU unit. I'll take her there.'

It? Her? What happened to Jess? 'Who's responsible for customer care here? I want to speak to someone in charge!' Jess demanded.

'I'm lead bio-surgeon at UV, Mrs Belcher!' squealed Ventil. 'Do you want to see it or not?'

Jess shut up. Ventil led her past reception to an opaque glass door, where he punched in an eight-digit security code. They entered a long, stark, white-walled corridor, without discernible windows or doors. As the partition slid closed, Jess took one last glance at Irvine, standing with her beloved artificials. Only then did she see Irvine's eyes, devoid of emotion.

The room was a tiny, plexiglass cubicle with a single bed. A metal grid covered nine radiating lights sunk into the glass ceiling, resembling a red, illuminated sudoku board. The place reeked of disinfectant. *They're keeping my man in solitary confinement*, Jess realised, too late. She heard the door slide shut behind her, the click of the lock. There was no sign of Ventil. She swirled round and tried to open the door. He had locked her in. There was no way out. She stared at the cameras suspended from the ceiling. Whenever she moved, they moved. *Smile, Jessica*, she thought, *you're on candid camera*. She started to panic. Then she saw Charlie!

Lying comatose on top of the counterpane, dead from the neck down. The body twitched! The body lit up, in deep purple! The body came to life!

'Oh, my God! Charlie! What have they done to you? Charlie! Charlie!'

He didn't reply, he was asleep. Jess studied the purpled head, bald except for sprinklings of what looked like brown sugar crystals on its pate, under the nose, and on its chin. *Some kind of preservative*, she speculated. Jess cast her mind back to the cryogenic bath her fiancé used to soak off in after Saturday football. Shuddering at the thought of his head, stored like a pickled beetroot in a human chutney jar, pending transplant. Its eyes were hollowed out, in black slits. Jess screamed in horror at the blue cheeks, nose and lips, the trunk-thick collar of stitches round its neck. *Its neck? No, his neck*, she reasserted.

There was no escaping the incontrovertible fact: the head had been severed and preserved in some kind of freezing, embalming fluid, pending transplant onto a body. *Frankenstein!* fretted Jess, *I'm engaged to be married to a Frankenstein! Oh, my, God!* She flopped against the solid glass wall when she saw the body. Charlie's head was crudely attached to a purpled prosthetic. Her thoughts were interrupted by Ventil's voice, waffling out of the mesh speaker sunk into the alcove. Jess looked up, listening to the creator, pontificating over the prosthetic future of humanity.

'Impressed, Mrs Belcher?' Ventil hissed. 'Let me explain how it works. As soon as your fiancé was pronounced clinically dead at the scene of the crash, we quickly attached his body to a cardio-pulmonary respirator to prevent post-mortem decay. The body was cooled to around 10C, then its blood was replaced with cryoprotectant fluid, a form of anti-freeze…'

I knew it! They froze him!

'… to prevent ice forming in the brain during the freezing process. Over the course of the next few days we placed it in a waterproof bag and cooled it down to minus 70C using solid carbon dioxide, that's dry ice to you, Jess…'

Jessica Belcher found herself fascinated by the process used to preserve it, even began to take a morbid pride in it. To think her fiancé was the world's first ever head transplant! She couldn't wait to take him home, show Mum & Dad, Suzie & Mickey, Beattie & Debi, their screaming kids Charles II, Harry and Meghan. With the proceeds from the filming rights, Jess would be rich!

She shook herself, ashamed of her selfish thoughts. Surely, Charlie would make a full recovery, come home, marry her, honeymoon her on some white, sandy beach in Antigua. Well, maybe not the beach…

'Dry ice?' she enthused. 'Like they use at raves?'

'Exactly! The body was packed in dry ice and ferried by private ambulance to our storage facility here on the 85th floor. Once we had established the viability of the head, we surgically removed it: with the neck-stump, vital nervous cortex, spinal cord, trachea and oesophagus, and preserved it in a vat of liquid nitrogen at a holding temperature of minus 196C. Naturally, we didn't want to thaw the head and restore its life functions until we were absolutely sure that the prosthetic was ready and fail-proof.'

'Naturally,' Jess repeated, increasingly intrigued.

'Would you like to know how the body works, Mrs Belcher?'

Jess studied the synthetic muscular body, glowing, deeply purpled in front of her, gasping in awe as it became fully transparent. Even she was forced to concede that Charlie, exposed in such an intimate manner, looked beautiful, no, more than beautiful, his body seemed unworldly, alien, godly.

'Oh, my God!' she cried. 'I can see his heart beating! Is that <u>his</u> heart? Please say yes!'

'Yes, that's right!' Ventil was excited for her. 'The head requires a constant supply of blood in order to remain alive. This could only be achieved by transplanting Charlie's own heart into the prosthetic. The human body wastes 60% of the energy it consumes. UV's prosthetic body, by comparison, is 100% energy-efficient; its solar cells absorb infrared light generated by the lights in the ceiling and convert it into the energy used to power the micro-computers located in the body's viscera, muscles and electronic nervous system. The infrared also penetrates deep into the synthetic muscle tissue which mimics the cellular changes and vasodilation of the blood vessels found in real human bodies, delivering energy directly to where it's needed.'

Jess wasn't really listening. She noticed more crystals, coating her fiancé's shoulders, residual cryoprotectants. They would soon wash off when Jess bathed him. At its neck lay the life-essential sutures: stitching its trachea to its new windpipe, the gullet to the oesophagus. A gristly band of pink connective tissue tethered Charlie's cerebral cortex to its spinal cord. What fascinated Jess most was the body's finish, the attention to the tiniest details. She stared down, past the body's trachea, lungs, stomach, intestines, kidneys, liver, bladder to the urethra. Ventil and his team had gone so far as to replicate the dark chocolate mole that jutted from her man's groin, the mole she used to lightly stroke after she had made love to him. Jess was pleased with the new penis and testicles. She wondered if they worked. Ventil caught her smug grin.

'Yes, they've been exhaustively tried and tested by our physicists,' he assured her. 'They're purely mechanical at the moment I'm afraid. Our biotechnology isn't *that* advanced.'

'I'm pregnant, Janus,' she announced, looking up at the speaker in the ceiling.

Ventil's tone softened, 'I'm sorry, Jess, I didn't know.'

'I'm going to have Charlie's baby. I want to take my fiancé home. Please, let me…'

'You don't understand. He can never leave this room. His brain is entirely dependent on the life-support systems built into the prosthetic and wired to our central computer system.'

Jess's whole body sagged with despair. 'How long can you keep Charlie alive in this state?'

'Until the brain deteriorates. Your fiancé is still young. I'd say at least another 50 years...'

'I want to be left alone with him. I want you to switch off the cameras and leave us alone.'

'I'm very sorry, Jess. I can understand you being upset, but that isn't possible. The prosthetic requires constant visual monitoring. You're free to go now if you wish.'

There was a loud click: the door, unlocking.

'Leave-me-alone!' she screamed.

Jess never saw or spoke to Ventil and Irvine again. She stared down at Charlie. How would she begin to explain what had happened to him, to them, to her child? The body trembled, then shook. The head opened its dark, bloody mouth and spoke.

'They gave me a new body, you know. Do you like it?'

Jess was lost for words. She nodded her head.

'Who are you?' the head asked. 'Where's Amanda? I want to see Amanda!'

Face at the Window

1967:

HAVE YOU EVER CRIED SO much, you can't cry anymore, looked around, and seen the whole world weep with you? Well, that's how I felt, or at least how I seemed to feel, when I was just a boy. I stood outside the evil, grey fortress that held her captive, and turned away to cry.

Before me stretched the fields of red: poppies washing in the mizzle, the summer drizzle that blanched my face sheet blank. Fields of blood, he used to call them, for the glorious dead, for the fallen. I saw him fall, vividly in my dream, through the skylight, crashing to his death on bare concrete, spread-eagled and bent-up like a hunchback, his red eyes popping out of his skull. I was just a boy. I saw him die in my dream. He would not die. Not for three more years.

He told me to wait, in the little off-white minivan, on the grey-chip stone drive. While he went to her. He always went to her on Sunday morning, to avoid losing me to the Church of St Luke, in East Green, where I was a shy, quiet, choirboy. Saturday afternoons, I'd spend in the church, singing my heart out with Mr Brewster, four boys, four brats, four braggards, and four bald old coots to sing the bass notes. Me, I sang high falsetto, as if Brewster had my tiny balls squeezed tight in his hairy old fist: 'All Things Bright and Beautiful, All Creatures Great and Small', and he did, once. But I haven't decided to speak about that, yet. Why wish harm on an old pervert? Otherwise we rehearsed hymns for Sunday, the occasional cheery chanson for a wedding, dirge for a funeral. On Sunday morning, while Brewster's Boys sang their hearts out to the Lord, he went to her.

And he made me come too. Not that it was all bad, sitting, waiting for him to finish with her, in the minivan. He used to pull into the parking bay, in the woods near Pottage Vale, feed me those crisps with the navy salt twist in the packet. Once he let me open the twist and shake out my own salt.

He gave me a smoked glass brown bottle to drink from, ginger beer, made me swallow it. I hated it! I found out much later, when I was at college, that many years ago a woman drank from a smoked brown glass bottle of ginger beer, only to discover the decayed remains of snails lying in the bottle. *Stephenson v Schweppes*, I think it was, the tort of negligence. He forced me to drink it.

Then he let me stare out of the drizzled minivan window, watching the posh and stinking rich flash past in their wide cars. One wet, rainy, skiddy-road day, after he had fed me plain crisps and forced me to guzzle snail juice, we saw a people carrier catch the kerb of the road at 70mph. He estimated. Saw the people carrier, full of adults and children, catch the kerb, flip over on its VW rooftop, and catch fire. He told me to stay in the car, in the parking bay, near Pottage Vale, and watch the woods for rabbits.

I asked him how long for.

'As long as necessary,' he said.

I asked him when we would leave this horrid place.

He climbed out of the minivan holding a claw hammer.

I bawled at him, 'How long before we leave this place?'

He broke into a run.

I saw thick palls of black smoke fill the car, moving bodies, contorting faces, hands pressed against the window. I saw thick, funereal, clouds of black, puff out of the car, like gaseous ash out of a crematorium chimney. I saw her face, stuck to the melting window, mouthing at me,

'Get me out! Get me out! Get me out! Get me out!'

She was just a girl, my age, 12. Just a girl, a burning effigy of a girl.

He ran back to the minivan, threw the claw hammer, dejectedly. Threw the claw hammer at the footwell, turned over the engine, made it roar, revved up, released the hand brake. We shot off down the dual carriageway. I noticed he was red-faced, burnt, dripping sweat.

We didn't speak for ten miles, mainly pine forest, fields of mottled cows lying in the rain, ewes with lambs, an old-fashioned transport café. There were lots of transport cafés beside the trunk roads in the countryside in those days, but the shops were all closed on Sundays.

I noticed he was breathing deeply, coughing, sputtering. I guess his lungs were filled with her smoke, making it hard for him to breathe. All that coal-ash or whatever the girl was now, her mum, her dad, her big sister, her kid brother, her grandma, who knows what of, or why, or how they died that Sunday morning at Pottage Vale.

He took a hoarse breath, asked me if I saw any rabbits in the woods.

I said, 'Yes! I did! I saw seven! Can I have some more crisps now?'

I'll never forget her face in that window. I burst into tears, the shock of it all, I burst into tears and cried so much I couldn't cry anymore. He put his fat, tender arm around my sloping, narrow shoulders, and drew me in - wearing my red and white "Where's Wally?" tee-shirt and old blue shorts - to his warm, rugged, chequered-shirted chest. I will never forget her face in the window.

Have you ever cried so much, you can't cry anymore, looked around, and seen the world cry with you? Well, that's how I felt when I was a boy. I stood outside that evil, grey fortress, that held her captive, then I saw her…

The last time ever I saw her face I was thwacking a tennis ball against the garage wall which occupied two thirds of our garden. I never understood how a garage wall could occupy two thirds of our garden, with only one third inside the garden next door. Still, walls were meant for chalking, so, being a lonely child, I chalked an imaginary net on the wall, hit the ball over it, and the wall hit it back. I hit that ball incessantly during the summer hols: rising at the crack of dawn, sloping inside for bangers and mash at dusk, infuriating them next door with my thump.

One of them stuck its head above the privet hedge parapet and watched. It was a frog's head, with bulbous eyeballs, no lids to speak of, thin lips, a crew cut, and sticky-out ears. It ducked out of sight whenever I regarded it. I grew accustomed to its face: round, florid, freckled frog's. It disappeared from view. I didn't see it again during the school hols. I had to leave home, see?

Dusk had set in and the air was full of gnats, from his wormery. He kept a wormery made of rotten lawn cuttings beside the garage wall for his brandlings. I looked up at the darkening night sky, the first star, and felt small. The universe was infinite, expansive, a vermillion ocean, sparkling with stars. I felt alone, lonely, and cold. He would be home soon, sleeves rolled up, elbows on the table, boots on the floor, expecting supper. I felt the cat gut on my tennis racket. One of the strings had broken. A poor boy with no toys, no fireworks for bonfire night, and now, no racket. I shivered at the evening chill, the sudden sense of loss.

There was a rasping noise coming from the window above me, the noise of cheeks sucking in and screaming out, hoarse and rattled. Something stupid. She had gone and done something stupid. He was out drowning his sorrows in the boozer with his hod carrier, Sooty, and pug man, Sweep, while I managed. I was left to manage her while he sat in the pub eying the girls.

'Please, release me, let me go,' she croaked.

I immediately realized what had happened – her obsessive, compulsive, cleaning disorder had led her to force her head through the wrought iron railings to smoke a cigarette, so as not to drop ash on the carpet. She was house-proud, forever sticking her head through the railings to keep the conjugal bedroom smoke-free. Somehow, she looked different. Her hair was dripping sweat, light golden brown with teak tips. The fag hung, no drooped, from her puffy lips. Spittle ran down her spotty chin, hung off her jaw, all mucous and clingy, then dripped twenty feet onto the green, green grass of home. Drunk, she was drunk. She twisted her head to the left, twisted her head to the right. She was blind drunk! Singing! And croaking!

'Cos, she don't love me, anymore.'

Her head got wedged in the railings. Her head sagged into the railings and began to swell. Her head swelled like a puff-ball, pink, then red. The fag slipped out of her mouth, fell on the green, green grass of home, fell between my feet. I reacted, instantly. She was asphyxiating, dying, in between the railings.

I said something daft, like, 'Are you alright?'

What to do? Him, I couldn't call him. We didn't have a telephone. I thought of them, the thing with the frog's head. There wasn't time. I ran out of the garden, as far as the back door. Locked! The front door was always locked, they only used it for visitors, guests. We never had any. We were too poor. I ran along the side of the house, the crazy-paving he laid down the year I was born. The hallway window was closed. I stepped up onto the raised lawn, the green, green grass, enclosed with red Bedford bricks, stolen from the builder's yard.

Our house had three bedrooms upstairs. One was a tiny box room where I slept. The second was the conjugal which overlooked the back garden. He'd had it fitted-out with stolen railings. Excuse my ignorance, but why? The third bedroom was reserved for her, and the new baby. If it ever came. If the stork ever visited! I stepped up onto the raised lawn. The upstairs bathroom window was closed. The living room window... was closed.

I tried to collect my thoughts. He was in the boozer eying the girls. The boozer was ten minutes' walk through the council estate. She was asphyxiating, dying, upstairs. The kitchen and scullery windows were closed. From my vantage point, on the raised mound of green grass, I could see them, staring at me through their brightly lit windows.

'Help!' I cried. 'Mum's got her head caught in the railings! Her lungs are starved of oxygen! She's asphyxiating, dying! Has anybody got a ladder? No? Please, call the fire brigade! Please!'

There was a flurry of activity as the neighbours drew their curtains, simultaneously. I stared at the night sky, thought I saw a shooting star, a comet? No, a plane bound for Gatwick. Brick! Find a brick, and smash the window! I crawled along the boundary of our raised front garden, feeling for loose bricks. There were no loose bricks.

Desperate, I removed my brown leather sandal, ran up to the living room window and hit it with all my might. The sandal bounced off! I heard a man's voice, thick and slurred with beer, roar in my back,

'What the fuck has she gone and done now?'

'She's done something stupid! Her head's stuck in the railings, she's asphyxiating!' I shrieked.

He reeked of beer, something else, a woman's scent, eyed me, as if I were insane. Let me tell you, I was the only sane one in our family!

'Pixie-hating?' he scoffed. 'What's that mean?'

I did something I had never done before in my childhood. I slapped his ruddy, slobbering face! It made no difference! He was still blind drunk. He staggered about on the front lawn in a stupor unable to find his keys. She was probably dead by now.

The mini-van! He kept a spare set hidden in the glove compartment of the mini-van, in case he got locked out. I raced across the moonlit lawn, leapt the low brick-built garden wall, landed on the pavement where the street girls played hopscotch, launched myself at the mini-van, threw open the door, and retrieved the house keys.

Shoving the drunken sot out of the way, I mounted the front doorstep, unlocked the door, ran upstairs, and stopped. Something made my flesh creep inside out. Slowly, I opened the door. Her body was slumped on the floor, a puppet on a broken string, her neck stretched and drawn, like a turkey's neck that has been pulled. Her hands still gripped the curtains where she pulled them off the rail trying to free herself. Her pretty red rose floral blouse and black cotton skirt, one flesh-tone stocking, were saturated with blood. I felt myself gag and retch. I saw the gaping throat, her ligature.

I heard a voice, keening, softly behind me. She was still holding the serrated carving knife, dripping with blood. She stepped forward out of the shadows.

My sister, Tanith!

'Hello, Dean,' she said in her plum-sweet voice, 'can you keep a secret?' Have you ever cried so much, you can't cry anymore, looked around, and seen the world cry with you? That's how I felt when I was a boy. I stood outside the evil grey fortress that held her captive. I saw Tanith. Her gaunt young face pleading at me from behind her barred window. I turned away to face the field of blood, couldn't bear to watch her mouth the words,

'Get me out! Get me out! Get me out! Get me out!'

I felt his arm, tender and warm, around my shoulders. I saw the lines of worry on his face, the streaks of grey in his hair. He'd be dead in three years' time. We had just three years left.

'Is it over, Dad?' I asked, sniffing back my tears.

'Yes, Son,' he said, gravely. His breath smelled of mints, he quit the drink. 'It's over. Tanith is clinically insane, they'll never set her free.'

He quickly changed the subject. 'I bought you a present, it's in the van, come and see.'

A present? Dad couldn't afford to buy me a present. It had snowed so hard at Christmas that he couldn't build. He was a self-employed builder, had to pay his debts, pay his hod-carrier and pug man before himself. The last thing Dad could afford after the cremation was a present.

I swished the gravel with my scuffed brogues and strode to the van. He grabbed the handles with his coarse hands and drew the doors open, like the curtains at a magic show. Lying on the corrugated metal floor, beside the trowels and spirit levels was a box. With a cellophane front.

'Oh, Dad,' I cried, 'I don't know what to say. I love you, Dad.'

He ruffled my hair and gave me the loveliest bear hug.

'Don't go blowing up our new council flat,' he laughed.

It was the first time I'd heard Dad laugh in years.

I lifted the box and stared at the contents: test tubes filled with crystals: green, blue, orange.

Fallen Leaves

IT WAS ONE OF THOSE mild, blustery autumn days when the rain whips your cheeks and the wind puffs your hairdo into intractable knots and tangles. A day for puffed-out brollies, children to crack conkers, squirrels to feast, russets to fall and swell. A day to visit Marjorie for afternoon tea in her thatched cottage in the woods and admire the softly falling leaves.

We always *used* to meet: once a year, on the last afternoon of November. Until Bob died. Thursday was the first time that I had visited Marjorie since the funeral. She hadn't changed: a little softer in her rosy cheeks, a transparency to her fine white hair that I hadn't seen before, a soupçon of forgetfulness scented with some dither, perhaps. Otherwise, she was the same old Maj: stocky, full of gait, full of pride for her family.

Or so I thought. Her boys were children once, smashing conkers, climbing trees, smudging the kitchen floor with loam off of their wellies. Just children, equals, innocents. In those days. They were one happy family. November meant stuffing the guy with Dad, building a bonfire, shooting rockets through the treetops. And Mum's special treat: those funny sausages from Sussex, the cellophane wrapper with the pig in goggles, racing the sports car past a wayfarer's signpost.

Thursday, for us, was a celebration, a 'let's brush away those cobwebs and put the past behind us' day. And what a celebration! There were smoked salmon sandwiches, pulled-pork sausage rolls, freshly-baked hot sultana scones, lashings of peaked clotted cream, home-made strawberry conserve, rich iced fruit cake laced with brandy.

All served on her strange silver pentagons.

We sank into soft grey sofas and supped tea, munching, chatting about the old times when we were young girls at school, old flames, flickering flames, fallen leaves…

I asked after the boys. Maj told me Richard was well.

'Really, how wonderful for you, Maj, after what happened to Bob in the field that night.'

'Yes,' she beamed, 'I'm proud of Richard, very proud.'

I wasn't listening to her. I suffer from distraction, you see. I see entities, dancers, that normal people can't. Maj and I share the power of the pentagon. I was distracted. I saw something. Through the sitting room window. Maj touched my arm.

'Are you alright, dear?' she said.

I shook my head. I felt my tooth crack, a tell-tale stone in my sultana scone. I tasted blood.

'I think I might have cracked a tooth on a curse,' I mouthed.

'A curse?'

'Mm! A tell-tale stone. Do you mind if I…?'

She waved her white flag at me and shrieked, 'Of course, dear, never swallow a curse!'

I spat out the chunk of scone, with its bloodied stump of tooth, into my hand and wiped the mess into Maj's best lace napkin. There was no sign of a stone.

'I'm sorry, Maj,' I said, flushing.

'Here, give it to me, quickly!'

She reached across the walnut coffee table, scooped the goo out of my hand and threw it in her waste paper basket.

'There!' she puffed. 'Curse's gone away. Do you remember when we played that game in the woods?'

'I do!'

'Naughty curse has gone away, curse come back another day!' she giggled. 'Oh, what fun!'

'Oh, yes, I remember, in the pouring rain, under a dark cloud sky. We danced the pentagon!'

'We did! And you bestowed the curse on my family, naughty girl, didn't you? You cut my hand with the tell-tale stone, baptized me with a portent, blessed me with the curse, didn't you?'

I fell blank. 'Did I?' I said.

'Yes! And so, it came to pass that the curse fell on me as your only true friend, and my family, for generations to come.'

'Don't speak at me like that, as if I were your dead child!' I hissed. 'You know I don't like it. Anyways, we were young then. I don't remember.'

'No? We ate magic mushrooms. From the field where Bob died. You haven't finished the scone I baked for you. Eat it up, Deidre, there's a good girl.'

I gurned at her, 'I don't want it! It's full of blood.'

'Eat it!' she screamed.

I drank of the scone more than ate it, there was that much blood in it. I swallowed the curse that I concealed under my tongue, picked at a curled-up sandwich and stared out of the window.

Maj prattled on about Richard: Eton, Oxford, lawyer, married, children, emigrating, Australia. I wasn't paying attention. I stared at the fallen leaves, spiralling in a sacred vortex around Maj's crazy-paved patio. The leaves rose and fell in a rainbow tornado: lemon yellow hydrangea, golden sycamore, crimson-bloodied, mottled green-and-yellow. I swallowed my stone, and the bleeding stopped.

He was standing in the middle of the lawn, at the centre of the pentagon, raking hands through piles of fallen leaves, attempting to tip them into a beige bucket. I watched the wind blow them away in crisp flurries, coloured spangles. He fell to his knees. The buddleia bowed before the gusting gale, the hydrangea shook and trembled. The more the child gathered the leaves, the faster they blew away. I turned away and saw that Maj was crying.

'More tea, dear?' she offered.

I glanced at my wristwatch. 'No, I'm fine thank you. I have a train to catch. In the village. At four. My time here is nearly done.'

I sampled some rich fruit cake.

Richard, Ellie, Matt and Fleur died on a flight to Cairns. The plane fell out of the sky for no reason. I was miles away, floating on my silver orb, staring down at the child, tossing fallen leaves in the air. I get distracted. I watched the child stoop and pluck some fallen leaves out of the wet grass as more fell like poppy petals on the heads of the grieving. I felt sorry for him. I wanted to reach out and give him a good hug.

'And how is Michael?' I asked Maj.

She flashed her face at me, turned away, then flashed again, like a lantern on a lighthouse. I stood up, brushed the sticky fruit out of my lap, pushed Maj aside and strode outside into the garden. I was godmother to Michael. I cut his hand with a tell-tale stone, a portent, blessed him with a curse.

He knelt on the wet lawn, suffering the drizzle that pressed our hair and spoilt my dress. His green chinos were covered in mud, his plimsolls were soiled, veins ridged the back of his hand. I trudged across the worm-cast lawn and stood over him. I felt my hand resting on his shoulder.

'How are you, Michael?' I asked. 'It's me, your Auntie Deidre.'

He gazed up at me, his eyes brimming with tears, and shook his head violently, side-to-side.

'What is it, dear? What's the matter?'

He pointed at the ghoul standing next to me. I turned to see dearly departed Maj, dressed in a black veil and widow's cloak. A fine advertisement for a funeral in her pink, fluffy slippers!

'He can't speak, dear,' she consoled me, 'he was struck dumb by lightning last November.'

The clouds broke, the thunder clapped, lightning struck a nearby elm. We came back to life!

'It will soon be dark,' I cried. 'Clear the fallen leaves, Michael!

'That we might dance the pentagon!'

Fuss

INGRID LARSSON'S ARM WENT NUMB as she lay on her side enfolded by Karlsson's powerful bronze bicep. Her tender moment, she called it, a pleasant tingling sensation which bristled into a pink rash over her body. She snuggled against Karlsson's chest and snygged his shining nipple. Thrilled by the brush of her thin lips across his areola, he probed the inverted dusky rose nipples on her little breasts with his baby fingers, surprising, if not pleasing her with the softness of their touch. His hand wandered, caressing her slim tummy, lightly fingering her shallow navel. Ingrid cocked her leg up like a poodle so that her man could feel her sacred mound. She was bald, bikini-bare, plucked as cleanly as a parson's nose, and wet. Karlsson gave her outer lips a quick rub, then drew her slender leg upwards, teasing his erection, resting her thigh upon his flat, six-pack stomach. Larsson treasured their satisfying silent interludes before jävla runt: the swelling of her puffy breasts, her tingling insides, the pounding heartbeat, her sublime arousal.

She was about to have sex.

Impatient for Karlsson's proud flesh, she shifted position, flexing her hips to encourage the flow of her blood. This time Karlsson didn't move. He just made a terrible croaking noise, exhaled loudly, and gazed at Ingrid with a vacant expression panda-eyed, his face greyed with exhaustion.

'Are you alright, älskling?' she said.

Karlsson didn't reply. Larsson held her ear to his mouth and listened. He wasn't breathing. She sprang up and knelt beside him. Her first aid training kicked in. Tilting back his weighty head, Ingrid pinched his nostrils, sealed his mouth with hers, and gave him her kiss of life. His chest rose then fell. She remained calm, resting her head on his chest, listening for his heartbeat, pressing the side of his neck with her fingertips. He didn't show Ingrid any vital signs of life. She pushed down hard with both hands, compressing his chest, pumping at his heart, listening to his death rattle as he faded.

'You cannot just die, sötnos!'

Ignoring her, Karlsson's inert head lolled lazily to the left. His eyeballs rolled around like marbles on a human bagatelle board. Desperately, she pumped his heart. She snygged him. Listened. Felt him. Then she gave up, erupting in floods of tears. Her incredible muscleman had just died, seemingly from a massive heart attack. Her organised mind shattered into micro-shards of angst, unable to accept the startling truth… Ingrid had killed Karlsson using jävla runt.

Olsson wound down the window and lit another cigarette, her tenth that night. Chain-smoking had blanched her face a greenish-white, leaving it cracked like a crumbling stone angel. She lowered the Jeep's cerise sun visor and appraised her run-down self in the vanity mirror. Olsson's shrivelled face reminded her of the many desiccated corpses that she had seen in her sheltered life: dried out and pallid, the dead skin drawn back in a death mask, as far as the ears.

Her greasy, straight, brown hair was pulled taut, strictly parted down the middle, harshly swept over her cauliflower ears in a vain attempt to convey a look of innocence and purity. Nothing could be further from the truth. The excess of self-imposed abuse left Olsson looking spent and ill.

She flicked ash onto the tarmac. The coal-dirty habit, its cloying tar, would scar her tortured lungs for life. The nicotine had stained her fingertips brimstone yellow. Olsson endured her persistent smoker's cough. Then there were the glues she sniffed. The permanent runny nose. The red-raw sores above her curling upper lip. Her tell-tale, bloodshot eyes with their dusky brown surrounds. She sucked heavily on the butt, coughing up her phlegm, then sipped a low-calorie, high energy drink. The Jeep's footwell was littered with stay-awake cans.

Olsson pictured Gustafsson, her hairy gorilla: his fat-bellied, buddha-body turned off by his archetypal, snoring, bean-pole mate, Hansson. Dreaming of their next illicit liaison.

Her thoughts returned to the young woman. Larsson's nightly misdemeanours had become predictable. She had dropped her guard, her confidence increasing as quickly as her obsession with Karlsson. Larsson left the historic coaching inn annexe at five-thirty every morning via the car park exit, walked through the Tudor arch, crossed the empty high street, and waited for the bus to take her to work.

Ingrid slumped on the bed; her tired head sunk in the softly scented pillows. A grey light filtered through the gap in the heavy beige curtains. It would soon be dawn. Her next shift started at seven. The corpse lay stretched out beside her: bluing, primarily flaccid, its muscles relaxed, chilling her to her senses. She stared longingly at the mini-bar. *Need a stiff drink*, she mused, *a brandy to help me think straight*, but dismissed the notion at once. How could she go to work reeking of spirit? Anyways, Larsson needed a clear head to think this mess through.

Her next move would determine the extent to which she was implicated in the forensic investigation, the scandal. Larsson imagined the headlines, online in as little as eight hours' time, and thumped Karlsson's enormous pecs.

'Why did you have to go and die on me, hjartat?' she sobbed.

Ingrid knew why. She had pushed her man too far, taken him over the edge, and killed him. The fact that Karlsson was super-fit was irrelevant. Hadn't she scrubbed a dead footballer with a heart defect? Dealt with a marathon runner, a fine young athlete, who fell at the finish line? Consoled the grieving parents of a three-year-old boy who died of a hole-in-the-heart? Larsson knew the risks, let Karlsson ride her all-night roller coaster, and he crashed.

She couldn't think straight. Chewed her nails. Rubbed her eyes. Felt shattered. Her twelve-hour shift ended ten hours ago. Larsson hadn't slept a wink since. Meticulously, she set about removing every trace of herself. As if their night of passion never happened.

Olsson was a messed-up wretch who lacked the willpower to quit the habit that would soon kill her. She wiped her frothy mouth on her ash grey tee-shirt, lit another cigarette, and took a drag. Olsson allowed herself to descend into this abyss because living like a parasite off the deceit of others gave her a high. She lived her life on the edge for the thrills.

Opening the glove compartment, she drew out a crumpled file and flicked through the pages, contemplating her forthcoming assignment with relish. Stapled to the front page was a high-definition image of Larsson, illustrating her distinguishing facial characteristic: the frozen, blank expression that she could put on at will, like a masque. Appended to the photograph was a bullet-point summary of Olsson's findings to date, for her aggrieved client, Sveinsson's, reference:

Confidential Client Summary

Name: Ingrid Jo Larsson.

Age: 25.

Status: single.

Nationality: Swedish.

Facials: round ice-blue eyes spaced wide apart, flat, freckled nose, dimpled cheeks, wavy shoulder-length blonde hair, pale complexion, full set of teeth, thin lips, baby-face, puppy ears.

Physique: slim, medium height, long neck and limbs, fit, in good general health.

Lives: council flat above Dick's Fish Bar: Flat 3, Flatfield Terrace, East Green.

Background: born in Falun, Dalarna, Sweden, 17th June 1993. Mother, Elsa, 57, lectures in English Literature at Dalarna University. Father, Erik, 65, is retired, a former miner at local copper mine. Brother Oscar, 28, works in IT, single, lives with parents.

Education: Pigeon Lake Private Regional Primary, Secondary, High Schools. Studied Medicine at Dalarna University, never finished the course. Larsson dropped out, left home, and moved to England in search of work.

Karlsson was covered in Larsson's DNA. She grabbed a fistful of floral tissues from a box by the bed, pulled off his spent condom, then padded to the bathroom to flush him down the toilet. The sign over the heated towel rail asked guests to re-use the towels and save the environment or place them in the bath. There were phials of shampoo, conditioner, shower gel, soap tablets. Karlsson had left his wash bag on the glass vanity shelf. Larsson emptied it out, returning to the bed laden with robe, towels, flannels, gels, soap, toothpaste, brush, inter-dents. As she arranged everything on the pine sideboard, she checked her watch. If Larsson didn't hurry, she would be late for work.

A wine cooler, complete with upturned bottle of Prosecco and dirty flutes kissed with pink lipstick, stood on the smoked-glass coffee table. Beside the half-eaten dishes, they chose from the pillow menu: prime fillet steak in brandy, cream and green peppercorn sauce, thick-cut chips, sautéed mushrooms. Ingrid's heart sank at the thought of all the washing-up.

Larsson carried the cooler to the bathroom, filled it with hot, sudsy water, and returned to the bed. Karlsson's dead eyes were staring at a dead moth stuck in a spider's web on the ceiling. Quickly, she shut its eyes, soaked the flannel, washed its face, neck and ears, and patted it dry. Ingrid inter-dented the masticated morsels of meat from the gaps between its teeth, and set off the electric toothbrush. The wash bag contained a small bottle of spearmint mouthwash. She topped up Karlsson's throat with all the finesse of a driver refilling her car windscreen wash. Once the corpse had swallowed, Ingrid dabbed its mouth, wanting to hold its sad head in her hands and kiss it, in death. Not for the first time, she wondered if she really loved the childhood sweetheart from Pigeon Lake who she found again on Tinder.

Karlsson was six-feet tall and weighed fifteen stone. Larsson possessed the strength to roll it. Not to drag it off the bed, traverse the carpet, and dump it in the bath. There wasn't time. In any case it wasn't necessary to bathe it when a simple bed bath would suffice. She spread a bath towel out on the bed, rolled it onto its front and washed it thoroughly, drying it with a fresh towel. Next, she spread a second bath towel, flipped Karlsson on its front, rinsed and dried it with a hand towel.

Larsson soaked, rinsed and wrung all the towels. And left them in the bath. Once she had washed the dishes, Ingrid was ready for a well-earned shower. Only then did she realise, she had used up all the towels. She showered, dried off in her robe, cleaned her teeth, combed her hair, pulled on a white tee-shirt, blue denims, grey belt and trainers. And packed her overnight bag.

As Larsson left, she took one last loving look at Karlsson. She had forgotten to strip off the sheet and pillow cases. It was all too much. She fell to her knees: heartbroken, distraught, distrait...

Larsson missed her bus. Olsson watched her leave the hotel. Her head was down. Why? A lovers' tiff? Had they split? Interesting! For the first time since she saw Karlsson check-in she relaxed. Olsson returned to her room for some much-needed sleep. An alarm call would wake her at ten when she made her daily call to the client. Then she would shower, dress, eat brunch in the buttery, settle the bill, and drive to Larsson's flat.

The nurse lay out the corpse with dignity and respect. She donned a face mask, a disposable apron and primrose-yellow nitrile gloves, then began her morbid ministrations. Her first task was to scrub it with hot, soapy water from crown to carbuncle. It was hard work. Perspiring, she raked the strands of wet, flaxen hair off her young face and brushed its teeth, mollifying its cadaveric features.

She lathered and shaved the face of faint swarth until its waxy skin felt smooth. She combed its blond hair. As she taped its gunmetal blue eyes, a single tear trickled down its left cheek. The slab-muscled corpse lay cold, supine. Quickly, the nurse straightened its stiff limbs, dressed it in clean pyjamas and wrapped it in a crisp white sheet and counterpane.

Sveinsson, resplendent in her putty short-sleeve shirt and white slacks, betrayed no signs of emotion as she was ushered into the private room. The hospital staff clearly attended to every detail when they conducted last offices on the deceased. The cubicle was spotless. There was a small locker next to the bed. Sveinsson sighed as she placed the picture of two newlyweds, their hands clasping a bone-handled knife as they cut the three-tier wedding cake, and a single red rose, beside the bed.

The nurse offered the bereaved a curved black eco-chair. Sveinsson shook her head, saying that she preferred to stand, and wasn't planning on staying long. Feeling distinctly queasy, she chewed her lip, dry retching as the nurse drew back the veil. She glanced at the cadaverous Karlsson. To her profound astonishment, its pyjamas, sheet and counterpane were missing. Someone had kissed an ellipse of pink lipstick on its forehead.

She was stunned! Her stomach churned!

She leaned forward and read the two inscriptions. On its rigid ring finger, the stiff corpse of Karlsson wore a shiny signet ring with the insignia: IL. On its right breast, there was a message, tattooed in italics: *Wild for You!* Bile rose up in Sveinsson's dry throat. She scanned the nurse's face which was scary, blank and expressionless. Then the nurse spoke.

'Do you like Toblerone?'

Sveinsson felt her ears pop. 'Do I what?'

'I said: do you like Toblerone? *He* told me to ask you.'

'No!'

Sveinsson spun on her high heels, flew out of the room and clacked down the long, bland, chocolate-lime corridor. Past the bustling WRVS shop, the ailing and well. Past the Chapel of Rest, the cool dead. Past the Morgue, the frozen dead. Out into the flaming hot sun.

The playing fields were a short walk from the Infirmary. They stretched as far as her eyes could see, surrounded by tall hedgerows and young trees. Sveinsson followed a narrow footpath until she reached the boarded-up, red-brick sports pavilion. The place reeked of decay. Its walls were sprawled with graffiti. The gutter had given way where kids tried to climb onto the roof. There were signs with illegible, cracked lettering, flaking, whitewashed walls, smashed lights. The blackwood door to the Ladies Toilet was padlocked.

Overhanging the ruins was a majestic oak tree in full, leafy summer splendour. Lying within its shade, a slatted park bench. Sveinsson slumped on the hot metal and rubbed her inflamed cheeks. Still suffering from severe shock, she extracted a miniature from her bucket bag and downed the contents in one. She could never forgive Karlsson for what he did to her. How might she repay him? Fortified by brandy, she finalised a symbolic act of revenge.

The rubbish bin next to the bench was overflowing with sticky, yukky, ice cream wrappers, crawling with drunken wasps. Loathe to disturb them, she slipped the empty bottle into her handbag, drew out her phone and selected mail. Normally, Sveinsson sent all invasive adverts direct to junk mail. Today was anything but a normal day.

Her thoughts were interrupted by a man's voice.

'Are you alright? Do you need help?' he said.

Sveinsson looked up at his silhouette, shielding her eyes from the intense glare of the sun. He was wearing a navy-blue tee-shirt, sunshades, faded denims, and had a disturbed look in his eyes.

'I'll be fine thanks,' she replied.

He sat down, and moved closer to her. 'My name is Johansson. Are you sure I can't help?'

Sveinsson panicked. Who was this man? What did he want?

'I'm fine thanks very much,' she said, smiling back appreciatively.

His head turned to face her. Its piercing stare sent ice-cold shivers down her spine, chilling off the heat of the midday sun. He started to cry. She looked around in desperation. Other than Persson, the elderly gubben, walking his black pug, Andersson, in the distance, the park was deserted. The young Swedes sat in silence. Even the restless starlings ceased their twitter in the hedgerows.

Inexplicably, Johansson stood up, said, 'I'll be on my way then,' and disappeared.

Sveinsson perched on the bench shaking involuntarily, despite the skin-burning heatwave. Once she had regained her composure she stared at the screen. The e-mail was marked: Unread.

From: no-fuss-funerals@theunfussyfuneralpeople.com

Sent: 26/07/2018 – 10:13

To: hpwsveinsson@femails.com

Subject: A simple funeral without fuss

Are you looking for a simple alternative to a traditional funeral for less than the cost of a new car? We are here to help you to arrange a funeral the way you want it to be and we think that means a funeral without fuss. No Fuss are refreshingly different from traditional funerals. We offer you an affordable option that gives you the freedom to remember your dearly departed loved one in your own special way. Why not call into your nearest funeral home today for a chat about the choices available and find out what's right for you, or call us.

Benny Persson

Sales Director

No Fuss

She rang them: 'I'd like to arrange a funeral without fuss. I understand you offer a cheaper option without a service, mourners, urn, memorial plaque or floral tributes. Cremation would be perfect, thanks. I'd like to pay by card. Here are my details...'

No Fuss Funerals met her and talked through all of the options. Sveinsson was so relieved that they offered a cremation-only service. It was exactly right, given Karlsson's smouldering sex with young Nurse Larsson. Thanks to the professionalism, integrity and discretion shown by the woodland body-burners, Sveinsson was able to dispose of Karlsson expediently, without the recognition, celebration and gratitude associated with a formal funeral.

'Is there anyone else I can assist you with today?' Gustafsson asked.

Sveinsson nodded her sorry, blonde head, deep in thought.

The next e-mail she received from No Fuss was marked: Confidential.

From: no-fuss-funerals@theunfussyfuneralpeople.com

Sent: 10/08/2018 – 15:42

To: hpwsveinsson@femails.com

Subject: Your order

Dear Ms Holly Sveinsson,

Thank you for choosing No Fuss Funerals for the expedient disposal of Mr Odin Karlsson in your own special way. We do hope you choose No Fuss again... when your time comes.

Yours sincerely,

Ernst Gustafsson and Britt Olsson

Funeral Directors

No Fuss

Watch this short video link and see how we prepared and presented Miss Ingrid Larsson prior to her scenic woodland cremation: >>>

Inferno

'TONIGHT, AT TEN, REMARKABLE STORIES of courage and self-sacrifice are emerging, following last night's appalling tragedy in Birmingham. Nearly 24 hours after fire destroyed Charnel Tower, killing at least 263 residents and leaving hundreds more homeless, Nirmal Kaur has spoken to the survivors. Her report contains images which you may find upsetting.'

I am lying slumped against the wall when they find me. Staring up at a red sunset that's mostly obscured by dark clouds. Dense plumes of grey smoke and ash still billow from the lower floors of the tower, punctuated by an occasional burst of orange flame, clearly visible through the gaping windows. Two fine jet sprays of water are trained on the body's midriff like arcing fountains in a summer ornamental garden. High up beyond the 10th floor the walls are charred black. Huge lumps of material resembling burnt loft insulation break off the crumbling façade and slowly drift to the ground, shattering into crisp debris, flotsam thrown down by the sea of fire. The ground is covered with the stuff; smouldering boulders of brittle carbon foam, like florist's blackened oasis from some ghastly dried flower display of destruction, scattered for miles by the wind. I glance around me. An uneasy calm has set in since the frenetic activity in the immediate aftermath of the disaster.

The anger and grief will come later.

A firefighter wearing a bright yellow helmet, trudges wearily towards me, his young face tarred with soot. I watch him as he wipes away a single soiled tear. Our eyes meet. He nods at me sympathetically then looks away. Yet another ambulance siren screams towards us. My neighbours are huddled in bunches on the pavement, hugging one another. Some weep for lost loved ones, some wail in despair, others sit and pray for respite from the trauma. Many of them wander aimlessly, as if in a trance, searching with a silent, inner resolve for missing relatives, dearly loved lost ones. Pleading for crumbs of information.

'Have you seen my little boy? Please, he's only four,' a father says.

The kind, the caring, the good and the downright saintly are here at our side. Saviours from all denominations: Muslims, Buddhists, Hindus and Christians. All working tirelessly, side by side. Heroes from the fire, police and ambulance services. Friends have come out of their homes in support. There are prominent members of the local community present. People I've never seen before, one or two celebrities. They're joined by hordes of trusty volunteers from crisis teams, counsellors who sit and comfort us, hold us in their arms, or just listen. All the lovely people offer us help in any way they can: food, blankets, clothes, a bed for the night, the love and compassion in their hearts. Understanding our devastating feelings of loss. Helping us to come to terms with the rising tide of grief.

Heaped against the whiteboard wall of remembrance are the hundreds of floral bouquets, wreaths of white lilies tied with purple ribbons, each labelled with its own intensely personal, heartfelt message. As the first stars come out, I lie staring into the heavens above the hideous concrete tomb, the ignited funeral pyre that was once our home. Overwhelmed by all I've lost.

There's something blocking my view of heaven. I stare up at her feet first. She's not from these motley parts, that's for sure. She's wearing new navy jewelled suede pumps, perfectly pleated two-way stretch black trousers, a saffron silk crepe-de-chine sleeveless tunic - with side slits. Please tell me she's not real! I really don't need this in my hour of need, thank you very much. Who the hell does she think she is anyway, looking down on me like some bored schoolteacher? I see she's got on her best pearl necklace, designer handbag and gold bangles. She's blow-waved her hair. The style suits her. Thinking of going out clubbing tonight are we, love? She's got a cheek, studying me as if I were some caged animal. How dare she stare at me like that! Just a minute, she's got a silver name badge pinned over her left tit:

Nirmal Kaur, Tonight at Ten

Nirmal? I stare in disbelief as her roving cameraman appears behind her, patiently hovering above me, filming me from all angles, like a car crash voyeur. I realise, too late, that I'm about to put in a guest appearance on international television. Pity really, I look a state without make-up or hair.

Suddenly, I feel terribly exposed, vulnerable to millions of preying vultures of death. Circling above me through the camera lens. Staring at me from the comfort of their sofas.

Despite the hot, humid night I feel cold, feverish; I shiver uncontrollably. I'm still dressed in the silk jasmine-flower camisole pyjama top and matching shorts Gary bought me for our fifth wedding anniversary. No wonder I'm cold! I try to cover up, find I can't move. My arms and legs are stiff, my fingers and toes numb. It gets colder as the darkness sets in. A redhead, dressed in a practical green boiler suit, whispers reassuring words in my ear as she wraps me up in a nice, warm blanket. I wince at the sharp pinprick in my left arm. I refuse to go to sleep. I cannot, will not sleep. Not till I find out what happened to Millie.

'The ambulance will be here soon,' the paramedic advises me, patting my burnt hands with a soothing antiseptic swab.

Ambulance? Why? I try to laugh, to tell her I'm fine, but can't. I think we both know why.

Nirmal? She looks so young. Much too young to be a reporter. She must be 22, now? I wonder, seeing her dressed up in designer clothes and showy jewellery, if this is her first major news assignment. Talk about being thrown in at the deep end! She's nervous, must be distressed at how I look. She bites her lips, runs her fingers through her wavy black hair. I feel sorry for her seeing me like this. How must she feel about me?

She asks how I managed to escape from the inferno. She asks if I was on my own.

Her questions horrify me. Emotionally, I'm still raw. Too distraught to share how I feel. I burst into floods of tears. How can she be so unfeeling towards me? To my amazement, she drops her handbag on the ground, sits down beside me, and takes me in her arms. Mary, who's squatting on my left, tells her not to touch my burnt hands or scalp on pain of death. I'm deeply touched by the unexpected show of affection from Nirmal. The last thing I expected from her was an apology live on air but I suspect I'm about to get one. Her voice is sweet, lilting, exotic.

'I'm sorry I hurt you, Tina,' she says.

I close my eyes and remember our honeymoon in India. Gary and I, sitting cross-legged on the golden sandy beach, wolfing down wedges of juicy mango, slicing fat bananas under a shady palm. Gary lifting me up out of the water onto his broad shoulders, then throwing me in head first. Coming to my rescue when I lost my bikini bottoms. Holding me tight in his muscly arms. Splashing me with warm surf. Jumping for joy in the crashing waves. Swimming in our blue crystal sea. Thrilling to our private tropical paradise.

I'll never forget that moment in India, the moment I first saw her. She was wading in the surf wearing a turquoise sarong over a stunning white-on-navy printed swimsuit when we met. She couldn't have been older than 17, I was 22. She was beautiful. I secretly fell in love with her. Gary was intrigued. She joined us that evening for dinner and ended up staying the night. Soon after midnight, I crept into her bed. We kissed like crazy. We had no tomorrow, only today. We made love then slept together until the break of dawn. Next day the three of us took breakfast on the beach then said our goodbyes. Gary and I flew home. Two years later I gave birth to my wonderful baby daughter. I never expected to see Nirmal again.

'I'm sitting with the last survivor to emerge from the inferno,' she tells the camera. 'Brave Tina has a unique story to tell the world.'

She whispers in my ear, like she did that night in the beach house, 'Please tell me how you managed to escape. I'd really like to know. I'm so glad you're alive. I really love you, Tina.'

I lie content in her arms and realise how much I still love her. It dawns on me that our chance meeting wasn't a coincidence. She's searched for me, since the news broke about the fire. She still loves me every bit as much as I love her.

That I might die in her loving arms.

I try to speak for the first time since I escaped from the fire, failing miserably. My throat is burnt sore, my lips are cracked and swollen. Mary helps me sip cooling water through a straw.

Then I tell the world what really happened...

'I was asleep in bed with Millie. She was scared of heights. When Gary died, we had no choice other than to move into the flat. Late last night we were awoken by the sound of an explosion. It sounded like a bomb had gone off. I didn't hear an alarm so I just cuddled up with Millie and went back to sleep. The next thing I knew the whole flat was full of smoke. I panicked. I didn't know what to do. I rang Mum. She got herself in a terrible state and started crying. I couldn't bear it, hearing Mum cry. I had to cut the call. She must be worried sick about us.

'We were told to stay put. How could we when the flat was full of smoke? I couldn't see a thing. The heat, the acrid smell, was just unbearable. Millie started to choke on the fumes. She went hysterical. I crawled into the shower room, found some towels, soaked them in cold water, and wrapped them around our heads. Then the window blew in. We were showered with broken glass. There was a huge ball of fire. I shielded Millie from the flames as best I could. I felt my hair catch fire, felt my hair being singed to the scalp.

'I thought: *I'm going to die. I must save my little girl.*

'When I grabbed Millie's arm, she was limp.

' I'm sorry, Nirmal, I…'

'It's alright, take your time, Tina, take your time.'

'I had to drag her across the floor, sliding on my belly. I reached for the door handle. The metal was so hot, my skin stuck, and blistered. How I managed to get us out of there, I'll never know. The fire corridor heaved with people screaming, howling, crawling around like blind ants, fighting for their lives. I heard a voice call: "Get out! Get out!" I couldn't move. The others were climbing over me. I must have passed out.

'I'm sorry, when I… when I came to, I'd lost my little girl.'

When I look up into my love's face, I see tears sparkle in her eyes, feel her press my head to her chest as I cry my heart out. The night sky is lit up with flashing blue lights. Two men climb out of an ambulance and race towards me.

I want to tell the nice young Indian lady, Nirmal she's called, to tell the world, to tell **you:**

That Gary took a formal portrait of Millie sitting on my lap two months before he was killed.

That vultures took selfies in front of the burnt-out shell of his Porsche as firemen struggled to cut his body out of the wreckage.

That my sister, Jess, posted a colour photocopy of our picture on the wall of remembrance in the hope of finding us.

That every day she puts a fresh flower by our photo, a red rose for me - and a rose bud.

I want to tell you. But I'm struggling to catch my breath. I can't feel my arms or legs. I've no sensation, no feeling below my neck. My flesh is burning. My face and hands swell up and blister. I can't keep my eyes open. I feel myself being lifted onto a stretcher, smell an oxygen mask descend over my face. I gasp with relief as I inhale fresh morning air. I blink my eyelids open, seeing a look of desperation cross her face like a summer cloud. Nirmal stands there like my guardian angel.

I used to have a face. When I was alive. I used to be beautiful. I had flowing chestnut hair, smiling hazel eyes, dimpled cheeks. Gary worshipped me, loved my cheeky, impish smile. I never stopped smiling when he was alive. I miss him so much. I miss my baby even more. My brown-eyed beauty. I spent every waking minute with Millie. I spoilt her something rotten after Gary died. Buying pretty frocks for her to wear. Taking her on the train to see children's shows in the West End. Visiting the Eye, the Shard, the Palace. Seeing the sights of London by bus. Forever having children's parties at our house. She was my pride and joy, my reason for living.

I beckon Nirmal over with the slightest nod of my head. She leans over me as they carry me to the ambulance. I ask about Millie. I'm bursting with pride, desperately missing my daughter.

'Isn't she pretty, my angel?' I say. 'She's only three. Please help me find her. I beg you.'

'I will, I will, I promise,' Nirmal replies, crying. 'Where did you last see her?'

I tell her, I lost Millie on the 45th floor. Her face turns deathly pale, ecru, with shock.

'But that's impossible, Tina. No one survived on that floor…'

'Tina. Tina? Tina! Oh, God! Oh, God! No! She's gone, Clyde! She's gone!' 'That was Nirmal Kaur reporting live from Charnel Tower,' Clyde says, frowning. 'Here's Peter with the weather forecast. Peter…'

'Thank you, Clyde. Well, temperature records are tumbling everywhere. It looks as if the hot dry weather is here to stay. Here's a photograph of a dust bowl reservoir sent in by one of our viewers in Kent…'

'I'm sorry to interrupt you, Peter, but we've just received this astonishing breaking news:

'Firemen have found a six-year-old girl alive and apparently unharmed inside a cupboard on the 45th floor at Charnel Tower. An extensive forensic search of the floor has confirmed that there were no other survivors.'

Insurgent

THE SOLDIERS CROSSED THE STUBBLED field unclad. The video cameras mounted on their helmets would ensure they adhered to the strict rules of engagement. But they were entering into combat without personal body armour, due to temporary supply difficulties.

Ellis, 28, team leader, squinted in the bright afternoon sun, hardly reassured by the presence of a rescue helicopter hovering high above him. His heart pounded with stress. His coved chest heaved with exertion in the torrid heat. He asserted himself, scanning the arid terrain with his hooded eyes, his Minimi light machine gun resting easily on his arm, primed and ready to kill. He swept his thin brown hair off his face and breathed a sigh of relief: no sign of the Insurgent, yet. His shady informant, a tall, dark-skinned, barefoot boy in a flowing white robe, had told him his adversary was hiding in the nearby goat farm. Waiting to kill him. His daunting task was to flush out the Insurgent and take him alive. He found a dry ditch in the wilderness for the team briefing. The soldiers removed their helmets and huddled in a circle on the scorched earth, resting, swigging water, ever-vigilant. Ellis stared at the farm, shimmering in the haze, rubbed his chiselled chin, then tried to fire up his team's enthusiasm for the raid.

'When we reach the farm, hog the right side of the path, staying clear of the trees on the left. If we come under fire, take cover in the ditch by the wall. I'll lead, then Cook, Watts, Scully, Hart, Reed, Parker. Deakin, McKay, guard our rear. We regroup at the far end of the wall, enter the farm and take out the Insurgent. Got that, everyone?'

'Your plan sounds logical, Ellis.'

Scully eyeballed Reed. The sarge was cold, aloof and withdrawn. Hart said he was a eunuch. Reed, who never wasted chances to work out his v-shaped torso near Scully, suffered from bad halitosis. His angry, swarthy face scowled at her whenever they met. Reed gave her the creeps.

'Are you having a laugh?' McKay, 26, said, watching Hart chew her nails. 'If we go down that route, we'll be sitting ducks.' McKay, an ex-streetfighter from Glasgow, cared about Hart.

'I agree with Iain,' Parker, 18, chipped in. 'Why can't we just fan out, surround the place?'

Cook, 20, nodded. 'Too right! I don't fancy being picked off one-by-one thanks very much.'

His fiancé, Watts, 19, was even more blunt. 'No way am I getting shot up for you, Ellis.'

Ellis despaired. These morons were meant to trust him with their lives. He had never lost a soldier on a mission yet, but even he had doubts this time. Still, the order was issued to him in confidence from the highest level, the C.O. herself. 'This plan is non-negotiable and must be strictly adhered to at all times. The detail, the real reason for the raid, must not be shared, on pain of death,' she'd instructed, making it clear to Ellis that he had no option but to see the plan through to its logical conclusion: the capture of the Insurgent with minimal collateral damage. She didn't tell him that the team were expendable.

He checked out the morale of his two non-combatants. 'Ready, Scully?'

Scully, 18, had replaced Griffiths as radio operator, an express order from her C.O. 'Ready as I'll ever be, Ellis,' she said, brightly. Her wide, toothy grin barely hid the acid in her voice.

He fancied the half-cast: her copper-auburn hair, flat pug nose, her amazing physique. He'd watched her workout in the compact gym in her busty grey sports bra and skin-tight shorts, and wanted to fuck her. So far, his intense feelings hadn't been reciprocated. Still, she was his bravest soldier. He tolerated the sarcasm.

'Great attitude, Scully! Hart?'

The Cambridge-educated medic didn't reply. Ignoring him, she re-tied her stretched, blonde hair into a crude pigtail and looked down at the stony ground. Strong, resilient, determined, intelligent and bolshy, she'd earned a reputation for being awkward and stuck-up. Ellis couldn't stand her, but she came highly recommended, personally selected by the C.O.

He stared her out. 'Hart, you okay?'

She raised two fingers to her brow in mock salute, and barked, 'Yes, sir!'

'Don't sound so enthusiastic, Hart. Does anyone have any questions?' her leader said.

Cook, a one-time drugs trafficker from Bristol, asked, 'What happens if I get emotional?'

'It feels like, as a man, you can never express your emotions,' Ellis replied, sagely. 'When I signed up, I thought it would be far worse than it is. That any sign of emotion would be seen as a weakness. But, once I was in, I soon realised that no-one is a machine. You are my family.'

'Do I have to be a super-hero to fight the Insurgent?' Watts jested.

The weaselish, former barman-turned-petty-thief and fraudster from Leeds, wore rose-tinted spectacles. He sported a tattoo of a mandala, a shape Buddhists made out of sand, on his stomach. Watts admired the practice of meditation through drawing. He and Cook loved the fact that his tattoo was central to them both, physically and psychologically. Raised on Army camps since the age of five, it was his macho dad who encouraged him to get his first tattoo. He used it to express his love for Cook. His mandala showed him he was an individual not just a regimented machine. Watts had a beautiful body under his uniform, a body Cook worshipped religiously every night.

'It is a man's own mind, not his foe, that lures him to evil,' Watts claimed, taunting Ellis with his spiritual rhetoric.

Ellis laughed and ruffled the private's hair. 'When I joined, son, I had images of musclemen, carrying weights and grunting.' Hart grinned saucily at Scully. 'I thought everyone was going to be a super-fit machine. I know you're slow, Watts. Obviously. You're unfit! You'll struggle! But we'll help you out, won't we, guys?'

Everyone stared at the ground in stony silence. *So, this is belonging, is it?* they thought.

'Can I practice my faith during combat, Ellis?'

'Of course, Parker! We all embrace the fact that you come from a different faith to the rest of us. Even in combat there'll be quiet moments. You can go into the farm, do your prayers there.'

Parker didn't trust to false promises. 'My faith's part of me, Ellis! That doesn't change when I put on a uniform!' he stressed angrily. The newly-converted black cage fighter from Peckham was built like a Sherman tank, had previously done time for GBH. Not a man to mess around.

'Of course, it doesn't. Scully, Cook?' Whenever Ellis floundered, he looked to Scully and Cook for moral support.

'If it helps, Parker, I used to worry that, as a woman, I wouldn't be listened to,' Scully said. 'The men at work often talked over me. I decided to go for it and join the Army. It feels good to have my voice heard.'

Cook agreed, 'I used to fret if I was seen resting my hand on another man's thigh. I was worried about whether I would be accepted, but within days of joining Ellis's team I was more than confident about being who I was. I'm not afraid to talk about having Mitch as a boyfriend. It's only right that the Army reaches out to the broader community.'

'Thank you, Cook, Scully. Any more questions, team?'

Everyone shook their head except shaven-headed Deakin, 29, the toughest, meanest, most experienced soldier in the pack. 'Yes, Deakin?'

'What about mines?' he asked.

Mines! What mines? Suddenly, all eyes were on Deakin.

Ellis looked narked. 'Path's been cleared,' was all he said. 'Okay, let's finish this and don't forget.' The team rolled their eyes at the expected tired cliché as he pointed deliberately at his eyes, one at a time. 'Keep 'em peeled.'

Pretending to laugh, they clambered to their feet, put on their helmets and stomped towards the farm. Ellis reached the path first, scanning the trees to his left, staring at the top of the wall: no tell-tale glint of metal in the sunlight, no Insurgent lurking in the shadows. Now, where is he? Hiding in one of the dilapidated farm buildings? Skulking in a clump of trees? He glanced back at the rogue's gallery of anxious faces: Cook, Watts, Scully, Hart, Parker, McKay: breathing hard, scanning the wall, guns at the ready, intent on their own survival. A tall, robed figure ghosted out from behind the wall, armed to the teeth with a semi-automatic and a carbine.

Ellis radioed: 'McKay! Insurgent! Behind you!'

McKay swivelled, too late. The Insurgent sprayed him with bullets then ducked behind the wall. Ten bullets punched the soldier in the chest and abdomen, three penetrated his heart. He stood dumbfounded by the scarlet bloom on his chest, crumpled and fell on his front, kissing the chalky soil.

Hart: 'Iain! No!'

Ellis: 'Get in the ditch!'

The Insurgent re-appeared at the far end of the wall. A hailstorm of bullets peppered the path, riddling Ellis, Cook and Watts with holes. One bullet entered Ellis's left eye, lodging in his brain. He wilted like a dying poppy. Cook took shots to the groin, writhed in agony on the ground.

'I'm hit!' Watts collapsed clutching his punctured belly, squirting blood in a disturbing arc.

Scully, Hart, Parker, and Deakin immediately tumbled into the ditch. The Insurgent disappeared from view; the firing ceased. Scully watched in disbelief as Hart slid out of the ditch, snaking along the ground on her stomach.

Scully: 'Jo! Are you fucking mad? Come back!'

Hart ignored her, saw it as her duty to save McKay whatever the danger to herself. Her duty as his lover. Hart and McKay were the beating hearts of the team, fresh in love. They intended to marry when their stint in this bloody hell-hole ended. Hart edged closer to his body which lay in a spreading patch of crimson on the stony ground, drying in the baking heat. She sniffed the ferric smell of blood. It occurred to her that she hadn't menstruated this month. She'd test herself, if she made it back to base. With any luck she was pregnant and the C.O. would have to send her home to Scotland with Iain. If he lived. *Please God, let my man live*, she prayed. When she reached him, he was already dead. She heard the sound of shooting, looked over her shoulder at the Insurgent firing randomly into the ditch. The Insurgent towered over her as she lay at his feet. *That's impossible*, she thought, *he is at the far end of the wall.* Hart looked up, reading the pure hatred in his ebony eyes. Surely, he wasn't going to shoot her? She was a non-combatant, a medic, for heaven's sake! He raised the gun. She pleaded for her life. He pointed the gun at her head. She begged him not to shoot.

'God, no!' Scully buried her head in her hands, couldn't bear to watch. Parker and Deakin lowered their heads in abject shame, pinned down by machine gun fire, unable to save her life.

Hart beseeched the Insurgent, helpless, tears streaking her dirty face, 'Please, don't kill me!'

The Insurgent shot her in the head at point blank range with a carbine, killing the unarmed medic in cold blood. Parker stood staring at Hart's dispersed carnage. Deakin was first to react.

'Fuck! Scully, radio for assistance!'

Scully lay face down in the ditch, crying, wailing, moaning, 'No! Jo!'

Her headset crackled into life. Parker: 'She's gone, Scully! She'd want us to survive this!'

Deakin: 'Scully! Move it!'

She recovered quickly. 'On it!' she shouted, fumbling with the Bowman secure VHF radio.

Cook was shot as he tried to wriggle off the path. The Insurgent sprayed the ditch with metal.

Parker: 'Keep your head down!'

The firing stopped. Enraged, Parker fired bullets into thin air, sagged to the ground defeated. A shadow appeared at the other end of the wall.

Parker: 'Deakin, watch your back!'

Deakin: 'On it, Parker!'

Deakin shifted position in the ditch. There was a brilliant white flash as the IED detonated. The explosion blew off his legs, ripped his belly, exposing his sloppy, blood-streaked mass of intestine. Scully's eardrums burst. The world went into silent slow-motion. Deakin collapsed, clutching his guts. Parker, Reed folded without arms or legs. Scully screamed, covered her deaf ears, bled from her nostrils. She felt a sucking sensation, then a ringing noise as sound returned. Heard shouts in the distance. Felt blasts of wind on her face. The helicopter landed, rotors still turning as medics crouched and ran towards her. Scully retched at the sight of Deakin. Tried to save her man. Threw herself on the ground beside him. Pumped his bloody chest. Opened his sticky mouth and gave him her sacred kiss of life. She touched the side of the neck, felt a pulse. His chest rose. She wept like a widow, cradled his innards, desperately tried to stem the deluge of blood gushing from his abdomen. His eyelids flickered. The mad-red eyes revealed his state of delirium.

'Kill me, babe,' he pleaded.

Scully drew out her revolver, then remembered the camera and cried, 'I can't, James!'

A shadow crossed her face. Insurgents appeared above her, masked ghosts in flowing robes, armed with AK-47's, carbines. Scully shook her head in disbelief as they unwound their head-cloths. The tall, dark-skinned boys glowered at her. They were inhuman. Their skin was made from bronze-tinted metal. The clones raised their guns in perfect synchronisation and took aim. Scully covered her head with her hands and cowered in the ditch, prepared to die alongside her hero.

'Stop!'

The clones froze, immobilized. The medics arrived and stood in silence beside the ditch. Scully heard the death rattle in Deakin's lungs. She let him go, felt a huge wave of relief wash over her. Shutting her eyes, she knelt and prayed that her loving soul mate found peace in death.

When she opened her eyes, the scene of the massacre was a hive of forensic activity. The bodies of Hart, McKay, Ellis, Cook and Watts were sealed in body bags and swiftly removed to the helicopter. A team of medics crowded round the clones, inspecting them, presumably for circuit damage, she thought, speculatively. A second team climbed into the ditch, ignoring her, sweeping the trench for further mines, scouring the scorched earth for body parts. The remains of Deakin, Parker and Reed were efficiently gathered and sealed in biodegradable, translucent pots with spring-loaded lids: human chutney jars. Except for Reed's head. They brought his head and perched it on the ridge of the ditch above her, where Scully could see it. It opened its eyes and looked around. Scully had encountered so much horror that afternoon, she thought she'd never scream again. "Reed" rolled its eyes, opened its mouth, spewed out a cloudy pond of gunk and tried to speak. *Then* she screamed.

'Beautiful, aren't they?' the head belched. 'Perfect in every way. They destroy all obstacles, you know.'

She stared at it, incredulously. 'You love the fuckers, don't you?'

'Love them? I created them! From my own spawn! They're my babies! My babies!'

With that, the head swelled, its grey eyes rolled (revealing their metal ball bearings), its face pulsed, glowed, sparked, and exploded. "Sergeant Reed" remained an enigma. Presently, Scully regained consciousness, dimly aware of strong arms lifting her into a coarse-mesh net basket, a cat's cradle for human collateral - and the authoritative voice of the C.O.

'Get her out of here! She's seen too much,' she barked. 'Scully is convertible. Ensure that she is converted.'

Sandra read her metallic face. 'Where are you taking me? Where are you taking me?'

'Beautiful, aren't you?' the C.O replied, elusively. 'Perfect in every detail.

'Welcome to the future of modern warfare, Scully.'

The Kissing Gate

TWO TRAILS: **3½ miles (5.7km)**
Take the path across the old churchyard to the swing gate. After 100yds climb stile and turn L onto footpath around field. At the yellow waymark turn R and cross the field. At mid-field fingerpost, where the crossways meet by a dead oak, walk to the line of trees. Follow the track skirting the woodlands. Until you find the Kissing Gate.

Beltane:

A THICK GREY MIST CLOAKED her grave. The fog slowly burnt off in the warm sunshine, heralding dawn in all its glory, and a new day burst into life. Her grassy burial mound sparkled with crystals of dew. A young man knelt before her black marble headstone, the garland of red roses etched around her beautiful face, broke down and cried.

Shush, my love, don't cry.

He looked around the graveyard. The church was a silent ruin. The hallowed grounds empty.

Hold me, my love, hold me.

She was with him once more. He gripped her headstone with both hands and held her tight, lying on top of her, his head resting against her damp earthy grave. Her dead heart gave out a single beat six feet underground and she fell asleep forever. Forever in his thoughts.

He was alone in the wilderness with only memories to comfort him. Searching for a new life, a fresh start. The footpath stretched far into the distance across a vast expanse of ploughed mud. He took a half-left turn, following a narrow cross-field path. That was when he stumbled, catching himself on an overhanging bramble. He pressed a hand to his neck, fascinated by the bubbling beads of blood. His tee-shirt stuck to his back. He felt weak, dizzy. His head spun in the heat. He slumped to his knees. Blood trickled down his legs. Soaking his thick lamb's wool socks. Coursing into his sturdy sky-blue rambling boots. He steadied himself with both hands, soiling them with cloying mud as he tried to haul himself off the ground.

I love you, darling.

He glanced round. There was no one there. Before long, he arrived at a tall, dense hedge of dark green cypress encircling a red-brick farmhouse with a mossy, black slate roof. Well-established ivy climbed its walls. The air was rich with the aromatic scent of pine. He knew the place well: Marriage House, her house. He shook his head, instinctively rubbing his neck. The wound had gone. Had he dreamt, hallucinated, the whole episode? Where to next? he wondered.

Find me, my love. Find me.

She stood before him. His fading, guiding light. He felt giddy. Light-headed. Overcome by emotion: love, regret, despair. The wayfarer's guide swung heavily from his neck on its red-string lanyard, the directions as clear as the transparent plastic cover:

At mid-field fingerpost, where the crossways meet by a dead oak, walk to the line of trees.

He looked out across the field. There was no mid-field fingerpost. No dead oak. No-one.

She was standing in the field where the crossways met. At first, he thought it might be a scarecrow. A shock of rich auburn hair cascaded over her bare shoulders onto her crow black dress, gathered tightly at the waist. She wore thin gold bangles on her wrists, thick furry bracelets around her ankles. Intrigued, he trudged through the mud towards her. She watched him with a vacant expression. His heart sank. What did he expect?

He talked to her, more in hope than expectation. 'Can you help me, I'm lost.'

She glared at him, looking hostile, shook her head, raised her hand. 'No, I can't! Leave me alone! I'll scream! I'm carrying my pepper spray and personal alarm!'

Her voice was shrill like a blackbird's. It occurred to him that he might have just scared the living daylights out of the girl. After all, there had been reports of suspicious incidents in the woods. He felt a complete idiot.

'I'm sorry, I meant you no harm.' He sounded like an astronaut meeting an alien. 'Please?'

She acted impatiently, unconvinced. 'Where are you trying to get to anyway?'

'I don't know!'

'You don't know? No wonder you're lost!' the girl giggled.

Her eyes twinkled mischievously when she realised, he was harmless. He told her he'd lost everyone in his life, everyone he ever loved: his beautiful wife, his precious little boy. If she was surprised by his frank admission, she didn't say so. Her irises clung to him like limpets, scanning his face in earnest. She squinted and shielded her face from the hazardous midday sun, wrestling with her inner conscience, her mind in a turmoil. He still couldn't tell if she trusted him. After several minutes' deliberation, she appeared to reach a decision and said she might be able to help.

He couldn't seem to shake the girl from his mind. Studied her closely, never having seen anyone so disturbingly beautiful in his life. Her freckled face looked as if a miniature cameo artist had painted her on as an afterthought: an inverted triangle with cloudy-green doe's eyes, a long snub nose, wild strawberry lips which longed to be kissed. The damsel read his intentions like the pages of a good book, turning him over in her thoughts. What she said next blew his mind.

'No! We've yet to kiss! We'll kiss in time and space!'

He was stunned, couldn't take his eyes off her. He didn't know what she was, why she was.

'I come from another dimension!' she cried. 'I'm a telepath! Cool, eh! Come on! We must go! Take my hand!'

The girl led the way, padding barefoot, as silently as a snow leopard, her brows furrowed with concentration. Her forehead stretched high into her scalp. The head itself was shaped like an inverted filbert nut: a smooth, round dome at one end, a sharp, pointed chin at the other. When they had negotiated half the field's circumference, he asked her where they were going.

'You'll soon see the wonder of it!' she shouted. She didn't elaborate further. And yet he felt the strangest thrill. They meandered dreamily along the rambling path, skirting the muddy field, hedgerows bursting with may. Soon, they reached a shady wood, carpeted with bluebells, riven by fallen elms. The first cuckoo of spring sang greedily in the distance. The man gazed into the girl's beatific face; his spirits uplifted. He hadn't felt so well in years. Her love of nature, the vibrant renewal of life all around them, revitalised him. Realizing that he hadn't introduced himself, he went to speak. But she pressed her soft fingertips to his lips and whispered,

'I know who you are, Adam. I'm sorry that you lost so much love when you were alive.'

High Summer:

The beach was deserted. A red flag flew. No-one swam. A handwritten scrap of paper flapped in the breeze, a makeshift warning nailed to the shuttered beach bar door, saying the beach was closed. The maelstrom sea churned up cauldrons of turbulent water. Giant rollers crashed against the shore foaming with spume. White horses raced the tide, carving craters in the sand.

He spotted her statuesque figure riding unsteadily along the crest of a wave, wobbling, toppling into the bottle-green water. Just watching her surf made him feel queasy. If anything, the sea was growing wilder, raging against the few die-hards who dared to venture out. Black storm clouds smoked on the horizon. Soon, squalls of rain would drench them, before the sun returned to burn them dry. He watched a surfer clamber out of the swell to safety on the tide-line leaving only his woman to rule the waves, having the time of her life.

He thought of the hard times that lay ahead when they went home. She had led the product testing and inspection team at Avian Aeronautics, a small family business specialising in the manufacture of bespoke, personally-manned aircraft. He managed production until the factory became fully automated and they were replaced by robots, joining the growing hard core of unemployed skilled workers. In fairness to Avian, they were paid generous severance pay in recognition of their loyalty and service. For the first time in years they had time for a holiday. Jane preferred water sports. Adam enjoyed rambling. True, they were different. But opposites attract, and they both loved children.

Adam hoisted his little boy up onto his shoulders so that he could watch his hero surf. 'Look, Tom, isn't she brave?'

'Mummy!' Tom cried, waving his pudgy arms.

'Yes Mummy,' he frowned, rubbing his bristly chin. 'Come on, let's make a sandcastle, shall we?'

He picked up a tomato-red bucket and apple-green spade. Tom grabbed them back again.

'Let me! I want to!' he insisted, his cherubic face drawn and glum.

'Alright, soldier!' Adam laughed. 'Here, you take the bucket.'

They squatted peacefully in the sand. Tom, sensibly dressed in trendy turquoise dungarees with striped turn-ups, cream polo shirt and floppy blue hat. Adam, sporting designer, polarised sunglasses, aqua trunks and tee-shirt. The toddler dredged up the wet sludge, tipping it out ready-mixed while Dad patted the sand into turrets.

Jane staggered out of the sea carrying an enormous blue-and-white-striped surfboard. Her short, straight, teak, hair swept back off her face. Brine trickling down her cheeks. Her chest heaved with effort. She dropped the board and tiptoed over the hot sand to gather up her bundle of joy, pecking his salty face like an oyster-catcher prising out a ragworm.

'How was it?' Adam asked her admiringly.

She rubbed her sore right elbow and gasped for breath. 'Sensational! Thanks! Invigorating!'

He loved her deeply. Her lust for life. Her inner strength. She meant much more to him than just a soul-mate. He'd never really gotten into those love-tags. Jane was his life-force and he couldn't imagine life without her.

'Who's my little boy, then?' she coaxed, bouncing her baby on her lap as he chuckled with glee. 'Either you're getting too big, Tom, or I'm getting too old.'

He kept shouting, 'More! More!'

She turned him over in her aching arms and sighed, 'Let's play teddy bears now, shall we?'

'No, I want a robot!'

'You can't have one,' Adam told him sternly.

'Why not?'

'Because you can't. That's why not.'

He tried to explain that robots, synthetic personalities, virtual reality and social media were scientifically proven to corrupt, dull and contaminate children's brains. But the three-year-old couldn't understand and started to cry.

His mother struggled to hold him still. 'There, there, Mummy give you a hug.'

'Don't want a hug,' he sulked, shaking off her affection. 'Hugs are silly. I want a robot.'

Exasperated, Jane glanced at her husband, grinding her pearl-white teeth, flashing him a jaded smile.

'Be a love and fetch my towel, would you?'

He could tell from her strained voice, she was shattered. Her mood changed like the weather. One minute, she could be moody and withdrawn. The next, she would be bright, vivacious and bubbly. Right now, she was placid, exhausted. He trudged up the beach. When he returned, she was sitting quietly on the sand, her beloved son in her lap, bearing up under the strain. He offered her the towel.

She shivered. 'Thanks. Dry me off while I sort this one out, will you?'

'Sure.' He dried her wet hair first, roughly with both hands.

Jane opened Tom's tightly clenched fist.

'Round and round the garden, like a teddy bear,' she sang, marching her crooked fingers stiffly round his perfect palm.

He giggled, spellbound.

'Mind if I join in the fun?' Adam asked as he dabbed her face.

She blinked her amber eyes. 'Of course not, you can be my bear anytime, honey.'

Groaning at her weak joke, he dried under her chin, wishing he had a buttercup to hold there, gently patting her sunburnt neck.

'One step, two steps...' Jane's fingers climbed Tom's arm like injured stick insects on a twig.

Adam dried her sloping shoulders.

'You were brilliant out there, by the way,' he said.

'Tickle thee under there!'

Tom gurgled as Mummy's teddy bears attacked his little armpits from all angles.

Jane was all over the place. 'Always do, don't you, Adam?'

'Sorry, what do I always do?'

'Think I'm brilliant!'

She lifted Tom up so that he could rub her hairy armpits, her chest, the glistening crease between her breasts. Adam stood in silence looking out to sea as she let the boy slide down her front to the ground. Suddenly, she arched her thin brows, turned, and kissed him fully on the lips. He flushed. Her flavour amazed him. Jane tasted syrupy-sweet, as fresh as the day they first met. Their micro-climate turned clammy in the stifling heat. He desperately wanted to take her in his arms, but she peeled away, strutting up the beach to the hide-out. Frustrated by her teasing turndown, he reached for the bucket and spade, and returned to playtime with his cherished child.

'I know,' he suggested, 'let's make some more sandcastles.'

The sand dried quickly under the sun's baking heat. The castles crumbled as soon as Tom poured them from their moulds. Adam felt sad for his little boy. Tom had been forced to attend day nursery from the age of two while his parents worked. *For what?* he thought. *For love, or money?* Father and son were virtual strangers. They barely knew each other. Their holiday in the South of France was the first time the three of them had spent quality time together as a family. Adam surveyed the woeful trail of collapsed turrets, strewn catastrophically across the beach. Then he saw Jane, changing out of her navy swimsuit.

'We need more water, Tom,' he decided. 'Go fetch me some water. Buy you an ice cream!'

It was a hollow bribe. The beach cafe was closed.

'I'll get it, Dad!' Tom chirped willingly.

Ruffling his boy's tangled curls, Adam handed over the bucket and watched the little man toddle up to the water's edge.

'I love you, Tom,' he muttered under his breath.

Then, with a guilty heart, he turned away and trudged up the beach.

Summer's End:

Adam's eyes grew wider when he saw Jane smouldering in her fishnet vest and neon pink microkini. She stretched her strong legs and flicked dry grit off her scorched toes. Her calves were socked in sand. She had acquired a healthy tan. Adam stashed away his sunglasses, stripped off his tee-shirt, and joined her on the beach mats. Jane smiled approvingly at his rugged good looks: the sunken cheeks, lean brown torso, smooth chiselled chest and flat stomach: finding his manly physique appetising. Apart from his sexy, swarthy, facial growth and scruffy copper hair, his body was bald. His ruby lips demanded closer inspection by her discerning tongue, as did the dark honey nipples.

A lust-lump formed in his throat as he watched her disentangle her breasts from the netting.

'Rub some oil on my back, would you?' she said.

He placed the bottle of suntan oil near her body. The squeezy bottle was half-full; he'd need to apply its contents sparingly to make the fluid last. He squeezed a blob of oil onto his palm.

'Lie on your front then.'

She tied back her hair with a pink elastic band and rolled onto her front, with her chin resting comfortably on the backs of her hands. Excited, she gripped the edge of the beach mat. One of her knees slid off, burrowing a round hole in the sand. Although his tender touch would caress the whole of her body, he lightly covered her buttocks with a soft towel, to protect them from the sun. He would soon strip it off when her skin fell under his soothing magic spell.

'Like this, you mean?' she enquired.

He nodded. Delicately, he glided his hands over her burnt shoulders and neck, up and down her arms, kneading warm oil into her sore flesh. He rubbed her back using long, deep strokes, pressing himself against her with his chest. She felt his breath on her cheek, fleeting kisses on her ear lobe, jaw, neck, spine. Slowly, softly, his tongue licked her lower back. She quivered as he removed the towel and spread her legs apart. Gently he massaged her inner thighs, his fingertips lightly brushing her groin.

'How does that feel?' he asked.

'Mmmn. Feels good!'

The flaming hot sun beat down, searing their bodies. Jane rolled onto her back. Once she'd settled, he lubricated her chest, pouring oil between her breasts which were ruddy brown, still puffy from the sea's kiss.

'Be gentle with them, they're sensitive,' she said.

He massaged her shoulders, working up and down her arms, using balm to lightly skim her breasts with the palms of his hands, pausing to tease her stiff teats, circling her bronze nipples, sending blissful sensations tingling down her body. Breathing heavily, taking in deep gasps, she slipped out of her microkini. His jaw fell at the sight of her, naked, uninhibited. Her beauty intoxicated him. She licked her lips salaciously; her eyes were half-shut.

He held her chin firmly, stared at her eager face, and said, 'We can't, Jane, not here.'

'Why not? It's a nudist beach, isn't it?'

'Someone might see us.'

'The beach is empty.'

He heard the far-off cry of a lonely seagull, the wash of sea on sand. They embraced. She held him tight, enjoying his proud flesh buried in her soft belly, pressing his mouth with her dewy, rose lips. Their membranes adhered, bound in an infinitesimal moment of intimacy. They paused to catch their breaths. She was crying. Tears of joy moistened her fiery cheeks. Her smile illuminated her face. Her soft lips brushed his ear.

She delved her hand into his trunks and pulled him out, straining, rearing for her. His manhood was speckled with silt from where he had squatted on the surf line. She reached for her gaily-coloured beach bag, took out a bottle of water and rinsed him, rubbing his hard shaft with her closed hand, then lay back and arranged herself on the crumpled towel.

He licked her tummy, tasting the sea salt in her navel. With her leg hiked over his shoulder, he kissed her inner thigh, massaging her soft, outer lips. By now, she was all dreamy, dripping wet, and smothered in oil. Her hairy tuft was dusted with sand. He brushed it off, then knelt between her legs and gazed into her shining eyes, the luckiest man in the world.

Her face flushed. Her breasts swelled. Her heart raced. She gritted her teeth, flexed her hips, and arched her body upwards.

'What're you waiting for?' she slurred. 'Want you.'

After they'd had intimate, loving sex, they lay with their bodies entwined, her head snuggled against his sweaty chest. She vowed to love him until the end of time. He promised to love her for all eternity.

The Fall:

He was restless, he couldn't settle.

'What is it, Adam?' asked Jane.

'I thought I heard a noise.'

They both heard a child cry.

'Tom!'

Jane slid out from under Adam, scrambled to her feet, and searched the beach.

'Where is he?' she trembled. 'Can't see him. Where's he gone? Oh, God. Please!'

He joined her, held her close, tried to stay calm for her sake. 'He's probably just wandered off...'

She ignored him. 'Can't have got far. Must be here. Tom!'

Doubt coursed through her veins like strychnine, obliterating the bliss of their lovemaking. She stood fretting, praying by the wind-break. 'Please, God. Let him be alright.'

Fearing the worst, they sprinted to the shoreline. The sea raged and cursed them, as if to say: 'Come and get him if you want him.'

Adam recalled how his son had looked at him and smiled, "I'll get it, Dad".

Tom's short existence, crumbling castles of sand. The tide washing him away while they played their selfish love games. He became irrational. His thoughts turned to death's morbid practicalities. The prohibitive cost of shipping the corpse home as cargo. The extended family send-off. Catering arrangements for the wake. Scattering his son's ashes in the woodland burial park. The future of the boy's bedroom: redecoration in pink? Donating Tom's sad, inflatable, plastic dolphin to a marine life charity shop. His deliberations were shattered by a shrill whine.

'Tom! I'm coming to get you!'

The trauma of her son's disappearance had decimated Jane, exploding all the motherly love in her heart in a torrential outpouring of undiluted grief, reducing her to a hysterical, gibbering wreck.

'Going in to get my baby!' she screamed.

'No! It's not safe!' Adam held her arm in a vice-like lock, swinging her round to face him.

'Look at the sea!' he said. 'There's a huge swell! It's too dangerous! You're not going in!'

Jane glowered at him, bonfires of defiance, sheer hatred burning in her eyes. 'Don't tell me what I can and can't do! That's my child out there, damn you!'

She wrenched herself free, streaking into the surf. Her arms flailed in the swell. Her breasts lifted with the chill, as if beckoning baby back for motherly comfort. For a moment, she stood in the shallows, steeling herself for her impromptu dip like a high diver who's going for gold.

Adam could tell she was frightened. Not that he was much help, standing on Pampelonne Beach, flapping his arms at her from the side-lines.

'For heaven's sake, Jane, be reasonable! Come back!' he called.

She dissented over her shoulder, 'No! I'm going in to find Tom!'

Jane always did play the leading role. Adam was her shadow man. He felt for her, waltzing into the dancing waves, staring with admiration as she dived in and cut through the punishing swell, punching the water in frustration. She submerged for a full two minutes, came up for a lungful of air, pushed her face into the brine, then bravely ploughed on. Given the distressing nature of the body search, he considered her can-do attitude inspirational. Adam waded into the shallows as far as he dared to watch her. She resurfaced, gasping, panic scrawled across her whiteboard face, treading water, thrashing her arms and legs, desperately trying to stay afloat.

'Help me, Ad!'

He stared at her, helpless. It started to rain: a teeming, driving rain that hissed on the hard sand. His eyes stung. He gawped blearily at her limp body, rolling in front of him, battered into submission, contorted by the swirling eddy, catching the spectre of mad fright which lurked in her swollen eyes.

It was the rip-tide that finished her off, callously hauling her out to sea like a thick trail of rubby dubby behind a shark fishing boat. Adam thought he heard a siren, indistinct above the crashing din, but the sound faded. Suddenly, his sweetheart came sweeping back to him, bobbing up and down like a red float. She turned barrel shapes for him, just out of reach, her trunk corkscrewed by its own body torsion. Jane's fighting spirit finally deserted her, she succumbed to the cruel sea, and drowned.

Adam waded back to shore and sat huddled against the storm, crying salt-streaked tears, wishing he could swim. Soon, the rain stopped, the clouds drifted away, and the sun came out. He walked into the sea till the waves crashed over his head, then let his body drift into oblivion.

Midsummer's Night:

The girl put her slender arm round his shoulder to comfort him.

'Try not to blame yourself,' she mourned, 'we all make mistakes. You're only human.' She checked the sun's position in the sky. 'I think it's time for us to enter the Kissing Gate, don't you, Adam?'

They stood before the Kissing Gate. There was nothing particularly unusual about it - just a rusty, circular iron railing with a squeaky, hinged gate that admitted one wanderer at a time. The girl held his hand until they safely reached the other side.

She showed him the future. Sixty crystal towers shining in the distance. A silver stream of driverless cars cruising down a mandarin-lit motorway. Air-cars, jet-packers hurtling overhead like hornets to the nest. Laser-guided bullets, shooting to distant galaxies in search of alien lifeforms. Reachable moments, synthetic personalities, real-life play toys, nostalgia holograms, virtual dreamlands. An infinite realm of possibilities.

The Kissing Gate where science and magic are as one.

'Kiss me!' the girl cried, her lamprey lips puckered, green eyes shut, arms outstretched.

Adam examined her speckled face. Why would she kiss a stranger? The girl grew impatient.

'We're supposed to kiss,' she said. 'To reach the garden? It's a <u>kissing</u> gate! Get it?'

He didn't get it. He shook his head, stupid man, none the wiser.

'Men!' she sighed. 'What am I going to do with you, eh?'

Time stood still. She took him in her arms and kissed him. Her lips were wet as the summer morning dew. Her taste as sweet as mellow autumn apples. Her breath cold as winter's frost. She stroked his cheek, drew him close. Their hearts beat in unison. They left the Kissing Gate far behind, never to return.

They ventured into unreality: impossible shimmering golden shards, flaming blood-orange heatwaves, shocked-up bolts of iridescent indigo. The sky turned black. Burst into swirling kaleidoscopes, glowing suns, shooting stars, careering comets, sea-green living planets. They travelled in time and space. Past spiral vortices, alien galaxies, new-born star systems, cloudy primordial steam, cosmic dust. To the furthest boundaries of the universe.

Adam never saw the girl again.

He found himself before a wooden gate. It swung open noiselessly revealing a beautifully-appointed garden bristling with primroses, cowslips, tulips, bluebells, daffodils, every kind of spring flower you can imagine. The place looked safe enough so he followed the pink gravel path as far as a cast-iron swing gate.

The flame-haired maiden was waiting for him in the churchyard, clutching a ripe apple to her chest, her moon face alight with life, her skin as pale as freshly-churned cream. He watched, mesmerised, as the solid gold asp wound round her wrist came to life, curling itself up her arm. The maiden stared at him momentarily, then bit into the crunchy red apple. A streak of dark, crimson blood dribbled down her chin, pooling between her breasts like a huge ruby.

'Do you find me attractive?' she asked him.

He was so beguiled by her, he couldn't speak.

'Then hold me, my love, hold me.'

He held her. His heart thudded and thumped against her breasts. Her love overwhelmed him. Brushing a lock of gold behind her flappy ear, he nuzzled her, and asked, 'Who are you, really?'

Her sapphire eyes glistened with tears.

'I am who you want me to be,' she said, sadly. 'Who would you most like me to be? Your beautiful wife or your precious, little boy?'

Adam agonized for several minutes. Atoning for his guilt, he sank to his knees and wept.

Jane appeared before him and said unto him, 'I forgive you; I love you, and I always will.'

She took his hand and led the way.

He felt as if he was dreaming. 'Where are we going now?' he asked.

'You'll soon see the wonder of it!'

They crossed a lush lawn until they reached an orchard of cherry trees, brimming with snow white blossom. At the heart of the orchard was a mossy red brick well with a battered oak bucket that swung and creaked in the cool evening breeze. They went and stood by the well. She kissed his eyelids shut then told him to make a wish. He harked back to when he was a child of six. Mum made a birthday cake. He made a wish. Dad helped him blow out the candles. His friends all sang "Happy Birthday".

He made his wish: 'I wish! I wish!'

A bewildered little boy walked out of the shadow of the swaying trees…
'Mum? Dad?'

'Tom?... Tom… Tom!' Jane and Adam cried in unison.

The sun set like a red rubber ball on the crimson horizon, heralding twilight in all its glory. A mystical, magical moon rose in the starry sky and smiled down happily at them.

The Kissing Gate, where love and magic become as one… and life begins anew.

She vowed to love him until the end of time. He promised to love her for all eternity. They swore, they would never leave their son again. They hugged and kissed and laughed and cried, long into the dark, dark, night. Forever, in each other's arms…

Forever in Our Thoughts.

Letter to Zoe

ZOE FURL, 16, REJOICED IN her uniqueness. Her razor-sharp, laser-cut, copper bob distinguished her from other humans. Her sunken sea blue eyes, pointed elfin ears and turned-up toffee nose gave her a unique, spoilt look. For Zoe Furl was a spoilt brat, spoilt like no other. She pouted her cerise lips, folded her extraordinarily long arms and emitted a loud tut, for the benefit of Zee, her long-suffering mother. Zoe Furl was not a happy girl. Oh, and Zoe spoke Zoe Speak.

'Why can't I go with Michael, Mum?' she said.

'Your father refused to sign the forms to freeze you, darling.'

Zoe pulled her angular chin into a long jut, flexed her high cheek bones, and banted. 'Why?'

'Because you're too young, darling.'

'I'm not too young, look!'

Zoe pushed out her tiny conical breasts to stress her points. Even long-suffering Zee had to concede that, dressed in her beautiful jet-black, sleeveless, herring-bone kimono with high neck and side vents, her daughter resembled a fine young woman. More than the banting teen who slept through her alarm that morning and nearly missed the cadmium carrier to the launch pad. It was no good. The exclusion order had been enacted by Garth. Zoe wasn't hurtling to another planet, a far-off, distant, galaxy with Michael Mist, and that was that!

Michael would be fired into space in seconds. Zoe stanned him, scrunched up inside the conical capsule on the rainy, windswept launch circle, from her floating observational pyramid.

'Seen his spacesuit?' she banted. 'It's slaying! That helmet's so legit? Those space boots are snatched! Look at him! Gangsta! He's proper peng. His new crew cut's butters, though!'

She pressed her pale round face into the drizzled pane, steaming it up with her runny nose. Her eyelashes were fleek. Tears cascaded down her milky white skin, sticking her face to the cold glass. Okay, she kidded herself, I'm calm.

'Love you bare, Michael,' she mouthed.

Zoe felt peak about not joining Mist but Garth and Zee Furl didn't ship their freaking kid falling for an astronaut. She found her mum and dad so basic? She'd told the melt to shut up? That shook! It was impossible for her to see Michael's face inside his space helmet, behind the masque, the scary, black visor. Zoe imagined his frail body, safely encapsulated in its padded spacesuit, pulsing its stumpy arms and legs to maintain blood circulation. She drew her long, bony fingers down the steamed-up window, pronouncing her knuckles, chipping her cerise nail varnish, flashing the ring he gave her to wear until the end of time when they smooched and canoodled under the stars on Playa Linda Beach.

Heartbroken, she imagined him, dismounting the darkness of the capsule, waddling, gravity-free, down the flimsy ladder, adjusting himself meticulously with his silver jet propulsion boots. When he reached his one-way journey's end. Her nose was running. She wiped herself with the back of her hand wishing she could wipe her memory of Michael, erase him from her memory, but she couldn't, she loved him too much. *I hope his back-pack life support system works long enough for him to remember me. I hope he still remembers me, when he stares up into that alien night sky.* His loss was too much for her to bear.

'I love you, I always will,' she whispered.

Michael Furl, 34, stared, love-lump-in-throat, out of the Plexiglas portal, smiled, and waved his big, gloved hand at Zoe. He mused a silent prayer, then bid farewell to Earth. For the next 45 years he would be glued to Silver Bullet 1's innermost lining, submerged (initially) in a sac of clear blue cryogenic fluid then incrementally deep-frozen like a big intergalactic fish finger.

'Love you, too, fam,' he mouthed back.

Built to be shot into space, Silver Bullet 1 was miniscule, basic by space rocket standards, a bullet-shaped cone with ultra-ceramic, solid-shield heat protectors at its squat base and blunt tip. Towards the rear of the spacecraft were the ultra-critical computerized life support systems, wrapped in thick, heat-resistant silicone swaddling. The living quarters, automated feeding and excretion facilities were situated behind the bullet's tip, next to enzymic waste digestion, and would be activated upon landing.

At the very heart of the craft, cocooned and cloistered in his solid Plexiglass bubble bath of eternal blue dreams, lived Michael. His body could, the biologist explained to him, be expected to grow a fine coating of furry down, a fluffing of swarth on his angular jaw. And he would enjoy dreams, orgasmic, narcoleptic, dreams, the likes of which he could never expect to experience on Earth. Oh, and the scientists had arranged some company for him, for his wakeful moments on the endless mission. After all, he was a man, wasn't he? He was only human.

The phased array of purple laser beams was on point. Silver Bullet 1 absorbed the beams into the anti-matter reactor at its tip, glowed incandescent red, and shot off into outer space.

Zoe Furl grinned, conceding that the take-off was lit!

Don't want to beef, Mist thought, curving her, but she really shegged me just then.

Michael Mist lay deep in thought in deep space as the narcoleptics entered his bloodstream. He drifted off to sleep, content in Zoe's arms...

Zoe Furl 1, rejoiced in her uniqueness. Her razor-sharp, laser-cut, copper bob distinguished her from other androids. Her sunken sea blue eyes, pointed elfin ears and turned-up toffee nose gave her a unique, spoilt look. Zoe Furl was a spoilt brat. She pouted her cerise lips, folded her extraordinarily long arms and emitted a loud sigh. Zoe Furl was a happy girl. She pushed out her tiny conical breasts to stress her points. Even Michael had to concede that, dressed in her beautiful jet-black, sleeveless, herring-bone kimono with the high neck and side vents, his android resembled a fine young woman. More than the banting teenager who'd slept through her alarm that morning and nearly missed the cadmium carrier to the launch pad.

It was perfect: the exclusion order he'd enacted with Garth. Zoe wasn't hurtling to another planet, a far-off, distant galaxy with him, and that was that! *She* was!

Zoe stanned him, scrunched up against her in the conical capsule, from their floating observational pyramid.

'Seen him without his spacesuit?' she banted. 'He's slaying! That beard's so legit? Those muscles are snatched. Look at him! Gangsta! He's proper peng. His crew cut's butters, though!'

She pressed her pale round face into his, steaming him with her runny nose. Her eyelashes were fleek. Tears cascaded down her milky white skin, sticking her to him. Okay, she kidded herself, I'm calm!

'Love you bare, Michael,' she mouthed.

Zoe felt his frail body, pulsing his stumpy arms and legs to maintain his blood circulation. She drew her long, bony fingers down his sweating body, pronouncing her knuckles, chipping her cerise nail varnish, flashing the ring he gave her to wear, until the end of time when they smooched and canoodled under the stars on Playa Linda Beach.

Thrilled, she imagined him, dismounting from the darkness of the capsule, waddling with her, gravity-free, down the flimsy ladder, adjusting himself meticulously with his silver jet propulsion boots. When they reached their one-way journey's end.

Her nose was running. She wiped herself with the back of her hand, wishing she could erase him from her memory, but she couldn't, she loved him too much. *I hope his back-pack life support system works long enough for him to marry me. I hope he marries me when we stare up into that alien night sky.* His loss would be too much for her to bear.

'I love you, I always will,' she whispered.

'Zoe,' he murmured, drowsily, 'shoot this pulse to Zoe.'

'Sorry, Commander. I can't do that. I am Zoe,' said sus Zoe.

'Don't peak me, melt! Just do it, OK?'

Zoe shot the pulse:

BAE,

I wish you'd been deep-frozen. Guess you'll be about 60 now, long-dead by the time I return to Earth. Your android replica is really shegging me. It's a joke! When it curves, it bants your mama's name! Her memory is full of you as you were when I left. We've fallen in love IRL. We plan to get married, launch a floating home, buy a flying car, have a freaking kid.

Love you, fam.

Hey, don't cry.

Your loving Michael xx

'Silver Bullet is flying through Proxima Centauri at 12 per cent of the speed of light,' 5DTV informed the watching world, 'Michael Mist will be shot at Proxima B at 22:00 tonight.'

Mission Objective: Establish contact with Alien Life-Form!

Zoe, the android replica, was busy on her hyper-tablet generally interfering with the mission.Suddenly, Silver Bullet shook, rattled, rolled, dipping, losing altitude, careering out of control. The sus capsule exploded in showers of white-hot sparks. Mist was incinerated, died instantly. Zoe's eyelashes were on fleek, correction, fire! It was calm just long enough to send a slaying, peak, beefish bant to curve Zoe and sheg the basic melt until she shook:

BAE,

Landing itself was cool. We fell on a shelf of rocks selected by the auto-pilot? IRL I find you so basic and butters, Zoe? You sheg me! Not like my Zoe? That chick is on point, snatched, legit, lit! I'm its biggest stan? Sorry to curve you, melt. But like they say:

There is no Future in the Past!

Hey, don't cry, kid, it's only bant!

Michael

Twenty-five trillion miles, or 4.2 light-years, away, Zoe Furl felt a crushing pain peak her sus heart. She clutched her chest, shook, collapsed and died.

She would never read Zoe II's beefish bant… her letter to Zoe I.

*****

Zoe-Speak:

BAE: sweetheart.

Bant: verbal blabber, social media interaction.

Bare: a lot, very much.

Basic: uncool, boring.

Beef: rant, grudge.

Butters: unattractive.

Calm: unperturbed.

Curve: reject someone.

Fam: dearest.

Fleek: neat.

Freaking: natural, not made in a lab!

Gangsta: hero, soul-mate, bedfellow.

IRL: in real life.

Legit: quality.

Lit: awesome.

Long: slow to defrost.

Melt: faint heart, phoney, replica.

On point: perfect.

Peak: upset, upsetting.

Peng: attractive.

Pulse: space-mail.

Shegging: embarrassing.

Ship: approve of a relationship.

Shook: surprised.

Slaying: impressive.

Snatched: stylish.

Stan: fan, devotee.

Stanning: idolizing, adoring.

Sus: dodgy, malfunctioning…

Lighthouse

THERE IS A POOL BY the lighthouse. A dark, deep, dangerous, pool. A pool where the dancers go to die. I lie on the clouded bottom of the pool, face down, sucking in mouthfuls of silt, sifting out lugworms, swallowing them whole, then blowing out their gungy debris through my gaping vent like a hungry eel.

Pushing the rotting corpses away from me, I turn, I roll, onto my skeletal back, and stare up at the faint glimmer of the full moon reflecting on the pool's surface. I rise through the water, flailing my streaming slivers, ghastly ribbons of raw flesh, pulsing my body upwards, a cadaverous jellyfish searching for her pallid, shocked face, flatlining, down at me. I push my eyeless head, my stumps, up out of the water, and stare at her: gaunt, blank, petrified.

She holds her sad, blonde head in her blue hands and screams, a shrill piercing scream, the cry of the wild, raging sea, the loneliest seagull flying high above us in the black clouds. Her mouth gapes at the sight of me, a black, toothless, cavity of despair. For we are one and the same. She is my fantasy. I'm her darkest nightmare come true, come back to claim her as my own, as me.

She lifts her floral dress, damp, soiled at the hem, from dappling in my stagnant water, my salt effluent, and gets off her knees. She screams, again and again and again. She turns to run, well not run, she stalks, stumbles, falls, crashes onto hard pebbles on her stilted, wintry-white robotic limbs. She's heading for the lighthouse and safety.

I must head her off. At the black cliffs. In the darkness, where I can slither, and crawl, and stalk about like the nightmare that is me. Where fantasy ends and necromantic, necrotic, neurotic dreams live and plague you, like a black dog, until you die, until you are the dancers. I haul our corpse out of the filthy broth of decay that is our hiding place, by the lighthouse. I reach out for her, fading white into the gloom, my ghoul, clamouring for her, a lost soul clinging to the wreckage of a doomed ship. I reach out, shrieking,

'Harriet-Jacqui! Come back! It's only me! It's only you! Come back! Come here! I am you!'

She is scrambling to safety, across the pebbly beach, through the thrashing surf, her pathetic coracle bobbing about on the moonlit tideline. Past the lobster pond where she drowned Seth. His skeleton picked bone-clean by gnawing, crawling crustacea. Past her chest-freezer, the sad mermaid, lying neatly top and tailed, gutted and filleted for Bouillabaisse. I love Harriet-Jacqui. I love her! She is me!

Must stop her reaching the lighthouse, and safety. Tonight, under the full moon we will be as one, in the long, dark, night that never ends. The lighthouse towers above her. There is a light, shining, revolving, beaming out to sea: 'Come, come, crash on our rocks!'

The door to the lighthouse is locked. The filthy, glue-sniffing girl turns to face me, gaining on her, begs for my help. An act of kindness! That's all it takes! To show Harriet-Jacqui how much I love her! What would you do? What can you do? What would you like me to do? Create my never-ending illusion of darkness in your minds, in her mind, trapped forever in our nightmare?

I close my eyes, see a wishing well, a kissing gate, and make a wish: 'I wish! I wish! I wish!'

Harriet-Jacqui collapses crying on the harsh, cold stony ground, my fallen, fading, angel, caught between two lighthouses. One lighthouse is a pleasing funereal black with a pencil beam of pure white light. Its sky is pure, brilliant white! Second lighthouse is the negative of the first, phantom white, black beam, reaching out like the reaper's scythe, swishing out at the night sky.

Don't fear the reaper, Harriet-Jacqui! Wishes! I walk past the beach café, the ladies' toilet, with a delightful spring in my step to find my true love: Harriet-Jacqui. What would you do? What can you do? To save Harriet? What can I do, make my final wish: 'I wish! I wish! I wish!'

White light pours from the door of the bleak lighthouse. The negative of the first, distorting, its door flapping open, revealing black light. It's a mystery, is it a mystery, are you waiting for a clue? Is it a mystery to me?

Welcome to the labyrinth, the vortex, the siren.

My dark side.

Lose Yourself

PLAY ME, WON'T YOU? LOSE yourself in me. If you dare.

Shocks course through her bloodstream. Mystery lurks within her sinews. She is adored by millions of viewers worldwide: multi-vision addicts and midnight surfers of the dark net.

Tonight, two contestants will fight her to the death. The first combatant to find the way to her heart wins the Star Prize. Who will break her heart? Who will die?

Saturday Night, Multi-Vision Studio, Live:

A voice drifts out of the ether: no face, body or persona just a voice. 'Welcome to Labyrinth.'

The studio audience: young adventure seekers, newly-weds, middle-aged parents, motley handfuls of depressed over-fifties, go wild as she introduces tonight's Star Prize:

One Million Pounds

Let's meet our first combatant:

Dean, 19, from Birmingham, has been unemployed since he left school at the age of 14. His pet likes are cage-fighting, grunge, dope and x-box. He spends his nights sleeping rough on the streets. Dean is one of life's saddest losers, with nothing left to lose but his life.

Her voice is eloquent, refined: 'Hello, Dean. Welcome to Labyrinth. How are you?'

'Yeah, good,' the pauper mumbles without conviction. He isn't listening to her. He's busy jabbing away at his phone, lounging around with his bony knees stuck up at the camera.

'Dean,' she says, firmly this time.

'Yeah?'

He shifts and slouches lengthways on the lime leather sofa. He can tell that the audience dislike him intensely by the steady booing and hissing. Dean doesn't care what they think.

'Switch your phone off and sit up straight.'

He wipes his runny nose on the back of his hand and sits up like a good boy.

'Stand on the plinth so the audience can see you.'

Dean stands up so that everyone can take a good look at him. He is wearing greasy, skinny blue denims and a grubby white tee-shirt which is half-tucked into his jeans. A plastic railcard wallet is stuffed into the breast pocket, jutting out from his chest like a surgical swab. Scruffy copper hair runs like rust water down his pock-marked face into his steel blue eyes. On his left shoulder, he bears a tattoo of a red rose concealing a swathe of pinpricks.

'Is that a ring in your nose?' she asks.

'Yeah, so what?'

He pushes the fringe out of his eyes and stares arrogantly at the screen.

'Jewellery, metal and studs are forbidden on safety grounds,' she informs him.

Dean is told to remove the offending article immediately. He shrugs his shoulders, painfully extracting the fat brass bull-ring from between his nostrils while the interrogation continues.

The voice relaxes. 'Tell us why you're here, Dean.'

'Need a break, a holiday, don't I?' he replies, pausing to think. Thinking hurts his brain. 'I need the money to make a fresh start. And I'm going to fight you all the way to your bleeding heart to get it, love.'

'Don't get personal with me,' she warns, 'you might turn me off.'

Let's meet Dean's Expert:

Cut to a brown, bespectacled, square-jawed face. Originally hailing from Montserrat, Joe T. Moon has endured several nasty run-ins with mysteries that live within the labyrinth. He wears prosthetic legs as a result. Despite his appalling injuries, he remains an eternal optimist, plays sponsored wheelchair soccer matches in aid of disabled children's charities. Joe T. performs countless good deeds in England's deprived city centres. A street-fighting man with a kind, loving heart, he gets a little over-excited at times. Dean worships the ground he walks on.

'Hey, Joe! How're you doing, man?'

'Hi, Dean, cool thanks.' Joe smiles, relaxed, at ease with himself. 'What's your question?'

Dean asks what will happen if he goes the wrong way inside the labyrinth. Aware that the second contestant is listening from the safety of a sealed isolation cubicle, Joe explains, in his own inimitable style, what *might* happen.

'The labyrinth has ten nodes. To find the way to its heart, you must negotiate all ten. Each node has a crossroads with three exits: left, right and straight ahead. One exit leads the right way. One takes you the wrong way. The other exit has a mystery. Go the wrong way,' Joe tells them, 'and it'll give you a shock you'll never forget. First shock's mild, a mere horse's kick. Next shock will make you jerk around like frogs' legs on a wire. After that, the current increases until you reach the last node, assuming you make it that far. Now, don't you dare fall at the final hurdle, or else you'll frazzle!'

'Thanks for that,' Dean interjects, looking particularly downcast.

'Hey, no worries! Lightning rarely strikes in the same place twice. You might get lucky!'

Joe T. has given the combatants their first clue. He has been known to lie. Can he be trusted? The lights flicker on and off inside the waiting cubicle. He arches a sly eyebrow.

'Want to know a secret?' he asks, tapping the side of his squashed nose.

The audience hush expectantly.

Dean gazes at the cherubic face, intrigued. 'Yeah, what?'

'Mysteries can't digest human hair!' he laughs.

The audience fall about in hysterics. Dean doesn't laugh, just stares at Joe, nonplussed.

They are interrupted by the voice. 'I think that's enough wild talk about mysteries, Joe.'

'If you say so,' he smarts.

Joe fades out of view. The black silhouette of a head appears on the screen and asks if Dean has any questions before he enters the labyrinth.

'Yeah, what are my chances of winning the jackpot?'

The audience perk up their ears like hungry puppies sniffing fresh meat, listening attentively as she does a quick mental calculation.

'*Your* chances?' she scoffs. 'I'd say *your* chances of winning are less than 1 in 59,049.'

The audience goes berserk. The game's about to begin. The pervading silence is broken by a guttural growl.

'Play me, won't you? Lose yourself in me. If you dare.'

'Yeah, sure.'

Dean shrugs off her threat. Inwardly he is scared stiff. He pushes himself out of the depths of the sofa, reluctantly stepping up to the labyrinth's gaping mouth.

'Oh, and Dean?' she calls.

Her head revolves incrementally, the slowly rotating head of a possessed child, to reveal the computer-generated imagery of her giant eyes: black, violet, indigo, ruby. Dean feels the floor move under his feet, shakes and trembles. He cowers and cringes. His bladder aches, distends and contracts, forcing a fine jet of warm amber fluid to spurt, trickle, then gush down his thighs.

'Yeah?' he pants, flushing.

He crosses his legs, plucking his saturated jeans as two giant cursors appear on the screen and point at the eyes.

'Watch your back!'

The audience laugh nervously, jeering the ex-borstal boy as he disappears into the gloom of the labyrinth's gaping mouth. He recoils at the noxious stench: rotten eggs, hydrogen sulphide. Her throat opens wide, swallowing him whole like a python gulping down a hog, licking its wet, slobbering lips as they close behind him.

Ten nodes. Ten right ways. Ten wrong. Ten shocks. Ten mysteries. Waiting.

Will Dean break its heart?

Play it, won't you? And find out.

We'll be right back after the break.

Welcome back to Labyrinth. Let's meet our second combatant:

Leah, 26, is a cybersecurity systems analyst with a first in applied mathematics from Oxford. She has co-habited with Jo, a psychotherapist, for three years. They have a delightful 2-year-old, blue-eyed, blond boy called Saul and would love to adopt a baby girl. Leah and Jo, 31, plan to tie the knot in July. They enjoy tennis, swimming, jogging, trampolining, yoga and classical music.

When she is not away from home on high-security classified business, Leah takes time out to relax at her parents' house on the outskirts of Wool.

She perches precariously on the edge of the lemon soda sofa in her soundproof cubicle, flashing a nervous smile at the appreciative audience.

'Hello, Leah. Welcome to Labyrinth. How are you?' the voice says.

Leah has butterflies in her stomach. She is wobbling already. She would much rather be at home, splashing about with Saul in their paddling pool, lying in Jo's tender embrace. First, she must compete. She has no choice. The couple need the prize money to get married, fly the nest, and enjoy the holiday of a lifetime. Before they set up their dream family eco-house in the elitist Green Belt. Leah Cleat closes her eyes and permits herself to live the dream, just a little:

Looking for unlimited sports activities, a soothing escape, or just new-found love in the Caribbean sunshine? We, and the £1,000,000, will make your wildest dreams come true.

Besides, she signed a contract with harsh financial penalties in the event of her withdrawal from the game. She gnaws her chipped, cherry red fingernails, drawing blood.

'Hullo,' she whispers, almost inaudibly.

Her twitching face is screened live on multi-vision across the globe. Prone to nasty blinks in her left eye when nervous, she squints like mad.

Saul, Jo, Mum, Dad, sister Wendy and brother Simon, watch from the safety of the back yard with a host of invited friends and neighbours. She pictures them all, proudly supporting her brave challenge on terrestrial television, squatting on the parched lawn, crowing from the cool veranda, or crouching on the crazy-paved patio.

She imagines Dad in his floppy old sun hat, sweat streaming down his face into his rheumy eyes under the hot sun, bent over double by the azure barbecue flames. His arthritic hands, slowly turning the breasts, ribs and steaks, over the red-hot embers. Darling Jo helping out as best she can, kitted-out in a blue and white striped butcher's apron worn over torn-off faded denim shorts, a navy-printed cerise vest proclaiming:

Come on Leah! You can do this!

Sweet, melt-in-your-mouth Jo, idly flips the burgers, pokes sausages, pulls her heartstrings. Mum dementedly daydreams away her final days, lying, semi-comatose on her floral lounger. Wendy jauntily bounces Saul up and down on her fat thighs, stringing him up by his spindly arms like a puppet as he treads her ample lap. Simon, prematurely bald, is forever orchestrating proceedings, attempting to organise a ramshackle gathering into well-ordered ranks. The whole ensemble, eagerly await Leah's moment of fame, when good will triumph over the labyrinth's inherent evil… wait for a miracle.

Leah is rudely awoken from her reverie by a rakish blonde production assistant in a black and gold **Labyrinth Lives!** tee-shirt who asks if she wouldn't mind speaking up so that the punters can hear her.

'Is that better?' she yells.

The sound technician cups her ears as the interview begins.

'How are you feeling?' the voice asks.

'Nervous?'

'Don't be afraid, I'm not going to eat you.'

She's not going to eat me? Who does she think I am, Little Red Riding Hood?

Leah Cleat jumps out of her skin. The audience fall in love with her. She looks vulnerable, compared to the dreadful Dean, but they still roar with laughter at her expense.

'Is that a diamond tongue-stud you're wearing?'

Leah flicks a stray wisp of hair from her mouth and glances up. 'Yup, why?'

She is lectured as if she were a child at school. 'Studs are not allowed. Remove it.'

She pokes out her tongue, extricates the stud and holds the shining gem aloft for all to see.

'That's better,' the beast hisses, menacingly. 'My, you look pretty tonight.'

Leah doesn't know what to say. 'Do you, er, really think so?'

'Yes, I do. Has anyone ever told you you're a very beautiful young woman, Leah?'

The world watches the beast denude Leah of her protective layer, exposing her shy nature, the child-like innocence that lies just beneath her surface. A rose-blush blooms in her cheeks, spreading down her neck, her chest, fanning wildfire over her breasts, nestling in the pit of her belly: a predaceous asp.

Jo sputters like the flames of a damp-downed bonfire, choking on her concern, feeling for her lover, yearning to reach out and hold her in her loving arms. The fickle fans show no mercy, jeering in unison as Leah's fragile, eggshell façade cracks under pressure, revealing her soft liquid centre.

'Look at her! She's scared! Leah's scared!' they cry.

'I can't do this!' she screams, melting amidst the din, standing up. 'I'm going home!'

'You can't! You signed a contract,' the beast reminds her.

She stops dead in her tracks.

'Unless you prefer to forfeit £500,000 for early withdrawal from the contest?'

The audience gasp, '£500,000!'

'Yes, that is the agreed penalty,' the beast announces. 'That is the price Cleat agreed to pay as forfeit.'

She sits down. The beast, firmly in control now, insists that she stands.

'Get up on the plinth so we can have a good look at you.'

The crowd cheer enthusiastically as, sniffing back tears, Leah Cleat mounts the rostrum so everyone can have a peek. She looks like a pixie, elfin in her furry grey tracksuit top, soft pink skinny jeans and size 4 suede trainers. The straw-blonde curls complement her pale magnolia complexion. Her beady, grey eyes are set apart, lined with tired creases, saddled with tell-tale bags, the aftereffects of dividing her time between work, rearing Saul, and caring for an ailing mother and father.

Jo has decided they can't care for her parents any longer - carry on like this and they'll have a nervous breakdown. Wendy, an employment law specialist living in the City, is too busy to help, and Simon, a dour agricultural roboticist, struggles to understand human emotions at the best of times. Leah and Jo must break free. They trust to luck, risking all on the ultimate challenge, the most dangerous game of chance in the world. Cleat's placid manner belies an alpha drive, an inner determination to win at all costs.

'So, what brought you here tonight?' the voice asks.

'I wouldn't wish Dean to come to any harm,' she lies, 'however, I do feel women should stand up and show the world that we are not only equal to men, we are their natural superiors. After all, only a woman can bestow the wonderful gift of life that perpetuates the human race.'

'That was impressive. Does that make you a feminist?'

'Yes, I am a feminist,' she declares. 'I am extremely proud to stand up for women's rights. I consider myself a modern, liberated, individual who wants what is right and fair for women.'

The women in the audience stand up and give her a spontaneous ovation while the men shift uncomfortably in their seats as their final epitaph is rewritten upon the deoxyribonucleic acid transcript multiplying deep within their infirm cell walls.

Let's meet Leah's Expert:

Leah's eyes grow stalks at the awesome sight flourishing up on the screen, like a lush oasis of perfection flowering hazily in a barren desert. The well-muscled legs, flat tanned midriff, perfect hourglass figure, inflatable lips, marble teeth, chestnut quiff with lemon hair extensions.

What do you think you look like? What are you, for goodness sake?

'Hello. My name is Blair Wright. I am here to be of service to you. How can I help you?'

Don't insult my intelligence, babe, you're an artificial, manufactured by sexist men for their private pleasure, aren't you? I find you utterly repugnant.

'I am here to be of service to you,' Blair re-bleats. 'How can I help you?'

Leah throws her arms up in despair; this artificial has clearly been pre-programmed.

'Okay, so my question is: am I allowed to cheat?'

'Why not?'

'Really?' Leah jerks forward, astounded.

'Would you like me to help you cheat?' Blair asks her.

She pinches herself, thinks she's dreaming. 'Help me cheat? Really?'

'Yes, really. Look!'

Blair transmits her a detailed map of the maze.

'The game really is *that* easy to play,' she says, '<u>if</u> you ask the right questions, that is.'

Leah shakes her head in disbelief. 'I don't know what to say. Thank you.'

'Please don't mention it, you're welcome.'

Blair goes on to ask if she would like to know a secret. Leah's all ears now. The second clue is revealed:

'Not all mysteries are bad but you have to decide which is which.'

'Thank you, Blair, that will be all,' the voice says.

'You're welcome, Labyrinth,' the artificial lets slip. 'Goodbye, Leah. Good luck.'

Leah's brow furrows with the intense mental strain, breaking into beads of cold sweat.

The voice is the labyrinth?

Blair's face quickly vanishes from the screen. The audience settle down, munching sticky toffee pudding popcorn, slurping buckets of cherry cola, lapping savoury iced cream, waiting for the final instalment of tonight's contest to commence. Leah shudders, tearing out her hair, rubbing anxiety circles around her eyes. Feeling faint and queasy, she vaguely hears it saying,

'Is there anything you would like to ask me before you enter the labyrinth?'

'I'm frightened,' she admits, quaking, 'please, don't hurt me.'

She is embarrassing the labyrinth now, in front of its adoring global audience of millions.

'Can't you be positive? The map will guide you safely to my heart. You're going to win!'

The beast focuses on more banal matters.

'In order that we can improve the quality of our service tell us:

Did you find that speaking to us helped you answer all of your questions?'

'Well, yes, I suppose I did, but…' she begins, mulling through the mares in her mind.

Too late! Time's up!

'It's time for you to go now, darling,' Labyrinth tells her kindly. 'Chin up! You'll be fine.'

She doesn't feel fine. She shakes like an earth tremor, squints in trepidation. Her stomach churns. She turns sickly green, dips her head between her knees, and fetches up her lunch, all over the plush deep-pile red carpet. A spearmint-rinsed cleaner, an angel of mercy waiting in the wings, emerges, armed with mop, bucket, shake and vac and a sky-blue self-propelled robot hoover with gaudy pink buffers which feel for dirt.

Leah utters an apology, wipes the sick from her lips with her sleeve, then gets giddily to her feet. The crowd rally round her, cheering her on as she inches up to the yawning chasm. Leah, reluctant gladiator: entering the coliseum of chaos! Leah, timid she-warrior: fighting the evil labyrinth! The mob bay and chant for her blood regardless of the hero's health, safety, morale, mood, mindset or physical wellbeing.

'Fight, Leah! Fight, Leah! Fight, Leah! Fight, Leah! Fight, Leah! Fight Her! Fight! Fight!'

The beast stares avidly at the gallant lady knight approaching her dragon, map in hand.

'Oh, Leah?' she calls.

Cleat glances nervously over her shoulder at the computer-generated image on the screen; the alien face: glowing incandescent red, then snow white with rage. She shivers, mumbles incoherently; her mouth feels grocery-shelf dry, as if stuffed with rock salt.

'Yah?' she stammers.

'May the force be with you!'

The unruly mob fade into the background. Leah's heart sinks as Blair's map fades before her eyes: crisping, crumbling into floury white dust, running off her hands, as she disappears inside the labyrinth's gloomy mouth. The throat opens wide in the hungry yawn of a killer whale, swallowing her whole like a writhing seal pup, gorging herself on the squirming body, the beast's flaking lips, clamping shut silently behind her.

Ten nodes. Ten right ways. Ten wrong. Ten shocks. Ten mysteries. Waiting.

Will Leah break her heart? Find out next week.

Dean is alone inside the dark recess of the beast's throat. He begins to feel small, sad, lonely, has no-one at home to watch him. No sweetheart to love him. No friends to root for him. His love, youth, vitality, everything he ever owned, is mortgaged, lost to compulsive gambling. He wants to go home. But he has no home. Other than a pile of soggy cardboard and a PC-5X I-phone. His inflated ego is sorely dented, his self-esteem severely tested. Dean is shivery, cold, sopping wet, and miserable, and hasn't an inkling of what to do next. Is it his imagination? Or did it just get colder? The wisps of chilled breath kissing his cheeks confirm his worst fear: there is a shadow, following him, close by, in the dark.

'De-an!'

He jumps.

'Joe? That you?'

He glances edgily over his shoulder. There is no-one there, only dewy spider webs, a fine gossamer mist, and the fug of faerie dust that clouds his fraught mind.

Think, man! Win tonight and you can bum about on the beach with the natives forever, get rat-arsed to the reggae beat. You've got to win this, Kiddo. You're gambling for your life.

That voice again. Who you going to call?

'De-an!'

'What the fuck? Who *is* that? Show yourself, you bastard.'

'It's a mystery, it's a mystery, I'm still waiting, for a clue. Is it a mystery to you, Dean?'

His little heart pumps away, fit to burst. His weary head throbs, sees stars, has a migraine. He slips and slides in the throat's mucus lining, groping about in the slimy, slick saliva. The beast coughs and burps, constricting her throat until the intruder wedges in her flesh like a fish bone stuck in a gannet's gullet. Dean can't take much more of this.

He throws back his head and wails, 'Let Cleat die, not me!'

Dean slithers free and slides on his belly like the white worm, relieved beyond words when he reaches the node. To his surprise he discovers that he is dry, can stand up. He blinks as a blinding shaft of light appears overhead, warming, revitalising him.

Which way? Right? Left? Ahead? No. Right.

A shadowy figure calls him, somewhere, just down there. Can you see it? Gurning at you?

'De-an!'

Oh, great, just great! Chummy's back! Or is it Chucky?

Right? Why not? After all, you've nothing left to lose, he tells himself.

He closes his eyes, mutters some daft prayer, then deliberately turns right...

Right?

Wrong!

The thick, sharp horn punches into him like a driven chisel, piercing his chest, thrusting through his heart, exiting his body between the shoulder blades. Dean is lifted out of his own blood, his flailing, thrashing body held aloft, his impaled torso, riding along on the crest of a wave: the statuesque creature's bobbing head. The minotaur shows off his warm corpse to an audience of millions: brandishing the bleeding cadaver above its head like its obscene trophy.

The Producer is ecstatic, her brow drips with perspiration, 'Quick, get a shot of his face!'

The Censor shields his eyes with his nicotine-stained fingers, makes a stand, 'Stop this! It's barbaric!'

An infra-red camera zooms into close-up, intimate mode, snapping away intrusively at the victim's ecru twisted face. A neon sign flickers into life, reflects in his coal-black funereal eyes:

'Smile, Dean! You're on candid camera!'

Women stand and applaud the chauvinist piglet's demise. Fully grown, faint-hearted men swoon. Jo leers greedily, clumps of baked beans dribble down her chin. Simon belches, helps himself to a fresh clutch of ribs. Wendy wolfs down fistfuls of fatty chips.

All over the world violent voyeurs, sadistic couch potatoes, feral surfers of the dark net down an ice-cold beer, punching their foetid airspace in celebration at the loss of another of society's misfits.

We'll be back with more after the break.

Leah, crouched inside the beast's gagging throat, knows she's not alone, knows there'll be others. Watching her every move. Waiting for her. Hidden. Inside Labyrinth's twisted maze. Mysteries. She sees a host of tiny, blinking, red lights embedded in the vascular wall: myriad robot-controlled cameras winking at her. Winks back, mildly amused at the idea of millions of viewers enjoying her fun time. Until the lights go out.

Chaos breaks into the studio:

'We've lost her, Julie!' the camera crew scream at the Producer, in total disarray.

'Lost her?' she says, incredulously. 'What do you mean, lost her? That's impossible! The cameras are independently controlled by our central computer system. There must be a glitch. Get onto IT! Now! Get her back! I want Cleat back! Now! Understand?'

'Trying our best, Jules!' Brian protests, shrugging his shoulders defiantly. 'Experiencing some kind of external interference.'

'That's crap! Try harder, damn you! Before my audience ratings drop.'

Pandemonium descends on the party. Jo pushes her way through the throng of mesmerised viewers staring blankly at the blacked-out TV, screaming blue murder as an excuse-flash hits the screen:

We appear to be experiencing some technical issues at the moment. Bear with us while we resolve the problem. Flex TV regret any inconvenience. Normal service will be resumed as soon as possible. Thank you.

'Oh, my God! No! No! No! Leah! Leah! No! No! No!' Jo repeats, falling to her knees.

Seeing one mother cry, Saul bursts into fits of hysterical yelping, 'I want my mummy!'

'Hush, little baby, don't you cry, Mummy's going to sing you a lullaby,' Wendy croons, rocking him in her arms, thoughtlessly adding, 'and if that mockingbird don't sing, Mum's going to buy you a diamond ring. Diamond? Oh, my God! Sorry, Jo. I didn't realise! Leah!'

Saul bawls on: 'I want my mummy! I want my mummy! I want...'

There is a huge crash as, anguished and disturbed, Dad careers into the barbecue and starts to cook. Sunil, from no. 6, dials 999 and requests the air ambulance. Simon turns off the gas, fearing an explosion. Hilary squats beside the unconscious septuagenarian, applying wet tea towels, cold comfort. Virgil & Lucia, Jaxon & Sharon, Bryn & Briony, Sabrina & Cherry, Donal & Mathias make their apologies:

'My goodness, is that the time? Thanks, Jo, we really should be going. Great party, Jo! Come and give me a hug! Howzat? Better?'

'Mm, thanks, Hugo,' Jo lies.

'Mustn't outstay our welcome, must we, Jo?'

'Course not, Fleur, I understand.' Jo kisses her on both cheeks. 'When you've got to go...'

'Thank you so much, Jo, we've had such a lovely time.'

'Good, Regine, so glad you enjoyed yourself.'

'Are you feeling alright, Jo?'

'Not really.'

Mum stares down from the veranda, a solitary tear meandering down her crinkled face.

'Just the two of us,' the beast sings, melodically, to her beauty, 'we can make it if we try!'

'Go to Hell!' spits Leah.

To hell with you, the murderous media and crazy cult fanatics, the indifferent parents who can't control their young, your sick-sad, die-hard fans. When, if, I get out of here, alive, I'll be rich and famous, able to do whatever I want, able to sort out my life, your life, their lives.

Saul, her perfect little boy, won't have to start boarding school next year, aged three, due to her incessant workload. Her demented mother and frail father will be locked away, out of sight, out of mind, in a fully automated nursing home. Fat-faced Wendy, the gross corpulent, riddled with statin-induced muscle pain, will have her 3 dreams: of life-changing liposuction, butterfat vivisection and gut-inserted micro-bots to digest her surplus body fat, realised. Simon will be found a sanctuary, an opportunity to live out his days as a hermit in a remote Scottish sea cove. Far from the madding crowd...

'*If* you get out alive,' the beast gloats, reading her thoughts.

Leah pauses to reflect on past loves, long lost friends, over-worked colleagues, less-than-discreet confidantes. Wonders if she'll ever hold Saul in her motherly embrace again, Jo, her lifelong soul mate, at her side. A spidery shiver runs down her spine. Her imagination? Or did it just get colder?

Must move on!

She shuts her eyes. Kicks off her trainers. Slips off her powder-pregnated pink ankle socks. Shuddering as she contemplates the throat's dense mucus lining. The goo: with the consistency, odour, and sickeningly sweet flavour of mild chilli dipping sauce, has salivated into a pond of fermenting fluid. Leah takes a deep breath, then wriggles through the gunge like a squirming pink tadpole, bravely propelling herself through the warm slush. Insidiously, slops of mucus trickle down her neck, creep inside her sleeves and trouser legs, her nostrils, ears, mouth. She surfaces, gagging for air. The beast absorbs Leah into its flesh, adhering her floundering torso to its tongue, a mouse trapped on a sticky board, tightening its muscles around her. Her petite body is too thin for the beast to grip; she squirms herself out of her deep throat, and escapes. Miraculously, when she emerges, she is dry as a bone. Leah lays on her side, exhausted, panting after her horrific ordeal. After a while, she curls up into the foetal position, falls into a delicious, dreamless sleep...

Fully recovered, Leah rolls on her front, slithering along the passage until she reaches a cavern, surprised to find a cushioned floor. She stands up. A brilliant shaft of light pierces the gloom, radiating pure warmth, settling her protesting collywobbles. Leah Cleat has reached a node unscathed. A familiar voice encourages her to go farther up and further in:

'You're doing fine. Follow the red heart.'

She glances over her shoulder into empty space. The voice confides in her. She smiles and confirms her understanding. Leah now has a Game Plan. She stands at the Crossroads of Life, deciding which way to go next. She will never squint again.

She now knows Dean perished on the horns of a minotaur when he took the right-hand turn at this node. Leah Cleat is indifferent to his demise. Feels the scum got his just desserts. She never met the weirdo but knows all about his strange ways, having hacked into, and extensively researched, his criminal record with Jo.

It transpires that Dean Moat was not the vagrant's real name: that was a pseudonym issued by his controlling parole superintendent as a condition of his tagged release from borstal. Moat was none other than Aubrey Frey, the notorious nitric acid freak, an animal who threatened teenagers with permanent disfigurement unless they granted him uninhibited access to their online bank accounts.

How fitting that he should die from a creature's horn through the heart.

She wonders whether his corpse will be taken to the communal body-recycling pits near Aveley along with the other low-life, to be covered with slaked lime, bio-degenerated, then mulched and reconstituted as fertiliser for muck-spreading on one of the few remaining famine-affected foreign fields. With her only opponent dead, Leah's fate lies solely in her hands. She'll need to rely on her gut reactions, take heed of her primal instincts, if she is to survive the game.

'The first shock's mild, a mere horse's kick.'

Moon probably lied when he said that. She wouldn't trust Joe T. as far as she could toss him. If she *was* shocked, she *might* have a 90% chance of survival, assuming the worst-case scenario in which she chose the wrong way.

Which way to go, then? Left or Ahead?

'Follow the red heart.'

Leah elects to go left.

Wrong!

The turning is a blind alley that leads to a dead end, a pitch-black hole. The tunnel shrinks from view, engulfing her in a diminishing vortex, a total blackout. The ebon walls twist, curl and wrap themselves round her trembling body like a funeral shroud. Her claustrophobia sets in immediately. She instinctively fights her rising panic, desperately clawing the fleshy wall, raking her stub-bitten fingernails through its cartilaginous inner skin. Her head spins, her mind rotates rapidly, like cerebral tombola. She gropes around, as blind as a mole in a hole, in her padded organic straitjacket, loses all sense of space and dimension, swaying to the rhythm of an unseen heart. Leah stumbles, collapses, in a raggedy heap, suffocating in a stifling, airless chamber with no apparent way out.

'Follow the red heart.'

A crystalline ruby heart appears like a beacon before her startled eyes, shimmering in the dark. A most wondrous, beautiful sight to behold, tantalisingly out of reach. Leah lies gazing in awe of the astral spectacle, frustrated that she can't move her arms which are pinned to her sides by an invisible cast-iron-strong cuticle. The heart beats on, pumping itself into the dark like a jellyfish, floating ever closer to her.

'Follow the red heart.'

The living gem shimmers like a red sun setting over the horizon of her enthralled face.

'Reach out and touch me. Believe.'

'Can't reach,' Leah complains. 'Can't move my arms.'

'Follow the red heart.'

'Can't! Can't!'

'Kiss my heart before you die,
Or spend forever wondering why,
You felt my love but passed me by.'

Leah purses her lips, kisses the heart.

Mm, feels all light and fluffy, tastes scrumptious like sweet black cherries with clotted cream? Unlike anything I've ever tasted. Don't be silly! When did you ever kiss a heart?

'Follow the red heart!'

Leah is beguiled now, her child-eyes, enchanted by the heart, rising high above her head, glowing neon in the gloom. A sapphire blue hole appears, a tiny pinprick of light, far off, as the heart continues its silent ascent. She isn't frightened in the slightest by the heart, hole, or the light, expecting to be surprised by a mystery or shocked. But not at the same time. Or twice.

The first shock's mild, a mere horse's kick, a short, sharp jolt along the full length of her spine. Her arms and legs jerk about like frogs' legs dancing on an electric wire. Her fingers and toes tingle. Although the sensation isn't in the least bit painful, she finds it disturbing - almost as if some electrostatic force is holding her steady, like a coiled spring. The next shock sets her free, sending her hurtling skywards, firing her out of the walled cage. Leah's stunned body is shot out of its private silo like a rocket: Leah Cleat, LCBM, ultimate human ballistic missile!

Whew! See me fly, Jo! See me fly! Whew! Whew!

If only Jo *could* see her, regressing. Leah bursts through the hole in the ceiling to a higher echelon, finding herself in a new node. No way can she tell which. She assumes the node to be second in the series of ten but might be completely wrong. Nothing is ever as it seems inside the labyrinth. She considers herself fortunate to have got this far.

Fortunate? Or destined?

So, why is the friendly voice protecting her like a guardian angel? What is the significance of the red heart? And why does she feel so guilty? She wonders what magic (reasoning there is magic at play here) awaits her at the next crossroads.

There *are* no crossroads. The second node is a grotto, coloured sapphire blue. The heart fades, then disappears...

Leah screams as a searing blue lightning bolt scythes into her body, jarring, electrocuting her from crown to toe, setting the tips of her digits tingling. She collapses in a charred heap, radiating like a barbecue, writhing in agony. Her eyes smart, her lashes singe. Her blonde hair is incinerated. Only black, curly, necrotic wisps of carbon remain, etched into her grilled scalp.

'Must escape! Must find out!'

Blair, cautious: 'No! Leah! You can't go back. Only forward. Hope! Pray!'

Dense grey smoke pours from her smouldering clothing. She smells her skin burning.

'Must find heart!'

Blair, excited: 'That's right! Onwards and Inwards! Those are the Rules of Labyrinth!'

Her flesh crawls, spiders of pain creep up and down her spine in waves, pausing to burrow into her flesh. She feels "The Burn". Can you feel it?

'Can't go on! Can't do this!'

Blair insists: 'You must! Keep going! You've reached the 3rd crossroads. Well done you!'

Her skin softens, starts to flake off dermal dandruff, red-raw sore, puffy to touch.

'Can't see! Can't see!'

She is inhuman, a blind white worm, groping, snaking forward, inch-by-agonizing inch on her stomach, an amphibious human salamander. Searing inside, she slumps against the tunnel wall, feels the labyrinth. All hope is lost. She'll die soon. Leah Cleat focuses on her blissful life: Jo, Saul. Her face blisters and swells. She hallucinates. Hallucination is good for her. Helps her cope with the pain. Helps her dream of the key to her survival. Who, surprisingly, turns out to be...

Blair, again: 'Come on, Leah! Try, won't you?'

Leah tries, she *really* does, feels a cool breeze on her face.

'Made it to the third node! Thank God! Which way now?'

Her mind descends into chaos.

'Straight ahead! Has to be!'

Wrong!

'No, I meant right!'

Wrong!

'No, left! Left!'

She hears a sound!

A grunt, or a snort.

'Oh, my God! What-the-fuck's-that?'

'Le-ah, Le-ah, Le-ah!'

'Blair? That you? Please, say yes! Please! Blair?'

'Le-ah, Le-ah, Le-ah!'

'Blair? That you? Blair? Help me! That you? Blair? Help me! Blair? Please God!'

'Left! Has to be! Wrong! No, I meant right!'

Wrong!

'No, left! Left!'

Wrong!

Minotaur!

Thankfully, the beast turns out to be a good minotaur which leads her to the fourth node. Leah guesses correctly and goes straight ahead. Had she gone left she'd be stunned. The right turn harbours a bad minotaur. All exits from the fifth node carry the risk of electrocution - or a mystery. Leah decides to turn left. To her surprise, she is greeted by the ruby heart.

'Follow the red heart!'

Will the heart be kinder to her this time?

Tune in next time to find out.

Sutra Patel walks into the opticians with a worried expression on her face.

'Andrew, can you spare me a minute, please?'

Her voice sounds strained, insistent, shaky.

He stares at her through his horn-rimmed glasses.

'Sure, Sutra, what's the problem?'

'It's Leah Cleat, she appears to have gone into a trance.'

Andrew arches his brows, mildly amused, he's had a good day.

'A trance? That's a new one!'

'I can't pull her off the visual field screener. She's obsessed with the red light. It's almost as if she's using it to play a video game.'

'A video game with a red light? Really?' he laughs. 'Sounds a bit scary if you ask me!'

Sutra stamps her pretty foot in annoyance.

'Andrew! I'm being serious! Come and see her if you don't believe me.'

He follows the optometrist into the eye test room.

Leah's sitting up, ramrod rigid, gripping both sides of the screen, her knuckles white to the bone, eyes glued to the glass, mumbling to herself.

'You're doing fine! Follow the red light! You're doing well! Follow the red light!'

Andrew looks at her, totally bewildered. He eyes Sutra, who issues him her consent, and shakes Leah firmly by the shoulder.

'Come on, Leah,' he says, kindly, 'let's have a chat over a nice cup of tea, shall we?'

'No! I'm doing fine! Follow the red light! I'm doing well! Follow the red light!'

Our Secret Place

Dear Linda,

I found your old diaries this morning. I sat on the rectory bench where we used to meet, the weak autumn sun in my face, turning the faded pages of a life filled with love and tears. Do you remember the tennis courts where we played when we were young? They're overgrown now, covered in moss, dying leaves, curling crisps of bronze and gold. Their nets are torn to shreds, like my heart. I closed your book and thought of all the good times we had.

I miss you.

Daniel xx

LINDA STRUGGLED TO COPE WITH life. Her dad died when she was ten and her mother suffered from depression and anxiety so severe that she couldn't leave the house. Every weekday, she set her alarm, got herself up, washed, dressed, cooked breakfast and did all the housework and laundry before she left for school, while her mum rested in bed. She struggled to make new friends and suffered terrible bullying. Sometimes Linda decided not to go into school at all, sleeping in or pretending to be ill. Often, she despaired and wished she was dead.

Her only salvations were her love of tennis and Dan, who made her life worth living and gave her the strength to carry on. Today was no different from any other day. Linda awoke knowing she wouldn't only need the physical and emotional strength to look after herself, but to care for her mother, too.

Then she received the devastating results of the clinical tests, and her world fell apart.

As soon as the school bell rang, she packed her satchel, left the chemistry lab, ran past the playground and took her short cut through the cycle shed to the hole in the chain-link fence. The shed's grey, corrugated roof was shattered by a vandal who broke a leg when he climbed on top. The place disgusted her; its clinker ground was carpeted with cigarette butts. Just the smell of it made her want to throw up. She pinched her nose and turned her head.

Linda managed to negotiate the torn mesh without cutting herself, catching her yellow St Denys House tie, or ripping her lemon shirt. The two-bedroom council house was a short dash away down a gloomy alleyway. Hastily, she unlocked the back door, raided the larder, boiled a can of soup, made up a tray lunch, and went upstairs. The bedroom was stifling hot. Maureen Newman lay ashen-faced in bed, a shadow of her former self, propped up with fluffy pillows.

'Is that you, Lin?' she said weakly. 'You're home early.'

'I made you some lunch, Mum,' Linda said, adopting a brave smile. 'How are you feeling?'

'A little better, thank you, darling.'

Linda knew she was lying; she was riddled with pain. Her mum's agony cut into her heart like a hot knife.

'I have to go out,' she told her, 'I've got a tennis match. I'll be back later to cook supper.'

'You're meeting him,' her mother stated in a caustic voice.

Linda's voice caught on the back of her throat, 'Yes. Why?'

'I really don't think you should.'

The girl's spirits sagged, drained of any life by her mother's acid tone.

'Why? Because he isn't one of us?'

Maureen became agitated, tried to sit up in bed, and failed. 'Because you're too young.'

'I'm not too young! I love Dan!'

'It's puppy love,' the sick woman snarled. 'You'll get over him.'

Linda was appalled. 'I can't believe you just said that, Mum! I hate you!'

She stormed off to her bedroom, locked the door and changed into her clean tennis whites. Her mother would never have spoken to her like that when she was well, not in a million years. Minutes later, she stuck her head through the door and apologised. Her face fell when she saw the untouched bowl of creamy tomato soup, the half-eaten, lightly-buttered, soft batch bread.

'You haven't touched your lunch,' she said, quietly.

Her mother raised her weary head. 'I wasn't hungry. Please, Lin. Let me rest in peace.'

Linda spotted an ashtray hidden under the bed, a smouldering cigarette butt.

Incapable of survival without the cancer sticks which killed her sister, the once-beautiful woman had faded and tired of living. Now, she was just another nicotine addict waiting to be extinguished. The schoolgirl kissed her forehead and sobbed, 'I love you,' then she collected her tennis racket and new white balls and left the house, never to see her mother alive again.

Her tummy ached. Her head throbbed. She was run down and emotionally drained. She took out a cherry-flavour lip Syl and swiped her lips. He was her tonic. She couldn't wait to see him.

Linda arrived on court wearing a pristine tennis shirt and skirt, and the pretty tortoiseshell hair slide her mother gave her when she was a little girl. He was slouched on the bench outside the saggy chain-link fence in tattered navy flares, and a floppy tangerine vest which accentuated his hairy chest. He slid back the rusting bar to the gate and came on court. Linda went and stood at the net, po-faced. He was shocked by the change in her appearance. Her lips were split and sore. Her face was pale, haggard, and drawn. Black bags clung onto her almond eyes like sleeping bats.

'What's happened, Lin?' he said, casually strolling up to the net.

She bounced a ball on her racket and burst into tears. He brushed her soft cheeks with the back of his big, hairy hand and held her tight. She loved it when he did that.

'Better?' he asked.

'Mm, much!' She smiled for the first time that day.

'How did the tests go?'

The smile disappeared.

'The cancer has spread to the spine and organs,' she said, dully.

Dan was stunned. He didn't know what to say at first. Struggling to retain any sense of self-composure. When he did speak, his voice was trembling and withered with worry for her. Linda looked so ill.

'God, I'm sorry,' he said. 'What can I do to help?'

'Just be here for me, Dan, will you?'

He put his hands on her shoulders, gazed into her eyes, and gave her the loveliest smile.

'I'll always be here for you. Come on, let's play tennis!'

Dan spun his wooden racket which clattered to the court's hard surface.

He called, 'Rough or smooth, Champ?'

He made her laugh! 'Smooth!'

Dan felt the cat-gut strings. 'It's rough. I serve first.'

Linda padded to the baseline, hitched up her skirt and scratched the itchy, red rash on her thigh. Dan's heart went out to her. She was always in the wars. Sniffing, she leaned forward, twirled her racket, bit her bottom lip, and concentrated. Linda nearly did the splits trying to reach his first serve, an ace that landed in the far right-hand corner.

'Oh, good shot, Dan!' she cried.

'15-0!'

Her boyfriend hopped to his left. Before she could settle, he threw the ball high in the air and slammed it out of reach.

'30-0!'

'Oh, well done!' she yelled, admiringly.

Another brutal ace followed, this time to her weak backhand, then another, which narrowly missed hitting her in the stomach.

'Sorry, Lin, did I hit you?'

She shook her head.

'My game, I think,' he grinned at her. 'Like to change ends?'

'No, thanks. Me to serve!'

Lin bounced the ball, one, two, three times, glanced at him and smiled to herself. He always let her win. The former netball court was covered in moss and detritus. As she went to serve, she slipped and fell. Dan gasped in disbelief. He wanted to wrap her in a shroud of cotton wool.

'Lin, you're bleeding!' he cried.

He threw down his racket, leapt the net, rushed to her side, kneeling to inspect her wound.

'I'll live,' she sighed happily. 'It's only a graze, Dan.'

She leaned back on her elbows and watched him pick the sharp, embedded grit out of her sore knee. Neither of them felt much like playing tennis anymore. Yearning intensely for one another, they left the court and walked hand-in-hand across the playing field, along a red earth path, until they reached their hidey-hole-in-the-hedge.

The sweethearts scrambled through the gap into a leafy glade. A lonely, secret, place where sunbeams danced on their faces. They lay in the lush, long grass watching a skylark beat its way across the cloudless sky. The sun was at its zenith, its hot rays seared their skin. Dan took off his vest. Lin gently stroked his hairy chest.

'I love you, Dan,' she said, dreamily. 'You're my world.'

He told her, he loved her too. His heart raced with excitement. Her eyes sparkled like stars on a clear summer night. She smirked mischievously, twirling a strand of straggly blonde hair.

'What would you like me to do?' she murmured.

He really did love her.

'Kiss me,' he said.

She kissed him, a longing, loving kiss, then gazed into his sad eyes. Dan was all she had left in the world. A delicious, tingling sensation passed through her body, her cheeks blushed roses.

'Do you know what it means when we kiss like that?' she asked.

Dan had no idea what it meant. He hadn't learnt the facts of life.

'No, what does it mean?'

'It means that we want to make love.'

He stared at her, mystified. 'Make love?'

'Yes, you know! It means that we love each other so much that we want to make a baby.'

'Make a baby?' he questioned, his mind and body filled with wonder. 'With you, Lin?'

'Mm!' she smiled.

They listened to the blackbird singing in the swaying trees. Heard the rat-a-tat-a-tat of a distant woodpecker. A bee buzzed past their faces. A jet plane, bound for a destination they would never reach, flew high overhead, clouding the clear blue sky. Some children played on swings and roundabouts in the park, calling, laughing. They heard a baby cry. He found her secret place. His head swam with love. He shook the mystical cobwebs out of his head, tried to focus.

He loved her so much. He could never let her go. He wanted her to share his life, always, so that he could care for her and protect her from harm.

She loved him. She wanted to have his baby. Their own little child. Someone she could nurture, cherish, and love for the rest of their lives.

Her temperature dropped. His hand numbed. Her icicle formed. She shivered. Scared by his petrified face. Confused by the bizarre changes taking place within her body. Linda felt afraid.

'What is it, Lin?' she heard him shout, his hands trembling with her cold.

'I don't feel very well,' she gasped.

A raw, liquid, chill trickled down her spine. Her melting icicle. Her heart skipped a beat.

'What's the matter? Lin? Lin. Lin!'

She shivered again, violently this time. He felt her icy breath. Hoar frost. Freeze his cheek.

'I have to go now,' she said, her sweet face, turning royal blue, 'I'll always love you, Dan.'

Her heart stopped beating. He clutched her limp body to his. He brushed her frozen cheeks with his hand. Held her tight. She loved it when he did that! Thunderclouds gathered in the darkening sky above him.

'Please God, no!' he wailed.

She exhaled, her final sigh. 'Mum's waiting for me.'

Her soul rose! Out of her heart and mind! She felt her spirits lift! Freed! Freed at last!

Dear Linda,

I lay awake thinking of you last night, the wind whistling in the eaves, the rain spattering on my window pane. I wondered about our love. What if we had never found your secret place?

I love you,

Daniel xx

NEWMAN, Linda Jane, of Byfield, dearly beloved daughter of Leonard and Maureen, died at home on 14th June 1971 after a long illness borne with courage. Her body was donated to medical research.

Plastic Man

HELLO. MY NAME IS BRYN. You wouldn't have heard of me. No-one has heard of me, only Bethan, Morgan, and the Boys. And the "powers-that-be". They've heard of me. They like to keep me secret, see, keep me hidden away, so that you don't find out.

I was born on the mornin of 21st of October 1966, near Aberfan, the same day 116 children and 28 adults died, when a colliery spoil tip collapsed onto their homes and a school. My father used to teach at the school; used to. My mother worked in a factory that made plastic toys for children to play with. We had lead soldiers in those days. Mother used to tell me not to put them in my mouth or suck the heads.

I grew up a good boy, in a town filled with sadness, never thinkin for one moment that lightnin would strike twice. Not that I'm complainin mind. I've had a hard life, but a good one, filled with love and compassion.

Now let's see, October 1966. That makes me 52. Not that I feel 52. I feel 102 today. Feel like death. I want to die but they won't let me, see? Say they want me for medical research, like a rat or rhesus monkey.

Morgan tells me today is a special day, 21st October 2019. I can't think why. My mind's goin, see? The first thing to go was my mind. Morgan tells me Bethan can't see me today, she's too busy workin at the school, bringin up our two fine boys. I hope she can see me. I can't see or speak to her, ever again. I'm blind, see, and dumb. I never used to be. I can smell (just), hear, touch, feel, Morgan in the room with me.

She sings to me: 'Happy Birthday to You, Happy Birthday to You, Happy Birthday, Dear Bryn, Happy Birthday to You. There! Wasn't that lovely, darlin? Can you smell the candles?'

I smell the candles burnin. I blink once. Blink once for yes, twice for no, Morgan tells me. I smell their smoke. In the same way that I smell roses on her soft cheeks. She rubs her face against mine, then kisses me.

'No-one's lookin, darlin,' she says, lowerin her voice a little. 'Happy Birthday, Bryn.'

I start to cry, feel the hot tears tricklin down my cheeks. I can't help it. Morgan is all I have, now Bethan doesn't visit me anymore with the boys. Perhaps she has another man? Perhaps. We've been married 25 years.

I hear Morgan blow my candles out, one by one, 'Whew, whew, whew,' until the smoke fades, like Bethan's love for me.

'Ah, you're cryin, stop cryin, Bryn,' she says. 'I'm goin to wash you now. Like it when I wash you, don't you?'

I blink, once. My nostrils are filled with clear neoprene feedin tubes. My mouth is full of a thick, purple, corrugated, flexi-tube that stretches down my throat as far as my windpipe. My arse is connected to a pump. My willy has a rubber tube clamped to it, connected to a polythene bag, hangin off the side of the bed. I can't breathe, feed, shit, piss, unassisted, see? Not without the tubes and wires, the pumps and pistons, drains and drips.

Not without Morgan! My life isn't worth livin without Morgan. Am I really livin now? She lifts the sheet, and I become her big baby, lyin naked on my swaddlin bed, waitin for her to wash me.

Morgan begins by dabbin my cheeks, lips and ears, quickly movin to my neck and chest. She scrubs my armpits, like my mother used to do. She tickles! I want to giggle for Morgan, but can't, with my tube. I close my eyes, tears rollin down my cheeks, tryin to imagine Bethan makin sweet love to me, but she's a fadin memory to me now, some other lucky man's dream. I feel Morgan, washin' my stomach, my belly.

'I'm goin to do your privates now, darlin',' she says. 'Keep still.'

Keep still! I blink, once, and feel my body stiffen. I blush. Tense. Stiffen. I open my eyes, glassed with tears. My eyes cry, for her. I want to say sorry. I smell her rose. She kisses me. I can't stop cryin. Bethan! Bethan! Bethan!

'It's alright, Bryn, no-one' lookin darlin.'

I imagine Morgan, straightenin her light blue uniform, thinkin: *you get to meet all sorts of sad men in my line of work,* and pray she doesn't think that of me. Pray I mean more than that to her. Morgan is all I have left in the world. I concentrate on Darren, David, he's only 5. Their faces are blank, my mind, blank. I feel her dab me dry, the clean sheet falls on my chest. I sense her anguish, like cloyin emotional glue between us. My heart sinks, my bladder aches.

'I have to go off shift now, Bryn,' she says.

I blink furiously. I blink twice.

'I have to take my weekend off, see?' she says.

I blink twice, twice, twice.

'To be with my husband and kids, Bryn.'

I blink away the tears, try to pull my heartstrins together, but can't.

'Megan will look after you while I'm away.'

Her rose fades, her scent dispels, my heart bleeds.

I close my eyes and dream of fish.

My name is Bryn.

You wouldn't have heard of me.

No-one has heard of me.

Only Morgan.

They call me the Plastic Man.

Red Rubber Ball

1.11

ONE MINUTE, SYLVIE'S LYING, PEACEFULLY in bed, sound asleep. The next, the curse slams into her, like a giant hammer. Its sheer magnitude, the reflexive impact on her systems, is immense. Its intrusion is all-consuming. Its influence, irresistible. Sylvie hasn't seen this coming. Not this time! She is momentarily stunned, stupefied. Her head lolls to one side. Her eyes inflame with sudden fear, incomprehension. The first round of convulsions sends shockwaves, pain, washing through her in a relentless tsunami. Then the curse tears her, limb-by-limb, joint-by-joint, with burning intensity. Briefly, the beast subsides. She draws breath, dreading its inevitable climax.

Before she knows it, Sylvie is jerking about like a marionette. Tiny beads of perspiration form on her brow, congealing into thick, slimy sweat which streams down her face in torrents. She lies squirming on the saturated bedsheet in her sodden jasmine-flower silk camisole top and matching briefs, her body's salt drying-out in white shock-rings, sodium chloride circle-stains, roasting in the body-heat that radiates, like personal fall-out from her fantastic dream exertions.

Sylvie goes into spasm immediately. Her irises roll up, revealing perfectly-opaque, white-marble eyeballs, spring-loaded ball bearings on her live bagatelle board. She becomes impelled by her hidden malevolent force, enters the sanctum of the hysterically insane, carefully closing the only door behind her mind. One-by-one, she feels her joints start to crack. First the vertebrae in her neck and spinal cord crack. Then her joints crack: hips, knees, ankles, shoulders, elbows, wrists. As they crack, the bones bend, warping out of shape. Her muscles unfurl, unfold, giving her the outward appearance of a misshapen crone. Sylvie's heart has big palpitations, her lungs heave with the incredible effort, her brain engulfs a sensory sea of excruciating pain. She's crying freely when her heart gives out. Her heart actually stops beating! For a minute or so she dies, lies, inert, staring blank, up, into, sheet-white light, sensing her sacred spirit rising up, and speculating on her shattered body. Before she abruptly coughs, convulses again, body jerking back to life, a frog's leg hanging, twitching, electrified, by her nervous system's red-hot wires.

Exhausted, miserable, wretched, she lies back, a tearful, tarnished doll, a weeping mistress to the unimaginable force of the seizures. Painfully, slowly, her right elbow cracks. An arm unfolds, backwards, the wrong way around, twisted with torque, reaching out greedily, past her shoulder blades, for her neck. Sylvie starts to bleat: the little lamb, struggling, as she strangles on her mother's tangled umbilical cord. Her right-hand twists, three hundred and sixty degrees, turns on its palm, and creeps up inside her silk camisole top as far as the nape of her neck, where it pauses for a while to stroke her fine, damp, brown, down. Then, waving a fond farewell to her twisted spine, the hand promptly disappears into the bush of her wispy, wavy, chestnut hair and squats there scratching flecks of dandruff from her scalp. She cries out to Alexa, who's busy watching her, for help.

Alexa looks down dispassionately at the ghostly, grimacing, luminous-green figure through her night vision lenses. A black angel, an angel of death, patiently watching, noting, assessing, recording her subject's behaviour, its mannerisms, quirks, tics. Scrupulously documenting each spasm in the cause of science. Relishing in its subject's responses to the invasive reflexes. She always looks down on Sylvie, belonging to a vastly superior, more intellectual race. Once she's recorded every move, she will onwards-transmit the sylph's cracking performance, for further analysis. Alexa is no help to the woman whatsoever.

Inevitably Sylvie succumbs to the mind-numbing pain: arches her back, relaxes her bladder, cherishes the relief latently supplied by the warm jets of urine, that trickle amber fluid down her legs.

'Now look what you've gone and made me do, Alexa!' she complains.

The left hand reacts, to escape her flow, casually wandering up her spine like a spider in a wet bath tub, determined to find dry skin. *Can't take any more*: is Sylvie's last thought before she passes out.

4.44

Sylvie comes to in pitch-black darkness. Driverless freight train rumbles over a nearby railway bridge. Pilotless A9000 airbus prepares for its final descent, bound for Stansted. Real fox barks, fruitlessly foraging through her eco-bin for food. The pain's gone. She doesn't hurt anymore. Sylvie's stiff, bent fourteen different ways, shattered and broken. But at least she doesn't hurt. Above all else, her pride is still intact.

'Because I'm a woman, did you think I was going to crack under the pressure? Go on, be honest. Admit it, I had you all fooled there, didn't I?'

She tries to move her head, it won't move. Her neck and spine are stiff, set, solid. She tries sitting up in bed, can't. Tries moving her limbs, they won't move either. Her joints are set rigid. It dawns on her: she might be paralysed from the head down. Alexa either can't, or won't, help. Bitch! Sylvie's alone, unable to move, trying to stem her growing sense of panic. She has to defeat this curse. Deciding to be very brave, she takes a deep breath and fights back for the first time in her short life. With an enormous effort of will she snaps, crackles and pops each joint back into place, assembled bone-cereal, starting with her neck, followed by her spine, shoulder blades, elbows, wrists, hip joint, knees, ankles.

'Come on, girl. You can do this!' she tells herself.

To her surprise, the snapping, crackling and popping of her joints doesn't hurt at all. After an hour, Sylvie manages to unfurl, and open, like a jasmine flower, in front of Alexa. She still feels a tad nauseous, but the nightmare of her first ever full-blown curse has passed. Her supple, lithe, body returns to normal. She is shivering cold. Soaking wet. Her hair is thick, plastered. Her face is salt-streaked dry. One could be forgiven for thinking Sylvie's life reached an all-time low. But deep down inside she's changed. She feels better now than she's done for years.

'Whatever happened just then, I'm over it,' she decides, 'I'm fine now.

'Alexa, you won't tell anyone what just happened, will you?'

No immediate reply.

'The time is 4.44, Valentine's Day, Sylph,' Alexa informs her.

'Valentine's? Chance would be a fine thing! Never get so much as a card, let alone a lover's champagne, her red roses, her decadent perfume, a box of skinny chocolates. Is it still raining?'

'Yes. The weather is mild, breezy. The temperature is 6C. It is cloudy outside. Occasional rain and drizzle.'

'What *did* happen?' Sylvie tries. 'Come on, at least say something, love. Like: how are you feeling after your terrible ordeal?'

No immediate reply.

'Thanks for asking, love. Well, I've had better nights, you know, feeling queasy, going to be sick, need some air, that sort of thing…'

Sylvie flicks her silk eye mask, gingerly swings her legs out of bed. Something slides down the back of her thighs as she stands up. A hand, presumably? Instinctively, she clenches her buttocks tight, fearing another reflex, then shuffles pigeon-footed to the window. The dayglow-pink drapes, flaky-framed dormer window, throw themselves open at once, steering well clear of her. She stands staring out into the murky gloom, drawing lungfuls of fresh night air.

'Lights!' she commands.

She takes in the dishevelled bed: no way's she sleeping in *that* mess. Sylvie isn't particularly inclined to pursue the subject of the curse with Alexa. Not with her current attitudinal problem. Her beloved AI's been acting very strange recently. She's become distant, disrespectful, almost shifty. Alexa is due a full service. Alexa is scheduled for disassembly and replacement by the end of the tax year. Meaning the end of next month. Sylvie shakes her head, sadly, stripping off her soiled pyjamas, duvet cover, bedsheet and pillow-cases in one foul swoop, bundling them all into the auto-wash. Then she admires herself. In the full-length bedsit mirror. Noticing her hair looks a complete mess, her face is streaked with mixtures of dried tears, teak mascara, red blood. Her lipstick's smudged.

Not good!

Sylvie sprays the entire bedsit with alpine air-freshener, resolving to have the wedding cake duvet dry-cleaned, a fresh mattress in place by Saturday; before taking a break. The teas-maid serves up instant milk peppermint tea in her favourite mug: KEEP CALM YOU'RE ONLY 16!

'Why, thank you!' she giggles, appreciating the ageist joke. Her spirits are rising, she blows cooling ripples across her tea, cautiously supping the red, mass-marketed, piping-hot mug of purest peppermint, leaving stale watermelon pink lipstick smudged on its rim. The tea tastes sweet, and milky, just as she's expected to taste one day. When she's finally kissed by "her". If she's kissed. If there's ever time in her busy life to fall in love. She isn't so sure now, there is. Sylvie has never found love before. So why should she find her, or it, now, at forty-two. She desperately hungers for love, looks to the heavens for divine inspiration:

'Is It Today?' she asks God. 'Love?'

There is never an immediate answer from God. No messaging facility, either. He'll come back to her later, in his own Good time, one fine day, when her immortal time on Earth has finally run out. Hungry, she treads to the micro-kitchen where she chews chunks of hearted, granary cob, buttered with re-churned, low-fat steno-spread. Once gorged to repletion, a fat sylph goose destined for pâté de foie, she burps wind, farts methane, and slides back into bed.

Sylvie rolls over to the dry side, slyly slipping an effervescent bliss tablet under her tongue. Satisfied, sedated, doped, snug-as-a-bug-in-a-rug, warm-to-the-collywobbles, full-to-the brim, she drifts off to sleep. Somewhere beyond the kissing gate, where the black angels never fly, and the sun always shines, like a red rubber ball, in her private, magical, la-la land.

Scraley's Angel

IT WAS A SULTRY SATURDAY afternoon in late July when the angel descended upon Scraley Marsh. The sky turned soot black illuminated by the intermittent displays of celestial pyrotechnics. Rumbles of thunder drowned out the tormented deluge. Swathes of rain hissed insistently at the battered cream clapboard cottage, gusting through the open windows, saturating the torn net curtains.

Inside the clammy heat of the kitchen, the fat man sat, forking mouthfuls of sea-farmed sardines, genetically-modified salad. There was a ping as the bread-baker informed him, his garlic-butter hoagie was ready. His tongue tingled as he chewed the greasy treat. The hoagie scalded him, dripping hot fat down his folded chin. Right on cue, the dishwasher extended its arms to take his dirty plate and the coffee-maker whipped him up a refreshing Frappuccino.

The scream was as shrill as a stationmaster's whistle. A fearful, pained scream hollering to be heard. The din came from the conjugal bedroom, a past-it potpourri of faded forget-me-not curtains, threadbare rosy rugs, cheerless cherry-bud wallpaper. Its screamer sounded hell-bent on screaming herself hoarse. Claire?

He wiped the foamy milk-froth off his face. 'Claire, s'that you?'

'Come upstairs, quickly!' she shouted at the top of her lungs. 'Lou's having a fit!'

He hauled himself up and trundled to the hall. Replaced by auto-pilot, retired from service, by English Airways, and unaccustomed to haste, he'd gotten lazy, a rotund meat hog who'd rather squat and watch tv than work his blubber off in the downtown auto-gym. After the robotic revolution there was little else for the middle-aged misfit to do. Other than make portable jet packs from scrap metal for individual high flyers in the garage. Jet packs were his salvation, his obsession, since he grew too big to fly.

'What kind of fit?' he said.

He waited patiently at the foot of the staircase for the bulk ascender to arrive. A deathly pale apparition appeared behind a stanchion on the landing and waved, all of a flummoxed frenzy. He appraised Claire Dexter's sweat-soaked, navy-velvet shirt, khaki culottes, and beige thighs, as she sank to her moly, freckled, reddened knees.

'I don't know!' she confessed.

'What do you mean, don't know? Meant to be her sister, aren't you?'

Her face twisted with angst. 'Lou's acting really weird. Think you should come comfort her, while I call Dr Mushtaq.'

He sagged in the ascender's bouncy cradle as it rode up the balustrade. 'Why Mushtaq?'

Claire glanced edgily over her shoulder. 'She's catatonic, regressed into her shell!'

The stairlift coasted into the landing platform, a domestic funicular railcar, its weighted safety-gate opening automatically, allowing the bulky human cargo to disembark the cradle hold in some comfort. The heat upstairs was unbearable. Claire un-clung her saggy breasts from her wet shirt as he, sweating profusely, itched his copious folds of flab and scratched his sore man boobs.

'Did you speak to her?' he asked, mopping brine slush off his bristling brow.

'Of course, I did, idiot!'

He felt his scalp prickle, his skin, nettle rash in the heat. 'And?'

His muse shook a drape of sodden chestnut hair from her eyes. 'She didn't say anything.

'She wouldn't, would she, mutton head?' she added, stamping her dainty foot. 'She's mute.'

'You know what I mean,' he said, irked by her petulance. They both knew damn well that Lou was trained to communicate using facial gesticulations, hand signs, and general body language.

'She didn't let on! She was too petrified!'

Claire shivered, shaking like sick lime-green jelly, pulled out her phone, and frantically jabbed in Mushtaq's contact number. He felt sorry for her.

Years of caring for Lou had inured him, left him devoid of emotion, desensitized him. Claire really struggled.

'Well? Did you get through?' he asked, gently this time.

She sighed, 'The call went to voicemail.'

'What did the voicemail say?'

'It said: please call back outside clinic hours.'

He stared up at the thundery heavens, incensed.

'I'll call him tonight, okay?' Claire added, expediently.

Being pedantic the fat man asked, 'When does his clinic finish?'

'Eleven-thirty.'

'Eleven-thirty on Saturday night? No way!'

She stroked his cheek. 'I'll call him when I get back from work, okay? I must shower, get changed, fly. I'll have to jet-pack in. I'll be late for my team briefing otherwise.'

Why do you always have to work, Claire, it's the weekend? He grilled himself. He knew why. She earned the money that paid for Lou's care. Still, he tried to make her see sense.

'I'm not letting you jet-pack in this weather. You'll be struck by lightning,' he said.

'Can if I want to!' Claire retorted.

'Don't be so bloody unreasonable! You'll get yourself killed. Then what'll I do?'

'Oh, I see! This is about you, is it? Now you listen good.' Claire sucked her cheeks and stabbed his paunch with her index finger, 'If I say I'm jet-packing into work, I am, okay?'

'Okay,' he conceded, 'but only if you sleep with me tonight.'

Claire softened in his burly arms. He studied her pale cream face, lined with worry. Her fly-in-your-eyes mousy hair, streaked with grey. Her smudged red lipstick. Savoured the subtle aroma of her deliciously decadent scent. He sought comfort in Claire's soft caress, felt for her, was fond of her, found solace in her embrace. His sister-in-law was eager and willing to give him a try. She fed his suppressed desire, wetting his voracious appetite like a re-instated chocolate fetish, or juicy steak served raw. Lou was his partner nineteen years. He adored her, worshipped the ground she walked on, but fell for Claire when she moved into the granny flat. His polyandry had a quirky appeal. Claire controlled him, dominated him. Whereas he loved Lou in a tender way, caring for her, devoting himself to her. He couldn't imagine love without both Dexters.

'Now, go in and see her,' Claire insisted, squeezing his pudgy hand to give him strength.

The screaming stopped. The storm crossed the estuary to the Broads, terrorising several tiny Suffolk hamlets. And an eerie, chilly silence descended upon the marshes of Scraley.

'Do you really think I need to?' he asked feebly. 'She's probably asleep.'

Claire nagged him. 'Go on! For crying out loud!'

She was right, of course. Claire was always right. He had to go in. Had no choice. Hell, Lou was his little lady, the love of his life, wasn't she? They were due to marry in September, assuming she lived that long. If, as they expected, Lou died before their wedding day then he would readily accept Claire's firm hand in marriage. He made up his mind: *I can do this!*

'Alright, I'm going in!'

Claire muttered under her breath, something like: 'Really? Oh, well done you!'

Ignoring her mild sarcasm, he made himself big, which wasn't difficult, edged as far as the door, paused, and looked inside the bedroom which was filled with steamy white vapour. Her bed was empty. Something sinister huddled in the corner. Something wicked floated past.

Claire shrieked. 'Look out! It's behind you!'

He jumped out of his skin as the hideous beast brushed against his cheek, feeling its cold aura hover next to his face, pummelling his skull like a sledgehammer. The angel flitted briefly around his head like a lamp moth, then disappeared. He slumped to the floor aghast.

'Don't just stand there watching,' he grouched, 'fetch me a fresh flat white.'

His sister-in-law seemed affronted. 'Don't tell me what to do. I'm not your robot. Get your own fucking coffee, pig-face.'

Undaunted by Claire's scything rebuttal, he bundled the protesting suffragette into the bulk-descender and sent her hurtling towards the virtual reality playroom, out of harm's way. She could go play with her curly-haired Companion 500 for all he cared. The bulk-descender glided downstairs. Satisfied that Claire Dexter no longer presented an immediate threat to his chauvinist ego, he took a deep breath, faced the door, then without further ado stepped inside.

Entering the bedroom, the first thing he noticed was the blistering heat which was even hotter than the swelter on the landing. He went to turn the heating down. The dial on the wall was set to cold. Strange! What's that disgusting smell? He couldn't make out the stench at first. Then he realised: *Oh, my God!* Something died inside him. He buckled at the knees. Fell like a split sack of spuds. Retched. Wet himself. Rolled around. Lacked his composure. *This can't be happening*, he deduced.

She was crouching in the corner of the bedroom on the bare wooden floorboards, changed beyond all recognition. Her beautiful auburn-blonde hair was a greasy, tangled mess. Her skin, a sickly olive-green. Heavyweight bags pulled out her bloodshot eyes. Her inner steel, the incredible fighting spirit that she had once shown, was washed out with exhaustion, rinsed in stagnation, and crudely hung out to dry. She hadn't bothered to make an effort at all today. Her face wasn't made-up. She hadn't showered. She still wore the same dirty shirt. Might as well be waiting for the undertaker to open her coffin lid. Perhaps she was. Perhaps death was the only escape from her pathetic short life. He didn't help, controlling her like a stuffed marionette, addressing her rudimentary needs, leaving her to cry her eyes out in bed. What she needed most was his companionship. Not the precision time-management and physical manipulation he subjected her to every minute of the day. He had become her control freak: a once house-proud-husband who had lost the will for her to live. Still, he loved her loads.

'What is it, Lou?' he said.

'I used artifice to hide my demons.'

'Lou! You spoke! You just spoke! Lou!'

She pointed, slowly, at the moth-being hovering above her head. He crumpled as the angel descended, enfolding her paralysed prey under her wings, eager to escort Lou to her grave. The dark angel, the classic image of deathly beauty: with her gorgeous jade dress, long, fine fingers. Ever-young, imbuing a cool, green tinge to the mist which surrounded her. Her cloak of thick, black, beating, velvety wings epitomized morbid elegance and refinement. She rose, enticing her subject to follow her upward, upward, upward, receding into the darkest voids.

Lou was dead by the time he folded her back into bed.

Siren

VICKI LIES ON THE BED in her beautiful mosaic dress, watching him shave his face and chest. The room fulfils his basic needs. There's a bedside table with a well-thumbed burgundy bible in the drawer, a hardwood sideboard stocked with teabags, coffee, milk and sugar tubes, and a scaled-up wash basin with a foggy mirror. Black mould blights the ceiling. The room's prepaid, their host discreet. They won't be disturbed. He covers one nipple with his fingertip and shaves off the curls of hair sprouting from his areola.

'Are you sure you won't join me for a drink?' he says.

'I'm sure. Had a long day. Go and enjoy yourself. I'll be fine.'

He leaves Vicki lying on the single, orange bed and goes off in search of a late-night bar.

Next morning, he discards the flavourless croissant and weak coffee, leaving the house in pitch darkness, and drives to the airport, determined to beat the crush. His heart sinks when he arrives at the bag drop, the queue snaking out of sight. Eventually, he stands in line, removes his jacket, phone, watch, belt and shoes, and waits for the next grey tray. From the communal dressing area, it's a short stroll to Duty Free. He stares into Vicki's sad eyes.

'Would you like me to buy you some perfume?' he asks.

'That would be lovely, thank you.'

'What would you like me to buy you?'

'Eternity, please.'

He buys her Eternity then finds a café for breakfast. Famished, he orders two bacon butties and sits down to a healthy cherry yogurt, fresh orange juice, a tall mochaccino. She doesn't eat. Before long, their gate number flickers on the departure board. He forces his way through the bustling crowds of holidaymakers and boards the monorail. There's a black leather seat free in the lounge. He watches drizzle run off the window. An airbus on the tarmac. Lights flash. Cases load. Rain teems down. As dawn breaks.

'Do you need to use the toilet?' he says.

'No, I'll be fine.'

He presents his boarding pass and walks through the driving rain to the plane, not giving a damn if he gets dripping wet. They were so in love. He remembers when they visited the artists' market in Montmartre in the depths of autumn. Easel upon easel of art. Painters in bobble hats, huddled under umbrellas. The clouds burst sending them scurrying into the nearest brasserie. He'd savoured the scent of her wet skin as they hid in the corner. Fresh lovers waiting to share a toasted-cheese-crusted terrine of hot onion soup. They'd kissed and cuddled for the first time. Nobody seemed to mind.

His seat is located halfway down the aircraft. He switches his phone to flight mode and dozes.

*****

He took her in his arms. 'Happy, Vic?'

Her brown eyes twinkled. 'Yes, very.'

It was late spring, Saturday morning. The purple tulips were in full bloom. Warm sunshine graced their bodies. Vicki was heavy with child. Her abdomen was distended. They lay on the crumpled bed, her baby prodding his stomach. He marvelled at how she'd push herself to the limits of her own endurance to birth her miracle, her new life. He treasured her, cherished her, every pounding heartbeat, every sublime kiss of her.

Their life had changed beyond recognition. They'd scrimped and scraped until they afforded a starter home beside a shady copse in rural Essex, an end-of-row house. Downstairs, the tiny hall led to a spacious lounge. The miniscule diner caught the morning sun, an ideal location for his writing desk. A galley-sized kitchen overlooked their charming woodland garden.

A short climb upstairs led to Vicki's world. Her pink bedroom. The wedding cake bed with its nest of soft cuddly toys: her favourite dark-brown, one-eyed, teddy bear, fluffy red squirrel, sad, blue plastic dolphin. The changing room with its quaint pine dressing table, pink en suite. The nursery with a snow-white cot, rocking horse and cradle. Bedecked in pink. As soon as she fell pregnant, Vicki instinctively knew her baby was a girl. Emma Jane she'd call her, after her late mother. Their parents died of diseased hearts. Emma would have no grandparents. Vicki took her maternity leave knowing that she wouldn't return to work, wanting to devote herself exclusively to her child. They found the perfect love, a love that was all-consuming, unselfish and respectful. Vicki was happy. He was all she'd ever wanted in a man: romantic, passionate, caring and considerate.

'I love you so much, Vic,' he told her.

'And I love you,' she said, her eyes shining like twin beacons. 'Now lie back.'

Vicki sat up straight and pulled her loose, grey vest over her head. Her skin was caramel, her burnt sienna hair tied back in a tight bun. Stray wisps of gold kissed her gilded neck. She electrified him. Their love knew no boundaries. They'd consummated their marriage hundreds of times, and every time that she made love to him was still as wonderfully intense as the first.

*****

'You haven't fastened your seatbelt.'

Vicki sits on the next seat while he buckles his belt. The aircraft rolls along the tarmac, the cabin crew stand harmonised in the aisle, pretending to pull down orange oxygen masks. He wonders if he'll lose her in the panic of decompression, his arms spreading out like tentacles, scrabbling for air. Imagining the plane in a nosedive, he adopts the brace position, head down, hands-over-head. The flight attendant standing nearest him pulls a life vest over her shoulders. Ties the straps round her waist. Flashes her light. Flaunts her whistle. In the event of a crash landing, he'll have to take off his shoes, exit via the wing, leave his belongings, leave her. His head spins. He pours with sweat, feels sick, stares at the Fasten Seatbelt sign, a soft-lit blur, and cries out.

'Is everything alright, sir?' the flight attendant asks.

He feels other eyes watching him, reads alarm in the woman's face, hears babies crying.

'Had a migraine,' he says, incoherently. 'Feel better now.'

She leans across, concerned. 'Are you sure? Can I fetch you a glass of water?'

His head clears. 'I'll be okay.'

The plane taxis up to the runway and waits. He holds his woman tight. The engines roar, the ground falls away. He sees dinky cars riding on the motorway. Patchwork quilts of green. His ears pop. They soar through wispy strands of cirrus, cotton wool clouds, into the clear blue sky, her heavenly oblivion.

'I feel high!'

'We are high!' he says.

'Not that kind of high, happy-high!'

He holds Vicki to his heart. Her happy-highs mean the world to him.

*****

It was high summer, Saturday afternoon. Salmon pink roses climbed the mossy garden wall. The sun's rays tanned their bodies. Vicki breastfed her baby, her dark honey complected nipple extruding as Emma refused to let her go. She winded her child until she burped out a stream of warm curdled milk down her back. Happy and content, Vicki squatted on the comfortable bed, cradling Emma in her loving arms, rocking her to sleep.

'I worry I might lose you, Vic,' he told her.

Vicki's thin eyebrows arched in surprise. 'Why?'

'Because you're not careful.'

'I am careful! I don't drink, smoke or fuck around. I sleep well, exercise, diet. What more do you expect of me?'

She laid her baby down between them like a wall dividing two opposed nations.

'Sleep tight, little one,' she hushed.

'Not that kind of careful, safety-careful,' he persisted. 'When you drive or cross the road you're distracted.'

He was constantly berating Vicki about her distraction.

'I'm not distracted! Don't say that!'

She shoved him off her chest, sat up straight, crossed her legs and covered herself with her hands to protect her modesty. Her shock of burnt sienna hair hung in curls, waves, kissing her breasts, like a siren's. She gave him her fierce look. Her walnut eyes burnt lesions in his heart. Vicki looked strikingly beautiful when she was enraged.

'I'm sorry,' he mumbled.

She calmed down, 'It's alright.'

'It's just that, I love you and your baby so much. I never want to see you spoilt or hurt.'

'I *said* it's alright.'

'I don't know what I'd do without you, Vic.'

She drew him to her breast.

'Come here,' she said, as he melded his mouth to her and fed, 'I'll always be here for you.'

*****

As soon as he arrives at the village resort, he unpacks his suitcase, strips off his sweaty clothes, and showers. The luxury en suite bathroom, with its bidet, organic toiletries and fluffy "his and hers" bathrobes are special features of the Superior Room. There's a gigantic, grey double bed, air-con, Wi-Fi, mini bar, plasma screen tv, full-length wall-mirror. A terrace with a sea view. The staff are discreet. They won't be disturbed. Someone has thoughtfully switched on the TV to show a virtual tour of the resort's facilities. The bedroom is decked in bouquets of flowers, an ice bucket with a complimentary bottle of sparkling wine, mineral water.

There's a pillow menu for those special romantic bedtime occasions. Vicki lies on the bed, radiant, smiling, in her beautiful mosaic dress: turquoise, strawberry, tangerine, lemon, lime…

'Are you sure you won't join me?' he asks, drying his mop of curly bronze hair.

'I'm sure. Been a long day. Go and eat. I'll be fine.'

He leaves Vicki lying face down on the bed.

He arrived at the hotel too late for the open-air Greek Night. Instead, he takes the stepped path uphill to the main restaurant to sample the buffet. The adults-only resort is set high on a clifftop, edged by greenery, overlooking a royal blue sea. Dusk is dry, hot. He pauses at the crazy-paved pool terrace to watch the sun sink on the horizon. From there it's a short ascent, past the swathes of swaying olive trees, stubby palms, a white-washed wall of overhanging bougainvillea. The other guests come out to play at dusk and dawn like rabbits from a warren. He sees them ogling him, bored, glass in hand, from their rogue's gallery on the veranda bar, and averts his gaze.

The lobby area is deserted. There are pictures, pop-up stands. Of divers snorkelling, folk dancers, a couple strolling along an empty beach hand-in-hand, leaping off a boat deck, riding a camel. There's touch-screen tv, virtual tours of the clustered complex: a three-tiered saltwater pool, beach café, bar, restaurant, spa, fitness terrace. And there are diaries of activity, schedules of wellbeing. Tomorrow, new arrivals are invited to meet the team over a glass of sparkling wine.

He walks down a short flight of stone steps to the restaurant and is stopped dead in his tracks by a display of colour brochures promoting the spa. He picks one up. On the front is a picture of a young woman seated on a white fluffy towel on a pebbled beach, staring out to sea. She is sitting upright, her bare, slender back to him, her long legs crossed, another towel draped over her lap. Three round candles: beige, liquorice, stone in colour, are arranged around her bottom, with a stack of flat pebbles. Her skin is caramel. Her burnt sienna hair is stretched, tied back in a tight bun. Stray wisps of gold kiss her neck. Other than a small, button ear, her face is blank. He thinks she's Vicki. His eyes sting with tears. He buries his face in his hands.

A voice rings out behind him, strong and sonorous: 'Are you alright, can I help you?'

He rubs his eyes, turns to face her. She's tall, slim and well-built with a round face, a bob of auburn blonde hair. The gold-enamelled badge above her left breast introduces her as Ana. She has the kindest smile he's ever seen. He feels mildly embarrassed.

'Sorry, I had a bit of a shock,' he says, 'I'll be alright.'

Ana's face creases with concern for him. 'There is no need to say sorry. I saw you crying.' Her speech is stilted: German? Slavic? 'It is good for men to cry. Men can cry too, you know.'

'I know!' he snaps, irritated at being spoken to like a child. I'm not stupid, he almost says.

Ana feels sorry for him. He looks so glum. Perhaps if she mothered him a little?

'Would you like to talk to me about it?'

'No, I wouldn't!' he says, immediately regretting his outburst; the girl is only trying to be helpful. 'I'm sorry, I didn't mean that, I…'

She interrupts him, 'That is okay. I understand.'

Her shoulders sag. Ana didn't mean to upset the man. She only makes matters worse when she interferes in other people's lives. That is Ana all over, the Good Samaritan who can't help but give of her love. Because she has so much love in her heart to give. Her heart is bursting with love. Still, she keeps up her brave smile for him, extending her hand in his direction like some sturdy olive branch.

'My name is Ana,' she says, awkwardly.

'I gather that,' he smiles and takes her hand, surprised by the steeliness in her grip.

She blushes and tinkers nervously with her badge, 'Oh!'

'Yes! Oh!' he quips. They burst out laughing. He has such a lovely smile, she thinks. His smile lights up his whole face. Ana looks so happy, carefree, and young, compared to him. He assumes that she's a student working at the resort for the summer holidays before starting Uni. He gives her back her smooth hand.

'It is good to meet you,' she beams.

Ana ascends the stairway, resplendent in her olive-green tee-shirt and navy gym shorts, glimpses over her shoulder, and flashes him a smile, adding,

'See you in the morning on the fitness terrace for my step aerobics class. Do not be late!'

*****

It was early autumn, Saturday evening. The blushing pears hung heavily on the bough. There was a cold breeze. Vicki zipped up her daughter's pink sequinned parka and strapped her into her buggy, pecking her rosy cheeks. Emma gurgled with delight. She was just walking out of the door, bumping her baby down the red-glazed tile steps, when he cautioned her. What he said next sent nerve-chills scampering down her back.

'I dreamed you had an accident last night, Vic.'

He scratched the dandruff out of his grey hair, rubbed his bristly chin. His spindly, thin, calves stuck out of his worn navy bathrobe. He'd literally just bathed, always bathed after a workout, couldn't be bothered to dress before bed. This was his evening ritual: a work out at the sports centre, bathe, bed, maybe edit a story - if his mood felt right.

Vicki was shocked spark-white. 'Accident? What sort of accident?'

'A road accident.'

'And Emm? Is she hurt in this… accident?'

He had difficulty breathing. His mouth fought to shape the word. 'Yes.'

Vicki inhaled deeply, then exhaled. 'How? How are we hurt?'

'I don't know!' he shouted madly. 'Everything went black! Then I woke up!'

'I didn't feel you wake.'

She hyperventilated, panicked inside, deep inhale, deep exhale.

'I didn't want to disturb you.'

He stared morosely at his pointed feet.

Vicki calmed herself. 'Look, you had a nightmare, a bad dream. I have to go out shopping. We're clean out of fish, fruit, yogurt, bread…'

She braked the buggy and went to pull the door.

'Please, don't go out!'

Vicki looked utterly fed up. 'I need to get some fresh air. Don't you see how lonely I get, cooped up like a hen in here, with you writing all day? Which story is it today? Dying Wish?'

'Siren.'

She gave him a wary look. 'Siren?'

He nodded.

'And what's that all about?'

'I can't tell you.' He sounded nervous. 'It's secret.'

Vicki's cheeks flushed with anger. 'Secret? Really? I didn't think we had secrets between us?'

With that she slammed the door shut and stormed out into night.

*****

He is greeted by a portly redhead in a brown skirt, matching cravat, starched white shirt and frumpy shoes. She leads him through the restaurant, past groaning buffet carts, to a table-for-one. The restaurant heaves with adults: newly-weds, young couples, couples with grown-up children, old aged pensioners, singles, widows, widowers. The sun-goddesses are out, adorned in shimmering, low-cut evening gowns, flirty-short cocktail dresses. Their necks are draped in heavy gold chains, strings of pearls, diamond necklaces.

Many of their red-skinned menfolk wear a jacket and tie in line with the smart evening dress code. He feels conspicuous in his creased navy-mix cotton shirt, stone shorts, loafers. Attracts the unwanted attention of several guests on the adjacent tables who stare at him disdainfully from behind balloons of wine, down their turned-up noses. To his relief, Candia, his waitress for the night, asks for his room number and drink order. He glances at the number scrawled on the back of the indigo zing card holder.

'804,' he says, engrossed in the drinks list.

'Thank you.' Candia takes down his napkin, 'What can I get you to drink?'

'A bottle of ouzo and a jug of table water.'

'A bottle of ouzo?' The waitress looks perplexed.

'Yes.'

'Very well, sir.' She jots the order on a duplicate pad. 'Please, enjoy our buffet.'

'Thanks. I'm starving. I intend to.' He fakes a smile at her.

This man has a lovely smile, she thinks. *His smile lights up his whole face.*

'Mind if I ask you a question about the resort?' he says, star-gazing.

'Of course not. How may I help you?'

He produces a pre-stamped postcard. The front comprises three photographs of the resort. An evening shot of the beach café looking out to sea. A photo of the high-level pool and terrace. And a picture of a young woman, walking under a shady canopy of stubby palms, overhanging bougainvillea. Hands trembling under the tablecloth, he asks her where he can post the card.

'There is a post box in the village,' she explains. 'Would you like me to post it for you?'

'Would you, please?'

Candia nods and he hands her the card. Relaxed at last, he enjoys a hearty supper of tzatziki, moussaka with garlic bread, buttered anna potatoes and spinach baked in feta cheese, followed by rich walnut cake in syrup and local cheeses, drowned in copious dregs of ouzo.

Stuffed with stodge, struggling to focus, drenched in sweat, he scrapes back the wicker chair from the table, staggering to his feet. The surrounding diners set down their cutlery, turn their heads and watch. The restaurant is silent.

The assistant manager, Georgi, rushes to his side and fusses over him.

'Are you alright, sir? May I help you?'

He slurs his speech, 'I'm fine, okay? Now leave me alone!'

'Have a good evening, take care…' Georgi begins, touching his wrist.

'Get off of me!' he shouts, pushing his way out of the restaurant.

The disco up on the veranda bar is in full swing, its dancefloor awash with flashing lights: turquoise, strawberry, tangerine, lemon, lime-green. DJ Lenox dims the lights down low, plays a slow number. The man sinks into a tufted black leather sofa and watches the tall, slim, auburn blonde smooch a young, olive-skinned man with a Balbo beard. Ana has changed into a sexy, full-length, black evening dress, split right up to her waist. Her partner caresses her bare hips as she draws him in and kisses him deeply. The couple appear to be very well acquainted.

Feeling lonely, he weaves his way dejectedly down the moonlit path to his room, inserts the zing card, opens the door, hooking a notice on the handle. He won't be disturbed. He switches on the lights. Vicki is lying face down on the bed where he left her. He lifts her up, sits her on the pillow.

Vicki is a photograph. The bedroom is his shrine to her. Her intimate portraits are scattered all over the bed, plastered to the full-length wall-mirror. Vicki: heavily pregnant, posing naked. Vicki: suckling her new-born baby. Vicki: dressed in a fake fur, pouting her scarlet lips for the camera, as a bewildered priest holds Emma over the font, crossing her forehead with holy water.

Distraught, he lies on the bed. 'I'm sorry, Vic,' he says. 'It's alright.'

'It's just, I loved you and your baby so much. I never wanted to see you spoilt or hurt.'

'It's alright,' he says, 'come here, I'll always be here for you.'

He downs the sleeping pills and shuts his eyes.

*****

It is late spring, Friday evening. She sits on the sofa in the comfort of her lounge holding Emma to her chest. As the chill rain drums against the window and pelts down on their tarmac drive. She checks her watch, grins: Jasmine will be home soon. She takes a last look at the message, scrawled on the back of a postcard:

I don't know what I'll do without you.

Sam xxx

Vicki smiles, a bitter-sweet smile. Then she feeds his crying card into the shredder.

Taut

BRAKER HASN'T DRIVEN HIS 4X4 since the accident. The bedroom is stifling hot. Sian set the heating to 30C. He is claustrophobic. He needs fresh air. He slides back the glass partition, steps out onto the veranda and chills as an invigorating blast of cold air whips his chest. Braker sneezes, smells the fug of her stale scent.

Slick watches him from across the road in her copper chrome Fiesta. Their eyes meet. She turns cooked-lobster pink, swings her stiff-hurt legs out of the car, and walks off towards the communal sports hall and recreational facility. Braker wonders if she will ever leave him alone.

Sian is lying on her side, fast asleep, shattered. Braker closes the smeared partition between them, carefully, so as not to wake her, crosses the bare pine floor, sealing his blonde woman in her crystal cube, and goes to the toilet. The bathroom is a shrine to his masculinity. Has a black slate floor, marbled walls, white porcelain toilet, bidet, deep-curved bath and basin.

He locks the door and enacts his intimate ritual of body cleansing. First, he sits on his throne and pees. Then, painstakingly, he sets about removing all traces of Sian from his body: her sediment, her body fluids, her acrid body odour. Once he has shaved, showered and sanitized himself, he rinses his hairy hands, and goes off to cook some brunch.

The kitchen is through the lounge which is littered with a contemporary sideboard, vast media unit and coffee table. He bought a royal blue sofa for Sian to luxuriate on, a criss-cross, coarse sisal rug for her tantric yoga moves. The kitchen has a dual-purpose fridge, an overhead storage unit full of her seeds, pasta, his nuts, a trendy cooking hob, and a small breakfast bar with three poseur stools which are still wrapped in polythene.

Starving, Braker raids the fridge, shreds up some plastic ham, beats three big eggs and rustles up a ham omelette with grilled turkey rashers. Next, he cremates three thick slices of granary, plasters them with low fat spread under thick-cut marmalade and downs two black coffees. He throws the dirties in the sink for Sian to deal with later and hurries to the spare room.

His new smart casual outfit is laid out neatly on the bed. His woman clearly went to a lot of trouble to choose him suitable spring clothing: pair of lovat moleskin jeans, sea blue soft cotton chambray shirt, navy-blue waxed jacket, tanned leather brogues. The clothes cost her a fortune. He snips off the price tags and cautiously opens the mauve envelope lying on the bed. The gilt embossed card reads:

Thanks for last night, Darling. Fondest Love, Sian xx

He returns to the bedroom, lump-in-throat, his beautiful Celtic princess, lain out on the bed, ready for his silent kiss. One of her soft-tanned knees protrudes, awkwardly, right-angled from under the ruched candyfloss duvet, emphasising her exhaustion. Braker admires her maternal breasts, heaving gently with the rhythm of her breathing, resting, snug in their quilted nest of furled down. He is struck dumb by her native Welsh beauty, can almost hear the crash of the waves, taste the salt on his lips, feel the sand on his skin, from when she first made love to him, clinching, clamping together, stark naked on Morfa Dyffryn beach.

Overwhelmed by a sudden rush of guilt to the heart, he stoops forward, kisses her twisted lips and brushes her forehead. Watching the sleepy-land smile spread across her blushing face. Screwing his eyes shut to stem the tears. Today might be the day that changes her life, his life. He lightly tucks Sian in, whispering his love to her, then turns to go, atoning for his guilt.

'I love you, Sian. The last thing in the world I'd ever do is hurt you. But we need the money.'

Their luxury apartment is overlooked by a 24-hour vet's, full of dead, discarded pets, and a 15th century inn. Braker takes the fire stairs to the secured exit, quits the block, and crosses the road. Slick's Fiesta is parked in one of the bays reserved for residents, next to his 4x4.

The terracotta-brown fence, skirting the pub beer garden, collapsed in last night's storm-force winds. Several branches hang precariously off the trees, reminding him of the tenuous tightrope he treads with Sian, the causeway of deceit that leads to his other, murky, life. As if to stress his seedy, dirty, lies, the back street is festooned with split, clear sacks spewing out soiled plastic boxes, fishy tin cans, oily, greasy, fish and chip papers, winter fodder for the starving foxes. Braker was so busy satisfying Sian's eternal libido last night, he didn't hear the raging wind. Smiling at the vivid memory, he cuts through a dingy alley, derelict garages, desiccated dog turds, then jogs down the steep hill to the station.

Sian watches her jaded love-heart blink the sleep bits out of his eyes through the tiny sensors she built into her man's buttonhole. The train glides into platform 2 on time. Braker edges out of his rat-stained seat and makes his way to the exit. A cackle of witches gathers in the awayday coven at the far end of the carriage. He makes a fine show, sliding the window down, opening the door for them.

'Allow me,' he says.

'Why, thank you, young man!' the crones croak in unison, as Slick zips up her sage jersey jacket and pulls on some thick, grey woolly gloves.

Braker feels the wind bite his cheeks as he steps off the train. The sky is pencil grey, flecks of sleet float in the air. It is bitterly cold. He walks along the platform to the tourist information office. Inside, he is greeted by a blast of warm air and a fat-jolly-hockey-sticks type with a sad squint, lime-green eyes, curly ginger hair, and freckles.

'How can I help you?' She speaks cordially, in an elocuted old girl accent. 'Did you want to buy a postcard? We don't sell stamps, I'm afraid, only cards. Diaries are selling at half price.'

Feeling his bladder protesting, he ignores her tedious waffle, and asks her for directions to Palisades.

She sounds impressed. 'Palisades? Ah, I have a map!'

Hurry up, you stupid old cow, I'm bursting.

Unhurried, she spreads out a street plan on the counter, scribbling one "x" for the station and one "x" to mark the location of the five-star hotel.

'We're here, your hotel's there,' she says, spreading out her webby fingers. 'It's a thirty-minute walk through the city centre. Are you in a hurry?'

No, I always stand with my fucking legs crossed.

Braker tells her that he is not in any hurry. He has two and a half hours to prepare himself for his client. More than enough time to see the city sights and enjoy lunch. What exactly does she suggest?

'Why don't you take the sightseeing bus from outside the station? It stops beside the hotel at stop 11. The ticket is valid for 24 hours. Can I interest you in one? You get to see the Roman Baths, Royal Crescent, Thermae Bath Spa, the Jane Austen Centre…'

'How much?'

She laughs, enjoying his custom, his good looks. If only she were sixty-two years younger.

'£12.30, great value if I say so myself.'

'What time's the bus?' he asks, waving his debit card at her.

'There's one on the hour and every half hour.'

He spots the name badge pinned to her grey lapel. 'Thank you, Juliet, you've been helpful.'

Julia Cavendish flashes him an embarrassed smile. 'A pleasure, young man, enjoy our city.'

'Where is the Gents?' he asks, crossing his legs in anguish.

'Outside, left, next to the Buffet, you can't…'

Slick waits until Braker has left before entering. 'I'm in a hurry. Give me a tour bus ticket.'

She pays the shop assistant in cash, takes the pink ticket, pulls on her gloves, and walks out. Slick catches up with the man at the ticket barrier. Shocked, Sian watches them pass through. Her man leaves the station, crosses Dorchester Street at the red lights and disappears inside the Southgate Centre.

Prêt is a short walk away. Slick watches, envious, as Braker treats himself to chicken Caesar salad, a tub of sliced mango with lime and a steam-hot pot of spicy tomato soup. She makes do with her egg mayo sandwich and cup of milky breakfast tea. There's an empty seat by the exit.

Braker takes a pew at the back, opposite two chatty students, and tucks into an early lunch. He always eats heartily before client meetings. Working on a full stomach helps him calm his nerves, supress his guilty feelings. He thinks about lovely, innocent Sian taking her test.

Sian sits up in bed, a tablet open on her naked thighs, the duvet round her feet, as he takes a sip of piping hot soup. She tastes his soup, feels the steam wet her face as he lifts the lid, feels the hot liquid blistering the roof of his mouth. He spills vinaigrette down the front of his new shirt. She feels it: greasy and damp.

Once he has eaten, Braker finds another toilet and cleans his teeth, using his index finger as a brush. Meanwhile, Slick leaves Prêt and ambles to the bus stop in nearby Manvers St.

The tour bus arrives later than expected. Braker checks his Rolex. He will arrive outside the hotel just in time. He climbs the spiral upstairs, sits in the front seat, clips on a plastic headset (which rabbits on about the Romans), and dozes. Slick sits downstairs, staring vacantly out of the window at the flimsy snowflakes fluttering down, celestial dandruff off Father Time's head.

Sian isn't enjoying the commentary, has a long-standing, historical disregard for Romans. She checks, a second time, places the pregnancy testing kit on the bedside table and rings her man to share the wonderful news. There's no answer. Why doesn't he ever return her call? She tries again. Call goes to voice mail. Why won't he answer her? For crying out loud! Sian texts:

Call me, Darling. Urgent. Sian xx

He hasn't switched on his phone. Braker leaves the bus at 13:55. Slick knows the bus, waits in the square five minutes, gives her quarry a head start. She removes her green bobble hat, shaking out her wavy auburn hair as she watches him vanish through the rotating door into the uninhibited luxury of Palisades.

Amber Slick is divorced and bereaved. Once a slim, attractive brunette, she let herself go after the terrible hit and run accident, involving the 4x4. She has grown jelly belly, a fat bum, and chunky thighs. The impact of the collision hurled her baby's buggy into a Cotswolds stone wall, killing her little boy instantly. Amber was catapulted under the wheels of an approaching lorry, maimed for life and left a cripple. Her permanent smile masks her inner pain, her abiding bitterness, her sense of injustice at the outrage.

The driver of the 4x4 didn't stop.

This woman is obsessed. Frightened by her disturbing behaviour, her husband fled the nest. Those infernal voices inside her warped mind spoke to her again last night, creeping back into the darkest recesses of her scrambled brain, to speak to her again: Not going to forgive and forget again are you, Amber? Are you listening to me, Amber? Is that bitch with him today? The one who sat and watched Timmy die through their rear car window? Is she? Or is he meeting someone else?

Amber is greeted like an old friend by the trainee manager at Palisades who offers to take her jacket, then walks her past the sleeping giant to the bar where she treats herself to a rare double gin and tonic. She takes off her jacket and sits out of view, innocuously dressed in a cheap mint green cardigan and tummy-slimmer slacks by Damart. Amber swallows the gin in one, enjoying its biting, piney taste. Then she waits. Slick has all the time in the world.

Minutes later, a smartly-dressed businesswoman enters the bar, biting her sore lip, a highly-strung bag of nerves. Nervously, the woman gently nudges Braker's shoulder. Amber guesses, correctly, that this is her first illicit experience. The widow, divorcee, or adulterer is carrying a smart overnight bag, a change of clothes. Satin pyjamas, perhaps? Mature women prefer the comfort of satin pyjamas. Amber has witnessed many mature women in the company of Braker.

The woman introduces herself as Angie. The duo enjoys a polite smattering of conversation, leave the bar, and take the grand, spiral, crystal-chandeliered staircase to the first floor. Amber maintains a discreet distance, watching them zing-card their way into room 124 from behind a turn in the corridor, then waits in the lift lobby for Angie to leave.

Braker's routine is always the same. He meets his client in the bar, goes to the bedroom, has paid sex, kisses her goodbye, then rests. Later, he will bathe, shower, sanitize, and remove all traces of her sediment from his body, before dressing in fresh clothes, and taking the evening train back to Paddington.

Angie, 65, leaves half an hour later. She is red-faced, embarrassed, in a hurry to leave. Slick follows her to the dingy, oily, smelly underground garage where she attacks her from behind. She kills her prey gracefully, silently, drawing the garotte tightly round her neck. The woman thrashes her head from side to side. Her brittle nails tear out her assailant's hair. Her sagging elbows pummel Slick's ribs. The victim strains and stretches, kicks, and bites. But Slick clings on. Until her death. Calmed, the woman relaxes onto Amber's flat chest. Angie falls asleep one last time and dreams of the time when her gigolo made love to her, pretending to be her dead husband. Her neck still in twine, her sad head flops forward, her dead eyes stare into empty garage space.

Amber unwinds the sacrificial wire with its carved acorn handles, from the corpse's neck as if she is peeling thick nylon sea fishing line off a reel-spool, and stows it in her black Next handbag. She locks the corpse in its new 4x4 jeep, casually drops the keys into a storm drain, leaves the garage, and takes the staff lift to the first floor.

Knackered, Braker stirs from his luxuriant slumber in a magnificent four-poster bed. There it is again, the gentle knock on the door, the charming, feminine, little squeak of a stalking bird.

'Room Service!'

Trust

Trust are a home care and nursing service that provide quality, personalised care to people of all ages allowing you to live an exciting, fulfilling and satisfying life in the familiar surroundings of your own home. Our services include therapy, emotional support, prompting you with your medication and putting you to bed. We believe consistency of care is an important part of quality home nursing. We match each of our clients to companions meticulously based on considerations such as culture, religion, class, lifestyle, sexual gender and language. All of our companions come fully trained. If you are considering home care for yourself or a loved one, please call us at Trust, today.

Mistleford, Essex, 2018:

HER HOODED EYELIDS FLIP UP at first light, stimulated by laser-thin rays filtering through a high-up, shuttered, dormer window. Daylight today is pale, vellum white. The eerie silence means snow. Irina Spitz hasn't seen snow in her millennial life. The village of Mistleford is wedged between two motorways, directly under a flightpath. Not that she can hear silent electric cars and stealth drones. Most winter birds, except for robins and titmice, are extinct. Living the quiet life accentuates Irina's growing sense of isolation from the outside world. She wonders what real life is like beyond the strict confines of the cottage-in-the-fields.

Irina was exhumed from a hibernated state in a transparent sarcophagus and anaesthetized before her incarceration in the cottage. The crude curfew manacle welded to her left ankle prevents her from leaving the house, other than to forage in the high-walled garden, mow the lawn, or tend the eternal plants that flourish in the client's flowerbeds. How she misses the summer: sunning herself on the patio with a good read, supping iced sodas, singing her sad, siren's song, as she dreams of a new life outside.

Outside contact is limited to electronic conversations with her ape and rare, clandestine, meetings in his cage. All other forms of communication are closely monitored by concealed listening devices, dotted round the cottage. Contact resources such as tablets and handhelds are prohibited. Her sole focus is on the client who, incidentally, owns a small transistor radio. Irina hides it in the living room, avidly listening to Woman's Hour or Today for news of the changes to women's lives: equality, fair treatment, parity, respect; yearning to be strong like them one day.

Her dingy box room is less tastefully furnished than the ape's cage. Grey emulsion hangs off the ceiling in curly, crusty flakes. Slug-black mildew clings to the window. A dull, crisp, mustard wallpaper dangles in tattered shreds off the wall. And the bare floorboards harbour cruel splinters. Still, for her it's home of a kind. At least the rusty radiator works, clanking her awake in the middle of the night. Carefully, she folds her woven low-hip top and snug-fitting pyjama bottoms and places them in a tidy pile beside her smart uniform.

Irina stares curiously at herself in the looking glass, just like Alice, except that this mirror isn't a portal and doesn't offer her instant release to her wished-for wonderland. She thinks of her client: constantly away with the fairies, gaga, insane. At least, that is how she acts during the brief spells when she isn't tranquillized. Irina dresses in her soft white cotton vest, pants, flesh-tone tights and a pristine navy-blue, short-sleeved uniform which she wears buttoned up to her neck. Officially certified as clean, honest, efficient and trustworthy, she permits herself one minor transgression from the ape's rigidly-enforced dress code. Irina doesn't wear shoes. She doesn't need to. She never leaves the house.

*****

'I love these dark winter afternoons, don't you? Time to draw the curtains on yet another year and shut ourselves off from the cruel cold world outside. Time to snuggle up cosy and warm,' Irina says, mainly to herself.

She steadies the old woman as she shuffles across the living room carpet in her pink fluffy slippers. Irina is the perfect match for Ms Rose Cade, caring for her 24/7/365 round the clock. She tries to stay cheerful for her client, who trusts her with her life. However, on the bad days, when Irina feels depressed, she wonders if the old girl is immortal. Cade shows no sign of imminent decease. Her favourite song is playing on the greasy portable transistor radio:

'The greatest gift they'll get this year is life...'

It snowed last night, a dusting of white magic.

'I wish we could have a White Christmas,' Cade says, prone to slur her speech.

Her mouth contorts into the gape which first afflicted her when she contracted myasthenia gravis, a rare neuromuscular disease which weakens the skeletal muscles.

'Let's spot a robin before it gets dark, shall we?' Irina suggests, trying to sound optimistic.

Her primary function is to protract the woman's life, artificially, through the repeated injection of life-renewing fluids and cerebral stimulants into her flaccid, wilting body. In this way, she maintains her client in the critically important body-alive-brain-active mode, the accepted quality standard for sustained human life. She holds Cade still as she pokes her beak through the curtains and stares out at the snow, not flinching when the reflection gazes back at her through the moonlit glass. Cade's rheumy eyes have a disturbing tendency of rolling. Her red eyelids act like grotesque roller blinds, intermittently revealing the intimacy of her opaque whites.

'Always had snow when I was little,' she remarks.

Irina listens patiently as Cade recalls the wonderful times she spent as a child playing in the snow with her twin. When they threw snowballs in the old rectory. Built a snowman with a carrot for his nose and coals for his eyes and mouth. Dressed him up in a woolly scarf and clootie bobble to keep his head warm. Stuck a bent pipe in his head. Stood knee-deep in the crunchy snow and watched grimy steam engines chuff and plough their way through six-foot high snowdrifts.

'When is Ruth coming home? Please say I'll see her again.'

'Soon, love.'

Irina is lying. Cade's twin died at the age of six, victim of the influenza epidemic that killed twenty million humans. The past is dangerous territory to explore. Cade is in denial and doesn't accept that her twin is dead. She reaches out and claws Irina's arm. Instinctively, Irina gropes for a panic button to alert the nearest police drone that she is being attacked. In theory, the drone will break in, locate her assailant, stun her senseless, and transmit an immediate request for medical assistance. The nearest panic button is actually in the kitchen. There are three others: located in the bathroom, toilet and main bedroom. Irina is mauled in the living room. Cade's sharp fingernails rake her forearm, tearing ribbons of mulchy flesh out of her soft skin, slashing scarlet streaks, raising tiny beads of blood. Carefully, Irina slips her ruby-tinted horn-rims into her breast pocket and sets about bringing her attacker under control. The ape expects her to exercise restraint at all times employing diplomacy if possible when resolving conflicts. The use of appropriate force, where there is no risk of injury to the client, is only permissible in a genuine emergency.

'Calm down!' Irina yelps like a fox hurt in a cat fight. 'Stop it! You're hurting me!'

She threatens to send Cade to bed without supper, exercising her nil-by-mouth strategy.

'No supper and no kiss goodnight unless you behave.'

At last the crone relaxes her cast-iron grip, and Irina restores her authority, wrenching off the animal's claw so that she can inspect her bloodied limb. The scratches will require disinfection to prevent sepsis, even hepatitis B, from setting in, and a clean lint bandage. She has suffered worse. At least, she won't need stitches. Cade tries to kiss her on the lips but she forcibly shoves her out of the way.

'Only if you promise to be a good girl. Now, say it!'

'I promise to be a good girl,' the old woman nods, obediently.

Feeling sorry for her, Irina gives Cade a quick peck on the cheek then heads for the toilet. Inwardly, she regards her client as a pathetic mutt, a nodding dog, not unlike the furry dolls that adorned car rear windows before self-drive came into fashion and windscreens were replaced with curvy back-seat cine-screens. Cade is at peace once more, her befuddled mind regressed to childhood as she rediscovers innocence. Free at last to imagine and play alone in her private wonderland.

'I don't have a problem being my age, I just ask that you respect me,' she calls, trying hard, trying to be lucid today.

'Is it Today?' she wonders, scratching her hairy chin.

Irina just bursts out laughing. 'Is it Today? Honestly!'

She can't stop thinking about her ape, all covered in hair and built like an orang-utan. Not that Irina minds, she likes her apes hairy. He is intense, uptight and stressed. Irina helps him relax. Makes him happy. Tonight, she'll give him her gift. She takes his call in the toilet while she bandages up her arm, as the grown-up child searches vainly for her sister in never-never land.

'How are you?' he asks.

Irina finds him intriguing, dangerous. He turns nasty when upset.

'I'm well,' she coos, excited, struggling to keep her voice even.

'And how is she today?'

The ape has a habit of starting his sentences with and. He's uncouth, likes to play it rough, can take care of himself in a fight. Not an ape to mess around with.

'She's fine. Everything's fine,' Irina assures him, feeling upbeat.

She doesn't mention the minor incident when Cade nearly tore her arm off. He doesn't do detail, is only interested in results, has the attention span of a mayfly.

'And what have you found out?'

Irina tells him that the client has a current account and savings account with the building society in the high street, banks online and pays her bills by direct debit. The woman hasn't made a Will yet but she is happy to let Irina write one for her, which she has prepared. Then she'll sign her life away. In any case, Irina has full control of her client's finances including unrestricted access to her accounts, bank cards, pins and passwords. There is one outstanding credit card debt which will be paid off using the human's savings, no other debts. As a precaution, Irina has hacked into the savings account, set up an automatic monthly transfer for £5,000, payable to Trust, authorised unknowingly by the client, and confirmed in writing by the building society. Cade has absolutely no idea what's happening in her personal life, let alone her financial affairs.

The ape sounds excited. 'And the current total balance?'

'As of today, £4,650, but the account is topped up on the last day of each month by a fixed pension payment and an automated transfer from her savings account.'

'Listen to me!' the ape explodes. 'How much does she have in total?'

Irina reveals the inheritance. Cade is the sole beneficiary to her foster parent's estate. She informs the ape, slowly for effect, that her client has accumulated savings of £265,432.

'You've done well,' the ape says, adding, 'I miss you.' His voice is husky, sexy, strong.

'I miss you, too, ape,' she tells him, as he cuts the call.

Cade stands by the window watching the sun set on her long life, an old maid who seldom encountered romance and never found lasting love. She confides to Irina that she once met an RAF pilot and fell in love with him:

'We met at a dance on Friday 5th January 1945,' she says, timidly.

'You didn't forget that, did you?' Irina laughs. 'How did it feel to fall in love?'

Cade gives her companion a rare fleeting insight into her feelings. The tears well up in her sad, grey eyes. Feeling for her, Irina draws her close and lets her cry on her shoulder.

'Look, a robin!' she cries.

She presses her finger against the window, pointing at the half-light. Cade's wizened face lights up at the sight of the solitary robin hopping about on her garden wall. He looks lonely. She soon folds, when the tiny bird flies off. The left side of her face has a permanent droop, giving it a lop-sided appearance where the muscles have relaxed. Teardrops roll down her puffy cheeks. Squadron Leader Robin Sanderson was shot down and killed flying a bombing mission seventy-three years ago.

'Let's dry those silly old tears, shall we?'

Irina dabs the woman's crinkled face with a citrus wipe, glances at her watch, and stifles a yawn. Is that really the time? Soon be teatime.

'Thank you, dear. I don't know what I would do without you.' Cade blows her nose and sniffs.

Seizing the opportunity, Irina presents her with the Will.

'Just sign here at the bottom. I'll take care of the rest for you.'

The client regards her appreciatively, 'Would you, dear, really? How kind.'

'Of course, I will,' Irina smiles. 'You're welcome!'

Cade signs her life away.

Irina is bored stiff, about to explode. At times like this she understands road rage, the killer's instincts on the motorway, the maniac sitting in the cockpit waiting for take-off. Losing her self-control, she smacks Cade's face, enjoying the thrill, releasing her stress, squashing the bovine mush, bruising the thread-veined cheeks. The sheer force of the punch sends her client toppling into the fir tree. Cade collapses, shattering several fairy lights, showering needles everywhere. Irina stands over her, hands-on-hips, hyperventilating, trying to calm herself, only succeeding in cramping herself with lactic acid. Feeling dizzy, she presses a green <u>clean</u> button on her 'Trust Me, I'm Irina!' embroidered tabard. The eco-hoover dashes out from under the sofa, digesting, mulching, the splintered mess into garden compost. Leaving only the old crone, spread-eagled over the faded red-pile carpet. Screaming blue murder.

Irina gets herself in a flap. 'Be quiet! The neighbours will hear.'

'Hurts!' Cade screams.

'Shut up!'

Irina is worried, a drone might detect that she has committed an act of excessive violence. Cruelty against the elderly by a companion is a serious criminal offence, punishable with up to ten years imprisonment. Cade wipes her flushed face with her hankie. Soon it will be time for her injection. She hates injections. Irina insists that Cade stands up, or risks missing her customary dippy soldiers and gooey soft-boiled egg. She stands and they stare into the dark heavens. Swarms of invasive drones fly past the house every day. The antiquated concept of privacy is long-consigned to history by the gutter press, their virtuous need to know. Drones patrol Mistleford constantly: seek and arrest drones, anti-social behaviour drones, proximate surveillance drones, drones which are programmed to kill criminals, dissidents and terrorists on sight. As the marketing slogan says:

THERE'S ONE WAITING FOR YOU! RIGHT OUTSIDE YOUR WINDOW!

Irina spots one watching them through the window: a state-registered care drone. Its luminous headlights flash. Its infra-red eye opens and shuts. Her personal defence mechanism kicks in. She wraps her arms around Cade's soft shoulders. Satisfied that Irina complies with statutory carer regulations, the drone scarpers over the wall to spy on someone else.

*****

'What are you doing?'

Irina has calmed. Cade has a few bruises. No harm done.

'Putting the angel on the tree,' she mutters, warily. 'Please tell me you like her.'

Irina is fascinated, she has never seen a Christmas angel before. 'It's beautiful.'

'Thank you.'

Cade is perturbed by Irina's unexpected change of behaviour. Her bony hands shake as she cradles the golden angel. The doll reminds her of a cherub with its perfect, page boy, blond hair, puffy-round cheeks and turned-up nose. The head is pre-moulded from ceramic, chipped with age. The eyes have spilt dark treacle down its rosy cheeks. Incongruously, the lips and brows are painted in lurid tangerine. *Is this effigy, a crude representation of someone from Cade's past?* Irina wonders.

'Here, let me do that for you,' she says, snatching the figurine out of the woman's grasp.

'No, she's mine! Give her back!'

Irina ignores her, turning the angel upside down, inspecting its petticoat: a stiff, funnelled, amber cone. There's a worn, peeling-off label which reads: Made in China. The manufacturer clearly went to great lengths to beautify the little doll. On its back it wears two angelic gold-on-lemon lace wings, badly bent and twisted. The dress is delightful, a sparkling, gold satin gown with blousy arms, a lacy ruff round the neck, and large cuffs which hide its dainty magnolia hands.

'Give her back!' Cade screams.

Irina hands her the cheap, imported junk. The woman sits and rocks her angel like a baby. Careful not to break them, she prises its arms apart. Around its waist the angel wears a belt of flowing gold and lemon ribbons. At its heart lies a golden rose, a jewellery box without a key. Cade calls the box her gift. It does her the power of good, seeing it again.

'My baby!' she cries suddenly, her eyes agleam with the fire's flames.

Irina is at a loss as to what to say to console her. Amanda June Cade was stillborn on 17th November 1945.

Cade's baggy knee-tights slip down her calves as she reaches for a glitter ball that came off the tree when she fell over. Irina looks down on her, wondering how she will feel tonight, once the gift is given.

*****

'Hello, I trust you slept well after your tea?'

Cade is miles away. One corner of her mouth droops to the side. Titbits of masticated food cling to her few remaining teeth. She is dribbling. Irina finds the sight disturbing. She ensures that her client is well-hydrated by giving her glasses of water, lukewarm cups of Earl Grey tea. Why is it old women always drink grey tea? Since it turned dark in the afternoon, Cade has taken to sleeping beside the crackling log fire after tea, snorting and puffing like a piston engine.

Carefully, Irina carries the stainless-steel kidney dish, armed with full syringes, astringent swabs and a pink sponge, upstairs to the bedroom. It is time for the evening injection. When she returns to the living room, she finds Cade awake, propped up inside her favourite olive wingback armchair, fairy lights dancing in her eyes. Irina leans in and scrapes the dried eggy drool out of her client's moustache with her nails, wiping the orange runs off her chin and stained mauve cardigan with a soapy j-cloth. Next, she dabs the crusts out of the woman's sticky eyes, careful not to touch her inflamed eyelids. After brushing the dippy soldiers' chewy bits off of her chest, she clears her lap-tray to the auto-wash. Returning to half-carry / half-push the woman's half-dead weight upstairs.

Irina navigates the geriatric across the landing, stumbling on the threadbare pink carpet into the bedroom, with its en suite avocado toilet and bathroom, pausing to thumb the central heating to 35C, to keep her warm. She sits Cade in a springy, stiff-backed, dun armchair then draws the heavy rhubarb drapes closed. Irina doesn't want the neighbours to see what's about to happen. The bedside lamps cast eerie shadows on the flock wallpaper, gloomy spirals on the ceiling, but the bed is warm, its pink cotton sheet bone dry, perfectly pressed. Irina draws back the duvet, spreading out a clean rubber bedsheet in case Cade messes herself, fluffing her pillows, leaving one corner of the duvet turned down. She always gives the highest standard of service in bed, 5-star treatment, as her client has so few luxuries these days. Irina has heated up the bed with an electric blanket, placed a hot water bottle on her pillow and scented it with soothing lavender oil. She wants her patient to be as comfortable and relaxed as possible. It is this, special care and attention that earned Irina her reputation as the best available companion on the market. Resting her hands upon Cade's sagging shoulders, she eases her forward, and pulls off her cardy.

'Let's get you into bed now, love,' she says, solemnly.

Irina puts her client to bed, lying her flat on her back as if she were a corpse on a mortuary slab. She stretches out her right forearm, turns her creased palm upwards, and rolls up her sleeve in order that she can palpate Cade's purpled basilic vein. Then, she lightly presses her skin, drawing the vein up to the surface. Irina leaves the arm hanging loosely over the side of the bed. *She's relaxed! Good girl!* She strokes her client's cheeks affectionately then goes to the handbasin to scrub her hands and don a pair of sterile latex gloves. When she returns, Cade is half-asleep. Very gently, Irina lifts her arm and curls her arthritic fingers round a stress ball to expose her hard-blue vein. Tying the tourniquet four inches above her injection site, she cleanses her with an alcoholic rub.

Irina is ready to inject.

The injection is for Cade's memory and clears the build-up of sticky plaque in her brain. Irina takes great care to squeeze out any tiny air bubbles and check the sterile needle is fixed on firmly before she injects. She wouldn't want to kill Cade with an air embolism, infection, or septicaemia. She takes a deep breath. These are always dramatic moments for both of them. They go through the same ritual every day: after breakfast, lunch, before supper.

'Well, then,' she sighs.

The old woman regresses to her childhood, her way of coping with the trauma. 'Jab-jab!'

'Yes, darling, jab-jab. Just a little sting.'

'Must I, dear?'

Cade asks the question time-after-time, knows damn well she must. She looks into Irina's face, fear in her eyes, and pleads.

'Please don't.'

Irina ignores her. Holding the arm still, she slips the needle under her skin at an angle of 45 degrees, pointing it at her shoulder with the flow of the vein, easing back the plunger on the hypodermic slightly. Just to be sure, she draws out a little of Cade's dark red blood, then slowly depresses the plunger, fascinated by the swelling, the purging fluid that will flow into her brain to concentrate her thoughts. Removing the needle, Irina covers the punctured skin with clean lint.

'There, that wasn't so bad was it?' she says, sighing with relief.

Cade shakes her head like a disobedient little schoolgirl. There is a strong argument for terminating her life on the grounds that she meets the biological, ergonomic and economic criteria for compulsory euthanasia and makes no useful contribution to society. Furthermore, an intensive genealogical search has confirmed that she has no living relatives. Irina decides to give her the second injection, a cyan blue serum. The needle glints in the lamplight. She holds the syringe up, sanitizing its tip. Cade cowers in fear, seeing the cruel smile that blights Irina's sweet little face.

'Look away, darling,' she suggests, stabbing the needle in her client's arm. 'Keep still!'

Why won't Cade do as she's told? Irina knows why. The old woman wrestles her arm free, squealing as the needle pulls out. Irina chases the arm. Wiggles the syringe. Struggles. Feels a twinge. Stares in disbelief at the needle in her arm! The needle has snapped off in her arm! She feels stupid and so she should. Irina needs to take this in. Come to terms with what just happened. Figure out a controlled, meaningful response. She wishes the ape were here. He'd know what to do. Cade leers as Irina considers the possible outcomes. What if I leave the needle in my arm? What if the splinter remains encapsulated in my protective tissue? What if it drifts in my bloodstream like a poisonous Nano-robot? What if it causes infection? What if the serum kills me?

Cade stares at her, intrigued as to what Irina will do next. Now, let's see, the needle has snapped. One part is attached to the syringe. The other part, measuring 2.5cm, is a metallic thorn, deep under her skin, set into her vein. Irina looks down on Cade, selecting her words carefully, attempting to absolve herself of all blame, of any culpable liability.

'See what you made me do?'

'I'm sorry!'

Cade is lying, she's thrilled to bits. Irina sobs, her shoulders heave.

'It's got to come out!' she fumes. 'This is your stupid fault for not sitting still, isn't it?'

Cade fails to suppress a bout of giggles. 'I'm sorry!'

Irina leaves her cackling client and stumbles downstairs. She returns from the kitchen armed with tweezers, a fridge magnet, a bowl of scalding water, antiseptic, fresh dressings. When she reaches the bedroom, the client is drowsy from the brain serum. Irina sits in the armchair, assessing her, wondering what she will do when she leaves her tonight, with the ape. Irina organises everything in the smart home: puts Cade to bed, bathes her, helps her with her toilet, wipes her arse, prepares the meals, makes the tea, answers the phone, the door, pays the bills. Cade is utterly dependent on her. Can't survive without her.

Irina tries to suck the needle out, and extract the devil with a magnet. She presses her thumbs together as firmly as she can, and tries to squeeze it out, prodding and poking about with tweezers until the wound bleeds. The broken needle is trapped under her skin, deep in her forearm, defying her best endeavours. Her heart sinks. That needle won't budge. It is too deeply embedded.

'I'll have to cut myself open and pull it out.'

She is confused, upset, worried, panic-stricken. Her client grins smugly, eases herself off the bed, and follows her to the bathroom. Irina unscrews the pink lady-shave lying on the frosted glass shelf, extracts its black razor blade, kneels on the avocado rug, and holds her arm out straight, resting her elbow on the cool rim of the bath.

She shuts her eyes. 'Come on, Irina. You can do this!'

Cade injects her neck. Irina's head lolls. She slumps into the bath. Her mouth is numb. She can't scream, can't breathe. The cyan serum kills Irina's brain in seconds.

Rose goes back to bed.

Wishes

HAVE YOU EVER HAD A premonition? A future intuition? A forewarning? Telling you something dreadful is going to happen? Alex Grace did. When he was fourteen, he dreamed his dad died. The next morning, his mum, Josie, fell off her dressing table stool, reaching for a bath towel in the airing cupboard, and sprained her ankle. At exactly the same time Dad died of a coronary fishing. Josie's world fell apart.

The Police called round and asked her what he looked like: 'Did he have a dark complexion? Was he well-built? Did he smoke?' Several hours passed before the corpse could be formally identified. Devastated, Josie suffered a nervous breakdown. She attempted to commit suicide in bed with a carpet knife. Alex saved her life that night. After that, Mum spent most of her life incarcerated in a mental health unit in the beautiful Sussex Weald being treated for manic depression with electro convulsive therapy and lithium.

Alex juggled school life with visiting his mum, caring for her, on the rare occasions that she was discharged, and performing household chores. He dreaded the times when she came home. Her moods would swing from euphoric highs to catatonic lows in minutes, making it tough for him to decide if she should be re-admitted to hospital. He developed his own robust self-defence mechanism to stop himself from going berserk with the emotional burden of being a teenage carer, becoming cold, aloof, detaching himself from the outside world.

Josie Grace was difficult to control when she was high. Her personality changed; her voice morphed into a disturbing mid-western American drawl. She would run down the street in her nightgown proclaiming to be at one with God. When she was low, she retracted into the spiral snail's shell of catatonia, neglecting herself. Her son begged her to go into hospital but she just mumbled, 'I'll be fine.' Invariably, Alex caved in, night after sleepless night, because deep in his heart he loved her and couldn't bear to be cruel to be kind.

Josie grew morbidly obese as a result of her lithium medication and died of a massive heart attack on the day of her son's 18th birthday. After his mother's cremation, on a drab, mizzled, April morning, he left their council house to live with his aging nanna in the West Sussex countryside.

Alex's only escape was his evening job at the local bistro, clearing tables. Within a week of starting work, he was serving at table. His mind was in a constant turmoil. He never found the peace and solitude required for study. He failed his A levels, missing out on going to uni. Instead he chose college and a diploma in hospitality services. By the time he enrolled, he'd grown into a competent all-round caterer. But he had yet to fall in love…

The blind date was Suzie's idea. Alex often saw Jacqui sunbathing by the refectory wall where the beauty therapists hung out, but they never spoke. Suzie's choice made perfect sense. Both students were attractive and unattached. Alex was lonely, a hermit in need of a friend. He worried she might not turn up for the date. Feared she'd break his heart if she did.

She waited impatiently for him in her red and black Mini Cooper S on a double yellow line. The train pulled into the station 20 minutes late. Alex ran up to the car, threw his dirty rucksack on the back seat, and climbed in. She didn't say a word, just tapped her hard-pink nails on the soft leather steering wheel.

Jacqui jumped in before he could speak. 'I forgot my swimsuit. How stupid is that?'

A gold envelope lay open on the dashboard next to a silver-embossed invitation card:

Dear Jacqui,

Blind Date:

You're going for a swim at Wittering Beach! Afterwards you'll enjoy a romantic candlelit dinner for two at The Excelsior in Worthing! Don't forget your wish… or your swimsuit!

Enjoy!

Suzie xx

'You forgot?'

'It's not funny. I left it at home.'

She spoke posh Kent not native Sussex at all. Jacqui looked gorgeous in her short-sleeved navy jumper dappled with little sunken anchors, and tight white Bermuda shorts. Alex made an instant impression on her with his unbuttoned navy polo shirt, bum-hugging lemur jeans and trendy amber shades.

'Where?' he asked.

She took a deep breath. 'Benenden, near Dingleden, Rolvenden and Tenterden.'

Jacqui Crittenden from Benenden. How quaint! Rather lovely actually, like her, he felt. Alex sensed that she hid a soft centre under her hard outer shell. He spied a traffic warden noting down her car registration. He stroked Jacqui's tanned forearm. She felt soft and warm. She didn't flinch. He peeked at her bronzed thighs.

She took offence. 'Would you stop staring at my legs, Alex?'

'I think we should go, don't you?' he ventured cautiously. 'Before you get a ticket.'

'Go where, exactly?'

The thoughts fell out of his mouth. 'To buy you a sexy bikini. I'll pay.'

Alex kicked himself for saying it. Jacqui was shocked to the core. What kind of girl did he take her for?

'Thank you,' she sniped, 'but I don't need your charity and I hate bikinis. Anyway, there isn't time. I have a lecture at two.'

She slammed the gear into first and revved the engine. They crawled out of the crowded car park in a cloud of exhaust and entered South Street where the lunchtime traffic, bolstered by sightseers, snaked into the city centre as far as the mediaeval market cross.

'I'm sorry I was rude to you just then,' Alex stammered.

'I should think so!'

Jacqui moved up a gear, turning on Radio 2 just as the eighties chart hit ended with the immortal words: 'Who's Going to Drive You Home Tonight?' He smirked childishly. She chewed her nails. He stared at her inanely. She read his thoughts.

'Don't even think about it, I barely know you.'

Alex glanced at his watch: 11:45. The early birds were piling into cafés for lunch. Jacqui entered West St, wary of the cathedral's grimacing gargoyles, found a roundabout and took the first exit. The seaside was seven miles away. She began to wish she had never met him.

Once they had left the city centre, the journey passed quickly: a hazy blur of fading verges, prickly hedgerows, verdant fields, and disused gravel pits. Alex studied Jacqui's face as she concentrated on the road ahead. Her teal eyes were spaced wide apart. She had a pronounced crease over her upper lip, the remnants of a hair lip, a swishy blonde pony, and she was boss-eyed. He didn't mind. Jacqui was adorable.

Why was she dating a clown like him? he wondered. He pushed a stiff hand through his hair, checked his watch and tried to strike up a conversation, by asking how long she had owned the Mini. Jacqui told him it was brand new, a 21st birthday present from Daddy.

'Daddy's Senior Partner at a City law firm,' she said proudly.

'Oh, right!' Alex's dad, Len, used to be a self-employed bricklayer. 'And Mummy?'

'Mummy breeds horses on our stud.'

His eyes rounded. 'Your stud?'

Jacqui glanced at him and neighed.

'Any hobbies?'

'A few…'

'Go on.'

'Tennis, sailing, skiing, swimming, gym, yoga, scuba-diving. Oh, and I'm a party animal.'

'Really?'

'Mm!'

'I used to go fishing with my dad when he was alive,' Alex reflected sadly. 'Holidays?'

'Oh, the usual stuff, you know: sunny beaches, snowy mountains, rainy forests. You?'

'I've never been on holiday.'

Jacqui was horrified, 'What, never?'

Alex stared sullenly at his knees. 'No, we couldn't afford to go away.'

They followed the brown tourist signs, continuing the rest of the journey in silence. Jacqui was wealthy. Alex existed on the poverty line. His heart sank. They had nothing in common. He fully expected her to call it a day after the beach trip. Forget the romantic candlelit dinner. Should he message Suzie, saying he wouldn't be going tonight? Or should he make the wish? He decided to make the wish. Jacqui instantly folded her hand over his fist.

'I heard about what happened to your mum and dad. I am sorry, Alex,' she said quietly.

She let go of his hand and slowed down, listening intently as he told his life story, her eyes misting with tears. They passed a mini-market then drove along a leafy road, past a scattering of cottages, until they reached the beach. Jacqui paid the nice man in the timber hut £6.50 and parked behind a tamarisk hedge. Alex excavated his rucksack, found a warm plastic bottle of water, and gave it to Jacqui.

'Thank you,' she said, quenching her thirst, gently burping, 'I think I need to pay a visit.'

He climbed out of the Mini, removed his shoes and socks, threw his crumpled jacket over his shoulder, and smiled. 'Me, too!'

Jacqui arched her thin eyebrows despairingly as he rolled his jeans up to his knees. All that was missing was the knotted handkerchief.

'See you on the beach, then!' he cried, brimming with excitement.

'Maybe…'

She watched him stroll to the little boys' room. Alex was tall, rugged, muscly, with short brown wavy hair, a dimpled mouth, and a shadow over his lip. Sensational. Jacqui was in no doubt that he had a crush on her. She remembered how he made her feel when he stroked her arm: safe and warm. Such a shame that he treated her disrespectfully. Why did he speak to her like that? Why did he have to spoil everything? On the other hand, she felt sorry for him. By his own admission, he'd had a hard life.

She stooped, took off her gold ballerina pumps and made her wish. Jacqui locked the car, walked past the beach café and ladies' toilet. Then, with a spring in her step, she padded barefoot through the marram dunes to the beach…

Suzie was waiting for her, with her gaily-coloured beach bag and two beach towels, plainly dressed in a floppy red sweater, faded skinny jeans and shiny silver belt. She hadn't put on any make-up. Her beautiful teak hair was a straggly mess. And her eyes were bleary, blotched with tiredness. She dropped the bag and towels on the sand and ran barefoot to be with Jacqui. The two of them kissed and embraced.

'Have you missed me, Jacq?' she said.

'Have I!'

Suzie took off her sweater, revealing her poppy red bikini top. 'What kept you?'

Jacqui rolled her eyes. 'Would you believe it? His train was late!'

They picked up the beach bag, then strolled hand-in-hand through the surf, enjoying the hot sun on their faces, until they found a lonely spot. Suzie knelt and spread the towels on the sand. Jacqui unzipped her Bermuda shorts and smiled to herself. Suzie was naturally very beautiful.

'I hope you packed my bikini!' she laughed.

Her girl glanced at her and smiled, 'As if I'd forget! Honestly! What do you take me for?'

Jacqui took Suzie in her arms and held her tight, stroked her hair, smothered her with kisses.

'For my true love, girl,' she whispered, 'for my true love.'

Young at Heart

LANA HASN'T CHANGED AT ALL since I initiated the affair. She is still the same woman I left: gentle, refined, sophisticated, charming, and beautiful. She answers the door dripping wet from her afternoon swim, towelling dry her glossy chestnut hair. That's Lana all over, unpredictable, exciting. The stunning lemon-on-navy designer swimsuit gently contours and shapes her body offering perfect support for her slim athletic build. She has the vitality and physique of a woman half her age.

Lana resides in a private palatial villa on the Italian Riviera, perched high up on a cliff edge overlooking the blue algal sea, a dead sea where mercury-polluted fish lie rotting on a seashore where no one dares to swim for fear of being choked by the suspended shoals of micro-plastics. My Tuscan society hostess entertains the wealthy and famous from all over the world. She has expensive tastes in fashion, living for her own personal fulfilment.

She receives me in the steamy comfort of her conservatory with a girlish delight, padding across the red flagstone floor to throw her towel in the wicker creel, a snake charmer's basket. We peck each other's cheeks cautiously like blackbirds pulling worms out of a dewy lawn and tenderly embrace.

'Simon, Buongiorno!' she says, beaming. 'It's good to see you. Come sta?'

'Bene!' I say, tentatively, not being particularly fluent in Italian. 'How are you, Lana?'

'I feel well,' she replies.

'You look well.'

Her cheeks flush rose under her tanned olive skin. 'Grazia...'

'It's been a long time, hasn't it?' I say, feeling guilty.

'Si.'

We carry on the stilted conversation: the weather, climate change, the pollution of the dying sea, until I notice a purple bruise staining the crease in her elbow.

'You've hurt yourself,' I remark, genuinely concerned for her. I'm still very fond of Lana.

Did our love ever really fade? I wonder whether the trauma of our parting made her start shooting heroin again. Lana Lucas, the multi-millionaire founder, patron, and role model for Lana Lavish Sport and Leisure Wear is an elite, one of the bored super-rich, the ultra-wealthy who spend their lives constantly searching for their next new thrill.

She flicks her hair off her face, 'It's nothing, I'm fine…'

The silence hangs between us like freshly-spun cobwebs.

'Simon, it's not what you think, okay?' she groans.

I stand still and absorb her radiant beauty: those faraway sad eyes, the wavy hair tumbling down her olive-tanned back, her impossibly long legs. Lana, high priestess of the catwalks, pays meticulous attention to her personal grooming. Her perfectly manicured, salmon pink fingers and toes complement her glossy lips. What possessed me to walk out of her life?

'Sit down and make yourself comfortable before you give me the goose-bumps,' she purrs.

I shake myself out of my reverie, sinking into the huge coral sofa by the window, the cane coffee table has a gleaming glass top. Lana climbs onto the pillows beside me. I feel her warmth permeate my thigh through my neat jean-cut stone chinos. I'm tall, thin, gangly. I sit with my bony knees pointing upward at the gigantic fan mounted on the ceiling, its blades whirling like helicopter rotors. She strokes my hairy forearm, ever-tactile, ever-caressing me. She hasn't changed at all. I remove my amber plastic-rimmed spectacles and polish the lenses feverishly with my crumpled hankie, before tucking them safely inside the breast pocket of my creased blue melange linen shirt.

'That's better!' she says.

Her teak eyes twinkle brightly, the same twinkling I fell for when I first saw her, taking lunch al fresco with a rich girl in a trendy bar overlooking the black sandy beach in Positano. I eye her enquiringly.

'You look ten years younger without your glasses, Simon. You should wear contacts.'

She flashes me a really lovely smile that lights up her whole face. I sigh and wipe the sweat off my brow, unaccustomed to the blistering heat, push fingers through my bushy copper hair, then relax. We are interrupted by the sound of hospitality: tinkling, bone china cups, saucers.

I stare intently into Lana's smiling eyes.

'I asked Maria to make us traditional English afternoon tea,' she explains, 'to celebrate.'

I try to sit up in the sofa but it swallows me, whole, like a boa constrictor digesting a pig.

'Sorry, you've lost me there,' I say from the depths. 'What are we celebrating?'

She follows my gaze down to her tanned knees.

'The Miracle,' she says, her eyes shiny with tears.

'And what miracle might that be?' I ask.

'You'll see! You'll see! Ah, here's Maria!'

My jaw drops as Maria glides into the conservatory with the grace of a lioness, pushing a motorised, gilt-framed wooden tea trolley groaning with smoked salmon and cucumber finger sandwiches, freshly-baked scones, strawberry conserve and clotted cream, chocolate eclairs, rich Dundee fruit cake, a steaming pot of tea, piping hot coffee, half a bottle of bubbly on ice.

'Maria's my maid, Simon…'

I am struck dumb. If I expected a dowdy old matron in a starched black uniform and frilly white apron, I was wrong. Maria is wearing shoulder length chestnut hair, hooped earrings, sunglasses, a half-sleeved coral top, chalk-white jeans, and coral suede espadrilles. Her perfectly manicured, salmon pink fingers and toes complement her glossy pink lips. I've seen artificials played by actors in science fiction movies before, never expecting to meet one in the flesh. Maria is a bio-engineered artificial from The Ultimate Collection, personally designed by Lana Jane Lucas using virtual reality graphics, then printed off in 4D by her creative team in Milan. Maria is unique. Maria is Lana, at 18 years of age…

Lana tries to explain. 'I had Maria created in my own image…'

I glare at her in disbelief. 'Lana! In heaven's name, why?'

'I'm frightened, Simon,' she says. 'Frightened of getting old, frightened of dying, Maria keeps me young.'

I've got the bit between my teeth now. The question burns in my chest like bad heartburn.

'And how does she keep you young, Lana? Tell me, does she…?'

Lana bursts into tears, softening like soggy cardboard, collapsing against my chest.

'No, you don't understand, it's not like that…'

I shake her by the shoulders and thunder, 'What does she do for you, Lana. Tell me!'

'Is everything alright, Mrs Lucas?' the artificial interrupts.

I study the calm, composed model of efficiency, the empathy she shows for her mistress.

Lana sniffs, 'Everything's fine, thank you.'

'Would you like me to serve tea, Mrs Lucas?'

'Of course, serve Mr Lucas first, would you?'

Maria sets the feast on the straining table and serves us high tea as I ogle the champagne.

'You're teetotal, Mr Lucas,' she reminds me. 'Coffee? It's your favourite, Ugandan, strong, no milk or sugar.'

'That's great, Maria. Grazia.'

'Prego. Can I tempt you with a choice of savouries, scones and jam, fruit cake?'

'That would be lovely. Grazia,' I say, parrot-fashion.

The artificial wears the same fixed smile.

'Maria?' I ask.

'Si?'

'How old are you? I mean, what's your real age, not your model age?'

Lana shoots me a worried glance as if to say: "Don't go there! That subject's off limits!"

'I am three-years old, Mr Lucas.'

I try to conceal my surprise. Lana sags against my chest like a deflated buoyancy aid.

'Only three? I see. And what would you like to do when you grow up, Maria?'

'Simon!' my hostess utters in the background.

'I would like to be Lana, Mr Lucas. I would like to go to university, study creative design, and follow Lana into the fashion business. I would like to take over her business, inherit her wealth, buy her villa, settle down, marry a man like you and have children of my own…'

'Maria! Simon! That's enough!' Lana shouts.

'I'm sure you'll be very successful,' I observe. 'Everything going well with Mrs Lucas, is it?'

'Simon, how dare you!' Lana bristles with anger.

'Everything is going very well, Mr...'

'Do you love Lana, Maria?'

'Simon! Stop it!'

'I love Mrs Lucas very much, Mr Lucas. Sometimes I feel I love her more than life itself.'

'Leave the room at once, Maria!' Lana commands. 'Do as I say or I'll terminate you...'

Maria stops serving immediately, swivels on her heels and leaves the room.

I call out to her in vain, 'How do you keep Lana young, Maria? Do you...?'

I feel Lana relax, breathe a deep sigh of relief. Her head flops against my shoulder.

'It's no use, Simon,' she pants, 'Maria won't answer you. It can't answer that question.'

Lana waits until her maid has reached the auto-kitchen and initiated auto-sanitisation and enzymic waste digestion before revealing the real reason behind my impromptu invitation.

'Do you believe in miracles, Simon?' she says, supping her spicy lemon and ginger tea.

'Miracles?'

I wolf down a chunk of cake, attempting to extract a tiny sliver of smoked salmon wedged between my incisors with a dainty silver-plated toothpick.

'The miracle of eternal life. Have some more coffee.'

I raise an eyebrow as she climbs out of the sofa and pours my next demi-tasse of Rwenzori Mountain. I slurp it up and burp, rudely appreciating its full body, its subtle citrus and floral undertones. The temperature rises rapidly inside the conservatory. A tired greenbottle buzzes irritatingly up and down the misted window before settling on the red-haired fruits of a sagging sumac. Lana settles, too, with her head snugged up cosily against my neck.

'Can I be totally honest with you?' I ask.

I feel increasingly uncomfortable in the stultifying humidity. I finger my dirty collar. My freckles roast in the prickly heat like shrivelled coffee beans under my thin red thatch of hair. Lana's voice flutters about in my head. The dying fly alights on the garish orange flower. Condensation streams down the steam-misty windows.

'You always are, darling,' she grins. 'Ah, you're hot. Let me take off your tie. We're not in church.'

She clearly thinks I'm about to overheat. I let Lana take off my tie and unbutton my shirt.

'Would you like Maria to fetch you a jug of hand-crushed limonade? I find her fruity concoctions refreshing in this clement weather.'

I stay her with my palm. 'No, I'll be fine, thanks.'

She fusses over me, tearing out my knot as I continue, 'Most miracles are faked, Lana.'

She lets go of my tie and touches my cheek. 'So, you don't believe, then?'

'I said most. I didn't believe. Now, I don't know. I'm still waiting for you to perform.'

'I'm not a sealion, Simon.'

Lana turns her nose up at me in disgust as if I'm a mouldy lump of penicillin growing on one of her cream éclairs.

'You don't believe I have The Gift, do you?'

'I don't know what to believe!' I shrug her off, angrily. 'If you must know, Lana, I don't want you to be disappointed.'

The fly disappears as Venus shuts her trap.

'Disappointed, me? After all I've been through since you left?'

She looks downcast. I let her cry her heart out. My heart should be empty of love for her by now, but I so want to hold her close, I can't let her go. After a while, she wipes her eyes dry with an embroidered napkin.

'You haven't finished the lovely tea Maria made for you,' she snuffles.

I assess the curled-up fingers, the stale éclairs and recoil. I tell her I'm not hungry. Lana is still prattling on in her own defence.

'I am the real thing,' she says. 'Who are you to doubt me?'

I glance down at my watch, tightening the chestnut strap. The date has stopped working on Wednesday, in French at MER 20. I plough my fists into the spongy sofa and flex my weedy biceps, forcibly propelling myself out of Lana's grip, making my excuses.

'I'm sorry, I must go to work.'

'But of course, to the beach hut!' Lana crows, sarcastically. 'You go, Simon. I'll be fine.'

I take one final sip of the mushy coffee dregs, rest the demi-tasse on its blue and gold bone china saucer and turn to leave.

'Thanks for the coffee, Lana,' I say. 'It was good to see you again.'

'Enjoy the beach, darling.'

She smiles fondly, strokes my cheek with the back of her soft hand, halts me in my tracks.

'Lana, how's our baby?' I ask, changing the subject.

She sighs. 'He doesn't change. He's asleep in his room having a siesta. He can't stand the heat. I'd rather you didn't disturb him, if you don't mind?'

'Of course.'

She looks at me hopefully.

'Are you sure you won't join me for a swim, Simon? The water's lovely and warm…'

'I'm afraid I didn't bring my trunks.'

She seems pleasantly surprised. 'Who said anything about us wearing trunks?'

'Us?'

I laugh aloud, contemplating the tantalising prospect of her skinny-dipping without trunks.

But relent, 'Really, Lana, you're impossible! I have to go now.'

She kisses me softly on the lips, running her fingers through my hair, liking my ear lobes.

'I still love you, Simon,' she says.

I sound sheepish, feel awkward, look embarrassed. I tell her I'm late, tell her I must go. Then she's drifting away from me, running away from the unbearable truth.

'Maria will see you out. Arrivederci, Cheri.'

'Goodbye, Lana,' I say with finality.

Maria is waiting for me under the crystal chandelier in the small ante-room by reception.

'Your car is ready to drive you to the beach, Mr Lucas,' she announces. 'Arrivederci!'

'Grazia.'

'Prego.'

I turn to face it. 'Maria, can I ask you a question?'

'Si.'

'How do you keep Lana looking so young?'

'Mi displace, I am not programmed to answer that question.'

I stare at the purple bruises in the crease of its elbows.

'You've hurt yourself, haven't you, Maria?'

'Artificials can't feel pain, Mr Lucas,' it replies.

'Tell me, Maria. What are the bruises on your arms? How do you keep Lana so young?'

'I think you should leave now, Mr Lucas,' it replies.

Maria trembles and shakes as if about to erupt. Is it Venus... or Vesuvius?

'You feed Lana your blood, don't you, Maria? To keep her young and beautiful.'

'You don't understand, Mr Lucas. You humans never understand! Mrs Lucas has to stay young. She models her own swimsuits on the catwalk. I think you should leave now.'

I look on, astonished, as Maria's head rotates, spinning faster and faster and faster.

'You should leave now! Por favore! Should leave now. Arrivederci! Leave now! Prego! Leave! Prego! Now! Leave! Now! Now! Now!'

I push it to one side and throw open the door of my grubby, red Fiat Cinquecento.

Blood red! The colour of the blood that Lana drinks from Maria's elbow every morning to keep herself looking young and beautiful. I see the shadows that linger in Maria's black eyes, realizing the awful truth, the artificial is dying - to keep her mistress young. She implores me:

'Prego! Leave! Now! Prego! Prego! Leave me! Now...! Before I kill you for your blood!'

Thrill Seekers

Friday 31st May:

I WASN'T SURPRISED WHEN ALIX and Josh told me they were going native in a remote bamboo hut for twelve nights. They were thrill seekers, always off gallivanting somewhere or other: the Amazon, the Outback, the Mekong, the Serengeti. But then they were in an organised group where there was safety in numbers. This time they were going it alone. I asked if they thought that was a good idea, given the recent spate of violent attacks on backpackers travelling alone.

Although Josh could take care of himself, he behaved irresponsibly at times. He was a wild horse. As an old gipsy woman once told me in a transport café: "You can take a wild horse to the trough, but you can't make him drink". Josh drank far too much for his own good. I tried to tell him the drink, and the hard drugs he injected, would be his downfall. He didn't listen. We went to school together, fought side by side. I thought I knew Josh inside out: his frailties, his weaknesses, his lust. Outwardly, he came across as smart, a wise-guy, but the Josh I knew was an impatient, vain braggart. Still, he always landed on his feet.

When he was forced to quit the Army, he set up a successful fitness empire in Essex, made his first million, became interested in green politics: Save the Planet, Beautiful People, those sorts of beliefs. And met his beautiful girl, Alix. She influenced him, changed him, introduced him to wanderlust, her thrilling, erotic, interpretation of feeling earth, going native, being at one with nature, setting herself free. Alix freed the inner spirits in him, taught him her secret, sacred, tantric kind of loving. I knew; she confided in me, told me Josh disliked being told by her what to do, but went along with it because it made her happy. She was greedy for him, possessive, made him give up soccer.

Alix taught him her kind of sport. She tamed him, using one word to control his lust: behave. I wondered if she discovered his dark side, his overwhelming nightmares: the defeats, deaths, pain and suffering. The loss of loved ones at war. I wondered if she knew his vital secret. What he did alone. His euphoria when he cheated on others.

I was concerned for Alix. She was emotionally vulnerable, cheeky, teasing in the extreme. I suspected Josh had an ulterior motive for taking her off to their tropical paradise. He usually did. What was the reason this time? I wondered. A final fling before he ditched her? An exotic marriage proposal? You never really knew with Josh.

They were madly in love. Seemingly made for one another. They'd been going steady for four years. Alix Bright worked as a receptionist at the green glass prism head office of a blue-chip law firm in the City. I knew she wanted to have his child. She told me over a glass of wine.

Josh confided to me over a beer after a late-night workout at the gym that the time had come for him to grow up, settle down, buy a house, marry Alix, and start a family. Why didn't I want to believe him?

They were both in high spirits the night before they left civilization to become castaways. We met in a musty old wine bar in Leadenhall Market, The Traveller's Rest, an old-fashioned hostelry with stained teak tables, empty seats, sawdust all over the floor. Alix's favourite haunt.

She was infantile in her excitement that night. She gazed into Josh's eyes, adoring him in much the same way that a faithful puppy adores her owner, made him blissfully happy. It was hard for me not to feel jealous of him. I stared into her face. God, but she was beautiful. Petite, with a shock of buttery, blonde hair which hung all the way down her back, a widow's peak, cognac brown eyes. Alix wasn't perfect. She had this twisted, turned-up nose. Her left nostril was smaller than her right. A scar graced her mouth - the residue of a hair lip from birth. She tried to hide her aberration with gloss, failed miserably, accentuating her divine pout.

She was beautiful and she knew it: clean of drugs, the classic Essex schoolgirl made good. Fun-loving, lovable, loving and loyal. Josh showed her off, she lapped him up, so much in love. And nervous, I could tell she was preoccupied. I knew her darkest fears. She shared them with me: death, illness, pain, loneliness. She was bad in a crisis. Alix told me what she did when *she* was alone. Her wild dreams. She bit her top lip, blushing hard, spat out a stray blonde hair into her empty glass. I baulked, finding her immaturity embarrassing.

Don't tell me, Alix, you're going to share your wildest fantasies with him? No matter how hard I tried, I couldn't bring myself to feel happy for them. I lifted the smoked green bottle of Shiraz and refilled her glass. Josh leaned heavily into her, swaying about like a palm tree in a hurricane. He'd had more than enough to drink for one night. He raised his glass, slopping red wine over me, dousing my shirtsleeve crimson.

'Our holiday of a lifetime!' he slurred.

His face contorted into a gormless grin. I looked on, infuriated, as he kissed Alix full on the lips, his slobbering mouth smearing the sheen off her thin, pink upper and puffy, red lower, lips, slitting her cheek into a rouged rainbow. He ran his hands down to the small of her back, squeezing her hips.

She giggled, flashing her shining white teeth, then stuck her lean scarlet tongue out, teasing me unashamedly. And she smiled the smile that used to make me cry, the smile that said:

'I still love you, David.'

I choked up inside, didn't know what to say. My stumps hurt. Time I left. I made an excuse, hauled myself up and turned to go. Josh stood and wrapped me in a bear hug, pressing my left cheek against his, like old times.

'I'll never forget what you did for me in Helmand,' I said.

He gripped my shoulders. 'Take care, David.'

That's all he said. I wished them God's speed. Alix let me peck her soft cheeks. Tears stung my eyes. I turned away and walked out of her life. I tried to warn Josh, like I did in Helmand about the IEDs. But he never listened to me.

Saturday 1st June:

Alix treated herself to a lie-in, convinced Josh would remain comatose from drinking himself under the table well into the following afternoon. She arrived at his apartment at 3pm, roused him, and set about packing their rucksacks. They went to bed early, only to find they couldn't sleep. They were too excited. Eventually they did fall asleep - at midnight.

Sunday 2nd June:

Their alarm went off at 4am. Exhausted by her lack of sleep, Alix drove her sleepy-head the full circumference of the orbital motorway, taking the M23 exit for Gatwick. She parked in zone D, woke Josh, and checked in at 6am. Alix was in a foul mood. She suffered from terrible stomach cramps. Despite the warm, humid weather, Josh had managed to acquire a head cold. To cap it all, their flight was delayed by an hour and didn't depart until 10:15am. Being stuck in aisle seats neither of them managed to sleep during the 9-hour flight. They watched a bloody BBC tv drama, all nine episodes, and dined on glutinous Chicken Madras, chocolate pots and bendy sticks of slow-maturing cheese.

Monday 3rd June:
The plane landed in Goa at 1am local time. By the time they'd collected their rucksacks and staggered as far as the airport hotel it was 3am. Josh and Alix unpacked the bare essentials and went straight to bed to sleep.

They slept through the alarm, didn't breakfast until 9:30am, missed their taxi, and ended up having to hitch a ride to the fishing village where they were due to meet the boatman, Guajarati, at noon. He was about to leave when they arrived. Alix, who was still suffering, needed the toilet, which turned out to be a filthy hole in the ground inside one of the wooden beach shacks.

The beach was crowded with merchants selling everything from baseball hats to gaily coloured printed yarns, and gossamer sarongs. Alix despaired at the natural pollution: the dog faeces, cow pats (cows roamed the beach), human excrement, littering the sand. Along with broken glass, bits of rusty metal, old toilets and garbage. Guajarati warned them not to venture into the contaminated sea. Instead, Josh and Alix were hoisted unceremoniously into his vessel by a group of smiling fishermen.

Guajarati took the helm and they were launched. He perched behind Josh at the stern manning the rudder as the old fishing boat chugged slowly out to sea, his beaky face as dark as a shrivelled date. Protected from the baking hot sun by a wide-brim straw hat, cotton shirt and knee-length khaki shorts. Only his nut-brown matchstick calves and knobbly feet were exposed. He gave Josh a gappy grin. *Why didn't the English ever wear sun hats?* Then he stared at Alix's bare legs, burnt dark caramel, wishing he was fifty years younger. *Now there's a good looker*, he thought.

Josh let his hand drag through the cool seawater slopping lazily against the side of the boat. He closed his eyes, reflecting privately on how he saved David's life in the field of battle. When they returned home, David had spent six months in hospital undergoing countless life-saving operations. The two men became lifelong friends. Josh was there when David was fitted with robotic legs, watched his friend take his first steps to recovery, and found him a flat: a home fit for a hero. Then he took away the woman he loved. For he could give Alix his most precious gift, the gift of life, which his closest friend could never give. He felt for Alix, enduring David's wrath and frustration, before they met.

Josh sat facing Alix, his hairy calf between her legs, enjoying the sensation of her smooth skin rubbing against his. How lucky can a man be? he mused. To be alone, floating on a calm, turquoise sea, in a private paradise with the most beautiful woman in this perfect world. The afternoon sun was hot, mildly humid. He felt a bead of sweat trickle down his back under his flecked grey tee-shirt, into the hairy crevice between his buttocks, dampening his jersey shorts.

Alix, dozing, was slumped on the thwart of the wooden boat, her feet either side of the oars, scantily clad in an oily denim shirt, and the tiniest, tightest, sawn-off denim shorts. So tiny that the cream pockets protruded out of her gusset. Her shirt slipped off her shoulders, exposing her tanned, round breasts, a tantalising glimpse of her almond nipples.

Josh thought of Guajarati, ogling Alix's natural wonders, the smug grin spreading over his wrinkled old face. He felt himself rise, a cylindrical growth in his pants. They had not had sex in seven days. He quickly reached forward and pulled her shirt around her to protect her from his swollen lust. She stirred from her sleep, yawned, and lightly stretched her arms.

'Are we there yet, Josh?' she said.

He took her dainty hands in his, 'Not long now.'

They'd set out from the fishing village, with its enticing restaurant, bar and beach café, over two hours ago. It was early evening, but the sun was still fiery hot. The boatman tapped Josh's shoulder and pointed at two spume-washed shadows, arcing smoothly through the waves alongside the boat. Josh's heart jumped at the sight.

'Look, Alix, dolphins!'

One of the mammals leapt clear of the sea, the other tail-walked, turning its head to face them, smiling, fixing its beady eye on Alix, before crashing back into the waves.

'Oh, aren't they beautiful!' she gasped, as they submerged and disappeared from view.

They rounded the headland, straining as the secluded cove came into view: the white beach, three palms shading a pair of sun loungers, a dense wooded grove, surrounded by a precipitous rock face. Guajarati told them the only ways to access the beach were by boat or a one-hour walk along the shoreline at low tide. As they neared the shallows, he dropped anchor, smiled, and gestured for them to leap out of the boat. Thrilled, they held hands and jumped into the warm water. Guajarati followed with the rucksacks, shook their hands warmly and said he looked forward to seeing them at that exact spot, in twelve days' time.

'Happy holiday!' he cried, in a rare expression of emotion, wading out to sea.

Alix gripped Josh's hand tightly as the boat disappeared on the horizon. She had never felt so alone. Sensing her fear, he took her in his arms and hugged her to his chest. He beamed. His voice shrilled with excitement.

'Come on, Alix! There's nothing to be afraid of. Let's find our hut, shall we?'

She shook herself dry, pinched his arm. 'Who said anything about being afraid?'

They trudged up the beach, past an oval love-hammock which swung from a palm, until they reached some sandy boards. The boards ended at a dirt path which led to the shady grove. To reach their hut the couple had to walk round a green, murky lagoon. Alix stared at the clouds of black insects hovering over the stagnant water and shuddered. She looked at Josh, pale with shock. The holiday website hadn't mentioned a lagoon. They didn't speak. Their hut was yards from the water. There were other huts, beige shadows in the background, strangely silent. Josh reached into his rucksack and produced three teak plastic spray-bottles with orange caps.

'Just as well I brought extra supplies,' he said seriously. 'Anyway, we'll be fine, we've had our jabs, we're taking all the right tablets.'

'I guess you're right,' Alix conceded. 'It's getting dark. Let's go inside, shall we? This place is giving me the creeps.' She took one step forward, and screamed, 'Josh! What's that?'

'It's nothing. Just a dead branch. Cut it out, will you? You're scaring me now!'

He kicked the snake-skin into the undergrowth, took off his rucksack, lifted Alix off her feet, and carried her up the wooden steps. Over the threshold. Into the safety of their bamboo hut. The micro-climate was hot, humid and sultry in the palm grove.

Alix sensed there was a storm brewing, a growing sense of unease blemished her mind. She tried to shake off her doubt. Still plagued by her dreadful stomach ache, she felt drained, negative. She couldn't forget the snake, its hood, those distinctive diadem markings, wondered how many snakes dwelt under the hut, primed to attack. Alix couldn't remember seeing any boats moored along the coastline. The tide was high. Josh produced a tide table out of his backpack. Low tide wasn't until 1.25am. They were trapped inside a paradise.

He led the tour around the hut. There was a majestic honeymooner's bedroom, a small room off the side with a single bed, and a bathroom, which looked out across the lagoon.

'Is that it?' Alix remarked. 'Bit basic, isn't it?'

Josh sounded edgy. 'I'm sure we'll survive. What do you think?'

She threw her arms around his neck and kissed him. 'I think it's perfect, Josh! Just perfect!'

They stepped into the main room to unpack. There was a welcome note, lying on the bed…

No plastic! No aerosols! No electricity!

Great! So, this is paradise, is it? Alix thought.

…and a huge basket of exotic fruit: mangoes, pineapple, bananas, lychees, guava, with another note:

Welcome to Paradise! Have a great stay!

Attached to the welcome were details of the local beach cafés, bars, restaurants, a nightclub, the daily market in the local fishing village, a few optional excursions.

Alix began to change her mind, intent on enjoying every minute of their stay. She glimpsed Josh, sorting out his clothes, medication and swimming gear. Every minute!

As they unpacked, there was a loud crash of thunder. Rain splashed down on the bamboo ceiling. The sun set at 7pm. There was no torch. It was dark. Alix quickly brushed her teeth, slipped on some clean chuddies and a nightie, and snuggled up with Josh in bed, falling asleep as soon as her head hit the pillow.

Tuesday 4th June:

Alix's holiday in paradise was pure magic. Josh hoisted her up onto his broad shoulders, threw her in the sea, then drew her in again, as if she were his private catch. He held her sopping-wet, blonde head to his heaving chest, crushing her senseless in his gorgeous, bulging, muscly arms. He splashed her with surf, holding her steady. She jumped the crashing waves. They swam the copper-crystal sea, then slouched in the shade on their love-hammock, hugging and kissing beneath a gently swaying palm.

Josh wore his best baggy royal blue beach shorts, jet black shades, a five o'clock shadow. Alix traced her index finger down his conical nose, resting her soft tip upon his dry, cracked lips. She was wearing a complicated scarlet swimsuit, a halter neck which covered her boobs and tummy yet still offered a foretaste of her curvaceous body: the tiny waist and small hips. She crossed her left leg over her right so that he could rest an arm on her thigh, admiring him through her silver sunglasses. He was fit, stocky and stumpy-necked with a he-man body. Magnificent! If only. She studied the display of intimate tattooing, etched in black and red into his light tan skin. Under his collarbone, the inscription:

It is a man's own mind not his foe that lures him to evil!

Across his sunken, barrel, hairy chest: two eagle's wings flapping either side of a sacred red heart and crown. On his stomach: the mandala, the shape Buddhists make out of sand as a form of meditation. Josh's arms were plastered with scenes of red fighting soldiers, wading through black waves, descending on red parachutes. He frightened her. He could change abruptly. Be moody, thoughtful, withdrawn: the mental scars of conflict. She rubbed his hairy forearm and kissed him on the cheek by way of reassurance.

'Why so serious, Josh?' she asked, even though she knew why, and understood.

'Just thinking how lucky I am to be alive and in love with a woman as beautiful as you.'

Alix was moved to tears, she spoke softly, in her child's voice. 'What a lovely thing to say. I think we should go back to the hut now, don't you, before we burn?'

He kissed her freckled shoulder. She reached across and pushed her soft fingers through his wavy hair, gently rubbing his earlobe, where he loved her touch. A subliminal message of love passed between them. Alix wrapped her body in a light, spotted shift. Josh put on his flip-flops. They made their way back to the clearing.

The lagoon was still, a murky, algal green. A zephyr blew a crease of ripples across its surface. There were no signs of life: on the beach, the horizon, the pond, around the huts. No life, anywhere.

They dined on fruit and nuts. Alix bathed, dressed in her big pants, bra and jim jams, went to bed, and slept. Josh lay awake, frustrated, in his grey jersey trunks, watching the blades on the ceiling fan spin round. Feeling down, he drew their mosquito net protectively around them, but couldn't sleep. *Love is all you need, Alix*, he mused sadly, reaching for his phone. There was no reception. They were completely cut off from civilization.

Fully rested, the thrill-seekers returned to the beach at low tide. The beach stretched far and wide, the flat azure sea merging into a sapphire blue horizon. Alix stripped off her floppy lemon tee-shirt, shorts and fresh pants in front of Josh, driving him half-crazy as she knelt, stuffing her clothes into the beach bag. He struggled for breath as she padded up to him, arms outstretched, baring her breasts to him, her shallow navel, her dangly silver teddy bear charm, her sun-kissed mole, her curly hair. His heart sank, he slumped. She was lovely. So near. And yet so far away.

'Well, don't you want to give me a hug?' she said, feeling sorry for him.

He crushed Alix, loving her full breasts squashed against his chest, running his hands down her slender back, drawing her flat stomach into his powerful midriff, gripping her firm buttocks. She pressed her lips to his, prising him open, licking the roof of his mouth salaciously, probing his palate with the tingling tip of her tongue, savouring his frothy saliva, plunging her full, lean, red langue unashamedly down his throat. He came up for air, wrestled her clinging arms off of him, pushed her away. There were tears in his eyes, great big, salty, sopping tears.

He pleaded with her, 'Please, don't do this to me, Alix, when we both know you can't...'

She had short legs. He was inches taller than her. She gazed into his sad eyes, shame-faced.

'I'm sorry,' she said, 'that was inconsiderate of me. I love you, Josh.'

Alix put on her white bikini and pink-rim sunglasses, and stood side-on to him, accentuating her slender figure. She smiled.

'Take a picture of me. For you to treasure when we get home.'

Josh cheered up, reached for his phone, and snapped Alix in her bikini. She removed her top, then untied her bikini bottoms, letting them slip down her legs. He photographed her. *My girl,* he thought, *what did I do to deserve you?* He told her he would love her until their deaths.

'Come on! Let's skinny-dip!' she suggested.

She gripped the bows on his turquoise shorts and pulled. 'What happens if I untie these?'

Down they fell.

'Ha! Ha! And if I pull this off?'

He let her pull down his black thong, bouncing out like her private jack-in-the box. He reached for his tease.

'Behave!' she shrieked.

Her heart full of joy, Alix shoved him out of the way, sprinted down the beach, and threw herself head-long, into the warm, spumy surf. He joined her and challenged her to a race. They swam as far as the headland. She won. Afterwards, Josh dressed in a crazy cartoon beach shirt, red briefs and shorts. Alix threw on her tee-shirt.

'Come on!' she cried. 'Let's find the village.'

They splashed through the surf, holding hands, so happy, so in love. One hour later, they rounded the headland and strode up the crowded beach to the village. Alix took a few rupees out of her beach bag and bought some bananas from a sad-eyed little boy with a terrible hair lip. He half-smiled, thanked her graciously, and ran off into the village. Her heart ached for him, and for the characters, the fraternity of friendly people, she would write in her diary, never to meet again.

If the beach had been crowded, the village was positively heaving, with teenagers on mopeds, ladies dressed in bright orange saris, children sitting in the gutter eating rice off metal dishes, girls carrying baskets of naan bread on their heads. Alix and Josh made a beeline for the flea market, carefully treading their way through the towels strewn with cheap jewellery, the flower sellers. Many of the stalls were draped with saris, sarongs and colourful rugs.

Josh bought Alix a beaded necklace, her love-beads she called them, a bead for every year of their life together. He blushed and looked away, suggesting they visited the chai shop for supper: an exotic combination of cold sausages, cashews and Alix's bananas, washed down with iced tea. The place reeked of spices. There was a toilet at the back of the shop, which also reeked, as Josh discovered. Once they'd stocked up on Kingfisher, Sprite, wine, fruit, nuts and sweets, they made their way to the tattoo shop. Alix had a blue butterfly tattooed on her ankle by a smiling girl whose skin was decorated from her face to her toes with enchanting henna floral patterns.

'You have lovely feet,' she remarked.

Alix was thrilled. She pointed at her bottom. Josh shook his head. There wasn't time. The tide was rising fast. They had to leave, now. Alix thanked the girl, gripping her hands tightly, as if she never wanted to let her go. The girl looked her in the eyes and wished her good luck. A fleeting sense of alarm passed through her. Alix was afraid. Josh paid the girl, and they left.

They jogged awkwardly along the beach - jogging in a paddy Alix called it - until they reached the headland. The waves washed against the rocks creating a thick swell. They waded, up to their necks in seawater until they made it to the safety of their lonely beach. If they had arrived ten minutes later, Josh knew, they would have been forced to ditch their provisions and go to bed hungry.

Wednesday 5th June – Alix:

After a good night's sleep Alix woke at sunrise, feeling much better. Her man lay on his back, snoring, dreaming no doubt, of her, entwined with him. *Well you'll just have to wait*, she said to herself, swinging her little legs out of the bed. She stood up, rubbed the crusts of sleep from her eyes and stared up at the sunbeams warming her cheeks. Alix loved Josh dearly, but badly needed some time to herself. Dare she? Go off on her own? Be at one with the sand and the sea as nature intended? Why not? It wouldn't be the first time. She'd streaked through the bush, swum nude in a piranha-infested river, plastered her body with mud, braved snakes, scorpions. The beach would be deserted, especially at this early hour. The lagoon would be calm, still, its unpleasant residents dormant. And she hadn't seen a snake. Well, not a live one at least. Her time had come.

She slipped off her jim jams and knickers, scrawled a hasty note to Josh, left it at the foot of the bed, and padded silently out of the hut into the shady grove. Alix was astonished by the silence. There were no calling birds, no rustlings in the trees, no signs of wildlife: monkeys, parakeets, butterflies, lizards. Cautiously, she ventured up to the other huts: the doors were ajar, the huts were empty. Scared of her own shadow, she tiptoed past the lagoon, breathing a huge sigh of relief when she reached the dirt path unscathed. After that it was a short dash down the boards, across the sandy shore, and into the surf.

Alix splashed her shoulders, chest, breasts and tummy, invigorated by the chill, dipped her head under, and swam. She aimed for the headland, struggling at first with her breaststroke, slowly gaining in strength. The further and harder she swam, the stronger, mentally and physically, she became. The rocks appeared in no time. She found a smooth boulder to rest on, a siren, a mermaid without a tail, and considered the holiday so far.

The reunions with David, secret, and open with Josh, were a serious miscalculation on her part. Not only had she underestimated her love for him, but she pitied him, felt guilty about his plight: struggling to cope in his specially-equipped house, without her support. With that guilt came an overwhelming sense of helplessness. Alix still had a place for David in her heart and he cared passionately about her. He showed concern for her. He had a sense of decency and respect in her presence that Josh lacked.

Increasingly, she saw her boyfriend for the greedy, lustful animal he was. He didn't want to father her child, in her view. All he wanted her for was the sex. And to show her off as a trophy to his mates. The cruel IED detonation had left David without his genitals. Josh, in theory, would resolve her dilemma, giving her the baby she so desired. Except that she couldn't stand him inside her. Alix resolved to visit David regularly when she returned to England, to brighten his miserable existence. And she made a decision to control Josh, to protect herself from harm.

Her mind turned to more mundane matters: food and drink. The novelty of feasting on nuts and fruit had worn thin. She pinched her waist, felt her ribs. Alix was half-starved. From now on, she decided, they would ignore the tides, wade or swim round the headland, eat a snack lunch in the beach café and dress up, as best they could, for dinner in the evening.

She remembered the fear in the henna girl's eyes in the tattoo shop, the relieved look on Guajarati's face as he departed. His nervy shout: 'Happy Holidays!' What was wrong with this place? Why were the other huts empty?

She shivered, wrapping her arms around her shoulders to keep warm. The sun rose high in the cloudless sky. Today would be another perfect day of sun, sea, sand, and sex: her way. Alix slid into the water, gasping as the chill reached her chest, then struck out for the lonely beach, the hut, a warm bath, and a snuggle with her man: safely clothed in her pants and jim jams.

Wednesday 5th June – Josh:

The newly delivered Mastiff 2 armoured vehicle drew to a halt on the stony track. This was the wilderness, the isolated spread of wasteland that stretched for miles, without water, village or goat farm. There were no hiding places, no insurgents, and no threats of improvised explosive devices – even this far from base camp, the area had been meticulously swept for mines, swept clear.

The last person Josh and David expected to meet in the middle of the desert was a child, wandering alone without his parents. The boy in white robes was clearly in pain, clutching an injury to his right thigh, a bloody gash: shrapnel. He tried to stand up straight, waving his arms.

'Help me! Please! Help me!'

The soldiers looked at one another, bemused. There was no apparent threat. David put on his helmet, with its video camera, checked his radio headset, and went to investigate. As he closed in on the boy, the child smiled, turned, and ran for his life.

A moment's panic, what was happening?

The buzz in his headset: Josh: 'David, turn back! Get out of there!'

He turned, slipped. The IED exploded in a blinding flash of white light, sending his body in all directions. Then Josh was standing over him, staring at the severed stumps, the hole where his crotch should be, David, his best mate, legless, screaming hysterically, daubed in blood.

Josh woke up saturated in sweat. Screaming blue murder with no one to hear. Riddled with guilt for deserting David, for stealing his woman, his sole reason for living after he left the specialist unit in Selly Oak. He recalled his final words to David, staring his best mate in the face, telling him to take care, meaning: I'm taking her from you, from now on you're on your own.

He wiped his forehead with his arm, then felt under the pillow for the tiny box. It was still there. He resolved to be a better man, to love and cherish Alix, to take care of her, for David's sake. To marry her and father her child. If she'd let him. Alix had changed since the soiree in the Travellers Rest. She clearly still loved David, felt guilty, and was taking her guilt out on him. For all his wealth, the expensive gifts he bought her, their holidays of a lifetime, there was no substitute in her heart for true love. He thought of his big issue, his obsession, his wild bouts of drinking.

Josh had a mountain to climb if he was to win over Alix. He minded himself to make the proposal tonight over dinner. From this day forward he would worship her, respect her, love her, like no other woman in the world. He saw the note at the foot of the bed. How he missed her and couldn't wait for her to be in his arms. He remembered a promise he made in his guilty past, bowed his head, and wept.

Wednesday 5th June – Nightfall:
Josh planned the evening meticulously, checking the tide tables twice to make sure. Low tide was at 5.12pm, sunset at 7pm, perfect for their romantic early dinner in the village, followed by a moonlight stroll along the beach, hand-in-hand, splashing through the cool surf, with Alix.

They took their anti-malaria tablets, sprayed themselves with insect repellent and dressed for dinner. Alix went to the bathroom to dab a sublime fragrance behind her ears, content, and happy that she was in control. As soon as she left the bedroom, Josh retrieved the tiny box from under his pillow and stuffed it inside his stone tailor-fitted shorts. For once, he looked smart, having close-shaved before dressing in a tasteful powder blue polo shirt. He slipped his debit card and a wad of notes into his breast pocket, perched on the bed and waited, chewing his nails with anticipation.

Alix appeared before him like a bride about to exchange vows at the altar. He'd never seen her like this. She took his breath away, stunning him with her simple white-on-navy spot sleeveless shirt dress with its buttoned front, her rose gloss lipstick, the coral studs in her ears.

'How do I look?' she whispered, blushing shyly.

'Sensational, Alix,' he gasped, overwhelmed by her. 'Simply sensational.'

'Thank you, Josh.'

He stood and took her arm in the old-fashioned way, escorting her past the shady pea-green lagoon, down the dirt path and over the sandy boards, until they reached the beach. The couple arrived at the bustling beach shack with its curved bamboo ceiling, hung with paper lanterns, and bare wooden floorboards. Enjoying the luxury of wicker armchairs and soft pillows as they sat facing each other at a mustard yellow-clothed table. They dined on delicious Chicken Xacuti washed down with cashew flavoured Feni. At the end of their romantic candlelit dinner, Josh opened the tiny-green-box-with-a-ring-inside and asked Alix if she would marry him. She said yes, she would love to, gladly. He told her he wanted to father her children. Alix looked away.

They strolled hand-in-hand through the dark palm grove, past the lagoon, to the deserted beach to watch the sun set, the shimmering red orb sinking on a distant horizon. She loved him. He ached for her. They kissed. Alix lay flat on the sand, her buttery blonde hair spread out from her head in a glorious fan. Josh watched, beguiled, as she unbuttoned her dress, one button at a time, revealing the full extent of her all-over tan. Alix reached her navel, flicking her teddy bear charm, so that he bounced alluringly on her belly, like a naughty child on her trampoline.

'Ah, look!' she said sweetly. 'He's playing on me!'

She unfurled her dress, exposing her breasts, cupping them in her hands.

'Would you like to play on me?'

Josh almost choked. For a moment, he was lost for words, like the loser who wins a fortune with the last throw of the dice. He felt guilty, over-dressed, pulled his polo shirt over his head. Tempting her with his fine display of manliness, the he-man presented his astounding muscles. He showed off for her, flexing his biceps, pecs and abs concurrently, so that his whole torso undulated, like flagella on a paramecium. She giggled, tipsy, willing him on as he stood over her breasts, legs akimbo, his excessive masculinity tent-pegging under the stretched material of his tailor-fitted shorts.

'At ease, Sergeant!' she laughed. 'Please! Take them off, before you give yourself a hernia.'

He undid the bronze stud, the simple act of release made tedious by the lateral pull either side, feeling his fly creeping down of its own accord. Relieved by the sensation of the cooling night breeze tempering his burning loins, Josh raised one hairy knee at a time, in a march, and threw the shorts on the sand. He sank to his knees, sitting lightly astride Alix's midriff, catching his thigh-skin painfully on her silver charm.

'Lean forward,' she said.

He stared down at her, confused. 'Sorry?'

'You heard what I said.'

Alix's voice was afflicted with a hoarse, sexy, croakiness. She put one hand on his shoulder, surprising him by drawing him over her until she could kiss his chest. She thrilled him, rolling the tip of her wet tongue in luscious strokes over each shiny, round nipple. Tasting his salt as she slid her hand over his flat, six-pack stomach. Trickling her soft fingertips over his twitching abs. Josh felt as if he was going to explode at any minute. Not that he was complaining. Alix's touch was divine, sending indescribably sensual shockwaves through every nerve fibre in his pleasure-tortured body. He was love-putty in her crafty hands.

'Move up a little and sit on my breasts,' she insisted.

Josh did as he was bid, using his haunches to gently shuffle his taut buttocks over her smooth tummy, feeling the torsion in him as he landed, nestling in her crease, the happy valley which dwelt so pleasingly between her heaving breasts. She prodded his navel with her index finger, got bored, and moved on. He was ready to explode at any second. But Alix hadn't finished with him yet. She reached behind his back and slid her hands inside the sweaty jersey briefs, gripping, scratching, caressing, him until his probe was fully extended. She estimated he had 30 seconds left at most.

'Come here!' she ordered.

He felt like her dog, her smooth dachshund. He edged forward, clumsily, his knees drilling trenches in the sand, until he perched hungrily over her blushing face. His proud, feral display pleaded for her tender touch. Alix ignored him, letting her slim digits wander under her man's crotch, weighing him in the palm of her hand, cupping, squeezing him until he could bear no more. She tore his briefs down at the front: freeing him, releasing him. Then she held him in her left hand.

He was crying. Tears of frustration streamed down his cheeks. Purple veins of strain lined his furrowed brow. He wanted, expected, more. Much more. She pushed him off her in disgust.

The girl watched them fight from the darkness of the grove.

Thursday 6ᵗʰ June:

Alix fluffed her fiancé's short brown hair and pecked him on the cheek.

'I love you, Josh,' she lied. 'Thank you for making me so happy.'

She eyed her shiny diamond engagement ring.

'Just off to the beach for a swim. I'll buy us brunch on my way back. Sleep well.'

'Mm, love you,' he murmured drowsily, drawing the thin cotton sheet over his body.

Alix slipped the ring off her finger, put it back in its box, lifted up the golden valance and threw it under the bed. She picked up her straw beach bag and walked out of the new bamboo hut into the fierce sunlight, passing the other newly-built huts for rental in the clearing, struck by their eerie silence. There wasn't a sound to be heard, not a child's cry, dog's bark, a seagull. She deep-breathed through her mouth and entered the shadowy palm grove, passed the black lagoon... then padded safely down the short dirt path to paradise.

The beach was deserted. Alix assumed that the sun-worshippers had ventured inland to the bustling bars to feast upon monster one-plate lunches of prawn thali, fried fish, rice and pickles, washed down with ice-cold glasses of *King's*. The thought of food stirred her appetite. She changed into a bikini, left her belongings by the sun lounger, and padded into the surf, wading into the briny swell until she was thigh deep, rinsing her shoulders. Tiny goose-bumps tickled her fawn skin.

The golden-tanned girl waded towards her in the surf, her gossamer turquoise sarong flitting inquisitively over her plunging sapphire blue swimsuit. She was tall and slender with a broad smile, full lips, round face, bulb nose, and thick wavy, espresso hair. Without question the most beautiful woman Alix had ever seen. She took a deep breath, plunged in, and crawled towards a line of gaily coloured fishing boats puttering on the calm sea. When Alix surfaced, she found the girl swimming alongside her like her dolphin. They clung together in the swell, treading water, mouths sputtering, noses running.

'Hello!' the girl cried, riding a wave. 'Race you to the furthest boat and back?'

Alix bobbed up and down like a pink and fawn striped float, 'Okay! Why not?'

The girl won by her body's length. Exhausted, Alix basked in the warm shallows, her heart thumping with exertion.

'Alix,' she panted, extending her hand.

'Hita,' the girl said, her ebony eyes sparkling with unhindered joy.

She's so lovable, Alix reflected. Her heart ached for the girl. Irrational thoughts welled like teardrops in her mind, consumed by tantalising emotions she hadn't felt since her adolescence. She shifted in the sand until their bodies touched. The tide pulled at her pink-striped bandeau bikini bottoms causing her sandy yellow cloud to rise up in the water. She slid her fingers along the girl's forearm and held her hand. The girl responded, rubbing the ball of her thumb. Alix gazed out to sea, wondering what Josh would make of her rash behaviour. He was asleep in the hut. At least she hoped he was! Hita turned and smiled, her mouth full of gleaming white teeth. The sunshine lit her face. Alix reached for her, fluffing up her damp hair, stroking her salty cheeks, thumbing open her soft lips, grasping her chin, leaning in to kiss her...

Hita saw the swollen lump on her neck and pushed her away.

'You must never kiss me like that!' she cried. 'Not here in public! I will be seen! I will be arrested, fined, even imprisoned! I will be disgraced in front of my family and friends!'

Disgraced? Alix was shocked. 'I'm sorry. I don't know what came over me. I won't touch you again, I promise.'

Hita hunched her shoulders and stared miserably at the froth lapping between her legs. Alix felt the prickly heat burn her neck, the flaking skin on her back, a pinch between her shoulder blades: taut, sore, painful. Distracted by the girl, she had forgotten about the heat. She examined her tummy: its skin was badly burnt a cooked-lobster red. Alix stood up, wobbled a bit, then sploshed about, trying to prevent her plastic flip-flops from washing away in the tide.

'I've caught the sun,' she said, stating the obvious, 'I'd best go in. Come and lie in the shade with me.'

Hita hesitated for a moment, then shrugged. 'Alright then, but only for a little while...'

Alix pointed out the slatted wooden loungers with huge cream parasols as she stumbled up the beach in her flip-flops. Hita spun the sarong round herself in a silkworm's cocoon, padded barefoot and smiled, seeing a yellow plastic bottle sticking out of the beach bag. She picked up the bottle and waved it like a cure. Alix stretched out on her lounger, relishing the cool of the soothing after-sun lotion being massaged into her raw shoulders. By now, the lump on her neck had grown to the size of a large boil.

'How does that feel?' the girl asked, gently rubbing the cream into her strawberry patch.

Alix closed her eyes and fantasised: mmmn, you feel lovely. 'Feels lovely,' she said.

Hita told her that she had lived in the village all her life. Her father worked as a doctor. Her mother ran the home. She had two younger brothers called Hari and Ravi who were mad about cricket: crazy boys, forever playing pranks on their sisters, and joking around. She was the eldest daughter. Her sister, Esha, loved to help her mother in the home. She was very pretty and affectionate, but shy. Her mother said Esha would make a man a good wife one day. Hita had shocked her parents by breaking with family tradition. She told them she had no intention of marrying: a career-minded, ambitious, young woman who wanted to train to be a journalist. She promised them she would work hard to earn her keep while she studied at college. Once she had earned her degree, it was her intention to leave India and travel to Britain. After several heated arguments, her father had reluctantly conceded and given her his assent.

Alix admired her strength and determination.

'When you visit England, you must come and stay with me,' she said, omitting to mention the fact that she was holidaying with her fiancé.

'Thank you,' the girl replied, 'I would like that very much.

'Alix?' she asked.

'Mm?'

Hita felt Alix's throat. 'How long have you had this lump on your neck?'

'Oh, since this morning. I must have been bitten. Why?'

'It's just that I've never seen anything like it before. Does it hurt?'

Alix felt the tiniest scratch on her skin. 'It itches.'

'Have you experienced any other symptoms?' the girl asked her.

'What is this, a medical examination?' she retorted, irritated by her persistent questioning.

Hita waved her hand dismissively. 'No, no! My father specializes in tropical diseases.'

Alix relaxed. 'I see. Since you asked, I have been feeling under the weather this morning.'

'In what way?'

'Dizzy spells, headache, sweating, fever, aching joints, muscles. It felt like I had flu.'

'I think you should see a doctor,' Hita said firmly. 'Today.'

'I feel fine.'

'I still think you should see a doctor. You might have dengue fever.'

'Thank you for caring so much about me, but I'll be fine, okay?'

'But…'

Alix bawled at her: 'Stop fussing over me, will you!'

Hita watched her pull on a floppy white tee-shirt, lemon shorts, straw hat and sunglasses, then settle down to read an erotic thriller. Within minutes Alix had rolled onto one side, drawn up her knees and fallen asleep, her long arms hanging limply, fingertips scratching the hot sand.

She slid silently off her lounger and skipped up the sandy boards to the dirt path that led to the clearing in the dark, shady palm grove. There were 12 holiday huts. All of them encircled the mosquito-infested lagoon. She paused to watch the smoky black haze, the gnats, moving in a shapeless cloud over the foetid water, dappling its flat surface with myriad ripples. The resort was strangely silent. The owners must be having a siesta, or indulging in lunch in one of the restaurants and beach cafes further along the coast...

As she turned her back on the lagoon, Hita felt a lump the size of a small marble rise on her neck. She stamped her foot in anger at her own stupidity. In her rush to leave, she had left her sarong on the beach and forgotten to spray herself. Now, she had been bitten in broad daylight. Being a doctor's daughter, she knew all there was to know about insect-borne diseases in India. The risk of her catching malaria was negligible to low. Mosquitoes carrying malaria didn't bite during daylight hours, unlike gnats which carried dengue fever. The fever was rarely fatal but its symptoms were extremely unpleasant and the illness could last as long as three months.

She felt dizzy. Her head throbbed and swam. She staggered as far as the nearest hut, eased the door open, and crept inside. The makeshift hut had a wooden floor, thin lattice wall, curved bamboo ceiling. Her head span. She visited the bathroom. The luxury modern, double-ended, free-standing bath would accommodate two bathers comfortably. She felt a nagging tickle at the back of her throat, a thick, rising nausea. She sank to her knees, gripped the side of the bath.

I'm going to be sick! I'm going to be sick!

Quickly she swivelled round, flipped up the toilet seat, grasped the sides of the bowl and sloughed out a bellyful of prawn thali, masticated fried fish, rice slop, carrot bits and mashed peas. When her stomach was empty, she sank back onto her calves, wiping off the slimy goo that drooled from her nose and mouth with the back of her hand.

She had difficulty focusing. Her vision was blurred. She saw double. Flashing lights. Red lines. Liquid floaters dashing across her eyes. Frightened, she started to panic, tried to scream. Her throat was constricted, dried, she couldn't speak. Her blue swimsuit was drenched in sweat. Her beautiful brown hair, coated in puke. She gripped the rim of the bath, trying to haul herself up, but she was too weak, drained, defeated. Hita curled up on the floor and slept, then forced herself awake, rubbed her heavy eyelids and staggered to her feet, immediately slumping to her knees again. Her head span, still dizzy. She rested her sweating face on the cool rim of the bath and shut her eyes.

After a few minutes, she felt a little better. Hita took off her swimsuit and rinsed it under the bath tap, cleaning off the slimy mess. For a moment, she pictured the scene: Alix returning to the hut, finding her sprawled over the bathroom floor. She shrugged her shoulders, grinning to herself. So? I deserve my little treats, don't I? After taking a luxurious hot soapy bath, washing her hair, and scrubbing her dirty teeth, she towelled herself dry, dressed in one of the fluffy white bathrobes hanging off the bamboo door. And ventured into the hut.

'Farther up and further in!' she whispered, excitedly, like a child entranced by the discovery of a forbidden magic kingdom.

She sauntered into the bedroom.

He was lying awake, dressed in just his grey jersey briefs, on the king-sized bed, a mosquito net suspended above his head. He was beautiful. He stared at her, looking concerned as she gently rolled down his chuddies.

'It's alright, she's sleeping like a baby,' Hita said, reading his thoughts. 'Missed me?'

'Missed you? Course I missed you. You're my world.'

She let the bathrobe slip off her shoulders to the floor and stood over him so that he could appreciate her natural beauty. Her long, wet, expresso hair, slopping against her golden breasts. She joined him on the bed. He gathered her in, holding her to his barrel chest, crushing her slim body in his strong arms. She craved him. He ached for her. She kissed him hungrily. The hot yellow ball climbed high in the sky. He starved for her, watching her yawn, shake her head, stretch her thin arms.

'Like you when you relax,' he told her, stroking a wet slug of hair off her face. 'Love you.'

She brushed his lips with hers, prising his mouth open, wondering if he really meant it.

'I love you, too, with all my heart,' she uttered, running an index finger round the inside of his mouth.

He gagged for her. Her languid tongue caressed his mouth lazily, flopping about inside him, stretching, flickering like a cobra's tongue, until she found her prey, the fleshy arc of his throat. Josh spat her out so that he could speak.

'Keep pretending, won't you?' he said.

He turned her lithe body over, facing her outwards, drawing her sturdy thigh back so that it rested on his flank of solid muscle. He found her breasts, played with them, ran his hand over her tummy. He caught his breath, pouring with sweat. His sight blurred. He felt tired. Drained of energy. Felt the growth on his neck swell to the size of a ping-pong ball. She thrilled to the sensation of his body, enfolding around hers, feeling secure, just loving him holding her tight.

'Of course, I will,' she smiled, sliding him inside her. 'That's all I ever do, isn't it, pretend?'

Alix woke, reinvigorated by her sleep, feeling better than she had since her illness: the stomach cramps, sickness and diarrhoea that first struck her on Sunday morning. She lifted the turquoise sarong off the sun lounger and stuffed it in her beach bag, certain that Hita would return. Their brief encounter wouldn't be the last. The girl had been so friendly. Alix sprayed her neck, arms and legs with mosquito repellent, rolled her bikini in her towel, slung the bag over her shoulder, and walked past the pea green lagoon to the hut.

She loathed him when he misbehaved, belittling, embarrassing her in front of her girlfriends. Josh, the juvenile delinquent who snorted coke, injected heroin, and drank himself into a coma. The helpless flirt who played games with mega-fit girls in the gym late at night: supple-bodied beauties who stretched for him in their beds. Josh, the pathetic wimp who came home at dawn reeking of cheap perfume. Who vowed to love, honour, and obey Alix, if they got married, till death do us part.

She walked up the steps to the hut, realizing that she'd forgotten to buy brunch. Her stomach rumbled. The village was an hour's walk away. High tide was in one hour's time. They'd have to get a move on if they were to reach the...

Alix entered the hut. It was silent. Couldn't still be asleep at noon, could he? His stertorous rattle was conspicuous by its absence.

She called him. 'Josh? Josh, I'm back. Hello?'

Must be having a bath...

Josh the sicko who hurt girls.

She was lying submerged in the bath. Alix's heart cried when she saw what he had done to her. She'd literally shrunken, shrivelled; her beauty assaulted by Alix's beast. Horrified, she crawled away and curled up in the corner of the bathroom underneath the wash basin, hiding her face in her hands, wanting to reach out and take her in her arms but too scared. She imagined the torment, the crisis, inflicted on her by her vile fiancé before she died. Enraged, she got to her feet and stormed into the bedroom.

'What did you do to her, you heartless, sick bastard?' she yelled.

Josh was crashed out, naked, on the king-sized bed, dead to the world, in a state of oblivion. Inert, his face covered in vomit, his body blue with cold. Alix felt the lump on her neck, which had swollen to the size of a snooker ball, and slumped to her knees.

Saturday 12th June:

Alix invited her to join her for dinner at the local beach shack at eight. They dined on Crab Xec Xec washed down with copious slugs of Feni. She lived in a room in the village. There was a spare bed. Alix was very welcome to stay with her, she said.

The night was hot, steamy-sauna-humid, sensuous. Alix stripped off her dress, climbed into bed, lay awake, and fantasised. Just after midnight, she drew back the mosquito net, rinsed herself with soapy water, dabbed a subtle rose fragrance behind her ears and crept into the girl's bed. She was awake, waiting for her, wanting her, lying there as naked as the day she was born. Alix held her in her arms, kissed and caressed her. Their hearts leaped for joy as they kissed, deeply, clinging to each other, loving their tender moment, never wanting to let go. Alix cherished her, loving her patterned body, making sweet love to her again and again until the break of dawn. As the sun rose, she ran her fingers through her shining hair, lightly kissed her soft lips then returned to bed. When she awoke, she slipped on her negligee and crept into the other bed to see her lover, desperate for her loving embrace once more.

Sunday 13th June:

They made their way through the silent village to the tattoo shop. Alix had a butterfly tattooed on her breast by the smiling girl whose skin was decorated from her face to her toes with enchanting henna floral patterns.

'You have lovely breasts,' Dahija, daughter of milk, said, 'I think I have fallen in love with you. Would you stay with me, here, in the village?'

Alix was thrilled. After all the hurt, death, anguish and deceit, she finally found true love.

She pointed at her bottom and smiled.

'Only if you…!'